THE SAVAGERY OF MAN

- OPERATION HOMECOMING -

A Novel

By

Nikki Yanu Kanati

Black Bear Lucky Hunter
Publishing

THE SAVAGERY OF MAN - OPERATION HOMECOMING -

Copyright © Mark M. McMillin 02.12.2024
Release Date: 04.01.25
Book Cover Art by Julian Bauer

ISBN: 978-0-9838179-9-4
ISBN: 10: 0-9838179-9-4

Black Bear Lucky Hunter Publishing

The author wishes to acknowledge all those friends and colleagues who helped make this a better novel. I am most grateful. Thank you.

The Savagery of Man is a work of fiction. Apart from well-known actual people, events and locales described herein, all names, characters, places, and incidents are the product of the author's imagination. Any resemblance to current events or locales or to living persons is pure coincidence.

This book, in its printed form, is designed for the reading public only. All dramatic rights in it are fully protected by copyright, and no public or private performances, professional or amateur, and no public readings for profit may be given without the express written permission of the author and payment of a royalty. Those disregarding the author's rights expose themselves to prosecution.

This book has been printed in the United States of America. Without limiting the rights under copyright reserved above, no part of this publication (except for any artwork in the public domain used herein) may be reproduced, stored in, or introduced into a retrieval system, or transmitted in any form or by any means (electronic, mechanical, photocopying, recording or otherwise), without the prior written permission of both the copyright owner and the publisher.

Any pictures used in this book are faithful photographic reproductions of original works of art, which are in the public domain in the United States and in those countries with a copyright term of life of the artist plus one hundred years or fewer or either purchased on the internet or were offered as free downloads.

This is an original literary work created by the author, a human. No AI program was used, other than to check basic punctuation and grammar, in the creation of this book.

Praise for *The Savagery of Man*

"[A] ... riveting story ...
The author's concise, unadorned prose delivers keen dialogue and clear descriptions, and the seamless blend of real-world history and fiction gives this novel a welcome touch of plausibility. An exhilarating, realistic political tale with shades of SF."

- Kirkus Reviews

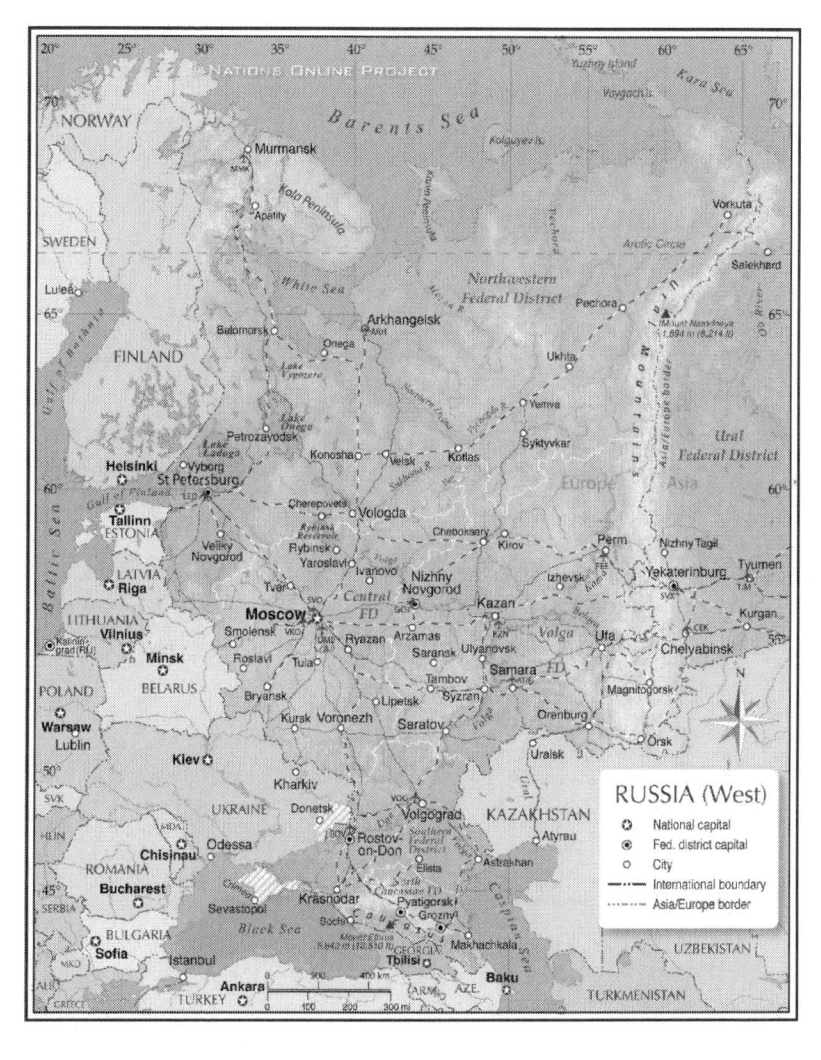

Reproduced with the permission of Credit Nations Online Project

Foreword

The King's Homecoming

After ten hard years of war, followed by another ten long years of trials and tribulations at sea, Odysseus, the father of the Trojan Horse, returns to the rocky shores of Ithaca to find over one hundred suitors, men of nobility, encamped inside his palace. Believing the hero of Troy is dead, the nobles plot to kill his son, Prince Telemachus, force his wife Penelope to remarry one of them, seize his throne, and then divide his riches between them. But the master of deception devises a murderous plot of his own. In his bloody homecoming Odysseus, with the help of Telemachus and his faithful swineherd and cowherd, will slaughter every vile suitor and kill every disloyal servant who collaborated with them to save his family and his kingdom.

Prologue

Excerpts from Hermann Adelman's private journal:
The Great Turmoil
(as edited by his loving daughter Gretchen Adelman after his death)

1954 - Hubat, Ethiopia

Dr. Harvey Winston, a young, tenured professor of archaeology at the University of Cambridge, used his soiled neckerchief to wipe the sweat and grime out of his eyes as the lorry, a Leyland Hippo, a rusty, squeaky old relic from World War II, bounced him up and down along a rugged, dusty trail. For months, Winston had been exploring various regions of central Ethiopia in sweltering heat and horrendous dust storms, looking for a promising archeological site without any luck. With his grant from Cambridge nearly exhausted, he was short on funds, supplies and time. But several Ethiopian hunters had restored his hope when they told him about an old human skull they had seen mixed in with a few other bones near Dire Dawa. Based on their descriptions of the skull, Winston concluded the remains could, possibly, be from a prehistoric age and decided to take a closer look for himself.

When Winston reached Dire Dawa, the locals directed him to the 13th-century ruins near Hubat, a small village not far from Dire Dawa, where, they informed him, a recent tornado, an exceedingly rare phenomenon in Africa, had uncovered the opening to a deep cave. Out of desperation Winston reluctantly decided to make the journey as he had, a season ago, already reconnoitered that territory and had discovered nothing of interest. With the last of his money, he bought additional supplies, hired a platoon of laborers from the locals, and headed for the cave.

An overwhelming sense of dejection smacked Winston hard in the face like a bucket of ice water when he first arrived at the place the hunters had described, when he saw children running amok and playing inside the cave with no skull or bones anywhere in sight. With time running out, he had no choice but to start digging. After three weeks of tedious work, removing countless baskets of sand, stones and dirt from the cave, Winston found himself standing triumphantly over a fully intact, incredibly old skeleton. He could hardly believe his good fortune. He had stumbled upon the bones of an ancient humanoid, an entirely new species of humanoid, along with several odd tools of extraordinary craftsmanship made from unusual materials he had never seen before. Winston immediately telegrammed the details of his find back to Cambridge and sent a copy of the telegram to a friend, Dr. Ludwig Papenfuss, a young professor at TUM, the Technical University of Munich, as Papenfuss had some expertise in exotic metals, compounds and other materials.

Winston was shocked when Papenfuss pulled up to the cave three weeks later with a small army in tow. Papenfuss had traveled from the port in Djibouti with scores of hardscrabble men, with men who looked like they had seen war, dressed in khaki pith helmets, khaki shorts and shirts. The Germans brought two dozen Land Rovers painted in desert camouflage with them, along with a dozen large trucks painted in beige towing trailers and long flatbeds loaded down with heavy equipment and assorted machinery for digging, drilling and excavation.

Winston extended his hand as his friend jumped off the lead Land Rover and approached him. "Ludwig, my dear fellow," he said cheerfully and forced a smile. "I had no idea you were coming."

"Harvey! It has been much too long," Papenfuss replied, and warmly embraced the Englishman. "I could not resist. The tools you described in your telegram simply sounded too extraordinary to ignore. And the bones! You'll be the toast of Europe, my good man, with this find of yours! One prestigious society or another will certainly honor you with a lifetime membership. The world will embrace you like a movie star."

"But what is all this now?" the Englishman asked, perplexed. "You brought enough men and equipment with you to outfit an army battalion."

"I have reason to believe Harvey," Papenfuss replied enthusiastically, "that you have only scratched the surface here. You'll be glad to have the resources I've brought with me. But do not be alarmed. I am not here for fame or fortune. All the credit, all the glory, shall be yours and yours alone, my friend."

To Winston's confusion - and utter dismay - Papenfuss's first undertaking, after carefully examining the exotic tools Winston had found, was to seal off the entire area with concertina wire and armed guards. No one was permitted to leave or enter the encampment. Then his men confiscated all the radios too. Papenfuss was imposing a total quarantine over the site. Once the Germans finished unloading their equipment and gear, after they pitched their military surplus tents, Papenfuss led his men deeper down into the cave while Winston and his team of Ethiopians were permitted to continue their excavation near the mouth of the cave.

For the next six days and nights, the Germans drilled and dug in shifts around the clock and when they had found what they were looking for, they began moving all of it out of the cave in sealed crates and containers and quickly loaded their booty onto the trucks. With the last item, something large and long, wrapped in tarps and rope to keep the object concealed, the Germans had to lay down iron rails and pull the thing out of the cave on an ingenious, makeshift trolley using diesel-powered winches, steel cables, block and tackle. Papenfuss's men had to string four long flatbeds together to transport the mysterious object.

During the past six days, Winston had reluctantly tolerated Papenfuss's cavalier dismissal of his objections and complaints. But now, appalled by Papenfuss's blatant pillaging of his site, the Englishman decided to put his foot down.

"Ludwig, this is outrageous! I must insist your men off-load the trucks immediately. I demand to see what you are trying to remove from my dig site - *my dig site!*"

"We have Harvey what we came for," Papenfuss said deliberately, as his men exited the cave with the last of their gear and equipment. "I shall now leave you to your own excavation in peace."

"Unacceptable!" Winston replied bitterly. "TUM shall hear of your cheekiness. I shall notify your rector directly. I shall file an official protest with the German government. Your conduct here has been incredibly unprofessional to be blunt, truly quite atrocious and will not go unanswered!"

"I'd say *auf wiedersehen*, Doctor Winston, but I fear we shall never meet again," Papenfuss replied coldly, then turned to his lead man, a grizzled, scarred giant molded by a hard life. "Leutnant Eichmann, our men are all accounted for, the cave is clear?"

"*Jawoll, Herr Doktor, alles ist klar,*" Eichmann replied as he clicked his heels together. Some old habits die hard.

"Good, then let us be finished with this unfortunate business and be on our way."

Eichmann suddenly produced a vintage World War II Wehrmacht Maschinenpistole 40 and pointed the muzzle at Winston's chest. After others armed with M-40s joined him, the Germans advanced in a skirmish line, forcing Winston and his Ethiopians far back into the cave.

"What is the meaning of this Ludwig?" Winston cried out in a shaky voice.

Papenfuss turned his back on the Englishman as he headed towards the long convoy of vehicles. But before he stepped aboard the first truck, he spun around to face the cave. "*Leutnant Eichmann, zerstöre jetzt den Eingang!*" he shouted without emotion.

Seconds later, after one thousand pounds of dynamite planted inside the cave explodes in a ball of dust and smoke, the entrance collapses and vanishes and the dozen souls trapped inside disappear forever, buried underneath tons of sand, soil and rock. After the Germans make one last sweep of the area to remove any evidence of foul play, they head back with haste for Djibouti and to a cargo ship standing by to return them to West Germany.

Chapter One

Unfathomable, gruesome violence. Explosions. Dozens of thunderous explosions shatter the serene, beautiful spring morning of a quaint Virginia town as smoke, flame and deadly shrapnel poison the air. Then the sharp crack of a single, high-powered rifle is heard, quickly followed by the drrrrrum - drrum - drrrrum - drrrrrrrrrrrrrum of multiple automatic weapons and the pop-pop-pop of semiautomatic weapons. These sounds are soon replaced with the sounds of sirens, screams and cries for help. As the smoke lifts, chunks of concrete and asphalt, mangled bodies, severed limbs and countless tattered, scorched American flags lay strewn across a town square soaked in blood, gore and filth. Men, women and children too, lost souls, stumble aimlessly about in shock. Chaos. Horror. Death.

The Beast, Cadillac One, the First Car, sometimes referred to as the Stagecoach, is a tangled heap of smoldering, twisted metal lying on its side. A few yards away from the presidential limo, the President of the United States is lying on the pavement in a pool of his own blood. There is no sign of life in him. Within seconds, men, presumably from the President's Secret Service detail, disappear into clouds of swirling white and green smoke, dragging the President's body with them.

As this depravity consumes the small rural town, the invisible enemy simultaneously launches a mix of a dozen armed drones and six smart missiles at the White House. All but one of the threats are intercepted and destroyed. One smart missile eludes the White House's elaborate defenses and strikes the North Portico, splitting the iconic entryway in two, killing or wounding an undisclosed number of civilians, mostly tourists, inside the grand Entrance Hall.

All this savagery and more is captured vividly on multiple high-definition security cameras for the entire world to see.

The woman offered the man a smug grin as he plopped down in a cheap plastic chair molded in a hideous shade of orange directly across the table from her. The table - government-issue crap, an ugly four-legged metal rectangle wrapped in chipped, gray paint, the kind of table found on every U.S. military installation across the world - had been bolted to the floor. Above the table hung a single light bulb on a black cord emitting a harsh, yellow glow.

"So here we are," the man said evenly with a deep, commanding voice.

The woman did not respond. She looked past the man with an air of indifference, focusing her attention on the two-way mirror behind him. But she and the man both knew her bravado was bullshit.

The woman was an attractive, nearly movie star-quality dirty blonde with large green eyes and Botox-perfect skin. She was prettier in person than on TV. Her stylish, custom-tailored suit looked as if it had been poured on. The raw, gray silk hugged every curve to near perfection. She wore her white blouse unbuttoned from her neck down to her sternum, revealing a good bit of cleavage, enough to entice anyone with a heartbeat to want to see more. Her shoes, wrapped in expensive black patent leather, one with a broken heel, sat off in a corner. Her ensemble exuded sexy though was still conservative, was still within the bounds of good taste.

The man placed a tall Starbucks in front of her, a cruel gesture considering her hands were shackled to the table. *Maybe I should have brought a straw* the man chuckled silently to himself.

She continued ignoring him, pretending that he wasn't even in the room.

"I shouldn't worry about the folks standing behind the mirror if I were you, Lucy," the man said. "I'd worry far more about the mysterious fellow now sitting across the table from you."

Her gaze suddenly shifted back to the man. She narrowed her eyes and set her jaw. Her arrogance reeked of aristocratic European boarding schools and exclusive American Ivy League.

She leaned forward. "That's Senator Brighton to you," she snapped in a harsh, condescending tone. "I don't waste my time with someone else's lackey. Be a good dog, go fetch your master for me."

"Senator?" the man asked nonchalantly. "No, no Lucy. I fear this is not quite true. You have forever forfeited that lofty title and all the power, prestige and perks that go with it."

"Ha!" she scoffed. "The people elected me. The Senate hasn't brought any expulsion proceedings against me. No court has stripped me of my office. None will. You and whoever the fuck you work for have abducted me without authority. You are detaining me illegally. You are violating my Constitutional rights. I demand you take me out of this fucking shithole - NOW!"

The man cracked a thin smile. "What you say is true, and yet here we are. A U.S. Senator handcuffed to a table in a dingy interrogation room sitting across from, well, me. Across from someone else's lackey, as you say."

"And who the fuck are you?"

"Ah, we shall come to that, all in good time. But I will be the one asking the questions and you, you Lucy will be the one answering them."

"Or what?"

Normally, this is when the man would have smashed in a nose with his fist and no one would have questioned his actions. But he maintained his composure. He pointed to the two beefy special ops goons - dressed in black fatigues, black boots and ski masks and armed with automatic carbines tipped in long silencers - standing behind her. He recognized the distinctive CZ Scorpion Evos chambered in 9mm the two men carried. The Czechs, he mused, knew how to make some nifty, badass weapons.

"*Or what* you ask, Lucy? Well, perhaps for starters I'll let Vinny and Guido standing behind you play piñata with your pretty head."

"This," Brighton said with a scowl, "is a bad joke. You're a bad joke. Spare me the buffoonery agent whoever the fuck you are. Spare me your idle threats. As you are detaining me, I'd like my call now and I can promise you, mystery man, you won't like the blowback that follows."

Despite the man's imposing size, his reflexes had always been quick. But for a bad knee he had suffered in an auto accident as a young boy, at six feet and two inches, every inch of him hard muscle, he might have been drafted by one professional football team or another. The army, though, had no qualms about his knee and had happily drafted him right out of college.

Brighton never saw him smack the Starbucks off the table with a swift flick of his wrist. The lid popped off in her lap, leaving a puddle of coffee spreading across her raw silk pants.

"You cock sucking pig!" she shouted, red-faced. "This is a Lalage Beaumont. This suit cost me more than your fucking paycheck."

"Ah Lucy, where you're headed, it won't matter. I hope you like denim. Don't think Uncle Sam contracts Lalage Beaumont to make jumpsuits. I'd prefer to continue our conversation dressed as you are over prison garb. Except for the deep shit you're in, you'd win my vote while you stood at the podium giving a speech dressed in that eye-popping outfit, even with the coffee stain across the crotch."

"Damn you. I want my call."

"Sure. Ok. I'm with the government and I'm just here to help. Who would you like to call? Your ex perhaps, Chuck Brighton? No, probably not. That old codger is not too fond of you from what I've read in those trashy supermarket tabloids. Oh yeah, I have a weakness for that kind of stuff. Is it true you left one of the country's ten richest men for your gym trainer? Ah, forgive me, I digress. Perhaps you'd like to call your chief of staff, Henry J. J. Gilmore? Nah, old J. J. is sitting in a room down the hall just like this one, shackled to a table just like this one. Perhaps he's putting on the same defiant act with his interrogators as you are with me. Then again... That spineless weasel more likely has pissed himself by now and is spilling his guts. No, he can't help you. Your attorney maybe? Nope, I'm afraid that's quite impossible. That silver-haired devil of the late-night talk shows, that legal darling of every radical whacko fringe group in the country, is dead. Good old Frank Weiss, Esq. shot himself in the head yesterday. He sure did, just as federal agents made a surprise visit to his D.C. apartment and stormed inside. Yep, old Frank is dead, dead, dead. He made quite a mess of things too while sitting at his desk watching the news. Some poor schmuck is spending his afternoon today scraping bits and pieces of Frank's brain off a wall."

The senator's face turned pale. The fire in her eyes suddenly died.

"Lucy, there will be no Congressional hearing, no trial. Haven't you heard? Our Commander-in-Chief suspended the writ of habeas corpus a few weeks ago under his new emergency war powers."

The man paused to toss a pack of smokes across the table. He had picked them up earlier just for her. He knew her brand. She frantically unwrapped the cellophane and removed a cigarillo. After the man reached over and lit the brown wrapper with a lighter, she took a long drag through the plastic filter, then blew a smoke ring towards the ceiling.

Except for an occasional cigar, the man despised the smell of tobacco. But the nicotine seemed to restore her poise - as he had intended. He needed Brighton to focus, but focus on his terms.

"You Nationalists will lose in the end," Brighton said in a haughty, sensuous tone. "I can wait out the storm until we win. Then you'll be the one sitting in my seat."

The man shook his head. "At least the secessionists of the old South knew what they were fighting for. What do you and your traitorous colleagues in the rebellious states hope to achieve by dividing the nation? No need to answer. We aren't here to debate politics or trade opinions on the looming civil war."

"I bet underneath this tough guy act of yours, you're a real pussy."

The urge to smack her again returned. Unlike many in his profession, the man took no pleasure in administering pain. But in the unfortunate scenario he now found himself, time was more precious than gold and he had little of it. He checked himself and didn't take the bait. He stared at the former senator dispassionately and said nothing.

She took another long drag from her cigarillo before leaning back in her chair, as much as her shackles would let her. "Nothing to say, Agent? Agent...? I didn't catch your name."

"I am not an agent, leastwise, not as you think of them. I am more, shall we say, freelance. I have many names. I can make a list for you and you can pick the one you like."

"I think I'll call you Agent Dickhead. That suits you."

"Poor Lucy, this misplaced bluster of yours is becoming tiresome. You may call me XMax5, my old code name, or just plain Max if you like, Max Doss."

"I'll remember the name, Mr. Max Doss."

"You do that."

"Odysseus is dead, isn't he?" she asked with a gleam in her eye.

Less than a hundred people in the world knew the answer to that question, and Doss was one of them. President Abraham Bancroft Calhoun, code name Odysseus, had reportedly died from his wounds on the streets of a small, Virginia town square though, with his body having been cremated only hours after the shootout without even a perfunctory autopsy, D.C. was awash in rumors that he might still be alive. Like his predecessor with the same given name and sharing the same 12th of February birthday, Calhoun had been determined to reunite the country regardless of the cost after he had been elected President the year before. He had been prepared to spill oceans of blood to do it too. But where the South had killed Lincoln at the end of the conflict, the Resistance, as they liked to call themselves - as if they were the heroes in one of those old Star Wars movies - apparently had decided an assassination would be more advantageous at the beginning. At least the militants within the Resistance were at the top of Doss's list of suspects.

Doss and Calhoun had history. When the U.S. sent a modest expeditionary force into Iran to support a people's rebellion - augmented with a token Israeli armored infantry brigade on the condition that the new government, once formed, recognize the State of Isreal and enter into strong trade and military alliances with the U.S. - Calhoun and Doss eagerly went with it. Full of vim and vigor, the two men thought they were invincible back then. Not as invincible as Superman they both soon discovered after Doss, a newly minted armored cavalry platoon leader, had to crawl into a burning Gen 4 Abrams-X tank lying on its side with mortar shells dropping all around to pull Lieutenant Colonel Calhoun's broken body out from the wreckage. Doss spent two weeks in a military hospital convalescing from his wounds. Calhoun spent three months recuperating. The two men became as close as brothers. After Calhoun left the military, he went straight into politics and rose through his party's ranks like a god, wading through deep cesspools of shit, piss, and blood until he, at the tender age of thirty-nine, ascended to the top of Mount Olympus to become *the man*. Doss had decided on a different career path after his discharge, one better suited to his particular talents.

Using the table as an ashtray, Brighton snuffed the stub of her cigarillo out and reached to grab another, until Doss snatched the pack out of her hand. She jerked back in fear when she saw that she had struck a nerve - when she saw the anger building in his eyes.

"Lucy, I've shown you great civility so far. But I swear, if you ask me one more question, I'll slap you so hard across the face your teeth will rattle and I can promise you the folks standing behind that mirror won't lift a finger to help you. We are short on time."

To give his words power, Doss nodded to the two special ops guys standing behind the senator. They grabbed Brighton by her armpits and yanked her up and out of her chair. They pulled until the shackles went taut; until she shrieked from a mix of fear and pain.

"This is outrageous!" she screamed. "I am a senior ranking member of Congress, a U.S. Senator, the Chairwoman of the powerful Select Committee on Intelligence!"

"We've covered this ground already, Lucy. Or would you prefer I call you, wait a moment..." Doss commanded, pausing to remove a laminated card from the inside breast pocket of his blazer. "Ah, here we are, prisoner bravo-charlie, double zero-one-six-eighty-seven?"

She stared at Doss wide-eyed, but kept her mouth shut as she processed her predicament and racked her brain, trying to find some bit of leverage. Nothing came to mind.

Doss was not looking forward to a long, tedious day of inflicting psychological and physical pain and despised being cooped up in small, windowless rooms. He switched tactics, decided to try the carrot approach and put the stick aside.

"Lucy, listen very carefully to me now. You only have one of two futures. Once we are finished here, you will be processed under the Extraordinary Seditious Crimes Act of 2044, or ESCA if you like acronyms, into a secret maximum-security facility where you will spend the rest of your days in a windowless, six-by-eight-foot cell fourteen hours a day, seven days a week, three hundred and sixty-five days a year with no friendly visitors and limited TV, phone and internet. As I have said, there will be no trial. You will be processed and transported to such a facility before week's end. There is however, another, albeit slim possibility available to you. Would you like me to elaborate?"

"Ye, yes."

With a nod from Doss, the two ops guys released their grip on the senator and let her slide back into her chair.

"I make no promises. There is this place up in the northwest that might accept you. You'll need the right recommendations from the right people to get there. Given your combative attitude and charming personality so far, this will not happen. The place I speak of isn't paradise. Your days of attending swank D.C. dancing balls and parties, lofty Congressional meetings and intermingling with powerbrokers and the rich and beautiful people are over. But this place isn't a Stalinist gulag in Siberia either. Once admitted, no citizen, that's what the residents are called, citizens - rather Orwellian, don't you think? - ever leaves the Village. I shit you not they call the place the Village. You'd have a small apartment to call your own. There are shops, a library and even a movie theater, I hear. The Village has a park with a lake too where citizens can walk, jog, or sit on a bench and feed the ducks while contemplating the meaning of life. Quaint, right? Of course, from time to time the government may want something from you in return. Lucy ... this ... is ... your ... moment ... of ... truth... You must tell me everything I want to know. Do you want a chance at becoming a citizen at the Village, or do you prefer to be a number inside a maximum-security penitentiary? Banishment or solitary confinement in a small cell? These are your only choices."

"Bullshit."

"Ok, we're done here," Doss said coldly and abruptly stood to leave. "I'll introduce you to your prisoner escort detail. I did my best to help you. I'm off to check on Gilmore."

"No, wait," Brighton mumbled in a pleading tone as Doss reached for the door. With a quivering lower lip and beads of sweat popping up across her brow, she bowed her head in defeat before looking back up at Doss. "I'll, I'll try answering your questions."

"A wise choice, Lucy. But just so we are clear, I have the authority to put a bullet in your brain, in this very room, if I think - in my sole and absolute discretion - you are wasting my time."

After Doss took his seat, he removed his service weapon from his shoulder holster and set the handgun on the table. He too liked CZs and carried a CZ 75 P01 semiautomatic 9mm, modified here and there to suit his particular needs. The CZ fit his hand like a glove, held more rounds than a .45 or .40, and was exceptionally accurate and insanely reliable.

"Are you ready to talk?" Doss asked while Brighton kept her eyes fixated on his handgun.

"Lucy?"

"Ok," she said and nodded vigorously.

"Let me hear you say it."

"Yes, yes."

"Yes, what?"

"Yes, I am ready to talk."

"Oh, you'll do more than talk. You'll answer all my questions completely, accurately, and honestly. Do be mindful that under Section II-B (a) (iii) of ESCA, any public official, elected or appointed, who knowingly lies to the public - by commission or by omission - for financial profit or political gain, for themselves or on behalf of any third party, or who unknowingly or unwittingly lies to the public for the same reasons when any reasonable person exercising ordinary due care would have known that their statements were, in fact, false, can be charged and convicted of Class B felony treason."

Doss paused to retrieve his handgun. He racked the slide back to eject a round. The gesture had the desired effect. Brighton flinched when the brass casing hit the floor with a sharp ping. He scooped the 9mm hollow point up in his hand and placed the live round in her hand. "You keep this memento as my gift. No lies, no holding back."

She wiped away a single tear from her cheek and silently nodded again.

"Let me hear you say it."

"No, no lies, no, no holding back."

"Very well, let's get to it then," Doss cheerfully said as he slid the pack of cigarillos back across the table.

Chapter Two

Excerpts from Hermann Adelman's private journal:
The Great Turmoil

A crusty, older gentleman with a deeply furrowed brow over a rugged, leathery face, a hard, unbending man by all appearances, wept when she finally opened her eyes during one of his frequent visits. He reached across the bed to take her hand in his and offered her a faint smile.

"Father?"

"Yes, my darling girl," the man answered with his heavy German accent. "How do you feel?"

She took a moment to take in her surroundings. She couldn't understand why she was lying in a hospital bed inside a hospital room, tied to machines and monitors by tubes and wires. She started to panic, pulled her hand away from her father's hand and tried to remove an IV attached to her arm.

Her father stopped her. "Gretchen, no. All will be well. I swear it."

"Where am I? What is this place? What happened to me?"

"You are in a hospital," her father answered flatly. "You were in an accident. Do you remember any of that?"

"An accident?"

"Yes. You were in a car with Charles, returning home from your prom."

"Oh. Yes, yes. I remember now. Prom Night. Charles. We swerved off the road to avoid the bright lights coming at us. The car rolled over and over again down an embankment. That's all I remember Father. Where is Charles? Is he here? Can I see him?"

Before her father could answer, a small gaggle of doctors and nurses rushed into the room.

"Gretchen," one of the doctors called out excitedly as he removed a small flashlight from his white jacket's breast pocket. "Welcome back," he said while he moved the light across her eyes. "I am Doctor Weitz. This other gentleman is my colleague, Dr. Fetterman. Doctor Fetterman is an expert in head trauma. He is assisting me today. How do you feel? Any pain?"

"No," Gretchen replied.

"No headaches?"

"No."

"Do you see any bright lights?"

"No."

"Any pain at all?"

"No."

"Raise your arms for me, good, good. Now wiggle your toes, excellent. Lift your right leg. Ok, now try lifting your left leg. Don't worry about that. We'll get your legs working again. Any dizziness, nausea?"

"No."

"Wonderful," Weitz said, then patted her reassuringly on the leg while two nurses moved around her bed to check the monitors and the IV. "Your vitals look good. You gave us quite a scare young lady."

"How long have I been here?"

Weitz turned to the old man for guidance.

"Gretchen, joy of my heart, we thought we had lost you," her father said gravely. "There is no easy way to say this," he continued and gently took her hand in his again. "So, I'll just say it. You've been in a coma for some time."

"What? How long?"

"Two years."

"No, no, no. This can't be. Fa, Father. Where, where is Charles?"

The old man leaned over and wrapped his daughter in his arms before answering. "Your friend was a good boy. I am so sorry Gretchen. Truly, it pains me to say this. I'm afraid Charles did not survive the accident."

After the doctors finished their examinations and informed the old man that they expected his daughter to make a full recovery, once they left the room with the nurses and after her tears subsided, the old man leaned over and kissed his daughter gently, lovingly on the forehead.

"How Father? I want to know how all of this happened."

The old man considered where to start. They had much to discuss. But before he could say more a handsome black fellow dressed in a dark blue suit with a sharp maroon tie stepped into the room.

"Herr Direktor, my apologies," the man said. "But I have urgent news which requires your immediate attention."

The stranger turned to Gretchen and smiled. "Gretchen, how very good to see you awake. Sarah and I have kept you in our prayers. Please forgive this rude intrusion. I won't keep your father long young lady, I promise."

The man looked vaguely familiar to her, but she couldn't quite place him. She couldn't remember anyone named Sarah either. She acknowledged the man with a simple nod and then closed her eyes, trying to remember other matters while the man and her father traded whispers. Soon she started drifting off and quickly fell into a deep, comfortable sleep.

When she awoke the next morning, she found her father snoring in a chair next to her bed. Then she noticed the tray over her lap with a bowl of melting ice and a plastic cup of red Jello with a note from Dr. Weitz with one simple word: *Try*.

"Good morning, Father," she said when the old man's neck suddenly snapped back in response to a loud gasp for air between his snoring.

"Gretchen!" he replied affectionately with a broad smile, something he rarely did. "How do you feel? You have a bit more color today."

"Fine, I'm fine or at least better. Tell me please Father, tell me about the accident. And why, why isn't Mother here?"

Her father recounted the terrible night when a presumably drunk driver had run the car Charles was driving off the highway and into a creek some one hundred feet below. Charles drowned, Gretchen didn't and the other driver was never found. Gretchen's mother, the old man's wife, had died a few weeks after the accident. The old man paused to let Gretchen collect herself after he told her. The real grieving, he knew, would come later after the initial shock wore off.

"How did Mother die?" she finally asked as she wiped the last of the tears from her face.

"From an aneurism," her father replied in a soft voice. But that wasn't true. The initial autopsy performed by the county coroner did indeed conclude that the cause of death was an aneurism but when he sent one of his own medical experts over to the morgue to take a second look, she concluded that the probable cause of death was from a rare, nearly impossible to detect poison, a poison that most likely had been meant for him.

"Two years!" Gretchen blurted out. "Mother is dead, Charles is dead," she mumbled to herself as a fresh wave of tears began cascading down her cheeks.

"Yes, but you are alive my darling girl! And you are still so very young. You only just turned eighteen a few days ago!"

"Why are so many folks here wearing uniforms Father? Is this a military hospital?"

"It is. You are safe here. A lot has happened since your accident. When you are strong enough to hear a story, I will tell you a story. I fear it is neither a short nor happy story. Much has changed in the world over the past two years. Our own country is at war with itself."

Gretchen, an only child, was every bit her father's daughter. Stubborn, strong-willed and curious about everything in the world around her, she was incredibly bright and hungry to learn.

"Tell me, tell me now Father."

The old man nodded. "Very well then," he said and smiled proudly.

Chapter Three

Doss didn't get much out of Senator Brighton, ex-Senator Brighton, because she did not know much. She was, as Doss had suspected even before stepping into the interrogation room, a disposable patsy for the party. Even so, she had some interesting things to disclose and unwittingly handed Doss one solid lead worth gold.

"Bravo," a tall, muscular woman with a dark complexion, dressed in black military boots, black cargo pants and a black, wool turtleneck sweater said as she clapped her hands together when Doss stepped into the observation booth behind the two-way mirror. "You did good, but you shoulda let me go to work on that bitch. She's got more to say. She knew you were bluffing when you laid your 9mm on the table."

Tactical Agent Alejandra Bijeau, a five-foot-nine, hundred-and-thirty-pound powerhouse with a figure somewhere between a gymnast and a weightlifter, was never shy about giving her opinion. She kept her raven, kinky hair - with faint purplish highlights - cut short. A tiny white scar on the right side of her nose, a barely visible dot, was the only evidence of a nose ring long ago discarded. Despite her tough guy image, the former force recon combat marine, with multiple decorations for heroism, was cute, even hot, and she knew it.

"I didn't think you liked white girls," Doss drolly replied.

Bijeau, a gum addict, continued chewing as she smiled. "As long as you got the goods, honey, this half Louisiana Creole, half Hispanic American bitch from the bad part of town ain't prejudice."

"Always the charmer."

She batted her eyes flirtatiously at Doss. "You know I like sweet pink, baby. But I'd make an exception for you, big guy. You're a fine-lookin' hunk of white boy meat and I'm bettin' you've got the goods that can make any girl swoon."

Bijeau, Doss was quickly learning, was a constant flirt - with everyone. But the *ah shucks I'm just a simple ghetto gal from the backwoods of Louisiana* schtick was only a façade. She was no lightweight. Doss had heard the gossip from her peers and they were not kind. She was no prom queen, either. But Doss had witnessed both her smarts and her fearlessness up close. When her service weapon had jammed during a raid up in Boston's gangland part of Chinatown a few months back, Doss had watched her charge at a two-hundred-pound plus gorilla, an enforcer for the brutal Fung Wu Squad. She took him down with her bare hands.

"I'm flattered," Doss said in jest, but with some truth.

"You suspect Brighton was involved in the assassination?"

"Not sure yet."

"Has her chief of staff flipped, that sleazy fellow, Henry J. J. Gilmore?"

"No. But they were plotting something. If they weren't in on the assassination, they at least knew something was afoot and did nothing to stop it. We're not finished with either of them, not by a long shot. We'll get the truth, eventually."

"Where to next, Doss?"

"Chicago."

"Why Chicago?"

"I'm off to see a man about some money."

"Let's get a move on then."

"Maybe you haven't heard, Bijeau. I work alone."

"Yeah, I know, I know. That's exactly what I told the VP, I mean the President, when she sent me here. I told her you work alone, you're the last of the lone wolves."

"Yeah? And what did Dreyfus have to say about that?"

"Ha! She said she didn't give a flying fuck how good you are. Ms. lily white Boston College said it just like that too, in her refined New England twang. She said I wasn't to let you out of my sight. She wanted to give us six goons for backup, but she couldn't spare the bodies, so you've just got me baby, bubblegum delicious. She also said if you had a problem with any of this, you could share a cell with the she-bitch chained to the table over there."

Doss sighed. He preferred working alone. He followed his own rules and had enjoyed a certain amount of autonomy, even untouchability, while Calhoun had been President. He knew he had been spoiled. At least Dreyfus had sent him Bijeau. He had pulled her file of course. Marine, Airborne with advanced recon and high-level interrogation training, and only the third woman to ever graduate from the Navy Seal program. She had superior marks on intelligence scores and exceptionally good proficiency ratings in the martial arts. She had seen action in Columbia, Venezuela and Iran. As an E-6 in command of a platoon, she had been awarded the Navy Cross, two Bronze Stars and a Purple Heart. Among her platoon she was known as the Terminatrix, or sometimes the Dominatrix. Her curriculum vitae was seriously hardcore. After processing out of the military a few years back, the Agency had enthusiastically recruited her.

A gal like that deserved some respect Doss told himself. But he knew Dreyfus hadn't sent her to help him as much as to keep a close eye on him and report back to her. That wasn't going to work for Doss.

"Ok, Bijeau. I've read your file. You have some marginal skill sets that might come in handy. But you do what I say when I say it. No questions. Got it?"

"Got it."

"Good, I hope you've got it. Your life will depend on it. And just to be clear, I don't answer to Dreyfus."

"How can you not answer to the President?"

"That's mistake number one, asking me a question you know I can't or won't answer. Clear?"

"Clear."

"You aren't squeamish, are you?"

Bijeau answered Doss with a look somewhere between indifference and boredom, blew a big pink bubble in his face and popped it.

Doss rented a compact sedan and headed to Chicago with Bijeau riding shotgun. From Fort Knox, the drive was about six hours straight up I-65.

Bijeau offered Doss a stick of gum and he accepted. "Pres said this is a top priority mission."

"Yep, C-1-A priority op."

Any operation designated C-1-A meant an open checkbook and

unlimited resources. There was nothing better than working a C-1-A op.

"So why are we taking this piece of shit to Chicago?"

"Because I like driving."

"Bullshit."

"Ok, Bijeau. Truth is, I like anonymity."

"I get it, avoid the airports, the trains, the buses and all the cameras. But you could've requisitioned one of those fancy Agency private jets for us."

"To requisition one would've taken too long and besides the Agency, your Agency, has been compromised. We're off the grid, so to speak, for now."

"Uh, huh. Dreyfus did mention something about that to me. So why am I here if you don't trust anyone at the Agency?"

"I didn't say I didn't trust anyone. You were the one who put the pieces together on Brighton, in record speed I might add. Impressive work. Besides, and God only knows why, Calhoun trusted you and now you seem to have the trust of Dreyfus."

"You know what they say?"

"No, what do they say Bijeau?"

"Once you taste black, you never go back..."

Doss glanced over at Bijeau and rolled his eyes with disapproval.

"What's your real name anyway handsome?"

"Don't have one."

"Right. Well, this Louisiana gal figures there's a good chance we're going to die together on this deal and that should at least entitle me to know what your given name is."

Doss smiled. "Fair point. You already know it."

"Baby, I don't even know who you work for and XMax5 ain't no name."

"Call me by my code name then, Telemachus."

"Uh, huh. What is a Telemachus?"

"You mean who is Telemachus? Google him when you get the chance."

"Google? Who uses Google anymore? I'll check the name out on KineticPro. I know you aren't with the Agency, NSA, or CIA. You must be with that outfit folks only whisper about."

"What outfit is that?"

"Section M3."

"Section M3? You mean the company that makes those yellow, blue, green and pink Post-it notes?"

"Ha, ha. That's 3M, the old Minnesota, Mining and Manufacturing Company. I think Section M3 though is just an alias."

"An alias? An alias for what?"

"For a double, triple, super-secret organization that officially doesn't exist run by that illusive fellow, that odd German dude who goes by Herr Direktor and sounds like Dr. Strangelove."

"What do the three Ms in 3M stand for in this fantasy secret fraternity of yours?"

"My guess: mischief, mayhem and murder."

"Good grief, Bijeau. You've been watching too many spy movies."

Bijeau mumbled one curse or another in French under her breath as she pushed her seat back and closed her eyes. She had no trouble drifting off to sleep.

Doss had briefly lived in Chicago once. Clean city that thrived on style as he recalled, a vibrant metropolis with a variety of wonderful cuisines and authentic ethnic dishes, with major league sports, world-class museums, art, finance, and business. Doss though had found the city too hot or too cold with very little spring or autumn for his liking. Chicago pretty much went from winter to summer and back to winter again - and everything in every direction was disturbingly flat.

With the sun just beginning to peak over Lake Michigan, Doss hit a sweet spot as they rolled into the Windy City. Traffic was light. The day promised to be warm, but not too hot and the humidity seemed unusually tolerable.

Doss pulled into a public garage off Wacker Drive and parked the rental on the highest level. He and Bijeau grabbed their things, Doss had brought only an overnight bag and Bijeau had brought something similar along with her laptop, and then Doss tossed the keys into the trunk. There was no need to wipe the vehicle down for fingerprints or DNA.

They took the garage elevator down to the building's ground floor level and from there they walked down a dingy stairwell into the basement where Doss led Bijeau over to a rusty metal door in one corner of the building with abused paint cans, tools, and boxes of junk stacked all around it. When Doss removed a loose brick from the wall and punched a code into a keypad the rust-covered door's electric locks clicked open.

Bijeau made a quick scan of the room after she stepped inside. "Dang Doss, this is a sweet pad. This is your place? Nice."

"Safe house. There's a shower in the other room with any toiletries you might need. Should be a change of clothing for you too."

"This damn sure isn't any government safe house."

"No. For our purposes, it's safer."

"Anything to eat?"

"The fridge is over there and should be stocked with some things. If you want a real breakfast, there's a decent place around the corner. We can grab something there after we shower, change and catch a few winks."

"Shower together? You drove a long way just to get me in the sack. *Ohlala* you horny dog!"

"Bijeau..."

"All right, all right, I'm going. I'll just have to find my pleasure elsewhere."

"How secure is your laptop?"

Bijeau understood what Doss was asking. Her IQ for information technologies was off the charts. That's the skill set that caught the Agency's attention first, more than her medals for valor. But she joined the Agency on the condition the Agency would assign her fieldwork. She didn't have the patience or the demeanor to work as an analyst, locked up in a windowless room somewhere. She knew her decision had cost her a promotion or two but she had no regrets.

The safe house had several sophisticated computers and communications equipment, equipment that could access just about any government network anywhere. But Doss wouldn't touch it.

Bijeau powered-up her laptop. "After Dreyfus informed me about certain, how did she put it, certain *irregularities* at the Agency, I layered my own protocols over theirs. You want to check out your porn baby-nobody in this world is going to know but you and me."

"BIJEAU!"

"Ok, ok, grumpy. Plain to see you need your caffeine fix and some sleep. I'll log you in and let you be while I clean up."

After a quick power nap, a shower and breakfast at the restaurant - Doss had a poppyseed bagel and black coffee while Bijeau ate a large stack of pancakes, two eggs and hash browns with a side of crispy bacon - they returned to the basement, grabbed their things, and walked up four flights of stairs to the garage. When Doss reached into his pocket and pressed a remote, the lights to a black, two-door coupe parked in a dark corner blinked and door locks popped open.

"Seriously?" Bijeau asked.

"Seriously," Doss replied.

"You have a Maserati?"

"A Gran Turismo Special."

"It's about time you treated this girl special. So much for traveling incognito. Any cool gadgets?"

"It's not an Agency car. It's not 007's Aston Martin. But she'll fly."

"Can I drive?"

"No."

Before they even made it to the interstate, Doss and Bijeau had company. Four government-issue black GMC sedans pulled out of two side streets and fell in behind them.

"Bijeau?"

"I see them."

"Your phone?"

"No way. I scanned my phone and laptop for trackers before we left."

"Your purse."

"Have you ever seen this foxy chick carrying a damn purse?"

Traffic was light. Doss accelerated to 55 in a 30 zone. The Maserati lurched forward with no perceptible vibration or noise. As Doss sped up, the sedans sped up too. Different options started racing through his head.

"What then Bijeau, think?"

"I'm telling you, Doss, I'm clean. Maybe the car?"

"No, not possible."

"Then I don't know. We ditch the tail and then the car and everything we have, including our clothes."

Doss pressed the accelerator pedal down to make the next light. The light turned red just as the Maserati flew through the intersection. The sedans behind them didn't stop or slow down.

Bijeau pulled and checked her Sig 226, a standard Agency piece.

"Are you really going to shoot at federal government vehicles," Doss asked, "in downtown Chicago?"

"The orders the Pres gave me, I suspect, are pretty much the same orders your boss gave you, whoever that is. She was pretty clear about it, too. The mission at *any* cost."

"You don't even know what the mission is Bijeau."

"Fuck if I don't. My mission is to keep you alive for the mission."

Lose the tail, ditch the car, ditch the clothes, ditch everything, Doss mumbled to himself. *Damn.* They didn't have the time.

"Bijeau, by chance, did you recently wake up one morning feeling nauseous?" Doss asked as he swerved onto the entrance ramp to the interstate doing 65. The tires didn't even squeal.

"What?"

"You heard me."

"I, I don't know. Maybe. Ah, yeah, yeah, I did wake up a week ago feeling sick to my stomach, but it passed."

Doss checked the review mirror. The sedans were continuing to keep pace with the Maserati.

"The night before your tummy ache, you went out for a drink and then slept like the dead, right?"

"Yeah, maybe. Ok, I think that's right. Why?"

"The tracker is in you somewhere. They drugged you, something that would knock you out a few hours later, slipped into your apartment when you were sleeping and injected a GPS tracker into you, a nano chip. Probably behind an ear or in the webbing between your toes. Maybe an armpit."

"How'd you figure that out?"

"We could ditch everything, as you suggested, and they'd still be on top of us."

"Fuck me sideways. That night I stopped at a local bar for a nightcap and some chick bought me a drink. Went home feeling woozy. Stupid, stupid, stupid."

"Don't sweat it. Happens to the best of 'em."

"Anyone ever slip you a high-tech mickey?"

"Nope."

"What do we do now?"

Doss pressed the phone connect button on the dashboard screen.

"Number please?" the Maserati's voice assistant asked.

"Mother," Doss replied.

"Dialing Mother."

"Doss."

"Mother."

"I see you're in town, dear boy. Traveling westbound on I-90."

"Yes, with four unwelcome guests."

"Ah, I have them. Destroy or disable?"

"Disable."

"ETA in ten, initiating - three, two, one, mark."

"Thank you, Mother."

"Always a pleasure. I see you have a passenger. She's quite attractive if you're into punkster."

"Mother, meet Tactical Agent Alejandra Bijeau."

"Ah, our war hero. Pleasure, Tactical Agent Bijeau."

Bijeau gave Doss a quizzical look.

"Bijeau, say hello to Mother lest you hurt her feelings."

"Hello, Mother."

"Do take care of XMax5, Tactical Agent Bijeau. I've grown rather fond of him, despite his eccentricities."

"What is XMax5? Doss won't share."

"Our fearless leader once upon a time assigned code names to certain field agents. X was for the experimental program they were in. The number five meant that our Max was the fifth Max in the program to graduate. The boss later discontinued the project along with these designations for reasons unknown."

"Goodbye, Mother," Doss said flippantly, then disconnected the signal.

"Who is Mother and who is your fearless leader?" Bijeau asked.

"Not now Bijeau."

"What happens in ten minutes?"

"Our entertainment for the morning."

"C'mon, at least tell me who Mother is?"

"Mother? Never heard of her."

Bijeau folded her arms and settled back in her seat annoyed but did not press Doss further. She was learning.

Mother uncharacteristically miscalculated the timing by a few seconds, probably because of an unexpected shift in the winds Doss figured. After he drove the Maserati through the toll booths at Plaza 17 in an I-Pass Lane near Devon Avenue, just before O'Hare, three of the sedans tailing them suddenly, magically, coasted to a stop. The fourth sedan slammed into a yellow plastic crash barrel in a cloud of black smoke.

"Whoa, that's some slick shit!" Bijeau exclaimed while watching the SUVs through the Maserati's back window. "How?"

Doss glanced up at the rearview mirror and saw 16 unhappy agents stepping out of their vehicles. "Drones."

"Drones? In the middle of Chicago, with only ten minutes to prep for the operation?"

"Yep, something new. Three RF military-grade drones utilizing radio frequency pulses to disrupt the vehicle's electronic systems, causing the engine to shut down, and one SE military-grade drone armed with a small explosive with just enough power to damage an axel or engine or pop a tire after the drone flies underneath the chassis and detonates. Looks like Mother only had three RF drones at her fingertips and had to send in one with explosives. The drones are standard, as you know. The delivery system is not. That's the new part."

Doss dialed Mother again.

"Max, how nice to hear from you so soon. Four for four I trust?"

"Four for four, Mother. I have another problem."

"Yes, you need to know how the government is tracking you."

"I'm fairly certain Bijeau was injected."

"Glove compartment, small blue kit," Mother said. "Use the scanner to find the point of entry. The kit comes with an extractor. Shouldn't leave much of a scar."

Bijeau opened the glove box and removed the kit. "After this is all over," she said with a trace of anger in her tone, "I'm gonna mess somebody's day up real bad. Payback's a bitch, as they say."

"You go girl," Mother said. "No half measures."

"Don't encourage her, Mother, bye-bye," Doss interjected and disconnected the call.

Bijeau activated a silver metal wand and located the tracker quickly. Someone had implanted the chip in her left butt cheek, which made her doubly mad.

Doss pulled off at Schaumburg, found a strip mall and circled around the back where the stores keep their dumpsters. As soon as he parked the car, Bijeau didn't hesitate. She undid her jeans and pulled them down around her ankles in front of Doss, even though she had decided to go commando for the day and wore no panties.

She seemed amused by Doss's close-up inspection of her butt as she turned her head around and gave him a huge grin, showing off a set of perfect, dazzling-white teeth. "You must admit, Doss," she said teasingly, "it's an exceptionally nice ass. Go on honey, show me some foreplay. Slap it around a few times or take a bite if you want. I showered real good just for you and won't tell a soul."

"Hold still," Doss ordered gruffly as he pinched a bit of flesh between his thumb and forefinger with one hand and, unconcerned about being gentle, stabbed her hard with the extractor with the other.

"Ouch!"

"*Semper Fi*, Marine," Doss said with a smile. "I don't have any band-aids, but I don't think you'll bleed out."

Doss tossed the nano chip, about the size of a pinhead, out the car window and headed back to the interstate.

"Why track me?" Bijeau asked as she pulled up her pants.

"Not sure," Doss replied. "Could be something unrelated to what we are doing. Could be to get to me."

"But who, other than Dreyfus, and now Mother, knows I'm with you?"

"Now there's an intelligent question."

Chapter Four

Excerpts from Hermann Adelman's private journal:
The Great Turmoil

Gretchen listened intently through the morning, mesmerized by her father's description of the most important domestic and world events impacting humankind since her accident. She listened until she could listen no more, until a heavy weariness spread throughout her body.

Her father began his tale with the general premise that the country had been hurtling towards secession for decades. Old prejudices and hatreds ran deep from sea to shining sea. The refusal of various cultures to assimilate, coupled with rising tribalism, coursed through the veins of the nation like a deadly, untreated cancer. After the spectacular meltdown of the old Republican Party not long after the end of the Trump era, conservatives, independents, libertarians, many industrialists and a few radical groups who disliked any form of government, joined together to form the new National Party and chose Abraham B. Calhoun, a hardliner in most things, to lead them. Not long after that, the old Democratic Party imploded too. Liberals and moderates from both old parties, new age socialists, a few radical fringe groups of all stripes, many elites and the wealthy, and even a few anarchists, found refuge within the newly constituted Citizen's Alliance Party, or CAP, though the anacronym never took and the secessionists continued calling themselves the Resistance. After Calhoun barely won the presidency, to the surprise of no one, all hell broke loose. What did surprise everyone was the surreal, breathtaking speed with which everything fell apart.

Calhoun was no Ghandi. He had no intention of looking for non-violent means that might heal the country. He had no appetite for appeasement with the Resistance. Calhoun would be, in his own words, a *fucking wrecking ball* on the issue of secession.

Soon after Calhoun's election, California was the first state to formally secede from the Union, followed quickly by Oregon, Washington and Nevada. Then New York bolted, taking Connecticut, Vermont, Massachusetts, Rhode Island, New Jersey, Maryland, and half of Virginia with her. Minnesota, part of western Idaho, Kentucky, and Colorado decided to join the Resistance a few days later. Most of the remaining states, still calling themselves the United States of America, or the Union, stood with the National Party. The rebellious states collectively decided to call themselves The League of North American States. The legislatures in three states, Pennsylvania, New Mexico, and Arizona, known as the Purple Territories, voted to remain neutral. Hawaii would have seceded had the Navy not intervened first. The Navy seized all communications and government buildings and imposed martial law across the islands before her political leaders could do anything about it.

America's abrupt and extraordinary implosion sent shock waves around the world, leaving behind a power vacuum of colossal, unimaginable proportions. There was one silver lining for America, one godsend. America's allies took neutral positions and decided collectively to let the Americans sort things out for themselves, while America's two greatest rivals, Russia and China, had their own problems, preventing either of them from taking any meaningful advantage of America's vulnerability.

The Russian Federation had already disintegrated into chaos following Premier Nicoli Kaminsky's mysterious disappearance. The government was dissolved, those supporting the old authoritarian dictatorship were arrested and the military, already in shambles following the costly debacles in Ukraine and Georgia, slipped into complete disarray. No one knew who had control of Russia's nuclear arsenal. Then the twelve richest oligarchs came together and carved Russia up into twelve independent states. Each family took one piece for themselves and all agreed to a loose confederation for defense and commerce. The families collectively became known as the Twelve Great Houses of Mother Russia.

China too, was in turmoil. Reeling from an unexpected collapse of her major financial institutions triggered by Calhoun's Executive Order 18,001, declaring the $42,000,000,000,000 of debt owed by

America to China null and void, China's teetering economy faced extinction. And then, after a group of well-armed, well-funded terrorists from parts unknown decided it was an opportune time to cripple Iran's oil refineries and blockade her harbors, which caused an abrupt, catastrophic disruption of China's access to Iranian oil, China's markets tumbled into a freefall. Thousands of businesses went under, decimating China's burgeoning middle class and unemployment exploded, killing off the working class. Famine, plague, and riots crippled China. Not even her vast reserves of gold and lithium could save her. Inexplicably, incredibly, the Chinese Communist Party somehow managed to maintain its iron grip over the people.

"The whole world," Gretchen observed when her father paused to take a sip of ice water, "is on fire."

"Sadly, yes."

"Do you still serve the President? Are we Nationalists, Father?"

The old man cleared his throat before answering. "We are with the Nationalists, of course, Gretchen. Could you imagine your old papa ever joining the Resistance? And yes, I still serve the President but Calhoun is no longer President. Two weeks ago, Dreyfus was sworn in as the new President of the United States."

"Elaine Dreyfus? What happened to President Calhoun?"

"Evil butchered him in the streets like an animal."

"Dear God! He was your friend. What will you do, Father?"

"Whatever is in my power to do, I will do."

"And that man, yesterday. I remember him now. Jeremiah something."

"Jerimiah Stone."

"Oh, yes, Mr. Stone. He works for you."

"Many people work for your papa, but yes, Jeremiah works for me. Do you remember what he does, Gretchen?"

Gretchen took a moment to search her memory. "I think you once told me that he is a, a fixer? He fixes things, yes?"

"That's my girl. And should anything ever happen to me, you find Jerimiah Stone. You run to him. He is a man we can trust. He will protect you from any harm."

And that was the moment when Gretchen sat back on her pillow and yawned, when she closed her eyes and slipped into a long and blissful sleep.

🔔

The President waved Herr Direktor into the Situation Room. The various TV screens and monitors along the wood-paneled walls were blank. The room's blue carpeting smelled new.

Hollywood's various portrayals of the White House's Situation Room, the President's intelligence management center located on the ground floor of the West Wing, were not too far off the mark, though it had been renovated multiple times, the last major renovation having happened under President Biden in '23. The Situation Room is not a single room. Staffed with roughly 130 National Security personnel, the Situation Room is a 5,000-square-foot operations center with three secure, adjacent conference rooms. The rooms are available for the President of course, but are also available to the Vice President, the President's Chief of Staff, senior advisors, and the directors of intelligence, national security, homeland security and FBI for monitoring and dealing with crises and for conducting secure communications with foreign governments or with certain key individuals. From the Situation Room, the President has complete command and control of all U.S. military forces and intelligence resources throughout the world.

"Herr Direktor, welcome back," Dreyfus said, then motioned him to take the last empty seat, one of 13 at the table. "I was so pleased to learn about your daughter. Gretchen is her name?"

"Yes, Madam President. Thank you."

"How is she?"

"We expect a full recovery."

"Good, good. I'm happy to hear this. My gosh, two years though! The emotional recovery from the loss of two years for a teenage girl I imagine will be a long and challenging road. Especially when she has lost her mother. Her physical, emotional and psychological well-being must be your first priority, Hermann."

"I assure you Madam President, Gretchen's well-being is and will always be my number one priority, along with the security of the nation."

"Well, to business then. You know everyone in the room except for Tom MacAfee, my new Chief of Staff. Tom, this is Hermann Adelman, the director, Herr Direktor, of Section M3. Hermann has been on loan to us from the *Bundesnachrichtendienst* for gosh, six, seven years or so I think Hermann? We just have never found the time to give him back. He was Germany's supremely capable Spymaster, which is why we poached him from our friends across the sea in the first place. Hermann holds PhDs in algebraic mathematics, quantum physics and electromagnetism, as I recall. So do be on your guard with this crafty one, Tom."

The Chief of Staff acknowledged Adelman with an unfriendly nod.

Conspicuously absent from the meeting, Adelman noted, were the directors of the FBI, Judd Brown, and the CIA, Christopher Nestle. Dreyfus began with General Barbara Ritter-Starling, the country's first female Chairman of the Joint Chiefs of Staff, and asked the general for a 30,000-foot overview of the country's military preparedness.

"Madam President," Ritter-Starling began as she flipped on one of the wall screens with a remote. A map soon materialized with the locations of all major U.S. military installations across the planet, some colored in red and others in blue.

"After California and the rest seceded from the Union, we moved swiftly to secure control of America's strategic nuclear weapons and America's anti-missile defense shield. We have one hundred percent control of the shield. However, the Resistance became a nuclear power when a squadron's worth of strategic bombers, older B-2s mostly but with nuclear payloads, the carrier *Gerald R. Ford*, recently rechristened *Liberty*, carrying nuclear-tipped Tyr M-3 missiles, and one aging Ohio Class ballistic missile submarine, *Maryland*, armed with twenty-four Trident-4 missiles, defected. Defections within the ranks of the Army and Marines have been significant, less so in the Navy and Air Force. Of America's conventual forces, including all active-duty personnel and reservists, roughly thirty percent have pledged allegiance to the Resistance."

No one was using the words *civil war*, leastwise, not officially.

Ritter-Starling next reported that minor skirmishes had occurred between Union forces and the Resistance here and there, but these had been inconsequential, contained matters. Americans across the country were still traveling, with very few restrictions, between the states for business, family and pleasure. States were still conducting business with each other too. The Navy's Columbia and Virginia class submarines, under construction by the General Dynamics Electric Boat Division, at Groton in Connecticut and Quonset Point in Rhode Island, along with Huntington Ingalls Industries in Newport News, Virginia - facilities all located in states pledged to the Resistance - were still expected to be delivered on time in exchange for the agreed contract price from the Union.

Then others around the table gave their reports on the economy, the nightmarish world of logistics, trade, energy, and various international matters. When Adelman failed to contribute anything, MacAfee pressed him.

"What news of the investigation, Dr. Adelman?" he asked. "What leads do you have into the assassination of President Calhoun and the murder of one-hundred and thirty-three American civilians, not to mention the murder of twenty-six law enforcement officers and seven Secret Service agents? Tell us what you know."

"I can only say what you already know," Adelman replied. "The investigation is in its infancy. We are only in the preliminary stages of fact-finding and not much in the way of meaningful clues or evidence has been recovered yet. We know that the perpetrators of these barbaric acts were sophisticated professionals, real pros. The attack was well-planned, well-funded and expertly executed. Beyond this I -."

"You are," interrupted MacAfee, "telling us nothing, Dr. Adelman."

"My Section's mission, Mr. MacAfee, is very narrow in scope. We are not the lead agency in this endeavor. We are not coordinating with any other federal, state, or local government agencies involved with the investigation. You should direct your questions to the Directors of the FBI, Secret Service, Homeland Security and CIA or maybe to the newly established Agency."

"What exactly is your Section's mission?" MacAfee asked testily.

"To protect the vital national security interests of the U.S. of course."

"That sounds like blatant obfuscation to me, not a meaningful answer, Dr. Adelman."

"Tom," the President interrupted. "We can discuss this offline. Section M3 is an off-the-books experiment created by Calhoun back when he was a U.S. Senator and one of the Gang of Five. I've tasked Hermann with a special assignment and he reports directly to me. Hermann, do you have any information at all about who or what may have been behind the assassination?"

"No, not at this time, Madam President," Adelman answered flatly, with a lie.

Chapter Five

Doss hopped on the interstate and headed west for Rockford, some 90 minutes away. When the Feds connected Chicago and Rockford with a high-speed rail system, Rockford, not Chicago, was the big beneficiary. Dozens of corporate headquarters flocked to Rockford so executives and their employees could enjoy less traffic, less crime, more land and a better life, or at least the illusion of a better life. Rockford enjoyed a renaissance of sorts with the influx of new money. Gleaming new skyscrapers, spacious new parks, ritzy new restaurants and high-end nightclubs were popping up everywhere along the Rock River and within the city's vibrant commercial district. The city had started breaking ground for a state-of-the-art monorail for mass transit and there was even talk of building an NFL stadium.

"It's a bit early for dinner, but are you hungry?" Doss asked Bijeau as they reached the city.

"Can you say *beef?*"

"Ok, let's grab a Mickey D's and find a place to kill some time."

"You drive this hot piece of ass around in a souped-up Maserati and then you want to buy her a fast-food burger?"

"If you survive tonight, I'll upgrade us to some swank, white tablecloth five-star place with candles later. I'll even throw in a dozen roses."

Bijeau smiled sweetly at him. "Candles and roses if I survive the night, Doss?" she asked as she batted her eyes for effect. "Deal. What kind of fun did you have in mind for us later this evening, lover?"

For the first time, Doss caught a glimpse of the cobra behind the façade. Maybe, he thought, just maybe, she would be an asset.

"Bijeau, put your game face on. You can stay behind and guard the car tonight, or you can tag along with me. If you're coming with me, I need you one hundred percent focused. Are we clear?"

Bijeau set her jaw; her smile vanished. "One hundred percent clear, bossman!"

"If you're a stickler for rank, a simple sir will do."

"Right, bossman..."

"Doss or Max, not bossman."

"Got it bossman."

They ate their burgers and fries on a park bench down by the river in silence. The early evening sky was bright and clear and beautiful. Doss had chosen a quiet, peaceful place to sit, a secluded area where he could go over the plan he had formed in his head. Bijeau for once was quiet and waited for his cue before asking the questions burning in her gut.

They agreed to take a stroll along the river walk to stretch their legs after supper and when the sun began melting below the western sky, they returned to the Maserati and drove into the heart of downtown. Doss eased the Maserati into a public garage and found an isolated spot to park. With most folks having left work for home, the garage was nearly empty.

"Another safe house?" Bijeau asked matter-of-factly.

"No," Doss replied while reaching behind his seat to retrieve a plastic container. "You up for some action?"

"Absolutely, bossman."

Doss switched on the overhead light and removed a set of blueprints from the container. "These are the security and floor blueprints for the Pfeifer Corporation Tower across the street. In that building is a man named Adolpho Pfeifer."

"I've heard of him. Young guy, play boy. Isn't he some kinda trillionaire?"

"Don't know if there are any trillionaires in the world, but he's got real fuck you money."

"*Fuck you* money?"

"Yeah, when you have enough money to tell anyone you want to fuck off and they can't do shit about it. Pfeifer inherited his daddy's AI software empire after he had his old man killed in an unfortunate skiing accident. A son any parent would be proud of, a real sweetheart."

"Charming. Never heard that before. Didn't know patricide was back in vogue among the rich and famous."

"Mother has confirmed Pfeifer is at his penthouse on the top floor of the Tower tonight. He'll be entertaining a small group of his intimate friends and a few business folks who serve on his board of directors."

"When did Mother do that?"

Doss showed Bijeau his watch. "She texted me, just now. At precisely twenty-two hundred hours tonight, the building's power and security systems will fail, then we go in."

Bijeau studied the blueprints briefly without asking any questions. That bought her one goodwill merit point from Doss.

"Is it true," Doss asked, "you have a photographic memory?"

"I am known as an eidetiker, been one since birth, I suppose. Been told that only children possess eidetic memory, but here I am. People associate eidetic memory and photographic memory with perfect memory, but it doesn't work like that."

"Eidetic memory - that's different from photographic memory?"

"Depends on who you ask. Some experts think there is a distinction, some don't. I can recall minute details of pictures and drawings, eidetic memorization, and I can remember words and numbers on paper with great precision, photographic memorization."

"So, after you study prints like these, you can recall most of what you've seen?"

"Go ahead. I know you want to. Test me."

"You've barely looked at the prints."

"I only need a few moments to study documents like these."

Doss grabbed the prints out of her hands. "Tenth floor, how many bathrooms and how wide is the hallway?"

"Um, twelve plus one private executive bathroom in the northeast corner office. The hallway is twelve and a half feet wide."

"Impressive. What's my driver's ID number?"

Bijeau gave Doss a wide grin. "There's no file on you. I admit I tried to find one."

"But you did go through my wallet back in Chicago while I was in the shower this morning," Doss said as he cracked a thin smile. "Bijeau, I can't tell for certain, but it almost looks like you're blushing."

"Ok, I confess I peeked. You have a VA license. License number zero-five-seven-three-four-six-five-seven, expiring on August 15, 2054. Huh, odd coincidence. Napoleon was born on August 15th."

Doss had to pull out his driver's license to validate her numbers. "Damn."

"I'm sorry for going through your things."

"Don't be, I respect you for it," Doss said and gave her two more merit points, one for her memory and one for doing a little recon on her new partner. The girl again showed promise. Doss started to hand the blueprints back to Bijeau, but then realized he needed them more than she did.

"Ok, we enter here at twenty-two hundred and use this stairwell to the twenty-fourth floor - hope you're good at climbing with a full rucksack of ammo and gear - and then we wait."

"Wait for what?"

"We wait for Pfeifer and his guests to show up."

"Pfeifer's penthouse is on the twenty-fifth floor. Won't he be there?"

"Yes, until the building's security system goes down. His security detail will escort him to his private apartment on the twenty-fourth floor after that happens. They could take the sky bridge from the twenty-fifth floor over to the adjacent building, but I doubt it. They'd be too exposed. Either way, we intercept him before he slips away."

"Why not go up to the helipad on the roof and take the chopper?"

"Even if the pilot is around, takes too long to get the chopper into motion - and the chopper would be an easy target for any fool with a SAM. For the same reason, I doubt they'll go down to the ground floor and try to reach the cars."

"Why not defend the penthouse and hunker down there until the help arrives?"

"His security team is pretty good. They're former Russian *Spetsnaz*, special forces of the GRU, and German KSK, the *Kommando Spezialkräfte*. Fun fact: certain elements of the KSK are infamous for their extreme political views, like flying swastikas. GRU are typically little more than sociopathic street thugs. Pfeifer's security likes to keep moving, avoid being pinned down, just like what you would do if you were still on the President's security detail and there was a situation. Even so, I think Pfeifer will insist on returning to his rooms on the twenty-fourth floor. Those rooms are the most secure place in the building, with power and security systems independent from the building's systems. If I'm wrong, we'll need a Plan B."

"How many in his detail?"

"Enough. Ten at least, maybe more."

"Guards on the first floor?"

"Only two, you'll take one and I'll take the other. They're civilians so..."

"Sleepy-bye for them, nothing permanent."

"Right."

"What about Pfeifer's guests?"

"Pfeifer will leave them behind in the penthouse to fend for themselves."

"And you are certain of all of this how?"

"I ran this drill a few months back - different mission back then - just to see what Pfeifer's people would do."

"How do you flip the power switch off and hack into the security codes to disarm the building?"

"Not our problem. If the doors are still locked at five minutes past twenty-two hundred, we call it a night, abort the mission and go grab a beer."

"What if Pfeifer's team reaches the twenty-fourth floor before we do?"

"Unlikely. They'll try to reestablish power first and then, when the security system goes offline, they'll try to reboot the system. When those efforts fail, they'll send an advance team down to the twenty-fourth floor to ensure the path is clear. At least that's what I hope, what I expect them to do."

"I'm good, damn good bossman. You'll see. But I've only got my service weapon and sixty rounds."

"Oh, ye of little faith. We have a trunk full of fun toys."

"Dang. Party time!"

"Don't be so cavalier, Bijeau. By twenty-two-thirty, things could turn pretty dicey for us. I need your head in the game. No Terminatrix type shit. I can't afford to lose you."

"Ah shucks, bossman. I didn't think you cared."

"One more thing," Doss said as he handed Bijeau a picture of Pfeifer. "And this is critically important. We must take Pfeifer alive and coherent, or this mission is a complete bust. Understood?"

"Understood."

Dressed in black fatigues over black coveralls coated in the military's newest lightweight Bodytec Armor, a real blessing, but loaded down with suppressed Sig SBRs, semi-automatic shotguns, M72E5 LAW rocket launchers and heavy rucksacks stuffed with ammo magazines, blocks of C-4, and a mix of fragmentation, concussion, smoke and incendiary grenades, Doss and Bijeau stood close to the outer lobby doors of the Pfeifer Corporation Tower and waited. At precisely 2200 hours, when the power systems suddenly failed, Doss and Bijeau raced inside, simultaneously hit the two uniformed security guards with 50,000 volts of electricity from two Taser X26Ms, secured their hands and legs with zip ties and then made their way up a back stairwell on the west side of the building.

Despite the extra 60 pounds she was carrying and Doss's longer strides, Bijeau kept pace with him, hardly breaking a sweat. Doss awarded her another merit point for stamina. The last three flights of stairs were a bitch and Doss was gasping for air and cursing himself for eating a burger with large fries before a mission. For a split second, he savored watching the beads of sweat finally rolling down Bijeau's cheeks, cheeks decorated in streaks of green and black camo face paint. She was flesh and blood after all.

Except for emergency lighting, the entire twenty-fourth floor was dark. The hallway was empty. *So far so good,* Doss told himself, but, as with any plan, a lot can go wrong.

Doss set his rucksack down. "Ok, I'm texting Mother to shut down the security systems five minutes from now. Let's set up near the six elevators in the center. Leave something for us at this stairwell in case everything goes to shit and we've got to make a quick exit. I'll be back in four."

"Where are you going, Doss?"

"I'm going to rig the south side stairwell. Once Pfeifer is on this floor, I'll set off a pair of incendiaries with a remote detonator. With a fire raging inside that stairwell, Pfeifer and his men won't have anywhere to go but forward towards the apartment. I'll drop down to the twenty-third floor before returning, do a quick recon below. Don't shoot me by accident when I return."

"I'd never shoot you, not by accident."

"Ah-ha. Good to know. You ready?"

"Don't I look ready?"

She did, Doss thought. She looked like the calm before the storm on a stifling summer day and nodded his approval.

Doss returned a few minutes later after disappearing down the north side stairwell just moments before Pfeifer's advance team emerged from the south side stairwell. Bijeau took up a position on the north side of the corridor on Doss's left and hid behind a Greek faux marble pillar near three elevators, while Doss did the same on the south wall. Bijeau had a clear line of sight along the south wall and the south side stairwell door, and Doss had a clear view of the north wall and the doors to Pfeifer's apartment. Together they had good crisscrossing fields of fire down the corridor.

Bijeau raised four fingers and tapped her Sig. Four men carrying submachine guns had emerged from the south side stairwell. Doss acknowledged her with a nod, crouched low to the floor, and chanced a quick peek through the leaves of a potted plant in front of the pillar. The men were dressed in dark suits, ties and dark blue shirts. Each man wore an earpiece. The men didn't bother sweeping the entire floor and went straight to Pfeifer's apartment some 25 yards away from Doss and Bijeau. Doss switched his Sig's safety off and set the selector switch to semi-automatic. Automatic fire is fun and looks cool in movies but is imprecise and is often a waste of ammo in the field.

Doss watched one man punch a code into a keypad on the wall next to the apartment's doors, a pair of large, elegant doors the color of cream with gold leaf trim. After the door locks clicked open, two men disappeared inside while the other two stood guard outside in the hallway. Doss knew that underneath the wood veneer, the doors were steel plate a half-inch thick. Maybe he could blow them, maybe not. They needed to grab Pfeifer before he entered his apartment and locked the doors behind him.

A minute passed before the two men inside the apartment stepped back into the corridor. One man started talking into his sleeve. "*Alles ist klar, boden gesichert*," Doss heard him say. Doss didn't speak much German, but he knew the German words for clear and secured.

A few minutes passed before Bijeau caught Doss's attention with a subtle wave of her hand. More men were pouring out of the south side stairwell. She raised her hands and began folding her thumbs and fingers one by one and then she gave Doss a thumbs up. Ten armed men plus Pfeifer were approaching the apartment.

When Doss hit the red button on a remote detonator, three minor explosions went off inside the south side stairwell, followed by a thin wall of white smoke rolling down the corridor. Doss raised his Sig, fired four 9mm hollow point rounds in rapid succession into the advance team, and watched four bodies slump to the carpet. Easy-breezy work at 25 yards.

Then Bijeau tossed a flashbang grenade down the hallway and covered her eyes before the *BOOM!* When Doss stepped into the middle of the corridor and started shooting, Bijeau did the same. She took the targets on the right and worked her way to the center while Doss started on the left and did the same. A textbook ambush. A small taste of American shock and awe.

Pfeifer's men never had a chance, though one man managed to get off a short burst at the ceiling before he doubled over and fell. Standing amid a pile of dead bodies, his face and clothing splattered in blood, Pfeifer watched in horror as Doss and Bijeau approached him. He sheepishly raised his hands.

A good kill, Doss told himself, but didn't gloat. Hubris is a dangerous trait. He knew that he and Bijeau had been incredibly lucky so far. A few years back, Doss had been an observer with a crack KSK team with a solid ops plan to extract an oil tzar from Kazakhstan. That op hadn't gone as well. Sometimes it just comes down to plain, dumb luck.

"You good, Bijeau?" Doss asked as he ejected the mag from his Sig and slapped in a fresh one.

"Good to go. You, bossman?"

"Good to go."

Doss and Bijeau paused here and there to make certain the bodies they were stepping over were dead before they reached Pfeifer. The heir to an empire was a young, fit, good-looking fellow, a dead ringer for one of Hollywood's old legends, Errol Flynn. Doss grabbed Pfeifer roughly by his yellow silk tie and dragged him down the hallway and through the apartment's blood-splattered doors.

Pfeifer's apartment took up the entire northeast corner of the twenty-fourth floor. The walls were white and unadorned with paintings, tapestries, decorations, or art of any kind. The rooms were spacious but surprisingly empty, even sterile. There was very little furniture or furnishings. The retro shag carpeting was white. The kitchen island, countertops and cabinets, along with the matching kitchen barstools and breakfast nook chairs, were white with chrome trim. The few accent tables they walked past were glass-top pieces with more chrome. Pfeifer's place appeared little used and had the look and feel of a hospital. Guys like Pfeifer owned dozens of homes, condos, and apartments across the world, but having money was no guarantee of having good taste.

"Your office?" Doss asked casually.

When Pfeifer pointed down a long, narrow hallway, Doss pulled him by his tie until they reached a room at the end. Along the way, they passed more white rooms with more chrome and glass.

Pfeifer's office was a surprise. A mahogany desk, an antique gaudy piece from England's Victorian Era, accompanied by a high-back, maroon leather executive swivel chair accented with brass nails, stood in the middle of a room paneled in rich, dark wood. A storm-gray laptop and a crystal lamp crowned with a white lampshade sat on the desk. An oil painting of a white clipper ship sailing through a blinding, white blizzard across a dark and ominous sea studded with whitecaps hung on the wall across from the desk.

Doss pushed Pfeifer into his chair. When he powered up Pfeifer's laptop, the entire desktop turned into a large, high-resolution touchscreen. He leaned over, came nose-to-nose with Pfeifer and snapped his fingers in Pfeifer's face as Pfeifer had all the signs of being high. "Listen closely, Adolpho. You have seven hundred and fifty billion euros stashed away in multiple accounts around the globe. You'll give me the access codes for each account and my associate here will assist you in transferring those monies into ten new accounts."

Pfeifer, who had avoided looking directly at Doss, looked up at him and smiled. "Who the fuck are you?"

Doss glanced at his watch. "Clock's ticking Adolpho. You don't have much time. We can do this with a lot of pain, or not, but I can promise you this: you'll give me what I want one way or the other."

Pfeifer laughed. "Surely you know who I am and what I can do."

"You should be far more concerned with who I am and what I can do, my friend."

"*Fick dich.*"

"No, Pfeifer, you're the one who's fucked," Doss said as he pulled his CZ out of its holster and placed the barrel against Pfeifer's left hand resting on top of the chair's armrest. "Last chance."

Doss took no pleasure but felt no guilt either when he pulled the trigger after Pfeifer refused to speak. He was simply in a hurry.

Pfeifer screamed when he felt the bullet tear into his flesh. The 9mm passed through his hand and nicked his big toe.

"A two-for-one shot," Doss whispered into Pfeifer's ear. "Not your lucky day."

Pfeifer pressed his bloody hand against his chest, a normal reflex action to deaden the nerve endings around a wound, and tried to stand on his good foot. "Fuck, fuck, fuck, fuck!" he cursed as the blood oozing from his toe seeped into a white throw rug underneath the desk. "You fucking animal!"

Pfeifer turned to Bijeau, apparently hoping she was the rational one. "You're wasting your time," he cried out. "You think this money is mine? It's not."

"I know," Doss replied calmly as he pushed Pfeifer back into his chair.

"*Du weisst scheisse.* You know shit, motherfucker."

"Oh? I know this money is mostly Council money."

"Ah, so you've heard of the Council."

"Yes."

"To know of the Council means little. To know the Council is to know unrestrained power and a relentless commitment to a sacred cause. If you knew the men and women who sit on the Council, individuals with unparalleled zeal and dedication, you'd never have come here. If you value the lives of your sweethearts, your children, you'll turn and run."

"Funny you should mention the men and women who sit on the Council, Adolpho. After you transfer the money, you're going to give me their names."

Pfeifer forced a brave laugh. "Impossible! Council members do not use names. And I can't access any accounts on my own. It takes two authorized persons working in tandem to access any account."

"Oh? My bad. Bijeau, time to go. Let's grab our gear and take Herr Pfeifer up to the twenty-fifth floor."

"Where are we going?" Pfeifer demanded.

"We, as in the three of us, aren't going anywhere. My associate and I are going to borrow your chopper to get off this building and then I'm going to buy her a drink for a job well done. You, my friend, unless you can fly, are taking a swan dive off the roof to the pavement twenty-five stories below. Compliments of Uncle Sam."

Bijeau grabbed the German by the arm and yanked him out of his chair. "Let's go, pretty boy. Never saw a rich man fly before."

"*Nein, nein, nein, warte*! Wait, wait, wait! Ok, ok, I'll give you the codes, but they won't do you any good. Monies exceeding one million euros can only be transferred from one authorized account into another authorized account - for reasons that should be obvious even to slow-witted oafs like you."

"No worries, I came prepared," Doss said smugly and removed a flash drive provided by Mother from his pocket. He plugged the drive into the laptop, handed Pfeifer a piece of paper with routing numbers for ten new accounts, and told him to proceed.

"Whatever you think you are doing won't work," Pfeiffer insisted.

"Then there is no reason for you not to do as I ask," Doss said as he handed Pfeifer a roll of gauze to wrap his hand. "Let's go."

Bijeau pushed Pfeifer back into his chair, whipped out a knife when Pfeiffer hesitated and placed the blade firmly against his crotch. "It's been a long day angel and this piece of ass needs her beauty sleep. You start typing or I start dicing starting with, well, you know."

Pfeifer quickly wrapped his hand with gauze and frantically started typing. He logged into a secure server located God knows where and began punching in codes with Bijeau leaning over his shoulder, closely observing every keystroke he made on his laptop as he accessed each bank account. Doss followed along, watching the transactions on the desktop touchscreen.

After the last transfer was completed Bijeau gave Doss a victory smile. "We're good, bossman. Got it all."

"You have the confirmation numbers?" Doss asked.

She replied by tapping her temple with her finger.

Doss nodded and set his phone on the desk. "Call Mother with the numbers, Alejandra. Adolpho, now I want you to scroll through these photos and names and tell me who you recognize. If you hold back on me - I'll know it."

With his injured hand beginning to throb and swell, and sweat dripping down his armpits, staining the sides of his suit jacket, Pfeifer gave Doss a quick, helpless look, then turned his attention to the photos. The pictures were of politicians mostly, high-level government bureaucrats and a few wealthy entrepreneur types. He stopped at one photo and pointed.

"You know this woman," Doss asked.

"No, but I recognize her face. I've seen her name mentioned in communiques."

"Communiques with the Council?"

"*Ya, ya.*"

"She wasn't on the Council?"

"No. Such an inferior person would never be considered. I only know she is on the payroll. She performs certain functions and provides certain information."

Doss did not need any more evidence against Brighton. She was history. But it was always nice to have confirmation.

"A U.S. Senator selling information? My, my, say it ain't so. She's the one who sold you out to me. Keep scrolling."

When Pfeifer brushed past one photo, Doss stopped him. "You skipped this fellow."

"I don't know him."

Doss pressed the CZ's muzzle against Pfeifer's thigh. "Don't fuck with me. You wouldn't begin to know how, but I already know the man's name and I know you know it too."

Only a handful of people in the world were capable of truly appreciating, at least in part, the incredibly rare and breathtaking genius of Billy Duc. Doss's boss was one of them.

"His name is Duc, Billy Duc."

"How do you know him?"

"I don't know him. I've never met him."

"But you've seen him?"

"Yes."

"Where?"

"In Vienna not long ago, during a gathering of the Council."

"What did he do for the Council?"

"He is a scientist. The Council offered him a position at TUM, for what reason I do not know."

"That's the Technical University of Munich?"

"Yes."

"Did he accept?"

"No, he left Vienna in a hurry. I think the Council spooked him."

"To where?"

"To the United States."

"Where in the States?"

"Seattle, Washington."

"How do you know this?"

"We have a team tracking him."

"To do what?"

"I don't know. I was simply instructed to provide funds for expenses and the like."

"Right. Keep looking through the photos."

When Pfeifer finished scrolling through the last of the photos, he handed Doss his phone back. "That man in the last photo. I saw him too, just once, with Duc in Vienna. I don't know his name - I swear it."

Doss raised an eyebrow at the photo of Jason Pollard, the Deputy Director of the FBI. "Who from the Council was present?"

"I told you. I don't know. Names are not used. I've never seen any faces. I've only met the hirelings, chauffeurs, bodyguards, couriers, lawyers, bankers and the like. Some people in these photos could be on the Council and I wouldn't know it."

"Ok. What was discussed at the meeting in Vienna?"

"I don't know. I was not summoned. It would be highly irregular for someone like me to be asked to attend such a gathering."

"You're just one of the Council's money men, right?"

"That's a rather crude way of putting it. I contribute to the facilitation of highly sophisticated, multinational financial transactions on behalf of my client."

"Ah, that's what it's called these days, *the facilitation of ...*

multinational financial transactions. Once upon a time folks simply called it laundering money for the mob."

"I am the majority shareholder of a global organization worth trillions. I'm a legitimate businessman. I'm not responsible for the activities of those who invest in my companies. To think otherwise is absurd."

"Open the safe."

"There is no -."

"Stop, Adolpho. This is not how to build trust between us. Open the safe, the one behind the painting on the wall."

As Pfeifer tapped numbers on the tabletop screen, the painting of the clipper ship swung out on hinges behind the painting and the door to a safe popped open with a sharp click.

"Bijeau, grab whatever is in the safe; Adolpho, I have one more picture to show you," Doss said, then removed a small photo from his fatigue jacket pocket and handed the photo to the German.

Pfeifer shifted uncomfortably in his chair. "President Calhoun? He had no association with the Council that I know of."

"No, of course, he didn't."

"What then? I did not know him. I never met the man."

"I have. He was my brother."

Pfeifer's face turned white as Doss placed the muzzle of his handgun against Pfeifer's skull.

"What was the Council's involvement in the assassination of the President of the United States?" Doss asked coldly.

"I know nothing about such matters!"

"What was your involvement?"

"I, I, I've already told you. I only move monies around from time to time when asked to fund this or that."

"Like monies to fund an assassination team sent to Washington, D.C.?"

"Please, please, please, no one says no to the Council. The Council for years has spent vast resources stirring up divisiveness, trying to undermine the stability of certain countries, including the United States. This is no secret. Calhoun threatened to undo all of that. My, my job is to move monies around, to maximize returns on investment. I'm no killer. I'm no assassin. I don't even have political views!"

"Well, Adolpho, my job is to clean up messes," Doss said and pulled the trigger. Pfeifer was dead before his head hit the desk.

"I take it," Bijeau asked sharply, clearly irritated, "we're done here?"

"It appears so. Poor Herr Pfeifer is the victim of a home invasion. Pity."

"With fourteen dead bodies outside?"

"He's dirty and double-crossed the wrong people. What was in the safe?"

"Multiple passports, cash, a bag of diamonds and a thumb drive."

"Leave the passports, take the rest. Can you swipe the laptop clean? Remove any trace of our involvement?"

"Can do," she said and started punching instructions into Pfeifer's laptop. "So, we came here on what Brighton told you?"

"Yes, though we already knew Pfeiffer was dirty. That's why I reconned this place a few months back, but we didn't know about his affiliation with the Council, not until Brighton talked."

"How did you know Pfeifer was lying about the safeguards on the accounts, that we could not transfer money into unauthorized accounts without a second authorized party?"

"He was telling the truth actually," Doss replied, smiling as he handed her the flash drive, the same drive he had inserted into the Pfeifer's laptop.

Her eyes lit up. "Fuck me sideways - I once gave the Agency a white paper on an experimental computer program. Theoretically, the insertion of one set of codes can manipulate a nearly identical set of codes ever so slightly to achieve an altered command without the system identifying the corruption, not unlike what you just did overriding the Council's account safeguards. I was told my paper was rejected."

"Apparently not Einstein. I have no clue what you just said but the geniuses at the new NSA complex in Atlanta dumbed it down this way for me: it's like substituting one slice of chocolate cake for another while your date turns her head for a split second, except the substitute is laced with a highly potent aphrodisiac coupled with a mild hallucinogen. One bite and she'll more than willing fulfill your every desire, she'll give up her secrets when asked."

"I bet the fool who told you that was a pimply-faced white boy named Gayle with coke-bottle glasses, a bad haircut and crooked teeth. That motherfucker's ass is mine."

Doss and Bijeau made a clean exit down a westside stairwell and returned to the car. The entire operation from start to finish had taken a little over an hour.

Doss turned to Bijeau after they tossed their weapons and gear into the trunk. "That was exceptional work, Tactical Agent Bijeau. You were calm under fire, smart and efficient."

"Thanks, I guess."

"Pardon? What does that mean?"

"What are we doing, Doss? I have no problem killing bad guys. But we just offed fourteen men and you executed Pfeifer without blinking an eye and I don't know why. What was the mission? Money? Whacking Pfeifer? Getting intel on this Council outfit? Was Pfeifer's execution even sanctioned? Dreyfus would never have approved of this. Never. Honestly, whose side are you on?"

"I'm on no one's side because no one is on my side."

"What?"

"Never mind. Just a corny line I once heard. As for the mission, all the above. You've been assigned a shitty job, Bijeau. The one man you trusted and respected in this world was brutally shot down in the streets of Virgina and now you work for a woman you barely know and she has handed you off to a rumor, a shadow, to a man you know nothing about whose pre-mission pep talk was to tell you that your odds of survival while working with him were slim. How am I doing so far?"

She nodded.

"If you're waiting for a speech from me about *truth, justice and the American Way*, you'll be waiting a long, long time. I know this much: the world has gone mad. Indian and Chinese troops are fighting along their common border in the Ladakh region - they aren't technically at war, but the casualties on both sides are in the thousands. Russia is slipping into anarchy. Germany has annexed Austria, Czechia and a small sliver of Slovakia. Unlike the 1930s when the Nazis gobbled up her neighbors by force, the Austrians, Czechia and a handful of towns in western Slovakia voted by large majorities to join a new German Democratic Republic, now known as Great Germany. The French, Italians, Portuguese and Spanish all distrust the expanding German empire and have formed their own joint defense pact, the Latin Federation. Africa is a mess. South America isn't much better. No one knows who is friend from foe. The map makers can't even keep pace with the daily changes to the world's political and national boundaries. And the most powerful, the most stable country in the world is on the brink of an all-out war with itself. Damned if I know who the enemy is."

"You paint a grim picture, Doss."

"It's a grim world, Alejandra. As for Pfeifer, after transferring the money to us, along with the intel he gave us, he wouldn't have survived the week and his end wouldn't have been clean or quick. I did the man a favor."

"I see, a mercy killing."

"Look, if none of this sits well with you, return to Dreyfus. But what you have seen and heard while working with me cannot be shared with anyone, not even with her. You gave me your word and I will hold you to it. There are many moving parts in play, a lot you, a lot I don't understand. I will share my official file with you when we return to Washington and you can decide for yourself whether I'm a patriot or not. There is trust between us or there isn't. You choose."

"In for a penny, in for a pound. I'm in Max. I just needed to know why. I've got your back. How did you know about my respect and trust for Calhoun?"

"You were on his security detail for a brief stint before joining the Agency. People talk, hear things."

"I see. I guess I need to learn to keep my opinions to myself. What is the Council?"

"Don't know yet, but their power and influence across the world is growing. I suspect we'll be hearing more from them very soon."

"Well, thank you for trusting me with your file. I look forward to reading it. Maybe I'll find your kryptonite."

Doss's lips curled into the mischievous grin of a schoolboy prankster. "Most of the information in that file is blacked out, the rest is rather boring..."

Chapter Six

Excerpts from Hermann Adelman's private journal:
The Great Turmoil

After leaving the White House, Adelman returned to his office and immediately took his private elevator down into the bowels of Section M3, into a nuclear, biological, chemical, electronic and cyber warfare-proof floor. He strolled through M3's nerve center at a brisk pace, acknowledging colleagues here and there with a nod along the way and then walked straight into the most secure room within the entire facility, perhaps the entire world.

"Mother."

"Herr Direktor."

"What news of our boy?"

"He found Pfeifer in Rockford, Illinois."

"Results?"

"Pfeifer is no longer with us. Seven hundred and fifty billion euros have been transferred into the Section's ghost accounts, spread across ten accounts in all."

"A tidy sum, Mother. We now have an impressive war chest to fund operations. IRS isn't hauling in much revenue these days. Give Doss my congratulations. Any loose ends in Rockford we need to be concerned about?"

"Doss left a mess behind, no loose ends."

"I swear that man enjoys leaving behind messes. He's never been subtle. Send in a crew. Sweep it all clean. What of Billy Duc?"

"Doss has a lead and is on his way to Seattle. One more thing Herr Direktor. The Deputy Director of the FBI may be compromised."

"Vienna, the Council?"

"Quite so, sir."

"The Bijeau woman, your assessment?"

"Thoroughly vetted on all levels. So far, she has exceeded

expectations. We have no reason to doubt her patriotism or her commitment. She shows great promise."

"Very well. Doss isn't complaining?"

"No."

"Good. He has access to the funds?"

"To one account as you instructed."

"How many assets are available to support him?"

"Depending on time and distance sir, one hundred fifty souls at most."

"Give Doss whatever he needs and quietly start recruiting more operatives. U.S. active duty or prior service only, no mercs. You know what to do. There's a man over at CIA named Ed Rice. I want him here."

"The one they call the Master of the Universe?"

"Why do they call him that?"

"His peers bestowed that regal title upon him because of his cutting-edge innovations in employing AI. He sees and hears all."

"He's the guy who worked the Papenfuss case?"

"Yes."

"He's the guy who incorporated his work into your systems?"

"Yes."

"He's the one. Buy him from the CIA if you must. With the federal coffers empty, CIA will gladly take the cash. It's time we gave this organization some teeth too. Quietly procure a dozen AH-64-E Apache attack helicopters for us, along with all the available enhancements and ordnance you can procure."

"And crews?"

"I know a guy who knows a guy who can help us with pilots, crews, and maintenance tech types. And Mother, get me the President."

"Which President, Herr Direktor?"

Chapter Seven

From Rockford, Doss and Bijeau headed west in a private jet procured by Mother. Doss was in a hurry. They landed at a small airfield outside of Seattle where a midnight blue Camaro SS with two suitcases in the back seat, one pink and one blue, along with two duffle bags in the trunk, had been parked at the end of the airfield with keys left in the ignition. They drove into the city and booked two rooms facing the water at the Four Seasons on Union Street. Mother, Doss chuckled to himself, should not have told him that he had access to 75,000,000,000 euros. His mind wandered at the possibilities. The thought of using the money to buy some remote island far, far away and falling off the grid forever caught his fancy and brought a smile.

"What's so amusing, Doss?" Bijeau asked as they took the hotel elevator up together.

"Nothing. Treat yourself to a quick shower and a change of clothing. Mother packed some necessities and clothes in your suitcase. Then stop by my room and we'll talk."

"God yes, this Marine loves her hot showers. See you in fifteen?"

"Let me tell you a story, Bijeau," Doss began as he stood next to a coffee table in his room and motioned Bijeau to take a seat on the sofa after she returned from her shower. "It is a fantastic but true story. Let me take you back in time to the year 1954 when a certain professor from Cambridge named Harvey Winston, an archeologist with no notable accomplishments, vanished in the wilds of Ethiopia while looking for his brand of treasure: old bones.

"Dr. Winston and his team of locals had made an astonishing find in a cave near the small village of Hubat. He immediately sent a telegram to the vice-chancellor of Cambridge informing his boss that he had not only discovered the bones of a new species of prehistoric humanoids but had also found several odd tools buried with them that rival or surpass anything we have now. Dr. Winston made a fateful decision that day when he decided to copy an old friend on the telegram, a German fellow named Dr. Ludwig Papenfuss, a brilliant young professor at the Technical University of Munich and an expert in metallurgy and exotic compounds. After Winston sent that telegram, he and his team were never heard from again.

"The Ethiopian authorities sent out search and rescue parties but never found the cave or any sign of Dr. Winston or his men. No one thought much about any of this back then. People disappear in the wilds of Africa all the time for all sorts of reasons. Now fast forward some seventy years later. Some bright, whiz kid from MIT named Ed Rice is recruited by the CIA on the very day of his graduation - and Rice's expertise is?"

"Archeology?"

"No, advanced metallurgy. Rice became an analyst for the CIA, a damn good one too, I'm told. One of his many assignments was to keep an eye out for anything in the public domain related to mysterious metals. Now, while Rice is honing his skills at CIA, which soar after AI becomes a thing, the great-grandson of Dr. Harvey Winston decides to write a book about his family after he learns that he is a distant relative of the Duke of Wellington, Sir Arthur Wellesley. Yeah, the same guy who took Napoleon down at Waterloo. Not sure anyone outside of the great-grandson's immediate family ever read the book, but the book was published. He only devoted a line or two to his poor, great grandfather - but he happened to include his great grandfather's curious 1954 telegram to Cambridge in the book's appendix and that telegram magically finds its way onto the internet. Rice stumbles upon the telegram and its reference to odd tools made from exotic metals buried with ancient bones. He also happens to be familiar with Papenfuss's work in metallurgy. Rice starts connecting the dots and eventually is able to convince his superiors to send a team to Ethiopia to further investigate matters."

"The plot thickens," Bijeau said, smiling.

"Yes. Rice's team discovers evidence of a sizable explosion, uncovers an extensive cave system underneath the rubble, and starts digging. They soon stumble upon the remains of Dr. Winston and recover his journal. Winston and a few of his men had survived the blast, but with no way out of the cave, and with few supplies, they contented themselves with writing farewells to loved ones using blank pages from Winston's journal before they expired. Rice's team also finds a fascinating item, a tool of sorts, made from a lightweight, seemingly indestructible metal not found on this planet. In the last entry of his journal Winston describes how Papenfuss cordoned off his site by force and how he removed a number of items packed in crates from the cave, including one mysterious object wrapped in tarps, about the length of four extra-long semi-trucks, that had to be hauled out of the cave on rails. It was Papenfuss, Winston wrote, who intentionally blew up the entrance to the cave to hide his pillaging."

"Doss, you're giving me goosebumps. Please don't tell me you're going to start talking about little green men. This rock we live on is bombarded by asteroids all the time. That's the more likely explanation as to the origin of such metal. As Einstein proved in his Theory of Relativity, nothing can exceed the speed of light. Interstellar travel is the stuff of science fiction."

"We'll get to Einstein in a moment. I have the discretion to, well, enlighten you on a few matters. You are risking your life on this mission and I think you deserve to be read in. But I must remind you first of your oath to your county, and then of your obligations of holding a security clearance level of Top Secret, Class Alpha-One."

"You nearly died for this country, bossman, as did I, on more than one occasion. That's my answer."

"You understand the consequences of betraying your country's trust, of betraying my trust, which, frankly, carries a much harsher penalty?"

"We've had this conversation already. I do."

"Right then, here we go... After the CIA's expedition to Ethiopia found what it found, it did not take the spooks over at Langley long to realize that they not only had uncovered the scene of a mass murder, and proof that Dr. Papenfuss was the mastermind behind it, but that they had solved another mystery. For some time, we've known that Germany acquired an alien spacecraft, the first, right around 1954 and now we know how -."

"What? You're joking!"

"I'm not."

"Alien spaceships? The first? There are others?"

"Bijeau, if you keep interrupting me at this pace, this is going to be a very long night."

"Ok, ok, but when I hear something as shocking as this, it makes me want to pee. Be right back."

After Bijeau returned from the bathroom, along with two Heinekens from the kitchenette, Doss nodded his thanks and resumed his tale. "Yeah, the Germans found the first. We found one some sixty years later. The Russians may have one, or part of one, and the Chinese have desperately been trying to find one for themselves and may have found something not long ago in the Mongolian Desert."

"So, the space race has taken on a whole new meaning? Area 51 is real? The military does autopsies on the bodies of little green men?"

"Yes, and yes, though we don't keep aliens or alien spacecraft at Area 51 and aliens aren't green or little. They look very much like us I'm told, though the average height of these beings, both male and female, is between seven to eight feet. Now, may I continue?"

"Sorry."

"There is a man named Billy Duc. Do you know anything about him?"

"Not much. You questioned Pfeifer about him. He is an inventor. I've heard rumors within the Agency. Something about batteries, small batteries, he invented that may be able to power a city like New York for several years before they need to be recharged."

"A small generator actually, no bigger than your average car, with supercharged proton technology might be able to power New York for decades, maybe centuries."

"And how does he fit into our story?"

"Billy Duc was born to poor peasant farmers in the slums outside Ho Chi Minh City. He has no formal education beyond the Vietnamese equivalent of high school. He is a nobody from nowhere. Some say this fellow is the greatest thinker since Einstein, perhaps even Newton. His brilliance in algebraic mathematics, they say, is the stuff of legend, but his true passion is quantum physics and mechanics. The Germans hired him to work on their clandestine UFO project after their best and brightest were unable to crack the mysteries of what they dubbed *das Zigarre*, the *Cigar*. When Duc fared no better, the Germans reminded him of his obligations of secrecy and released him from his contract. Duc, however, may have learned more about alien technology than he let on with the Germans and used that knowledge to further his own work."

"Like the designs for the generator he invented?"

"Possibly. As revolutionary as such an invention might be, Washington is more concerned about what he may have gleaned from his time in Munich in the areas of propulsion and weaponry."

"And what of our spacecraft? Have we been able to decipher anything of interest from it?"

"Our scientists and engineers caught a lucky break a few years back and were able to activate the craft's power - but only briefly."

"Why lucky?"

"Papenfuss salvaged a partially damaged spacecraft according to our intelligence. We apparently salvaged a fully intact spacecraft which allowed us to test and analyze certain critical, undamaged components. We've named our alien machine *Blue Swan* for reasons that will become obvious if ever you see it. I'm sure the folks at the Cheyenne Mountain Complex in Colorado would laugh at my explanation. Best this poor soldier can do."

"Ah, so Cheyenne is the facility where we keep all the supersecret alien shit we find?"

When Doss answered her with a broad smile and finished off his beer, Bijeau walked back into the kitchenette and grabbed two more. "So," she said and handed Doss another Heineken, "an evil German scientist finds the first alien spacecraft in Ethiopia back in '54 and transports the thing to Munich. The U.S. and possibly the Russians and the Chinese each have one. And now you are looking for a nobody from the slums of Vietnam, for a genius named Billy Duc. As an aside, I assume the German government was oblivious to how Papenfuss acquired the spacecraft? I assume Pfeiffer told the truth, others are looking for Duc too?"

"Yes, as to your last and most important question. As for Papenfuss's crimes, we have no reason to believe the German government had any involvement in his expedition to Ethiopia or knowledge of his evil doings there. The evidence suggests Papenfuss went rogue. The evidence suggests that towards the end of his life, he worked for or with the Council."

"And we know very little about this Council?"

"Very little."

"Apparently, its members are very powerful and secretive."

"Apparently."

"And Duc may hold the key to unlocking alien technology? If so, bossman, I get dibs on the first ray gun."

"Yes, Duc may - possibly - be the key. Don't know about any ray guns, don't even know if any of these extraterrestrial spacecrafts were armed. After all, they could have been just longboats used to ferry personnel and equipment down to the planet from larger vessels that remained in orbit. But think about the real possibility of colonizing the moon or Mars or even traveling to the stars if we could recreate their propulsion drives."

"Even if you could travel at the speed of light, the closest star system to Earth that has potential life is Proxima Centauri, and it's over four light years away. But Einstein concluded that traveling at the speed of light for humans is impossible."

"Did he? Let's talk about Einstein's Theory of Relativity - not that I am qualified to discuss the matter. I barely passed basic physics in high school. But I know what I need to know for the mission. Wait one, it's Mother calling."

"Max? Is Alejandra with you?"

"Yes Mother, she is."

"You may put me on speaker. Alejandra, Max, are you aware that the President is about to address the country, all fifty states, on national TV in a few minutes?"

Doss plopped down on the sofa next to Bijeau, grabbed the remote off the glass coffee table and turned on the TV. He flipped through a nauseating number of stations until he found the first national news channel.

Chapter Eight

Excerpts from Hermann Adelman's private journal:
The Great Turmoil

Adelman was just about to leave his office for the evening and pick Gretchen up from the hospital when Mother informed him that the President was about to address the nation. No one at the White House had thought to tell him about the speech. He returned to his desk with a heavy sigh, poured himself a bourbon, and turned the TV on.

"Good evening, America. I am Kaitlan Rafferty and this is CNN World News Live. Within the next few moments, we expect the President of the United States, Elaine Dreyfus, to address the country for the first time since she assumed office. The President's Press Secretary described tonight's speech earlier today at the White House Press Corps briefing as, and I quote, *a short but important speech with historic implications.* This is all we know. Oh? Ladies and gentlemen, I've just been informed by one of our producers that the President is about to speak from the Oval Office."

"Good evening, my fellow Americans. We are a house divided and we are living in perilous times. Since I assumed the Presidency following the tragic assassination of President Calhoun, I have concluded that our country will not survive much longer unless we take decisive action now, before our potential enemies and rivals across the world can overcome their own trials and tribulations and exploit our weakness.

"The only reason we still have a country - fractured as it may be - is because our potential enemies are themselves weak and in disarray. This is our bit of good fortune. But as I said, we cannot expect our good fortune to last much longer.

"What do we do? For now, we have avoided a shooting war between the states. As Commander-in-Chief, I can do what President

Abraham Lincoln did and force those states that now call themselves the League of North American States back into the Union by spilling oceans of blood. But we live in far different times than Lincoln. Lincoln was not governing the world's mightiest superpower, surrounded by powerful, envious foreign enemies. He had the luxury of being able to bludgeon the Confederacy into submission without interference from across the oceans.

"A hot war, a true second civil war between us will, I am convinced, destroy us all. Maintaining the present status quo will have the same result.

"To make matters worse, the League so far has failed to ratify a unifying constitution. They have failed to form a central, federal government. Many of the states within the League appear to be sliding towards their own nationhood. This is madness, sheer folly. The United States - sharing the continent with a dozen or so newly created independent countries? How long will it take before the world carves us up like a Thanksgiving turkey?

"My fellow Americans, it is clear to me, after much reflection, after much deliberation with my Cabinet and with many brilliant people both inside and outside of government, that there is but one rational solution. I propose, in exchange for a mutual defense pact and trade alliance with the League, alliances that will ensure we remain a military and economic powerhouse, that we recognize the League as a sovereign country and end the animosity and the looming civil war, this potentially suicidal conflict, between us. We are all Americans. There is much that binds us together as one people. If we give the League its independence, we shall still be one people living side-by-side in peace and harmony.

"In the morning, I shall, with a heavy heart, but with firmness of conviction, deliver a draft bill to Congress for its consideration that, if enacted, will recognize the independence of the League of States of North America. With this concession, I believe the states within the League will come together to form one nation. I believe the United States and the League of States will, as inseparable allies, have a better chance of survival within this hostile and dangerous world of ours. And I believe someday those things that bind us as one people will eventually bring us back together as one nation. As an ancient Greek philosopher once wrote, *time heals all wounds.*

"I realize my actions will cause some to take to the streets and dance with jubilation while others riot in rage. If I could preserve the Union and spare our people from unimaginable bloodshed, that is what I would do. But if I can only spare our people from terrible sufferings by letting go of the old Union, this is what we must do as decent, civilized human beings. May God watch over us all in these dark and troubling times. Thank you and good night."

"Herr Direktor, excuse me," Adelman's executive administrative assistant, a smart, savvy, young black woman named Brianna, said as she poked her head inside Adelman's office.

"Young lady, it is late, go home to your family. That's an order."

"Yes, sir, but first I have President Dreyfus on line one."

Adelman cleared his throat and picked up the phone. "Madam President. I just saw your speech to the nation. You intend to dissolve the United States?"

"I'm not calling about that," Dreyfus snapped. "I don't need or want your opinion on political issues, Hermann. I sent Tactical Agent Bijeau over to you, to Doss, to keep me apprised of whatever it is Doss is up to. But she hasn't informed me of anything lately. I'm pulling Bijeau from you and ordering Doss to stand down from whatever he is doing until I understand and approve whatever you have him involved in."

"That would be a mistake. Doss is in the middle of a highly sensitive mission involving national security."

"I don't care. I'm putting an end to these shenanigans over at your Section."

"But -."

"But nothing Herman. My decision is final."

"As you wish, Madam President."

After the President disconnected the call, Adelman had Mother dial Doss for him.

Chapter Nine

Doss and Bijeau looked at each other in shocked disbelief after the President finished her speech. Doss turned off the TV, went into the kitchenette and grabbed two waters.

"What the fuck, bossman?"

"What the fuck indeed, Bijeau."

"Does the mission change? Wait, I have a text from the White House. It's from Dreyfus's Chief of Staff. POTUS wants us to return to D.C. immediately."

"What about our mission?" Doss asked harshly. "Ask him."

"He says we are NOT, all caps, we are not to pursue any phase of any mission."

"Huh. Glad I don't work for him."

"Maybe, but we all work for POTUS and we must assume this order comes directly from her."

"This is true and yet I have my orders. I won't be returning to Washington."

"I don't understand. That would be gross insubordination."

"No, you wouldn't understand Bijeau. Alejandra, you've been ordered back to D.C. Go and thank you. Perhaps we'll work together again someday. I would welcome the opportunity."

"What the hell is wrong with you, Doss? Why would you disobey a Presidential order? What do you know that I don't?"

"Ah, that's my boss calling. Yes, sir? Yes, we watched the speech. How did you know? Uh, huh. Well, Bijeau just received a text to that effect from the White House Chief of Staff. She is about to pack her bags and I was about to call you. I could use her help. Good, thank you, sir. Understood, I will, sir."

Doss turned to Bijeau after the other party disconnected the call. "Have a seat Bijeau. You asked to know more?"

"Yes."

"If you're in, you're one hundred percent in. No half measures, no serving two masters any longer. You can leave for Washington tonight if that's your pleasure. No hard feelings."

"You're not going to tell me that you're one of those aliens now, that you have pointy ears and green blood?"

Doss smiled. "No."

While Doss wasn't watching, Bijeau subtly slid a knife strapped to her wrist underneath her sleeve into her hand. "Don't put me in an awkward position, bossman."

But Doss caught the sleight-of-hand while watching her from the corner of his eye. "You won't need the knife, Alejandra. I'd never ask you to betray your country. I will put it to you bluntly, he's alive."

"Who's alive?"

"Calhoun."

"What? Fuck me, I can see that you are serious. But -."

"The assassination attempt came from within our own government, at least in part. There were outside influences involved, too. Thus, all the secrecy. We need to understand and identify who the players are and what team they are playing for before Calhoun reemerges from the darkness."

"Does Dreyfus know Calhoun is alive?"

"Absolutely not."

"Who does?"

"Now you, me, Mother, my boss, of course, and a few dozen souls."

"Where is Calhoun now?"

"At a secret military medical facility recovering from his wounds."

"There are so many questions. I, I, I have so many questions. Damn."

"I bet you do. Frankly, I don't have many answers. I know that Calhoun is my President. I know that I have a job to do, a job that may have catastrophic consequences if we fail. Are you in?"

"You know the answer to that question already or we wouldn't be having this conversation. Yes, I'm in. For the last time, I'm in, I'm in. Do you think Calhoun will approve Dreyfus's plan to end the so-called civil war by recognizing the League as a separate nation?"

"If I know Calhoun, and I do, he is thinking about pulling out any IVs and tubes they've stuck in him, dressing, and driving himself to the White House right about now. Yep, I imagine his blood pressure is off the charts after watching Dreyfus's speech. But he knows, he knows we must bide our time. We must wait for the precise moment that gives us the maximum advantage possible."

"Right then. All caught up bossman. I suspect if there is an unredacted dossier on you somewhere, it contains the following warning across the cover in large, bold, red print: *Doesn't Play Well with Others.*"

Doss cracked a thin smile. "Nonsense. I'm a real charmer."

"Hmmm. Any more surprises now that I've sold my soul?"

"Nope, nothing that comes to mind."

"Now then, you were going to tell me something about Einstein."

"Before we talk about Einstein and space travel Bijeau, since we're now joined at the hip, so to speak, I'd like to know where you're from. Who are your people?"

"You testing me, Doss, to see if I have enough blue blood in my veins to be accepted into the Royal Order of the Garter?"

"Maybe."

"You read my file."

"I read your official file, yes. But prior to your enlistment with the Marines, your file is rather thin, as if it had been scrubbed."

"Ok, Doss. My past is hardly a national secret. I was born in New Orleans."

"I know that much. And?"

"And I had an unusual childhood."

"Go on."

"Ahem. Well... My daddy ran a crack house while my momma ran the girls."

"You're joking?"

"I don't think many folks would joke about that kind of upbringing. Yeah, that's the truth of it. While my daddy was dealing drugs, my momma was a madam selling sex and our house was always open for business, twenty-four-seven. On my twelfth birthday, my father sent me out to work the streets."

"Work?"

"Yeah, he handed me a gun, some cheap revolver of one kind or another and said, and I quote: *Baby, you a woman now. You needs to earn your keep, help support your baby sisters. Go down to the corner across from Jimmy D's Pharmacy and chill there. Bring home two hundred dollars cash each week, don't care how you get it. Ain't no reason for you to come home unless you got the green.*"

No one had ever accused Doss of being sensitive, but he reached over and squeezed Bijeau's hand affectionately when he noticed her eyes turning watery. "What did you do?"

The tough combat Marine, with medals for valor and hardened by unforgiving war, brushed back a single tear. "I went down to that corner. For three months, I went down to that corner each and every day. I made a little money here and there robbing the weak and helpless, shoplifting, selling drugs, or selling whatever I had stolen back on the streets. Gave a few hand jobs too, if I'm being honest. Then I robbed some dude I shouldn't have robbed. He came back with his homies a few days later and beat the living shit out of me. Fuckers left me for dead. That ended my days of thuggery. Sure did."

"And then?"

"Couldn't go home. Didn't want to go home. Had two baby sisters I knew I'd miss. I had stashed a hundred-dollar bill in my boot for an emergency. Went down to the bus station and bought a ticket for Biloxi, Mississippi, to look for my maternal grandmother. I had only met her a few times, but she had always been very sweet to me. When I found her, she was all smiles and took me into her home with a great bear hug. She was a good, bible-thumping, praise the lord kind of Christian woman. She cared for me and raised me right until I left one day to see the world with the Marines."

"Quite a story, Bijeau. Look at you now. Decorated war hero, Tactical Agent for the Agency and on a first-name basis with the President of the United States. I don't know if I would have had the strength to find my way out of that cesspool of a life you started out with. Few could. You've got some real grit, girl. You can't know the quality of a person when they're standing tall on top of the world. It's only when the world has beaten them down, when they're down and out, that's when a person reveals their true quality."

"Maybe. But there's always a price for escaping the ghettos. I lost both my sisters, one to drugs, one to a bullet. Had I stayed, maybe I could have protected them."

"I'm sorry for your loss. Perhaps you could have saved them, perhaps not. You have placed a heavy burden on your shoulders by second-guessing yourself. Maybe you're being a bit unfair to Alejandra Bijeau? Just a thought. Not my place to say. Well, it's getting late. Get some sleep."

"I thought we were in a rush?"

"We are. We are waiting on intel from Mother."

"Well, I'm wide awake now, Doss. Einstein, please."

"Ah, very well, Marine. They say that only a handful of people in the world truly understand Einstein's Theory of Relativity and I'm not one of them. But what little I do know might help you better understand what's at stake."

"I'm all ears."

"Good, light is made up of what?"

"Ah, protons."

"Right. And what are protons?"

"A proton is one of the three basic subatomic particles, along with neutrons and electrons they make up atoms, the basic building blocks of all matter and chemistry. A proton is a positively charged particle that, together with the electrically neutral particles called neutrons, make up the nucleus of an atom. The nucleus of the ordinary hydrogen atom is an exception as it contains one proton but no neutrons. The proton's positive charge is equal and opposite to the negative charge on an electron, meaning a neutral atom has an equal number of protons and electrons."

"You're cheating Bijeau. What memory data file in that cyborg brain of yours did you pull that out of?"

"Britannica."

"Jesus. And how fast does light travel?"

"In a vacuum, like space, one-hundred-eighty-six thousand miles per second or roughly three-hundred-thousand kilometers per second if you prefer."

"And what can travel faster than light?"

"Nothing can travel faster than light. Under the laws of physics, according to Einstein, the speed of light is the universal speed limit.

It's impossible to accelerate any material object even up to the speed of light because it would take an infinite amount of energy to do so."

"And then the good ship *Starship Enterprise* with her warp drive sailed into our world."

"Star Trek? That's not science, bossman. That's ancient Hollywood sci-fi crap."

"Maybe, but how did those aliens reach us from across the stars?"

"Maybe they didn't cross the starts. Maybe they were Atlanteans from the ancient civilization of Atlantis."

"Now who's talking trash? Still, I suppose that is just as plausible. Warp drive began as fiction, true, but scientists at NASA, MIT and other bastions of smart nerds think it may be possible, not by breaking the law of physics but by bending them. A physicist named Alcubierre back in '94 developed the Alcubierre Warp Drive on paper by bending the laws of physics. His theory is that by creating a bubble within space-time you can twist distances, making it possible for a ship to travel fantastic distances within the bubble at unimaginable speeds. Many of Alcubierre's peers applauded his theory but doubted its practicality because you'd need a ring of unbelievable amounts of negative mass around the spacecraft - something that may not even exist in the universe - to shrink space-time in front of the spacecraft and stretch space-time behind her to push her forward. And then there is the problem of weight. The faster matter travels, the heavier it becomes."

"No warp drive for you, Mr. Scott!"

"Not so fast. Some scientists now believe warp drive just might be feasible. Some interesting things are happening to solve the mass-energy issue. NASA built a White-Juday Warp Field Interferometer some years ago. It's some kind of equipment that can detect microscopic warp bubbles. Einstein's theory of general relativity and quantum mechanics have always been at odds. But there are scientists, engineers and professors around the world who are convinced that there must be a unifying theory between the two that describes how things really function in the universe and when they find that unifying theory, incredible new worlds may open up to us. But discovering that theory, if it exists, is decades, maybe centuries away. But what if Duc can crack the secrets of alien technology? Perhaps then we will be able to accelerate the process of finding that magical theory at lightning speed - pun intended."

"I see, I get it now. I assumed we were going after the Council after what Pfeifer told us. Duc is the mission."

"Duc is the mission, but not the entire mission. You are not wrong about the Council. Do you know the story of the Odyssey?"

"Vaguely."

"Well, Calhoun is a huge fan of ancient Greek history, of ancient Greek folklore and godlore. The story of Odysseus is one of his favorites."

"Odysseus was the great Greek tactician during the Trojan War? He's the guy who tricked the Trojans into opening their gates for the wooden Trojan Horse to end the war?"

"That's the guy. He was the King of Ithaca. When he returned home after the war, Odysseus found his palace besieged by jealous nobles, suitors, men who wanted to kill his son Telemachus and marry his wife and take his kingdom and his riches for themselves. Odysseus and his son plotted and bided their time and eventually lured the nobles into a room, had the doors locked from the outside, and slaughtered every man. Myth or legend, who can say when time distorts what is real from what is not? The President has asked me to help him destroy the suitors circling our country like vultures, people who want to pick her bones clean thinking the king is dead. Welcome to flying saucers and slaughtering suitors, Marine."

"Good to know the mission, Doss. I'm dying to know, is Mother human or AI or something in between?"

"Never met her. It is often unnerving to witness the breadth and depth of what she knows, seemingly off-the-cuff. I know she once worked for both Govini and Palantir."

"Who are they?"

"Two military government contract software companies who have been pioneering and developing innovative AI programs for years to modernize the military's most deadly high-tech weapons systems. Under the reincarnation of the Manhattan Project launched by President Calhoun, they've kept the U.S. in the AI game with China and what is left of Russia. Rumor has it Mother began her career with Mossad working with gifted autistics in Mossad's program known as *Ro'im Rachok*."

"Huh. One last thing. I need to know exactly who you and Mother work for."

"I'm freelance. Can't speak for Mother."

"Bullshit. Trust cuts both ways, Max. "You ever been to the DRC?"

"The Congo?"

"Yeah. The République démocratique du Congo. Not talking about the Disney Recreation Center in Orlando."

"Don't recall being there."

"You weren't with the special ops team that rescued Calhoun's niece when he was still a U.S. Senator from that Rwandan warlord named Kito after he kidnapped her a few years ago?"

"Where are you going with this Bijeau?"

"The team executed Kito, grabbed Calhoun's niece along with, or so the story goes, bags and bags of uncut, conflict diamonds worth hundreds of millions of dollars on the street. The team, with Calhoun's blessing, used the diamonds to fund their own operations through an off-the-books agency."

"Fairytales for ex-jarheads."

"If you say so. But with so many Citizen's Alliance Party diehard loyalists entrenched at all levels of government, it makes perfect sense for Calhoun to be suspicious of the Agency, the CIA, NSA, or any government agency. Not hard to imagine an instigator like Calhoun creating his very own phantom intel organization with people he can trust to run it."

"You're going to start talking about M3 again?"

"Don't have to. You're not the best liar, Doss. M3 was Calhoun's creation with the help of that German fellow people call Herr Direktor. Tell me I'm wrong. No? Nothing to say? That's it then. You work for M3, for Herr Direktor and Calhoun."

Doss couldn't help himself and started grinning. "You should know Herr Direktor's name is Hermann Adelman."

"Good to know. Now, WTF are we doing in Seattle?"

Billy Duc was sipping hot tea in a small, Japanese-style tavern while browsing through the sports section of USA Today. He casually perused the predictions for the upcoming NFL match-ups even though the leagues, like everything else in America, were a mess, he still enjoyed the game. His flight on Philippine Airlines would begin boarding soon, and he knew he should be walking instead of sitting. The flight from Seattle to Manila's Ninoy Aquino International Airport, with one refueling stop at Incheon International Airport, would take 17 hours and then some. At least his Chinese host, waiting for him in Manila, had thoughtfully booked him in first class.

Ever since leaving Vienna, though, he had an uneasy feeling in the pit of his stomach, a feeling that he was being followed. He had done his best to travel incognito. He brushed his anxiety aside after he made a quick glance around the tavern and saw nothing to concern him. When his phone pinged him, alerting him that his flight's boarding process had begun, Duc breathed a sigh of relief, left the newspaper and a generous tip on the table, grabbed his laptop bag and headed down a bustling concourse of sterile white tiles and antiseptic air towards his gate a few hundred feet away.

"Now," Doss whispered into his mic to Bijeau.

Bijeau, standing on the opposite side of the concourse, straddled up to Duc on his right just as Doss did the same on Duc's left.

"Mr. Duc," Doss said softly and flashed his fake FBI credentials in Duc's face. "We are U.S. federal agents. For your protection, you must accompany us. Don't resist, don't make a scene. We believe your life is in grave danger."

Duc instinctively clutched his laptop bag against his chest. "I break no law. I Vietnamese citizen. You no right to -."

But before Duc could say more, a burst of machine gun fire peppered the ceiling directly above their heads. Panic swept across the concourse. People screamed, dropped to the floor, or ran. Seconds later a dozen men dressed as airport security guards, large, burly men with heavy beards and dark sunglasses, appeared with their weapons trained on Doss and Bijeau, while two men dressed in business suits grabbed Duc by the arms and hustled him away. Once Duc was out of sight, the armed men simply disappeared through secure utility corridors in all the confusion. Powerless to stop them, Doss and Bijeau ditched their black suit jackets and ties and scurried out of the airport with everyone else. When they reached the Camaro, Doss called Mother.

"Max?"

"Mother."

"Have you secured the package?"

"No, a squad of professionals blindsided us."

"Wait, Max. Herr Direktor has just joined us."

"I'm watching the news alert from Seattle now, Max," Adelman said gruffly in his thick German accent. "How, how did this clusterfuck happen?"

"Well sir," Doss answered evenly, "we played the cards we were dealt. Mother was able to provide us with Duc's flight information at seven forty-five this morning. There was no time to marshal additional assets. There was no time to plan some elaborate, clandestine snatch and grab. I took Bijeau, and we were forced to improvise before Duc boarded his flight and left the country."

"Any clue who intruded on your ops?"

"The airport security men are obviously imposters, most likely mercenaries, maybe military. Two men dressed in civilian clothes, both Asian, Chinese, I suspect, grabbed Duc."

"We'll have access to the airport security videos of the incident shortly. Could you be compromised, Max?"

"I don't think so. Except for me, Bijeau and Mother, no one knew about our plan. I believe our paths crossed with the competition by sheer coincidence."

"How can you be certain about Bijeau?"

Doss glanced over at Bijeau. "Bijeau is solid, sir. She managed to tag Duc with a tracker. She is tracking his movements on her laptop now. We're still in the game."

"Where are they headed?"

"North by vehicle. Maybe Canada. Vancouver would be a smart play."

"Put me on speaker. Bijeau?"

"Yes, sir."

"Do you know who I am?"

"Herr Direktor?"

"That's correct. I've read your file. Impressive. Doss seems to trust you so I will trust you as time is short and the stakes are high. We live in a time infected with troubling ethics, where almost everyone is playing everyone else for money, sex, or power. When it comes to trust and betrayal, I am positively medieval and my reach is unbelievably long. Do we understand one another?"

"We do."

"Doss, Bijeau, whatever you need, Mother will provide. We are flush with cash, as you know. Finding men and women we can trust and rely upon is another matter. There is no higher priority in the country than this mission. I want Duc and I want him alive. But regardless of what I want - Duc does not leave the U.S. Are we clear?"

"Crystal," Doss replied.

Doss sped down the airport parking lot ramp with the engine revving and tires squealing, turned onto the airport road, and jumped onto I-5 North. "Quick thinking with the tracker, Bijeau."

"Tag 'em first and bag 'em later if things go wrong, is what I say. I learn from my past mistakes. What's the plan?"

"Can't trust the Canada Border Services Agency or U.S. CBP to help. We intercept them in Blaine before they cross into Canada. Calling Mother. Mother?"

"What do you need, Max?"

"We're on I-5 heading north, a few miles behind the target. My guess is that they'll cross the border and head for Vancouver. Can you procure a boat - something fast - and have it ready for us in Blaine should they try getting Duc out by sea?"

"On it."

"We have any assets in Blaine, or anywhere nearby for additional muscle?"

"Nothing."

"Hm. Rent a plane and a chopper too, have them fueled and ready to go, again something fast in case Duc's abductors take to the air. I want the plane sitting on the tarmac and the chopper in the air on standby. I can pilot the fixed-wing. We need a chopper pilot who won't turn tail and run at the first sign of trouble if you can find one.

Do your best to assure him that we're the good guys. Tell him there's an extra ten-thousand-dollar bonus in it for him if he lands that chopper where and when I tell him to. Hell, wire him the ten grand up front as a sign of good faith."

"On it, but it's high risk, Max."

"Yep, satellite?"

"Yes."

"Realtime?"

"Yes."

"Access to state and federal highway cameras?"

"Of course."

"Don't know how I ever did this job without you, Mother. All we have on our end is a red dot moving north across Bijeau's laptop screen. Link into Bijeau's laptop, keep tracking the car's exact position and then zoom in with the interstate cameras. I want a visual of the vehicle we're chasing. Get me the make, model, color - license plate number too if you can."

"On it."

The Camaro SS, Chevy's new reintroduction of the classic muscle car, lunged into action with impressive raw power produced by an 800-horsepower supercharged high-output V-8 engine as Doss stepped on the gas. He didn't ease off on the pedal until they were within a quarter mile of their prey, just south of Bellingham, where intermittent waves of rain greeted them.

"Dark gray S Class Mercedes up ahead with California tags," Bijeau said after exchanging text messages with Mother. "Mother confirms five males inside the vehicle, three in the back seat."

"Good. I'll pull ahead of them. Any sign of any escort vehicles, those thugs from the airport?"

"No, but can't be sure. I see one U-Haul behind us. I'll keep an eye on it."

"You any good with that M4 Daniels Defense carbine with the Trijicon 6x24 AccuPoint in the backseat?"

Bijeau smiled. "Yeah, engine block?" she asked as they zipped past the Mercedes.

"Yep."

"Automatic fire on an open interstate, that's your plan,

bossman?"

"You have a better one?"

"No, can't say I do. What about law enforcement? Can Mother keep them from interfering?"

"Not sure," Doss answered as they zipped past the Mercedes. He took a quick peek at the car but couldn't tell who was sitting in the back seat. "We're traveling through Washington State, in rebel, enemy territory. But we're out of options. Have Mother direct the chopper to our location. Tell the pilot we're in the midnight blue Camaro SS and have him shadow us. Find somewhere isolated before we reach Blaine, something with a nearby field where the chopper can set down after we disable the Mercedes and grab Duc."

"Not much open territory, Max. Here, how 'bout this, the Custer Northbound Rest Stop with an open field adjacent to a quarry to the east, approximately ten miles from the border. Looks like flat farm field, no power lines, close to the highway."

"That'll do. If things turn dicey, you get Duc on that chopper and then contact Mother for an extraction point."

"Who the hell is going to extract us?"

"Herr Direktor will have something headed our way."

"And you?"

"Be right behind you - but if I'm not don't wait on me. Your primary objective Marine, your only objective, is Duc and only Duc. Got it?"

"Roger that."

His plan would have landed him a solid 'F' at the Army's Armor Basic Officer Leader Course located in Fort Moore, Georgia. It was a horrible plan born of desperation and Doss knew it. He racked his brain trying to think of a better alternative. Nothing came to mind. Still, they had surprise in their favor. Still, the rain was a plus and traffic wasn't bad.

"Helo's a thousand yards off our starboard," Bijeau reported. "Pilot confirms he can land at the field. Mother has identified two state troopers ten miles north running a speed trap. Another police cruiser is heading south on I-5, about four miles from our location. Target is about two thousand feet behind us."

Doss took a quick look in the rearview mirror. "Can you confirm Duc is inside?"

"Negative."

"But the tracker still has him?"

"Affirmative."

"How far to the next exit?"

"Two, two and a half miles."

"Alright. I'm going to speed up, put some distance between us. See the J.B. Hunt semi off on the shoulder up ahead?"

"Yep."

"Time to ditch the laptop, Bijeau, and grab your carbine. Going to pull over to the semi, drop you off. You disable the Mercedes, take out the driver if you have the shot. I'll swing around in case you can't stop the vehicle and force them off the road. We take Duc, run through the rest stop over to the field and get on that chopper. We good?"

"Good to go."

After Doss pulled off on the shoulder, just a few feet in front of the eighteen-wheeler, Bijeau rolled out of the passenger seat with her carbine and her duffle bag, loaded down with all sorts of party favors for unwanted guests, and took a position in front of the semi. The driver stared at the crazy woman setting up a sniper rifle on a bipod over his truck's left fender wide-eyed, too stunned to say anything, and when she winked and smiled at him, he ducked below the steering wheel.

A moment later, Bijeau calmly put one burst of three high-velocity, armor-piercing rounds through the front grill of the Mercedes, then flipped her carbine's rate-of-fire selector switch to semi-automatic and put two rounds through the windshield. Black smoke and flame engulfed the engine as the Mercedes glided to a stop just as Doss threw the Camaro into reverse and slammed into the Mercedes to rattle the others inside. The two men in business suits from the airport sprang out of the back seat with short-barreled automatics and started peppering the Camaro with a hail of bullets. Bijeau dropped both men cleanly. When a third man jumped out of the front passenger seat and fired his automatic at her, she brought him down with a single shot to the head.

Doss rolled out of the Camaro and rushed over to the Mercedes. He found the driver slumped over the wheel and saw Duc sitting in the backseat, still clutching his laptop bag close to his chest.

"You, with me - now!" he ordered. When Duc refused to budge, he grabbed Duc by his bag's shoulder strap, yanked him out of the car and waved Bijeau to his side.

Then he heard the chopper, turned and saw the helo hovering nearby over the field Bijeau had described just as two cars suddenly flew past him at high speed to get past the burning Mercedes and the roadkill lying on the highway. Several more rational drivers screeched to a halt a short distance away and threw their vehicles into reverse.

"You good bossman?" Bijeau asked.

"All good. Thanks for saving my ass back there. Let's move."

Doss was relieved and a bit surprised that the pilot hadn't bolted. Maybe, he thought, between the trees and the noise from whirling rotor blades, the pilot simply hadn't seen or heard the shootout. Perhaps he was just desperate for cash, like so many other Americans across the county.

Then the driver of the semi put his rig into gear and drove off in a hurry. Behind him, northbound traffic was piling up behind the smoking Mercedes and the three dead bodies stretched across the pavement.

Bijeau slung her duffle bag over her shoulder. She cradled her carbine in her arms and took point. She hurried towards the rest stop with Duc a few steps behind her and Doss a few steps behind him. They could hear multiple sirens in the distance racing towards them. And then the U-Haul that had been trailing the Mercedes smashed through two parked cars on the interstate to get over to the shoulder where the eighteen-wheeler had been parked. The driver of the U-Haul didn't stop - he accelerated.

When Doss heard screeching tires and metal scraping against metal, he spun around, saw the U-Haul coming straight at him, raised his Benelli M4 semi-automatic and put three double-aught buckshot shells into the U-Haul's cabin. Big chunks of windshield exploded in a red mist across the ground. The truck suddenly swerved and flipped over on its side. Then the goons from the airport began crawling out of the back.

"Bijeau - to the chopper, now!" Doss screamed. "I'll cover you."

Bijeau hesitated for a moment. Marines don't leave Marines behind and today Doss was a Marine. But she knew Doss was right. She handcuffed Duc to herself and ran hard towards the chopper as Doss took a knee and fired more rounds at the truck.

Bijeau raced through the rest stop, ignoring a small gaggle of stunned onlookers while dragging Duc behind her. She kept running until they reached the trees, where she stopped to check on Doss. He had fallen back to one of the cars parked at the rest stop and was firing at the men from the U-Haul with his 9mm handgun. She started running again, pulling Duc with her, and made a mad dash through a small grove of pines and across the field where the chopper was hovering just a few feet off the ground. She heard a burst of automatic fire. She heard rounds zipping through the air above her head. Bijeau ignored the shots and ran harder.

Then she saw the pilot, a young woman, frantically waving at her to hurry. She was piloting an AgustaWestland AW109, a favorite rugged workhorse for SAR, for Search and Rescue missions. The pilot set the chopper down and opened a sliding back door as Bijeau ducked underneath the swirling main rotor blades and pushed Duc inside the cabin.

Bijeau heard a round slam into the chopper's tail boom after she hopped aboard. "Go, go, go!" she shouted.

The pilot jumped back into her seat and opened the throttle to increase power to the main rotors until the spin of their rotation reached sufficient speed to generate lift. She gently pulled up on the collective next to change the pitch of the blades while simultaneously depressing the left foot pedal controlling the tail rotors to counter the additional torque on the main rotors. As the chopper climbed into the air, she banked to the right to put some distance between the chopper and the men shooting at them.

The pilot craned her neck around to look at Bijeau. "What about him?" she asked, pointing towards the ground and at Doss.

With Duc now handcuffed to the rear seat, Bijeau, standing at the door, had a man in her sights trying to outflank Doss. She squeezed the trigger and cleanly dropped her target. Then she fired a second round at another man with the same result. And then the trees blocked her line of sight.

"You ex-military?" Bijeau called out, impressed with the pilot's poise under fire and her willingness to try and save a man left behind.

"Yeah, Navy. You?"

"Marine."

"You're paying for this ride, jarhead. What's your pleasure?"

Bijeau scanned what she could see of the rest stop. Civilians, some with young children, were ducking behind their cars, hiding behind the trees, or running for the restrooms. Flashing blue lights in the distance were racing towards the rest stop. She knew there was nothing more she could do for Doss and reluctantly secured the rear door. She looked Duc over for any holes, saw none, and forced him down on the chopper's steel floorboards. Bijeau wagged her index finger in his face, warning him not to move.

"This man I have with me, he's the priority. Let's hover a bit, see if my partner can reach the field. I want to help him if we can but I have strict orders..."

The pilot nodded, but as she eased the chopper up a few dozen feet for a better view, she and Bijeau could both see men hustling Doss into a parked SUV with his hands tied behind his back. Bijeau set her carbine aside, motioned the pilot to fly north towards the border and then called Mother.

"Mother, I'm in the helo with the package. The package is unharmed. The crew from the airport has Doss. They've stolen two vehicles, one is a late model, red Chevy Suburban with luggage stored on the roof and the other is a white sedan. They just hopped onto I-5 and are heading north from the Custer-Northbound Rest Area."

"I have acquired both vehicles," Mother said calmly. "ETA for your extraction team is approximately fifty minutes."

"Doss will be dead or out of reach by then."

"Maybe, but you have your orders."

"If I can save Doss and complete the mission, I gotta try. We have one advantage. No one else will be crossing the border today, leastwise, not with Doss."

"I'm beginning to like you, Bijeau. Be prepared for a severe tongue-lashing from Herr Direktor later, but even he has a bit of a soft spot when it comes to Doss."

Mother tracked the Suburban and the sedan to a house, presumably a safe house, close to Lincoln Park in Blaine and only a stone's throw away from the border. Bijeau checked her watch. Reinforcements were still 35 minutes out.

"What's your name?" she asked the pilot.

"Heidi."

"Heidi?"

"Heidi Wagner."

"Good grief, you'll fit right in."

"Beg pardon?"

"Your German family name - a little joke. I'm Alejandra, Alejandra Bijeau. How's our fuel situation, Heidi?"

"We're good. We have a minimum of two hours of air time unless we start pushing her hard."

"Ok Heidi, here's the deal, our sit rep. You're with the good guys. I hope you can take my word on that for now. The passenger may be a foreign agent, or not, but someone back in D.C. thinks he might have some intel that may be of high value to us - intel valuable to all Americans. So, regardless of what your political leanings are over secession, put them aside for now. Can you do that?"

"I can. I saw those merc types rushing out of the U-Haul, guns blazing, with civilians all around. Doubt they're friendly to anything American."

"Good, thanks. An extraction team is on its way to us, about thirty-five minutes out. I want you to ease us over to that house with the red Suburban and white sedan in the driveway. Not so close to spook anyone inside. Does the hoist and winch work?"

"Breeze-Eastern product, never had one fail."

"Good. Here's the plan. You're going to hover a bit while I repel down the winch line with my gear. Then move over to that park and wait for my signal to land."

"What's the signal?"

"With a little luck, you'll see me running towards you with my partner at my side, hopefully with no bad guys chasing us. Keep the motor running."

"And if things go wrong," Heidi asked and jerked her head towards Duc, "what do you want me to do with him?"

"The extraction team will take him off your hands and you'll be paid another ten grand for your troubles. Heidi, you don't know me and I don't know you. I'm in bit of a pickle here, I am at your mercy. So far, you've been a good sailor. If you leave me behind, if you try to take the passenger somewhere, well, fair warning, you will have pissed off some of the most dangerous and most powerful folks you can imagine back in D.C., folks with unimaginable resources."

"Don't die on me, badass," Wagner said and winked. "You owe me a drink or two."

"Roger that!"

With her carbine and duffle bag strapped to her back, Bijeau repelled down the winch line using some tall oaks for cover, then ran towards the house, a small, charming house among other small, charming houses within a quaint, quiet suburban neighborhood. With cold rains pelting the pavement and a fog bank rolling in off Boundary Bay, no one was out walking. She carefully made her way over to the house and saw that someone had drawn the window curtains and shut the blinds. She crawled on her belly over to the Suburban, removed a small block of C-4 from her duffle bag, set the fuse for remote detonation, removed the protective wrapping and gently pressed the adhesive side of the block up against the Suburban's gas tank then moved over to the white Honda parked next to it and prepared another block of C-4.

She kept low to the ground, circled the house, moving from window to window, but couldn't see a thing. She heard men speaking Chinese inside in what she figured was the living room and then someone said something in English, but she couldn't hear what. And then she heard Doss's voice and felt a wave of relief wash over her. She heard him, in a loud, rebellious tone, tell someone to "go fuck a duck, a Peking duck if you can find one."

She decided to go in through the backdoor and prepared another block of C-4. After she moved around the corner of the house with a remote detonator in one hand and a flashbang grenade in the other, she took a deep breath, smashed in a window with her elbow, tossed the grenade inside and then blew the backdoor. Both the door and an outer screen door flew off their hinges in a cloud of smoke followed an instant later by a flash of bright light and a deafening BANG inside the house. Bijeau rushed through the back entrance shooting. She saw Doss tied to a chair in the middle of a room, his face was a bloody, purple mess, and shot his interrogator in the chest. Then she sprayed the living room with bullets and bodies toppled over. Four men, still disoriented by the grenade, clumsily rushed to the front door and made it outside. And then Doss rolled his chair over and knocked the last man standing off his feet before he could draw his handgun. Bijeau finished him off with two bullets into the back of his head.

"Can you walk?" she asked while she cut the cord around Doss's wrists and ankles.

"I can run!" he shouted over the ringing in his ears from the blast of the grenade.

"Saving your ass is becoming wearisome, bossman."

"I had things under control here."

"Yeah, I could see that."

"Where's the helo?"

"Close by."

Bijeau helped Doss to his feet, thrust her 9mm sidearm into his hand, and then they heard the engine of one of the vehicles cranking over. "Let's go," she shouted.

"I have a couple of loose ends to deal with first," Doss said and racked the slide back on the 9mm.

Bijeau smiled and showed him the remote detonator in her hand. "Allow me," she replied and pressed the trigger. Two explosions followed.

When they stepped outside, they saw two smoldering vehicles in the driveway with four broken men sitting inside the Honda. They hurried across the street and over to the park where the chopper was sitting on the grass with rotors spinning.

"Doss, meet Heidi Wagner, former Navy aviator," Bijeau said as they climbed into the Agusta. "Heidi, meet my boss, Doss, Max Doss."

"Pleasure," Doss said.

"Likewise, sir," Heidi replied. "Forgive me sir, but you look like shit. Can we get the fuck out of here now? Haven't seen this much combat since Iran."

"By all means," Doss said and tried smiling, but regretted it. "Where to Alejandra?"

"Mother is sending us coordinates now for the rendezvous point. The extraction team is on the ground and waiting."

Doss nodded. "Very good. Heidi, you serve any booze up here in first class on this flight?"

"With what you are paying me, I suppose I should, but no. Backpack hanging on the bulkhead behind me - you'll find painkillers, some are off-the-shelf, others came with a script. Help yourself."

Heidi flew the AgustaWestland over the Georgia Sea, turned south over the Strait of Juan de Fuca and landed at Quillayute Airport, just a few miles west of the windswept City of Forks on the Olympic Peninsula. A party of special ops types was standing around an unmarked, black Dassault Falcon 50 EX at the far end of the runway.

Doss reached into the cockpit to shake Wagner's hand. "Heidi, I know we're paying you well, but I still feel indebted. You went above and beyond. If you ever need a job..."

"Thank you, sir. I just might take you up on that. I could use the extra hazardous duty pay. Besides, that kickass Marine back there owes me a drink."

"Never known her to welch on a debt. We'll be in touch. Fly safe Navy."

Wagner smiled. "Mr. Doss, Alejandra, thank you for choosing to fly with Cascadia Adventure Tours today. Your connecting flight appears to be on time. Do make sure you take all your belongings with you and watch your step as you exit the aircraft."

"You Doss?" one of the special ops guys called out as Doss, Bijeau and Duc walked towards the Falcon.

"Yeah," Doss answered and shook the man's hand. "This is Alejandra Bijeau and this fellow is our very special guest."

"Bijeau," the man replied and shook her hand too, then turned to Doss. "Paul Bryant. You look like shit, Doss."

"So, I've been told. Had a minor disagreement with a Chinaman."

"Any unfinished business we need to finish?"

"No."

"Well, you made quite a mess of things along I-5 and up in Blaine. Still leaving dead and mangled bodies wherever you go I see. All types of law enforcement are running amok, tripping over themselves trying to hunt down a large terrorist group."

"They'll find them too, all of them. But they won't be saying much. Any civilian casualties?"

"No. At least none have been reported."

"That's a damn lucky break."

"The cute blonde over in the Agusta - loose end?"

"No."

"I'm sure you're both exhausted, but my orders are to get you back to D.C. ASAP. That's from Herr Direktor himself, so don't shoot the messenger. The blackbird is fueled and ready to go."

Somewhere over Nebraska, Bryant shook Doss's shoulder to wake him. "Secure satellite, President wants a word with you."

Doss took a moment to stretch before taking the phone. "Madam President. Yes ma'am, I got it. Yes, ma'am, I am one hundred percent certain I got it loud and clear. That's an unfair assessment, Madam President. Yes, the killings were very public. Yes, regrettably, we endangered civilian lives. No, I wouldn't say this was a normal operation for me. No, I wasn't aware you ordered me to return to Washington immediately. Well, ma'am, if you are finished cursing, I'll tell you what this is all about. We had a lead on a Chinese terrorist cell and had to act before they blew up the airport. No, there was no time to brief you. I'm aware you are the President. Oh? Well, I'm sorry your call with the Chinese President was very unpleasant. No ma'am, the Chinese Ambassador's claim that we gunned down four innocent Chinese businessmen on the interstate is bullshit. How do I know? I know because they were carrying guns and shooting at us. Yes, ma'am, Bijeau is sitting next to me."

Doss set the phone down on the plastic seat tray, silently counted to five and then smiled at Bijeau. "She wants a word with you."

"How did she know to call you? Bijeau asked. "How did she even know how to call you?"

"Adelman is having some fun at my expense, I suspect."

"What is it with you and Dreyfus?" Bijeau asked. "You two snap at each other like an old married couple, like there is some history between you."

"Yep."

"Ah, so there is?"

"There is what?"

"History?"

"Yep."

"I knew it! She's attractive enough if you like bony, white chicks who visit a salon once a week for nails and hair instead of hitting the gym and a range. You could do worse than the President, I suppose."

"We don't have that kind of history."

"Dang, Doss. Then you're smarter than you look."

"Might interest you to know that bony, white chick once took first place in one of the more grueling national three-gun competitions not long ago."

"Fuck me sideways. You're joking, right? She has no military experience."

"Yep, I'm a regular late-night comedian."

"Respect! She didn't mention anything to me about your quick wit, but she did tell me that you have some sort of genius IQ and that I should be on my guard with you."

Doss laughed with no pain as the meds had kicked in. "If that were true, don't you think I'd be designing starships for NASA or teaching highfalutin physics at MIT instead of spending my Friday nights getting shot at and letting someone use my face as a punching bag?"

"Hello, Bijeau? Doss? Is anyone there? Hello? Someone answer the fucking phone. Damnit, this is the President! No one puts the President of the United States on hold! Answer me!"

Chapter Ten

Excerpts from Hermann Adelman's private journal:
The Great Turmoil

Billy Duc sipped his hot tea at a modest round wooden table in a small room that smelled of fresh paint while casually perusing the Wall Street Journal. Though they had blindfolded him before deplaning, he was certain that he was somewhere in Washington, D.C. He smiled as he set his paper aside and took in his surroundings. The Americans had left him in a room with red walls, the favorite color of every Communist Party in the world, and the decorative paintings around the room had a decidedly Asian flavor.

"Mr. Duc," an older man with an impressive mane of silver hair, with deep wrinkles and a German accent, said as he stepped into the room and offered his hand. "My name is Hermann Adelman. I am a great admirer of your work."

Duc ignored the man and resumed reading his paper. "I never hear of you," he replied dismissively.

"No matter."

"Where I am? Like I say to your man before, me commit no crime. You no right to steal me. When I leave? Ah, when can I leave?"

"You are in Washington, D.C. No one has charged you with any crimes. Not yet anyway. As for leaving well, we have quite a long road ahead of us, I suspect, before we can discuss such things. Who were those men in Seattle, the ones who tried to abduct you?"

"You know. They your people. Big, white man. Dark, pretty woman strong like water buffalo. They bring me here."

"No, I am referring to the airport."

"What is referring?"

"I am talking about the incident, the shooting, at the airport by the men dressed in airport security uniforms and the two Chinese men who grabbed you and took you away in a Mercedes."

"I don't know."
"Why did they want you?"
"I don't know."
"You don't know?"
"No."
"Why were you traveling to Manila?"
"See family."
"Oh? Not to meet a Chinese businessman named Wo Fat?"
"Who this man?"
"Mr. Duc, if we are going to play these silly games, you are going to be secluded, that is put away, in a small room like this one for a very, very long time. Fat bought your patent to your supercharged proton particle generator and made you a ridiculously rich man. But without you, he can't get the damn thing to work properly and you agreed to meet him in Manilla. Now do you remember?"

Duc looked away for a moment. "What you want?"
"You worked with our German friends for some time."
"So?"
"What kind of work did you do for them?"
"They design new military aircraft. I have wee knowledge of quantum mechanics Germans found useful."
"Huh, quantum mechanics, you say? How do you apply quantum mechanics to military aircraft?"
"I work on new propulsion system."
"I'd like to hear more about that."
Duc shook his head. "I sign no speak contract with German government. Me can no discuss."
"Ah, a nondisclosure agreement. Very well. Another time. Why did the Germans fire you?"
"They *NOT* fire me! I leave to start own business. This is Vietnamese way."
"According to my sources, you are from a poor family from the slums of Saigon. My dear fellow, you don't even have a high school diploma. Stop wasting my time. What could a simple, uneducated peasant like you possibly know about quantum mechanics?"

Duc took the bait and let his ego fly. He tore into Adelman with his brilliance, lectured the extraordinary spymaster and the holder of

THE SAVAGERY OF MAN

three PhDs as if he were a child.

"What do you think, Herr Direktor?" Doss asked Adelman after Adelman stepped outside of the Red Room.

"Stunning, astonishing, remarkable, unbelievably brilliant. All these adjectives barely begin to describe this man's grasp of higher evolution quantum physics, quantum mechanics and algebraic mathematics. I might, possibly, be able to hold my own on electromagnetism with him for a few short rounds. I feel it in my bones, Max. Duc has found, or is close to finding, the key to bridge, or reconcile, Einstein's work with quantum physics and mechanics. Duc is our man. Little wonder why everyone is after him."

"Where do we go from here?"

"We take him to Cheyenne Mountain, of course. We give him all the tools and resources he needs, including unlimited access to *Blue Swan* which is kept at Kings Bay, the Navy's submarine base near St. Marys, Georgia. We unleash him."

"Why Kings Bay?"

"Damn thing is too large to transport to Cheyenne Mountain, too big to move inside the mountain. Do you know the story of how we found *Swan*?"

"No."

"Some treasure hunters, deep-sea divers, found her off Cape Hatteras buried underneath tons of silt. They didn't know what they had found. They thought the thing might be a lost submarine and wisely called the Coast Guard, who turned the matter over to the Navy. Luckily no one imagined what the thing really was. The Navy brought in a salvage vessel, not unlike Howard Hughes's famous *Glomar Explorer*, to recover what the Navy assumed was some top-secret spy submarine for the CIA and took her to the naval shipyard in Newport News, Virginia as the shipyard was nearby. When the states began leaving the Union, Calhoun had the vessel moved to Kings Bay after the military informed him of what she actually was, though the Project Swan Team still works out of Cheyenne where all the other alien artifacts are kept."

"Good story. Any thoughts on Seattle? Pfeifer spoke as if the Council was behind Seattle, but that could have been misdirection."

"Indeed. The Chinese are the obvious suspects, but I have my doubts. China's Ministry of State Security prizes subtly and precision. I suppose one of Russia's Twelve Houses is capable of concocting such an incompetent, barbaric, untidy operation. Then again, the Russians are in a state of terrible disarray. I have my doubts there too. Once we ID the bodies, especially the men in the Mercedes, we may have something to go on. This mysterious group that calls itself the Council has certainly piqued my curiosity."

"Isn't that matter Herr Direktor with the Agency, CIA and NSA?"

"And when have I ever cared about stepping on their toes?"

"What do you need from me?"

"Get some rest Doss, heal up. It hurts me to look at you. I need you back in the field ASAP. And excellent work bringing Duc in."

"Bijeau is the real hero of that op."

"She risked the mission to save her partner. I was furious at first. Still, I find it hard to disagree with you. Under the circumstances, I'll let that bit of poor judgment pass this one time."

"What about Calhoun?"

"He's living up to his code name Odysseus. That wily old fox is planning and plotting and scheming while waiting for his body to heal. But then you already knew that. Don't think I am not aware he contacts you directly."

"Any leads into who planned the assassination?"

"Leads yes, incontrovertible evidence, no."

"May I know what the inconclusive evidence points to?"

"To some unholy alliance between this Council group out of Europe and a militant faction within the so-called Resistance."

"And Dreyfus remains in the dark?"

"That woman has never ventured into the light."

"What of Dreyfus's proposed bill recognizing the League's right to break away from the Union? Has Congress done anything with it?"

"Stalled in one committee or another thank God. Sometimes having a politician who is a master of procrastination in your hip pocket can be a wonderful thing. When you're up for it, I want you to quietly find out more about these bashful Council folk."

Chapter Eleven

Finding the Council had been surprisingly easy. Mother simply kept a close eye on the movements of Jason Pollard, the Deputy Director of the FBI, the man Pfeifer had identified to Doss as being in Vienna at the same time the Council had recently assembled there. A week after dropping Duc off in Washington, Doss decided to follow Pollard to Frankfurt, curious to see what he would do as there appeared to be no official government reason for Pollard to be in Germany.

This time Doss took a crack team of twenty operatives with him. He didn't need to ask Bijeau, she had eagerly insisted on tagging along. Doss, Bijeau and the others arrived in Frankfurt by private jet ahead of Pollard, set up shop at the Sofitel Frankfurt Opera and waited. After Pollard and his security escort of three FBI agents landed in Frankfurt on a commercial Lufthansa flight and cleared customs, they walked straight to the airport parking lot, piled into a black SUV, courtesy of the U.S. Embassy, and hopped onto the Autobahn. Mother tracked them by satellite to Mespelbrunn, a modest town due east of Frankfurt, and then to Mespelbrunn Castle, a 15th-century bastion nestled deep within Spessart Forest. The castle, isolated, peaceful, and surrounded by a deepwater moat, was an ideal retreat for corporations, associations, and various government and non-government organizations.

Doss led three, four-man surveillance teams into the Spessart Forest to observe the castle but security was extraordinarily tight with packs of armed men and dogs continuously roaming the grounds, forcing Doss and his men to watch the castle and adjacent buildings from some distance away. Numerous visitors came and went over the next few days, but Doss was unable to identify any of them, nor could he or his men see or hear what was taking place inside. The castle may have been over 500 years old, but the windows were high tech, protected by the latest in RF and IR-blocking film while a low-tech canvas canopy shielded guests walking to and from their cars and the castle. Mother couldn't even identify who had rented the castle. Doss needed a new plan.

When Pollard left the retreat four days later and started heading back to Frankfurt in his U.S. Embassy car, six men dressed in German police uniforms, driving two *Bundespolizei* motorcycles and two brand spanking new BMW 8 *Bundespolizei* cruisers, vehicles Doss's team had stolen two days before, stopped his SUV alongside a quiet forest road just a few miles away from the castle. Five of Doss's men took Pollard and his security detail quietly into custody, hustled them into a nearby van and drove them to a small apartment just outside Frankfurt while others disposed of the police vehicles and returned the SUV to the airport. After securing the three FBI agents in one room, they led Pollard down a rickety wooden staircase into a dreary, soundproof basement and left him there with a rustic wooden table, two crude, small wooden benches, and a laptop.

"Deputy Director Jason Pollard, we will try to keep this unfortunate encounter brief," Doss said as he stepped out of the shadows. He pulled a bench out for Pollard, and after Pollard took his seat, he handed him a stein filled to the brim with beer and took a seat across from him.

"You know who I am," Pollard said nonchalantly.

"Yes."

"And you are?"

"Doss, Max Doss."

Pollard shrugged his shoulders. "German name, but you're American. Who do you work for Doss? Certainly not for the BPOL, the *Bundespolizei*. The men who brought me here aren't really German police, are they?"

"The more interesting question, Pollard, is who do you work for?"

"I'm with the FBI, as you seem to know already."

"I suspect you serve more than one master."

"What does that mean?"

Doss turned the laptop around and opened the screen.

"What is this?" Pollard asked, confused.

"What does it look like?"

"Ah, um, a debris field floating on water, over a lake, I think. Looks like, eh, a plane crash?"

"Very good. Tragically, the world will soon learn you and your security detail perished in that crash."

Pollard roared with laughter. "Is this someone's idea of a joke? Ah, I'll wager some of the old gang from Skull and Bones put you up to this."

"No joke."

"Not a joke? Well then, know this: I'm protected. Perhaps you can fake a crash, but you can't fake the death of the Deputy Director of the FBI. No bodies, at least no bodies with matching DNA. The FBI, the full power of the United States, will devote enormous resources to find me. What is this all about? I fear someone has duped you, set you up. You've made a terrible mistake kidnapping me and bringing me here. If you free me now, you have a chance. If you don't, you'll be hunted down like a dog within the week and never seen or heard from again."

"Is that so? Employing international hunter-killer teams now, are we? That hardly sounds like the FBI."

"Wait..." Pollard said and paused for a moment, looking at Doss with a sly grin as if he finally understood. "A loyalty test! That's why I'm here. You came from Mespelbrunn Castle."

"Ah, there's no tricking a trickster!" Doss stated drolly. "To whom are you loyal?"

"I serve at the pleasure of the President," Pollard answered evasively.

"She'll be happy to hear it," Doss said and decided to roll the dice. "But it is your loyalty to the Council that interests me more."

Pollard shifted uncomfortably in his chair. He took a sip of beer, then took a moment to consider how to respond. He was a political appointee, the heir to a large fortune, not an agent, not a cop. He wasn't even a Washington insider. He had never been trained in interrogation techniques - on either side of the table.

"I'm loyal!" the Deputy Director of the FBI finally blurted out.

Doss couldn't help himself and smiled as he had snared his prey. "I'm sure, but to whom are you loyal? You're starting to sweat Pollard."

"I voiced my concerns over timing, that's all. Not the plan itself. Stromquist knows I'm loyal, I'm, I'm committed, I'm fully committed. Look at the millions I've contributed to the cause."

"We'll see. Some within the Council have quietly expressed their doubts about you to Stromquist. They have wondered about your motives. There are rumors."

"No. No, no, no! Who, who is spreading these lies about me?"

Doss got lucky. It happens. Someone once said you make your own luck. Doss wasn't sure about that but he had thoroughly reviewed the files Mother had sent him earlier on Pollard before interrogating him, including a psychological profile the FBI had worked up on Pollard - an unusual thing for the FBI to do - after Dreyfus's new Attorney General had forced the agency to accept a nonprofessional into its ranks as their number two. Pollard had no discernable skills Doss could find for the job. He was a rich, feckless party boy, a pretty boy, and had been since his days at Yale. He thought money made him untouchable. For the next 24 hours Doss and Bijeau took turns grilling Pollard hard and Pollard, having convinced himself that Doss was working for the Council at Stromquist's behest, that Doss was looking for a mole within the organization, talked willingly and candidly - all to prove his loyalty.

"Am I free to go now?" Pollard asked Bijeau wearily when the interrogation mercifully seemed to be at an end. He had been without sleep, without caffeine or any uppers for 36 hours. He could barely muster a clear thought.

Bijeau slowly walked over to him, lewdly spread her legs in front of him and eased herself down on his lap. She put her hands on his shoulders, nibbled on his ear, and began seductively grinding her body against his.

"Honey, you are free to go if you want," she said as she started moaning with pleasure. "I have a limo waiting for you outside. You sure you want to leave right now, baby?"

Pollard struggled, trying not to become aroused. The woman had a killer body though and was, in a sleazy, rugged way, quite attractive. And they were the only two in the room. He couldn't help himself. He gave in to his lust and started moving his body against her.

And then Doss walked in. "Bijeau, you're cruel," he said with a chuckle. "Teasing a condemned man like that is - ah - shameful!"

"A girl has needs," she replied as she stood away from Pollard. "Maybe," she said, looking down at Pollard, "we can finish this sometime in Siberia, handsome. Then again, I don't do traitors."

"What?" Pollard asked, confused.

"Jason Pollard," Doss stated in a formal tone. "You've committed high treason. Someone will explain the particulars to you later. Do you know Lucy Brighton, Senator Brighton? Of course, you do. You'll be joining her in a few days - that is if you choose to cooperate fully, otherwise, it's a deep, dark hole for you."

Confused, sleep-deprived and suddenly utterly terrified, Pollard started sobbing. "But I'm loyal!" he blurted out. "I'm loyal, I'm loyal, I tell you. I'm loyal! Take me to Stromquist. We can fix this."

"Stromquist? I don't work for Stromquist. Your treason is against your country."

"What? No, no. Let me talk to the President. She knows. She can clear up this misunderstanding."

"The President? You say the President will vouch for you?"

"Of course."

Doss turned to Bijeau. "Interesting. Bijeau, you and I will be returning to the U.S."

"And the agents upstairs?" she asked.

"Maybe they disappeared in that plane crash too, or maybe not. They stay here with the rest of the team until we know whether they're patriots, patsies, or something else."

"And what, what about me?" Pollard asked with a brittle voice, betraying his fear and desperation.

"That depends upon you," Doss replied. "You're coming with me. Though I am finished with you, your interrogation, your debriefing, is far from over. How well you cooperate will determine your fate."

"But I have rights! You can't do this!"

"Oh, but I can."

"The Council, they'll find me and kill me for talking to you. They have vast resources. There is no place you can hide from these people."

"You're in a fine pickle then. Not my problem. Let's go, our plane is ready."

The Council, Doss briefed Adelman by phone during the flight home, was not some ancient, secret society steeped in mysticism or religion, or charged with protecting the mysteries of the universe, or even with just preserving the order of things, of maintaining the status quo. The Council was a modern creation, conceived by an obscure

Swedish administrator at the United Nations named Kurt Stromquist, a man of limited accomplishments but who possessed two extraordinary gifts: the twin gifts of supernatural charisma and the power of cultlike seduction. With a jealous, jubilant world watching the startling, rapid disintegration of America as a military, industrial and economic powerhouse, as she slid towards civil war, Stromquist found his calling. From every corner of the globe, he quietly began assembling a following of the super-rich, the powerful, the gifted, the influential, the weak-minded and the easily manipulated and beguiled them with his grandiose vision of creating a new reality, of creating a united world under the single leadership of one universal government. Stromquist named his vision the New World Order, a term the Americans had coined after World War I when the League of Nations was formed, coincidently also governed by a Council, and was determined, obsessed, with saving humankind from itself.

Billy Duc never arrives at Cheyenne Mountain. After a pair of new, state-of-the-art F-51 Mustang Dominators flying escort are vaporized, presumably by a high-altitude satellite armed with some never-seen-before weapon, the aircraft carrying Duc, a JetZero C-BW-1 Starstriker military transport, the Air Force's newest, most sophisticated stealth, blended-wing body cargo plane, disappears 15 minutes later somewhere over Missouri. The Starstriker vanishes without a trace. There is no wreckage, no debris or bodies, no mayday calls or transponder signals. Nothing.

"Not a single clue, Herr Direktor?" Doss asked angrily as he took a seat in Adelman's office, disgusted that his work in Seattle was all for naught.

"No," Adelman replied gruffly. "Mother is working diligently on reacquiring Duc's location. We implanted a tracker on him, of course, but this time someone found and removed the device about an hour after the Starstriker disappeared. That's how we know he's still alive. We have no idea what kind of weapon vaporized the world's most advanced fighter jet or how a large cargo transport aircraft simply vanishes. Over at the Pentagon, the big brass is still reeling in shock.

The loss of Duc could be catastrophic. At least we have the man who tipped his abductors off in custody. That's something I suppose."

"Who is he?"

"He's Air Force, for Christ's sake, a twenty-year-old ground crewman, a lowly airman!"

"And he knows what?" Doss asked, shaking his head in disbelief.

"The only thing this kid knows is that he was approached by an attractive brunette, possibly Hispanic, maybe Asian, at a local bar. She gave him ten grand, a picture of Duc and a burner phone and promised him another ninety thousand dollars if he delivered information leading to Duc's whereabouts. Ninety thousand dollars was transferred into his bank account after he made the call. He has no useful description of the woman and the burner phone is useless. He has no clue who Duc is or why he is valuable."

"How did he find Duc?"

"Dumb luck. Duc slipped on a grease spot inside the aircraft hangar before boarding the Starstriker. His hat and sunglasses went flying when he fell. The kid just happened to be standing a few feet away and caught Duc before he hit the concrete. *Mein Gott, wie grausam die Schicksale sind!*"

"The Starstriker left from Andrews?"

"Yes."

"No street cameras near the bar or security cameras inside the bar?"

"The one street camera that could have been helpful for whatever reason wasn't working. The owner of the bar only turns the inside cameras on after he closes shop."

"My guess, Herr Direktor, is that this is a random shotgun approach operation. Whoever is behind this didn't just single out one airman. We could have transported Duc out of Washington any number of ways to any number of different destinations. Whoever these people are, I bet they have been spreading money all over town, hoping to get lucky. Not a bad approach, I suppose. The country has been up for sale for years and everyone wants a piece of her before there's nothing left."

"Sadly, I fear you are right, Max. The good news is that we don't need to look for a traitor inside our own house. Still, as a safeguard, I keep spies within spies within spies, not unlike those Russian Matryoshka dolls."

"Section 3M sounds like a real paradise to work at. Pollard is on Level Five. We should press him hard, see what he and the Council know about Duc."

"Yes, but I have other talent who can squeeze Pollard. You find Duc. Use whatever resources you need. I give you carte blanche. And remember what I told you before. If we can't have him, no one can have him. He's not a civilian. He's no innocent. Am I understood?"

"Understood, sir."

Twelve hours later, Mother came through. Mother always came through. Doss found Bijeau on Level 5 spread across a bunk bed in a deep sleep, still wearing her fatigues from Germany. He shook her gently on the shoulder.

"Pack your gear, Marine, no rest for the weary."

"Where to bossman?"

"Stop calling me that."

"Sure thing, bossman. Where we headed, bossman?"

"Your neck of the woods Alejandra, New Orleans."

"Fuck me. The mission?"

"Find Duc."

"You mean these shitheads have lost him already?"

"Afraid so. What was your rank in the Marines again?"

"Gunnery Sargent."

"Congrats. Adelman has agreed to bump you up a few notches. You now hold the rank of captain."

"Damn, a battlefield commission! That's quite a bump. He has that kind of authority?"

"You tell me when you get your next paycheck."

"You still a sir?"

"Yep. And I've asked Adelman to permanently assign you to me - if you want that. You do have a choice. You can let the President believe you are still working for her. You good with all this?"

"Shiiit... We taking a backup team again? The last team made this girl feel safe and special."

"We'll have a cavalry to the rescue team in place. You and I are running recon first, see if the intel Mother gave us has any value."

"How did she come by the intel?"

"How does Mother do anything? Let me know if you ever find out."

Doss and Bijeau were sitting at the bar in the Davenport Lounge of the Ritz Carlton Hotel on Canal Street, enjoying a cocktail as they waited. Mother had arranged a meet and greet with a local contact of interest. Doss didn't particularly care for jazz, but the band was good and the music wasn't bad. Then a young Cajan beauty dressed in a stunning, glittery black evening gown with high heel stiletto black patent leather pumps sauntered into the lounge. She walked towards the bar with confidence. She looked like royalty. She smelled of jasmine.

"Monsieur Doss?" she asked.

"Yes."

"Madame Veuve Delassixe from Exotic Temptations sent me," she said with the poise of a seasoned, successful businesswoman and took a seat on a barstool next to Doss. "I am Désirée."

"Of course you are," Doss replied, smiling as he took a moment to admire the body tucked neatly inside the bodycon, low-cut gown. "Drink?"

"Please, Monsieur Doss. They serve a perfect Vieux Carré here."

Doss nodded to the barkeep, then looked up to face the young beauty. "Call me Max, and this is my colleague, Alejandra Bijeau."

"Bijeau? New Orleans?" Désirée asked and reached across Doss for Bijeau's hand.

Bijeau nodded as she shook hands with Désirée. "*Il y a longtemps, mais oui, je suis originaire de la Nouvelle-Orléans.*"

"One's imagination runs wild," Doss said playfully, "wondering what type of enterprise Exotic Temptations is engaged in."

"I think Alejandra," Désirée said, pausing to take a sip of the cocktail the barkeep handed her, "your colleague is a naughty fellow."

"If only you knew the half of it," Bijeau replied, grinning. "I must confess, I've never heard of Exotic Temptations or Madame Veuve Delassixe."

"Madame runs an exclusive export-import business for a very select clientele. We specialize only in the rarest and most exquisite commodities. Madame understands you are prospective buyers for such things?"

"Indeed, we are," Doss replied. "And time is of the essence. As delightful as you are, Désirée, could you introduce us to Madame Veuve Delassixe without delay, preferably this evening?"

"There is the small matter of a nonrefundable deposit we discussed earlier with your factor in Washington."

Doss removed a black plastic card from his blue blazers inside breast pocket and handed the card to Désirée. When she nodded to the barkeep, he reached below the counter to retrieve a laptop with a card reader attached and placed both on the bar.

After she powered up the laptop and inserted Doss's card into the reader, she smiled approvingly at Doss. *"Excellent Monsieur Doss, cent mille dollars comme convenu."*

"Whoa, one hundred thousand dollars?" Bijeau asked, surprised. "That's a rather steep entrance fee."

"Hard to put a price on things of rare quality with timeless value," Désirée replied. "Now, I am required to neutralize any trackers you may have on your persons. I have a limo waiting for us outside. I will need to blindfold you and take your phones and the weapons you are carrying. These conditions are non-negotiable."

Doss wasn't happy about it, but he expected nothing less and nodded his consent. Désirée led Doss and Bijeau into a small private room in the back of the lounge, took a key from her handbag, unlocked a cabinet door along the wall and removed an electro-magnetic ring scanner. She scanned Doss first, then Bijeau and grabbed a kit from the cabinet, an extraction kit very much like the one Doss had used on Bijeau back in Schaumburg, and removed both tracking devices. Next, she took their weapons and locked them inside the cabinet.

As they rode in the limo blindfolded, Doss had no idea where they were headed. Bijeau thought they had jumped onto I-10 West and then exited onto I-55 North, but after that, she too was lost, though

THE SAVAGERY OF MAN

she was confident they hadn't crossed over Lake Pontchartrain.

When they turned onto gravel and stopped, Désirée helped them out of the limo, walked between them and led them arm-in-arm into a building. After she told them to remove their blindfolds, Doss and Bijeau found themselves standing inside the center of a dimly lit, empty warehouse with an attractive, middle-aged brunette accompanied by four burly men holding Uzis standing across from them. The woman, stylishly dressed in sleek, black slacks, black sandals and a low-cut, double-breasted black jacket decorated with brass buttons, let her cigarette fall to the floor and with an air of authority snuffed the stub out with her sandal.

"Mr. Doss, Ms. Bijeau, welcome," she said with a smoker's husky voice and the hint of a French accent.

"Do we," Doss asked, "have the pleasure of speaking with Madame Veuve Delassixe?"

"You have that privilege, yes," she answered while unabashedly looking Doss up and down.

"Veuve?" Doss asked rhetorically. "My condolences. I am sorry for your loss, Madame."

"Don't be, she said as she made the sign of the cross. "I am a widow by choice, may my poor, late husband rest in peace."

Doss raised an eyebrow at her audacity, at her candid admission, then took in the four corners of the warehouse. "By the looks of things, business appears to be off."

"Ah, this is not a place for storing things. I have other facilities for that. This is a place where problems disappear, Mr. Doss."

Doss and Bijeau instantly stiffened, fearing they had walked into a trap. They braced themselves for the worst.

"We've come in good faith," Doss offered without emotion.

"We shall see," Delassixe replied. "Tonight, we shall either part as friends or I shall have my companions dump your bodies in some remote bayou for the gators to feast on."

"Take heed, Madame -," Doss said until Delassixe cut him off with a wave of her hand.

"Save your threats, Mr. Doss. I have a fairly good idea of who and what you are but I too have dangerous, powerful friends in high places. The one hundred-thousand-dollar payment is a good start towards friendship. You may relax for now. To business then. You are looking for a man named Billy Duc, yes?"

"Yes, do you have him?"

"No."

"But you know where he is."

"No, but I know where he will be and when he will be there."

"May I ask how you know these things?"

"Because a new client, he goes by the name of Jack Conrad, an alias no doubt, has engaged my specialized set of services to smuggle Duc out of the country under a new identity. People across the country often come to me with difficult relocations, especially of high-profile individuals on the run."

"And why would you turn on this new client of yours to help us? Are you trying to spark a bidding war between us for Duc?"

"Ah, now that would be entertaining, but no. I like money. I am after all a businesswoman. Some would tell you that I am the boss of a substantial criminal syndicate. I make no apologies for who I am. This life was thrust upon me by my father and I do what I must to protect myself and those I love. As it happens, I also love my country. A conundrum, yes? I had a baby brother. He was the black sheep of the family because he turned down his future role in the family business, which greatly disappointed our father. My brother was a true patriot. He taught me why I should love my country and how to be a patriot. He died for this country. The people who have Duc, I'm quite certain, wish to harm America, perhaps even see her fall. Rumors abound about who these people work for. I always do my due diligence on prospective clients. This is why you and I are having this conversation. I don't need or want your money. I will even refund your deposit. Perhaps this will earn me a chit, some measure of goodwill with your people up in D.C., to be redeemed at some later time? The *enemy of my enemy is my friend*, after all."

"What do you want?"

"I want to help my country."

Doss took a moment to process everything Delassixe had said. "There is something you are not saying," he finally decided. "I suspect your motives are more complicated. Your brother, was he law enforcement, military?"

THE SAVAGERY OF MAN

"Air Force."

"I am sincerely sorry for your loss. Ms. Bijeau and I are both former military. We have seen combat. May I ask how your brother died?"

"I cannot reveal how I know, but I know. My brother, Major Daniel David Delassixe, was one of the F-51 fighter pilots killed while escorting a cargo plane transporting the curious Mr. Billy Duc."

Whoever said that fate is a fickle mistress knew what they were talking about, Doss mused to himself back at the hotel, in the dark, in the quiet dawn of a new day. By pure happenstance, a lowly airman of no importance unwittingly identifies Duc and then - by a bizarre twist of fate - the very folks who grabbed Duc decide to hire a woman to smuggle him out of the country who happens to be the sister of one of the pilots they murdered. Doss shook his head, bewildered by the confluence of such odd events. Coffee, he needed coffee and left his room for the Davenport Lounge to find some. He had five days to prepare.

This time, Doss assembled an elite team of 50 tried and true decorated combat and black ops veterans, the best, and all the weapons, equipment, and gadgets they could think of. He augmented his tactical ground force with six AH-64-E Apache attack helicopters from Adelman's new private air wing. Each Apache came armed with a 30mm M230LF Bushmaster Chain Gun mounted under the forward fuselage and four AGM-114 Hellfire missiles attached to the stub-wing pylons. He would get Duc back at any cost and this time, he would personally deliver Duc to Cheyenne Mountain.

Delassixe's new client, driving down from Saint Louis on I-55, agreed to deliver Duc to the same warehouse where Doss and Bijeau had first met Delassixe, a warehouse in Ponchatoula, just a few miles off I-55. Though the warehouse, with a mix of other commercial buildings and residential homes nearby, was not an ideal venue for a firefight - if it came to that - Doss decided to take Duc there. He did not know how many mercs the man named Conrad would bring or how his men would be armed, but he knew there would be at least ten as Conrad was paying Delassixe to transport Duc out of the U.S. plus ten.

Doss knew his plan was solid. He would keep everyone out of sight until Conrad and his men arrived. Once they pulled into the warehouse's gravel parking lot, once Doss confirmed that Duc was with them, he would launch twelve surveillance drones to cover a mile-wide perimeter around the warehouse and then send out four four-man teams with two vehicles each to tighten the noose, to seal off any escape points from the warehouse. His operatives, battle-tested men and women, were outfitted as an FBI tactical unit with FBI identifications in the event local law enforcement tried to intervene. The warehouse only had two cargo bay doors, one in the front and one in the back, and had no windows. Doss would approach the front with one team of ten while Bijeau would approach the rear of the warehouse with her team of ten. He would place two snipers in the front and two in the back to provide cover. The rest of his operatives would secure a tight perimeter around the area. Everyone had rehearsed their roles the day before. Everyone had familiarized themselves with the terrain and local roads. And Doss had Mother.

Yes, Doss knew he had a fine plan with top-notch professionals to execute his plan. But even the *best laid plans of mice and men* can go wrong. Twenty-four hours before the delivery date, a tropical storm brewing in the Gulf of Mexico, a real rainmaker, decided to make an unexpected sharp right turn up the Mississippi Delta. Delassixe contacted Conrad to suggest delaying the delivery, but he adamantly insisted on sticking to the agreed schedule.

When a caravan of six vehicles with dark tinted windows - three vans and three sedans of various makes and models so as not to attract attention - pulled into the warehouse parking lot the following day, the winds had intensified to gusts of 60 miles per hour and more and the intermittent rains and drizzle earlier had turned into a steady, blinding downpour. Doss, concealed underneath camouflage netting some 100 yards off, decided against launching the drones or the Apaches. And even with Synthetic Aperture Radar, the rough weather had badly degraded the ability of Mother's satellites to see. Doss's sophisticated op was fast turning low tech.

Delassixe, now dressed in a sexy, fitted denim jacket with tight cargo pants and hiking boots, had insisted on being present to greet Conrad and was waiting for him inside her warehouse along with eight of her own muscle. Both cargo bay doors had been left open.

A man with curly blonde hair, wearing a khaki windbreaker, casual navy-blue pants and loafers without socks, stepped out of the lead car. Doss counted 30 armed men stepping out of the vans to join him. He could not see how many remained behind inside the sedans. He whispered into his mic, relaying what he had observed to his team.

"What do you want to do, bossman?" Bijeau whispered back some 200 yards away on the opposite side of the warehouse. "They brought a lot of firepower. This could turn into a real shit show real fast."

"Wait. We must confirm Duc is here. All teams, hold in place. Do not engage."

Then Doss heard Delassixe's voice. His tech ops had bugged the warehouse with hidden microphones and installed additional mini cameras inside and out.

"Mr. Conrad?"

"Yes," the man with the curly blonde hair answered. "And you must be the shadowy Madame Veuve Delassixe of Exotic Temptations?" he asked with an exaggerated grin and offered his hand.

"I am," she answered and stepped forward to shake the hand of the man who had a part in her brother's death. "Shadowy?"

"As in mysterious. There is precious little information out there about you or your organization. I think you must prize anonymity."

"What woman doesn't crave a bit of mystery? What organization in my line of work doesn't prefer the shadows?"

"Touché, Madame. The people I work for are no different. Your reputation for quality and reliability, I must admit, is unmatched."

"Mr. Conrad, you've brought a lot of men with you with more, I suspect, outside. We agreed to transport eleven individuals out of the country, one man named Mr. Billy Duc and ten others. I cannot accommodate all of you. There simply is no time."

"I understand. One Mr. Duc, myself and nine others as agreed. Inasmuch as we have never done business before, I have brought a few additional associates with me to ensure things go smoothly. May I see the paperwork, passports, identifications, travel passes, etc. along with the details regarding the logistics you propose?"

When Delassixe nodded to one of her men holding a backpack, he stepped forward and handed the pack to Conrad. "You'll find eleven folders," Delassixe explained, "one for each traveler and one file containing all the logistical particulars. The ship leaves for Algeria at dawn tomorrow. Time is short. I've covered all your expenses in advance. I'll need proper photos of Duc, you and the other nine men to complete the documents. We brought the necessary equipment and can finalize the work here."

"Excellent," Conrad replied, then handed the pack to the man standing next to him. "Karl, position twenty men outside, then return to inspect the papers."

An uneasy tension filled the air after Conrad's man returned and started reviewing files. Neither Delassixe nor Conrad were much for idle chit-chat and both sides stood quietly staring at each other while listening to the hard rains ricocheting off the warehouse's metal roof. Then, without warning, a blinding flash of light lit up the entire warehouse, followed a split second later by a crack of bone-chilling thunder. Everyone flinched - then all breathed a sigh of relief that no one was trigger-happy.

"This is first-rate work, Mr. Conrad, really quite good," the man named Karl said. "The passports and visas are flawless. Duc's past has been thoroughly scrubbed. We board a container vessel under Maltese registry named *Oriental Star* tonight. The ship leaves the Port of New Orleans in the morning. All travel arrangements have been thoughtfully prepared with contingency arrangements for any mishaps or unacceptable delays along the way."

"Thank you, Karl. Shall we begin the photo process, Madame?"

"Of course, a glass of wine, perhaps while we wait?" Delassixe asked. "I brought something special for the occasion."

"How thoughtful, please. Karl, it is time to bring Mr. Duc inside."

Conrad's man nodded and stepped outside again as Delassixe simultaneously sent six of her men to a white box truck parked outside. Her men quickly returned with printers, photo, and lamination equipment, a folding table and two folding chairs. They set the equipment up in one corner of the warehouse and placed the chairs and table in the center of the warehouse, along with a charcuterie board and a pricy bottle of a Lafite-Rothschild Bordeaux with two wine glasses.

After Delassixe and Conrad took their seats, she began to pour the wine just as two men, propping Duc up between them, dragged him inside. Duc's hair was a matted, disheveled mess. His skin was pale. Delassixe watched him glance down at her with listless, bloodshot eyes.

At first, Delassixe thought he had been tortured but soon realized he had been drugged. "I think," she said after taking a sip of wine, "I better grab my makeup bag. We can't take this poor fellow's picture looking like that."

After all the photos were taken, after all the documents were finalized and the last of the wine had been sipped, Conrad stood and circled the air with his finger, signaling his men that it was time to leave.

"We have the small matter of payment," Delassixe said as she stood away from the table and reached into her handbag to grab her pistol. She wanted the pleasure of killing Conrad herself.

"Alas dear lady, leaving witnesses behind is not part of the plan," he replied and looked over at Karl. "Leave no trace of our presence."

"Move! Move! Move!" Doss shouted into his mic after he heard Conrad's last order. "All teams, MOVE! Snipers are hot, I say again, snipers are hot. We take Duc alive."

The storm was gathering strength. Ferocious, howling winds were whipping the rains around in every direction. Lightning and thunder hammered fear into every heart. Poor visibility made everything worse. Doss would have relished such conditions on the battlefield as he led an attack. But this was an extraction, not a battlefield, with civilians caught in the middle.

As Doss rushed forward with his team, he heard gunfire inside the warehouse. Bullets pelted the gravel all around his boots. A woman running next to him grasped his forearm before she collapsed. Doss raised his Scorpion and shot the man who had shot her. Then two flashbang grenades, thrown from inside the warehouse, exploded next to the cars, quickly followed by two smoke grenades.

"Hold your fire!" Doss shouted, certain Conrad was trying to flee. "Alpha Team, secure the vehicles. Bravo Team report."

"We've reached the rear of the warehouse," Bijeau answered.

"Hostiles outside neutralized. Hostiles inside have closed and locked the door. Permission to blow the door."

"Hold," Doss ordered when he heard tires screeching and kicking up gravel. Two sedans nearly clipped him as they flew by in the smoke. "All teams," he shouted into his mic, "a forest green Audi and a silver-gray Mercedes are on the move. Do not, I repeat, do not fire on the vehicles. Deploy the spike strips. Bravo Team, blow the rear door, Alpha Team move inside and secure the warehouse with Bravo Team."

Bijeau immediately blew the rear cargo door open and rushed into the warehouse with her team just as Doss and his team entered from the front. Three of Conrad's men dropped their weapons and raised their hands. The rest were dead or wounded. Duc was nowhere in sight. Then Doss saw Delassixe sprawled across the concrete floor over in a corner with her men lying dead around her and rushed over to her side.

Doss knelt next to her, found her still breathing and gently sat her up against the wall. "Madame."

"My daughter," she said, struggling to breathe, "your debt to me is now owed to her. She will inherit the business."

"Your daughter?" Doss asked as he raised her blouse to inspect her wound.

"You have already met."

"Of course, Désirée. We'll get you to the hospital. No need to die today. You have a collapsed lung, but I don't think your wound is fatal. The bullet passed through cleanly. Alejandra, any sign of Duc?"

"No, Duc and Conrad are gone."

"Madame, I need your car keys. Alejandra, see to Madame Delassixe, secure the area and keep any locals and law enforcement out. Don't take any crap from anyone. I'd prefer not to advertise our business, but play, *this is a federal national security matter; you'll be charged with treason if you interfere* card if you must. Understood? Good. Have Mother send the cleaners to this location."

Doss tore out of the parking lot in Delassixe's BMW M5 Special Edition Black Cheetah. He had tasked two of his men earlier with tagging every vehicle with a tracker using high-powered dart rifles once the real bullets started flying. Though the BMW's computer could not tie into any of the trackers without Doss pulling over and wasting time syncing his phone to the BMW, Mother was able to track both cars for him.

The Audi and the Mercedes blew past one of Doss's roadblocks with automatic weapons blazing, running over and crushing one man. The spike strips his team had tossed across the road did nothing. Doss thought about that as he waited for his team to pull the spike strips off the road so he could get by. Conrad had equipped his vehicles with high-performance, ballistic no-flat military grade tires, a controlled item under ITAR, the International Traffic in Arms Regulations, which made them nearly impossible to buy in the U.S. and exceedingly difficult to export or import. Doss concluded Conrad had American friends in high places.

Conrad avoided the interstate, took Wadesboro Road, a two-lane country road, and headed west. Doss pushed down on the accelerator pedal and with a 4.4-liter V8 twin-turbo engine producing 700 horsepower and 505 pounds of torque, the M5 launched itself down the road like a rocket.

"What's up ahead, Mother?"

"The cars have stopped at the JR Ponchatoula Boat Yard, a quarter mile down the road, Max."

Doss brought up a map of the area on his phone. "Damn, anything on satellite?"

"No."

"Well, if he can find a boat there and crank the engine over, he'll head south to Lake Maurepas and then on to Lake Pontchartrain."

"Why south, Max?"

"He'll either ditch the boat and hide in the swamps until help comes or he'll try to reach New Orleans, a place where he can easily blend in and disappear. Either way is bad for us."

"Max, the Audi and Mercedes are on the move again. He is heading for Route 22."

"I'm pulling into the boatyard now. It's deserted, no boats here. Connect me with Wagner. Heidi - glad you decided to join the family. I know it's risky in this weather, but I need your Apaches airborne. Mother, guide Heidi to my location. Heidi, once you have the two sedans I'm pursuing in your sights, do not lose them. I'm in the black BMW M5."

"On the way, Mission Leader," Wagner replied with a twinge of excitement in her voice, betraying the adrenaline spreading across her body.

The Audi and Mercedes were moving fast, but Doss had closed the gap. He could see the taillights of both cars about 500 yards in front of him. Then he glanced up and saw five black Apaches a few hundred feet away flying in close formation, struggling against a meanspirited storm still huffing and puffing and lashing out at the world.

"Wagner, Doss."

"Read you loud and clear, bossman," Wagner replied coolly.

"*Bossman?* You too? Jesus. Hey, I think you're missing a helo."

"Mechanical issues," Wagner explained. "She had to set down on a nearby soccer field."

"Gotcha. When Conrad turns onto I-10, get in front of him and force him off the road. We cannot allow him to reach New Orleans. Understood?"

"Copy that, will do, sir."

Both the Audi and Mercedes took the entrance ramp onto I-10 at 60 miles per hour. Doss raced up the ramp doing nearly 90.

"Max, Mother. The storm is breaking up over the city. I have a visual on one, no two helicopters taking off from Lakefront Airport."

"Armed helos? What direction?"

"Wait. Cannot confirm if armed, but both birds are flying straight up I-10 towards you."

"Wagner, peel off three of your Apaches and intercept. You and your wingman stay with me, help me box in the Audi and Mercedes."

"Executing now, sir."

When the winds abruptly shifted, they instantly lost their ferocity and the heavy rains suddenly turned to drizzle just as a brilliant shaft of golden sunlight unexpectedly poked a hole through the storm clouds over New Orleans. Not far off the three Apaches that Wagner had sent south to interdict the two choppers from the city were lighting up the sky while Wagner and her wingman flew past the two sedans, spun around, and flew straight at both cars with the tips of their main rotor blades nearly touching pavement. The Apaches forced the vehicles off the highway and into a ditch beyond the right shoulder.

Doss could see Conrad pulling Duc out of the Audi, and then he dragged Duc into the Conway Bayou. Doss pulled the M5 off to the side just as four men jumped out of the Mercedes, formed a picket line and started walking towards him. They opened fire and riddled the M5 with bullets.

"Wagner, a little help!" Doss shouted as he ducked below the dashboard with 9mm rounds whizzing by over his head, as shards of glass fell on top of him.

There is no mistaking the sound of a Bushmaster Chain Gun spitting out 30mm shells at 200 rounds per minute. When the Bushmaster went silent, Doss bolted out of the M5, ran past four torn, bloody heaps of flesh, guts and bone no longer recognizable as men, and disappeared into the swamp.

"Bossman, your three o'clock, thirty meters," Wagner, flying directly over him, reported. "Duc keeps stumbling. He is slowing Conrad down."

Doss easily caught up to Conrad. He raised his CZ carbine, selected semi-automatic mode, and placed Conrad's nose squarely in his sights after Conrad spun around to face him.

"Conrad enough! It's over. Release Duc and you can live."

Conrad smirked and pulled Duc - still clutching his laptop bag tightly against his chest - in front of him, using him as a shield. "I'm curious, how did you find me?"

"Wasn't hard."

"You fool, do you know who you're dealing with?" Conrad asked, as he placed his handgun against Duc's temple.

"No, enlighten me."

"I serve an organization you can't hope to win against."

"I don't care."

"Well then, if we can't have Duc -."

But before Conrad could utter another sound, Doss gently squeezed the hair trigger on his CZ, launching a 9mm hollow point at 800 miles per hour directly into the bridge of Conrad's nose, killing him instantly.

"To all teams, this is Doss. I have the prize. Bijeau, send twenty men to my location ASAP. Wagner, report."

"We signaled two UH-1N Hueys to turn back. After they fired on us with fifty calibers, we splashed both whirlybirds over the lake. No civilian casualties. Beaucoup police units rushing to your position."

"Bijeau, report."

"Warehouse secure, cleaners ten mikes out. Delassixe en route to Ochsner Medial in Baton Rouge. Condition stable. We've taken six hostiles into custody, three with gunshot wounds. Treating the wounded on site."

"Is the man named Karl among them?"

"Negative, he's dead."

"Damn, he could have been useful. Our casualties?"

"Two KIA, one in critical condition, three with non-lethal wounds. Sent the critically wounded man with Delassixe along with an escort to watch over them."

"Very well. Mother, please brief Herr Direktor. We need the local authorities to stand down. We must move Duc out of here immediately."

"I've been sitting on the sidelines listening in Max," Adelman said. "Congratulations on a job well done. Awe-inspiring work. Reinforcements are already en route. We'll chat soon. Adelman, out."

The I-10 corridor between Sorrento and the I-55 exchange had become the mother of all clusterfucks. Scores of LEOs from dozens of local, state and federal government agencies, hundreds of first responders and platoons of news folks had converged on the area like vultures. No one knew who was in charge. Everyone wanted to take Doss into custody and, but for the five Apache gunships circling overhead, along with the twenty heavily armed FBI agents surrounding him, someone would have. Thirty minutes later, Adelman's reinforcements arrived and ended the standoff with official-looking paperwork and lots of impressive, military-grade hardware and firepower.

Chapter Twelve

Excerpts from Hermann Adelman's private journal:
The Great Turmoil

No one knows quite how they managed it. For over 800 years the thirst of a nomadic, desert people from a small, poor country, a thirst for power and riches and a ravenous hunger to conquer the world, had laid undisturbed and dormant. And then came a man, a direct descendant of the great Genghis Khan, or so he claimed, who was inspiring countless millions - Russians from the north, Chinese from the east and Muslims from the west, the downtrodden, the disillusioned and the disenfranchised - to rally around his banner, the same banner, a plain white flag with nine blue ribbons sown along the fringes, the sublime, godlike Genghis once carried into battle.

Not since the year 1219 A.D., when Genghis invaded the Khwarazmian Empire, had the Mongols thought to march beyond their western borders. Imagine if you can merciless Mongolian hordes and their ruthless allies - a great and mighty host - assembling in the distance like locusts, stretching from one end of the horizon to the other for as far as the eye can see. The ground shakes beneath your feet as warriors beyond counting, wielding their brutal weapons of war, riding atop their enormous black engines of death, charge across the steppes of Eurasia. Their vast columns move swiftly, kicking up towering clouds of choking dust, dust so thick not even the sun can pierce the terrible veil.

Their confidence in their commander and themselves is unshakable. Their faith in the Eternal Blue Sky is unwavering. Hear their bone-chilling war cries. Witness the unbridled lust for blood in their eyes. The man who leads them knows no fear. He has no compassion. He will not parley. He will not compromise or bend. A mad craving consumes his soul, an unquenchable thirst, to bathe and purify the world in blood.

Prepare yourselves. Temüjin the Blessed is on the march. Go - hide your children, your wives and your elderly, hide your riches too, hide them all away in the deepest, darkest cave if you like - as if hiding in a hole can save you.

But first, like his legendary ancestor who robbed China of her revolutionary new weapon, what men today call gunpowder, before setting out to fulfill his destiny, Temüjin knows he must rob China of her newest revolutionary weapon before setting out to fulfill his destiny. In his first military campaign beyond Mongolia's borders, he leads his vast legions southwest into China towards a secret military installation, a base so secret it has no name, located deep within the remotest regions of the Taklamakan Desert.

His warriors easily brush aside China's pitiful border defenses and continue racing south until they reach China's super-secret base. They overwhelm the meager security forces there and sack the installation just as Genghis had once sacked the great cities of mighty empires. Hidden in massive concrete vaults deep below the surface, Temüjin finds China's most sacred treasure, he finds an alien spacecraft. His men crate the vessel and the laboratories up, they take the scientists too, and move their plunder up to the surface for transport. But before they leave, they round up what remains of the Chinese garrison, march them out into an open field and slaughter every soul, indifferent to any who might be watching. They brazenly leave behind a massive sign for the satellites to find, for the world to see, that reads when translated: *They stole what is ours, we punished them like horse thieves.*

"Well, aren't these pictures sobering?" President Dreyfus asked rhetorically as she stood away from her chair in the White House's Situation Room to grab a Coke from the credenza behind her.

The Joint Chiefs of Staff, the DNI, NSA, and CIA had all contributed something to the satellite images that captured a sizable army sweeping down from the southwestern border of Mongolia and into China. The images of Mongolian soldiers overrunning a highly secret Chinese military base in the remote regions of the Taklamakan Desert, and then removing truckloads of equipment and people from the base, were clear and detailed. The images of the Mongolians executing hundreds of prisoners and then destroying the base with explosives were unsettling.

"What is the readiness of our military?" the President asked as she resumed her seat at the head of the table.

"We are," explained General George Phillips, the Deputy Chairman of the Joint Chiefs of Staff, stepping in for General Ritter-Starling, "presently at DEFCON FIVE, Madam President, our lowest state of readiness." The general paused and stood to turn on one of the wall screens, using a remote. "I would suggest going to DEFCON FOUR, which means increasing intelligence gathering and strengthening our security measures. I'd also place both the 101st Air Assault Division at Fort Campbell and the 82nd Airborne Division at Fort Bragg at REDCON-TWO, which is full alert and ready to go into action but without deploying."

"DEFCON THREE would," the President asked, "increase our military readiness and the Air Force would be ready to mobilize in fifteen minutes?"

"Correct, ma'am."

"DEFCON ONE is easy enough, either we are already in a nuclear war or all parties involved have their fingers on the trigger."

"Correct, maximum readiness, immediate response."

"And DEFCON TWO?"

"We place all military units on maximum alert. They must be ready to deploy and fight within six hours or less."

"I'll need input from my Cabinet but your recommendations sound prudent to me, General," the President said, then turned to her Chief of Staff. "Tom, see to it my Cabinet is here by four."

"Your full Cabinet, Madam President?"

"God no. State, Defense, Homeland Security, Commerce, and I'd like each of you at the table to return at four. Invite the Director of the FBI and we should invite some folks from the House and Senate over too. Tom, we can discuss who after this meeting. What do you have up on the screen, General?"

"These are various charts and tables Madam President showing the locations, combat strength, and current state of readiness of our military forces across the world in the event you wish to consider moving certain units into South Korea, Japan, Taiwan, or the Philippines to reinforce our fighting capabilities in those countries or to beef-up our assets at our new base in Vietnam."

"Ah, ha," she mumbled, then took a moment to collect her thoughts. "How do we think the Chinese will respond to this invasion across her borders, to this blatant act of war? And what should our own response to the world be?"

Adelman cleared his throat. "Perhaps the first question should be why this base and why now?" he asked, though he was confident he already knew the answers to his own questions despite the attempts of his jealous colleagues sitting around the table to keep him, and what they perceived to be his lawless, rogue organization, in the dark.

"We think," offered the Director of the CIA, a career Washington bureaucrat named Christopher Nestle, "based on sound, reliable sources, this facility was where the Chinese kept their alien artifacts, their research teams and labs."

"DNI concurs with CIA," Harry Hanson, the Deputy Director of National Intelligence, serving as the acting director since the sudden departure of his boss to join the Resistance, interjected. "We believe it is safe to assume Mongolia now has unlimited access to extraterrestrial technology."

"What the fuck is wrong with the Chinese, how could the CPC be so fucking irresponsible?" the President asked with rising anger in her tone. "And how," she lashed out, "could you gentlemen sitting around this table let it happen?"

"Madam President, I think," General Phillips began saying, until the President cut him off.

"Save your excuses, your bullshit, George," she snapped. "I'm in no mood. The knives will be out. I can hear my political enemies, ah, my opponents, calling for my impeachment. They'll blame me for allowing a madman - on my watch - to gain access to alien technology!"

"Madam, may I remind you," Nestle offered in a soft, reassuring tone, "very few people know about the discovery of alien technology. Sure, there are lots of rumors and rumblings flying around, but the cat isn't out of the bag, not yet. Certainly, neither the public nor their representatives in Congress know anything of substance."

"Speaking about keeping cats in bags," Dreyfus warned, "the

meeting at four is strictly to discuss the Mongolian-China crisis, not a word about alien technology. Is that understood by everyone? Good. Remind me, who do we think is in the alien space race business?"

"We are in the race, of course," Hanson replied, "as are the Germans, possibly the Russians, now the Mongolians and I wouldn't discount the Chinese just yet. They would have redundancies in place to protect all their research. Just because they've lost the hardware doesn't mean they don't have what they need to design new weapons, new, unbelievably strong materials and new propulsion systems only seen in science fiction movies."

"What do we know about this clown who thinks he is Genghis Khan?"

"He is known to his followers as Temüjin the Blessed or Temüjin the Risen," Nestle answered. "And we know virtually nothing about the man. He claims to be a direct descendant of Genghis Khan and this may actually be true. Some historians believe the prolific old goat had hundreds of children. He had at least four official sons and five daughters with his wife, Börte, and she was far from his only wife. He may have had as many as five hundred wives and who knows how many offspring with each of them. What we do know is that in 2003, an evolutionary geneticist named Chris Tyler-Smith discovered that eight percent of the men across sixteen different Asian ethnic populations share the same Y-chromosome pattern. This pattern was traced back to a shared origin from close to one thousand years ago and to create so many descendants, it is thought that this origin, this man, would have had to produce an enormous number of sons."

"Good God, where did Genghis find the time, or the energy, to conquer half the known world?" Hanson asked to chuckles around the room.

"Is he a religious leader of sorts, maybe a fanatic with a messiah complex?" Dreyfus asked.

"We simply do not know, Madam President," Nestle answered. "The man is cloaked in mystery within a deeply closed society. We don't even know why some call him the Risen or the significance of the term."

"Let's find out Chris," Dreyfus said absently as if deep in thought and then turned to Phillips. "Now, General, what did you want to say?"

"Ahem. I would suggest, Madam President, that we treat the Mongolian move into China as a limited incursion, as a border squabble between neighbors. In our current weakened state, we don't have the military resources to cajole or demand anything from the Mongolians. In fact, the Mongolians may have done us a favor. China will be forced to put aside its focus on Taiwan and the Philippines. The Chinese military will need to redirect significant combat assets to the northwest to keep the Mongolians in Mongolia. I strongly urge us to stay well clear of this foreign mess, this potential flash point."

"Does China still have one hundred percent control over her tactical and strategic nukes?" Dreyfus asked.

"We," Hanson answered, "have no evidence to the contrary."

"That at least is some good news. This *squabble,* as you call it General, between Mongolia and China will do nothing to help my bill concerning the League. We are going to need a strong military alliance with the League if we are to preserve our American culture. We need a coalition, not a civil war with the League."

"I thought, Madam President," Adelman interjected dryly, "that this proposed bill of yours recognizing the sovereignty of the League was DOA with Congress?"

Dreyfus answered both Adelman's question and his sarcasm with an icy stare to show her displeasure. "What," she asked no one in particular, "was this mess down in New Orleans on the interstate all about? I called the governor of Louisiana. She suspects the incident was a spat between two cartel gangs over turf. But I don't trust that woman. FBI informs me that the FBI tactical unit involved were imposters. Speaking of the FBI, has anyone heard from Pollard? He isn't returning my calls. None of you have anything to say? Nothing? Jesus. Perhaps I should fire the lot of you."

When no one around the table offered any answers, when everyone refrained from even speaking, the President abruptly stood and adjourned the meeting.

Chapter Thirteen

Doss and his team played a shell game for a full week, moving Duc farther and farther west from place to place with multiple decoy convoys doing the same to confuse anyone trying to find and apprehend Duc. He would not trust the Air Force, or fly Duc out himself and risk being vaporized, and there were no other government agencies he had confidence in. America was returning to the days of the Old Wild West where laws could change on a whim, where it was often hard to tell the good guys from the bad and foremost on everyone's mind was simple survival.

Doss successfully delivered Duc unharmed to Cheyenne Mountain without incident seven days after the gunfight in New Orleans. When he saw the shocking news on TV about a Mongolian invasion into China, he immediately called Adelman.

"Yes, I quite agree Doss, the world has gone mad, and civilization as we know it may soon become extinct," Adleman said irritably after he had told Doss what he knew about the political crisis unfolding in Asia.

"What do we know about this Genghis Khan wannabe, this Temüjin fellow?"

"Not a damn thing."

"Why the sign planted in the ground about the Chinese stealing from them?"

"The Chinese found their alien ship in the Mongolian Desert and removed the thing to China. How the Mongolians learned of this and then discovered the location of the Chinese base is anyone's guess. What of your interrogation of Duc, did you learn anything useful?"

"I have a full written account, Herr Direktor, that I can transmit to you today. I didn't learn much because I don't think Duc knows much, apart from what he learned in Munich. He admitted the Council invited him to Vienna to discuss his work on *Cigar*. He claims he developed an uneasy feeling about the Council, told them he had learned nothing useful in Munich and had decided to return to Vietnam. As we know, he left Vienna in a hurry and made it as far as Seattle."

"Does he have any thoughts on who or what took out our two Dominators and disabled the Starstriker?"

"Duc was surprisingly chatty about that. I didn't understand much of the technical jargon, but according to Duc, he may be able to build a similar weapon for us. It is some sort of supercharged neutron particle plasma ray developed by the Germans that can vaporize matter, a crude byproduct from their alien technology research."

"The Germans are our friends and allies. I cannot believe they had a part in any of this. Perhaps the Council stole the weapon or the plans from them?"

"A strong possibility, Herr Direktor. Conrad did not say who he was working for and gave me no chance to interrogate him, but Pfeiffer, as you will recall, did disclose the Council was tracking Duc."

"Right. What else did Duc say about the weapon?"

"He believes the weapon is meant to be used in the vacuum of space and is less effective in the atmosphere with a reduced range. He said a similar, non-destructive plasma weapon could have jammed the Starstriker's communications, GPS, and transponders. He believes someone was able to hack into the autopilot and assumed control of the aircraft. Duc said they landed the Starstriker in a remote field somewhere. The people who took him executed the crew but left the aircraft intact. He seemed positively giddy about working for us."

"Interesting. I intend to leave for Cheyenne Mountain later today and interrogate Duc myself. He may hold the key to our survival in his hands."

"Who knows about the potential importance of this man in Washington?"

"Other than Calhoun, no one outside my Section and I intend to keep it that way. He wants to see you by the way."

"Understood. Do you have a new mission for me, or can I go decompress on a beach somewhere after I visit Calhoun?"

"Take a week, Doss, then report back. I want to know where the Mongolians have taken their new space toy and I want a feasibility study prepared on how to take it away from them or, alternatively, how to destroy the damn thing. I don't know who is the more dangerous threat to America, this megalomaniacal upstart from Mongolia with visions of world conquest, the Council, or Dreyfus."

"Mr. President."

Calhoun beamed with delight when Doss stepped into his room. He was out of the ICU and was no longer attached to any tubes, machines, or monitors. Those annoyances had been replaced with new annoyances, with exotic communications equipment, supercomputers and screens and various other high-tech stuff with a dozen people to work them. Calhoun's hospital room, with two adjacent rooms, had been converted into a cramped command-and-control center.

The President eased himself into a pair of cheap hospital slippers and left his bed to embrace his old friend. "I don't see any bullet holes in you, Max," he said with a friendly smile as he poked Doss in the chest several times with his finger before embracing him. "Between the two of us, you always were the tougher, luckier son-of-a-bitch."

Doss returned the President's embrace but was taken aback by how frail his once robust, energetic friend felt, how much older and worn he appeared despite his youth. "It's good to see you up and walking, Abe," Doss said. "'Bout time you got off your lazy ass trooper and did some honest work. I do like your new furnishings, though."

"Follow me, Max. We have our own secure situation room down the hall where there happens to be a small liquor cabinet if you know where to look."

Doss followed Calhoun down a long hallway with a pair of hulking Secret Service types and one Space Force colonel carrying a black briefcase tagging along. The hallway was empty of hospital staff and patients, as the entire floor had been closed for *emergency renovations*. Calhoun led Doss into a presidential situation room in miniature and closed the door. His security detail remained outside.

"The Colonel," Doss asked as Calhoun poured him a beer. "He has the football?"

"Sorry, I have no hard stuff to offer you, docs ignore the beer if I follow the rules. Yes, I have the nuclear football."

"What the hell does Dreyfus have?"

"For all I know, her military aide is lugging around his girlfriend's lingerie or a box of chocolates for Valentine's Day - whatever he's carrying, it won't give Dreyfus access to the nuclear launch codes."

"Sounds like the makings of a comedy. How are you healing?"

"I must admit, the road has been difficult at times and I have a ways to go yet, but I was lucky. I'm told I'll make a full recovery."

"Wonderful. And the investigation?"

"You know as much as I do, Max. We may be looking for a phantom shooter behind some grassy knoll for decades."

"Do you want me involved? Adelman will authorize it if you give the word."

"No one wants to see those killers of innocent men and women and children dangling from the end of a rope more than I do, but no. We have far more urgent matters to attend to, my friend, and our resources are already stretched thin. It's hard to tell friend from foe these days and time is against us. We must prioritize. My would-be assassins are low on my to-do list - for now."

The two friends sat and chatted for several hours. They talked about professional matters and private matters. They talked about everything. And when the President felt the urge to rest, Doss locked his arm around the President's arm and walked Calhoun back to his room.

"So, we have a plan, Max."

"We have a plan, Mr. President."

"Operation Homecoming, I like it."

"You would be pleased. Your love and admiration for ancient Greek stuff has always baffled me. I imagine you were probably a Spartan hoplite in a previous life."

"A lowly hoplite?" Calhoun chuckled. "Hell, I was at the very least one of Alexandar's lieutenants and no doubt one of his favorite drinking companions!"

The President's smile vanished when he rested a hand on Doss's shoulder. "I trust no one more than you, Max. I know the odds are long. I know how grim things look for America and for the world. I'm asking a lot from you and your team. We are standing at the edge of a great precipice and the view below is terrifying. But I won't let our country burn. I won't let her slip into chaos and ruin, not without a fight. And if it is a fight to the death, so be it. Bring it on, I say."

After leaving Calhoun, Doss took Adelman's advice and caught a flight to the Bahamas to relax, yes, but he did some of his best thinking walking along the beach and took his laptop with him. Before leaving for the airport, he sent Wagner and eleven of her pilots off to the 1st Air Cavalry Division at Fort Cavasos in Texas for three months of intense training in air cavalry combat tactics, special operations, and certification training on Bell's newest version of the Valor, the V-280A2 tiltrotor aircraft. He also wanted better answers from the two most prominent citizens in the Village and sent Bijeau there to get them which, for Bijeau, was better than a vacation.

"Well, well, well, former Senator Lucy Brighton and ex-Deputy Director of the FBI Jason Pollard," Bijeau said playfully, with an impish smile after she stepped into Brighton's apartment unannounced. There were no locks on apartment doors within the Village.

Brighton and Pollard, sitting next to each other on a sofa, both stared up at Bijeau with a mix of surprise and disdain.

"Brighton, take a seat over there in the chair. Do it now. Pollard, take that chair across from her. Good. I've heard you two are quite an item in the Village these days and here you are, cozy as two lovebirds. How sweet. You make an adorable couple. I can see your wedding photo splashed across the front cover of one of those supermarket tabloid rags with the caption: *Former Washington Power Juggernauts Find Love Inside Traitors' Cove!*"

"What do you want, Tactical Agent Bijeau?" Brighton asked indignantly.

Bijeau had to admire how Brighton had taken her seat, as if she were about to do an interview on Fox News or CNN. Where Brighton retained her poise and commanding presence, Pollard was slumped over his chair and looked like a neglected rag doll.

"Still have a pair of balls, Lucy - I figured you'd be the one wearing the pants in this family," Bijeau said with a sly grin, then took a step closer to Brighton and started wiggling her hips and waving her hands in the air. "Lucy and Jason sittin' in a tree, K-I-S-S-I-N-G, first comes love, then comes marriage, then comes a baby in a baby carriage!"

"What kind of child are you?" Brighton asked.

Bijeau could see the rage building in Brighton's eyes. *Good*, she thought. She ignored Brighton for the moment and turned to Pollard. "I'd still do you, handsome. Fuck, I'd do you too, Ms. Senate Beauty Queen, looking all so regal and mighty over there, or I could do you both together. Ohhh? You think I'm talking about getting naked, down and dirty with you? A ménage à trois? Nah, I'll pass. I told you back in Germany, Pollard, I don't do traitors. What I mean by *do you* is that I'd be happy to take you both out back and put a bullet in both your brains. I'd sleep like a baby afterward."

"I don't understand," Pollard said coyly. "What have we done wrong?"

"Have you two naughty little traitors been lying to your jailors? No? You sure about that? Lucy?"

"I've lied about nothing," Brighton replied coldly, baring her teeth.

"I've, I've told the truth too, I swear it, in every debriefing," Pollard mumbled nervously.

"Well, I happen to believe both of you. At least you may not have lied directly. But failing to disclose information is lying by omission. A lie is a lie is a lie, as they say in my line of work. I want both of you to turn and look at each other. Go on, do it! Good, good. Living out your miserable lives in the Village is a far better fate than either of you scumbags deserves. Now say goodbye to one another because one of you shit birds will be on your way tonight from this idyllic sanctuary to solitary confinement in a maximum-security facility - I kid you not. If I don't like the next words coming out of your mouths, one or both of you is about to get seriously screwed - and not in a good way."

After Doss checked in at the newly renovated Ocean Club on Paradise Island under one of his half-dozen aliases, he went directly to his room, showered and changed into casual linen slacks, a beige polo shirt and comfortable walking shoes. Then he headed for the hotel's outdoor bar. Mother was a notorious scrooge when it came to travel expenses with others, but she never questioned Doss's expenses because, she had once told him, he never stopped working.

The bar was nearly empty and Doss was able to take a seat at the bar facing the Caribbean's world-famous emerald green waters. He ordered a mojito and checked his text messages to kill some time while munching on a handful of cocktail nuts. He read Bijeau's messages first. It was obvious she was enjoying herself at the Village from what she had texted, though she had just started working on Brighton and Pollard and had learned nothing useful yet.

Then a striking brunette wearing a flattering red bikini with an inviting black, see-through coverup decorated in pearl rhinestones caught his eye as she took a seat on the opposite side of the bar. She removed her large sunglasses and a red, broad-brimmed beach hat, shook her hair out, then smiled sweetly at him. He acknowledged her smile with a polite nod and let his imagination run wild - until her husband or boyfriend plopped down on a stool next to her. A moment later when the couple stood and left the bar together, he sighed, went back to his phone, and started scrolling down a text message from Adelman. The Section, Adelman wrote, had several promising leads on the whereabouts of Mongolia's new toy from across the stars.

Doss treated himself to a second mojito, best he ever had outside of Havana, and then started to think about supper. He did a quick Google search and settled on a place called Graycliff in downtown Nassau. Doss had traveled all over the world, but had never been to the Bahamas and so with the sun dissolving into a fiery explosion of striking colors splattered across a deep blue sky, accompanied by a refreshing ocean breeze rolling across the islands, he decided to walk into town and do a little exploring before he went to the restaurant for dinner. After he took in the town, he went to the restaurant and enjoyed a pleasant, leisurely meal of roasted lamb with a good bottle of pinot noir from Oregon, followed by a decadent slice of chocolate mousse cake. Then he decided to treat himself to a snifter of Remey Martin Extra Cognac, vintage 1980, together with a Cuban Cohiba Pirámides Extra before heading back in the dark to the hotel.

Halfway across an empty causeway linking Paradise Island to New Providence Island, a dark tan sedan suddenly pulled up alongside him.

Three hulking black brutes, Schwarzenegger body builder types, sprang out of the car and started closing in on him. Out of the corner of his eye, he caught the striking brunette from the hotel bar sitting behind the wheel.

"In the car, now," one of the men with a Jamaican accent ordered.

"I don't think so," Doss calmly replied as he tossed his cigar to the sidewalk. Though he felt a bit naked without his 9mm, which he had to leave back in the States, he was hardly unarmed. "If you want money, take it. You can have what I am carrying on me."

When the man to his left raised a policeman's baton above his head and took a step closer, and the man on his right came at him wearing a pair of brass knuckles, Doss's years of grueling, advanced self-defense training, compliments of an intense program that catered to military black ops folks and field operatives from the various intelligence agencies, kicked in. He did a snap kick with his good leg, hitting the man with the baton in the groin, and caught the other with an openhanded blow to his larynx. The two men doubled over, gasping for air, and fell to their knees in pain. The man in the middle, a good six inches taller and fifty pounds heavier than Doss, and unfazed by Doss's martial arts skills, came lumbering towards him with clenched fists and a confident grin.

After his automobile accident as a young teenager, leaving him with a bad knee, the doors to competitive football, baseball and basketball had closed on Doss forever. But in college, a coach with a keen eye for talent gave him a shot at boxing - turned out he was a natural.

Doss assumed his stance, back straight, feet shoulder-width apart, right foot slightly in front of his left, and then shifted his weight to maintain good balance. He raised his large, powerful hands, hands with robust knuckles, knuckles that come from years of targeted conditioning drills that gave him better-hitting power, above his chin, made tight fists with his knuckles facing upwards and bent his knees slightly. He reminded himself to breathe properly, inhale before each punch, exhale through your mouth and keep your jaw closed lest the other guy breaks it.

When the Goliath threw several clumsy jabs at Doss and missed, Doss knew he was facing a street fighter, a brawler, not a boxer. Doss threw a few of his own jabs to the face and gut, just to keep his opponent off balance. The man retreated, shook the blows off and then resumed his attack, but with a less confident smile. He threw a wild hook and missed again as Doss slipped to his right and rolled to his left. Then Doss saw his opening and landed a powerful uppercut to the chin, a devastating knockout blow. Dazed and confused, the big man stumbled backward with a cracked jawbone, spitting out blood and bits of broken teeth before he went down on his back.

When Doss saw the fellow with the baton struggling to stand up, he knocked him out cold with a cross and hook combination. The man with the brass knuckles decided to flee just as the brunette hit the gas and sped off. Doss checked the pockets of the two men lying on the pavement but found no IDs.

"Robbers?" Mother asked after Doss called to inform her of the incident.

"No," Doss answered. "They didn't want my wallet. They wanted me to get into the car."

"I am accessing the security cameras along the causeway now. Reversing playback, ah. I see the fight. I see you haven't lost your edge, Ali. Don't have a good visual of the brunette, too dark. Can't ID the vehicle, either."

"How did you acquire access to security cameras outside the U.S.?"

"Really, Max?"

"Yeah, right. Another trade secret. I'll get you a photo."

"From the hotel's closed-circuit cameras?"

"Yes."

"Try not to break any more bones."

"I'll ask nicely, all laid back, Bahama-like."

"You have blood on your shirt, sir," the hotel's concierge said with genuine alarm when Doss stepped into the lobby. "Are you hurt? Should I call a doctor?"

"Not my blood. But I do need to see the manager on duty."

"How may I be of service?" a petite, young Hispanic woman with a friendly face and night manager's badge pinned to her red blazer asked a few minutes later as she strolled over to Doss.

"Several people tried to rob me, Ms. ah, Ms. Sanchz. One of them, a woman, was at the outdoor bar earlier today. I need to see your security camera files."

"Oh, that is terrible. Shall I call the police for you?"

"No need. They didn't get anything. I would just like to take a quick peek at the camera footage of the outdoor bar, at around four o'clock today."

"I am deeply sorry, sir, but without a proper court order, I cannot accommodate you. It is against hotel policy - for legal liability reasons, you understand. I am certain the police can help you with this matter. Shall I call them for you?"

Doss shook his head. "That won't be necessary. I think a stiff drink and a soak in a hot tub are what I need, but thank you."

"As you wish, sir. I trust the rest of your evening is more pleasant."

Doss was in a sovereign, foreign country. His National Security, CIA and FBI credentials were of no use. He would need to get the camera security files the hard way. He returned to his room and waited for Mother to send him the blueprints for the hotel. She delivered the prints fifteen minutes later, after he had asked by encrypted email.

The hotel kept its security equipment in an outside, standalone building, a small concrete shack, next to the HVAC units and a dump truck-sized emergency generator. At two in the morning, Doss grabbed his earpiece and went downstairs. He took a tire iron from the trunk of his rental car and cautiously walked over to the hotel's main fuse box bolted to an outside wall next to the security shack. When he was unable to pry the lock off with the tire iron, he pried the thin, rust-covered metal hinges off of the box instead. Then Mother walked him through the steps needed to fry the fuses without electrocuting himself. When the fuses blew and the power went out, the hotel generator kicked in as planned.

He had ten seconds to reach the door to the security shack before the generator started supplying standby power to the door's electric locks. If he was too slow, he decided he'd break the window's wired safety glass with his tire iron and hope the generator would muffle the sounds of any alarms he set off. But Doss was able to reach the door

THE SAVAGERY OF MAN

before the locks reengaged and found what he needed sitting on a shelf. He grabbed an old-fashioned compact disc with the date and time he needed, an antiquated portable DVD player, and returned to his room before dawn.

In the morning, he noticed a voucher underneath his door good for a free breakfast to offset any inconvenience caused by the power outage earlier. He smiled, showered, dressed, and headed to the hotel restaurant with his laptop bag slung over his shoulder.

"Thank you for the complimentary breakfast," he said cheerfully to Ms. Sanchez, the night manager, as they passed each other in the hallway.

"Our pleasure. Enjoy your day in paradise, Mr. Doss."

"Thank you, I will. Please give my warmest regards to Mr. Bond when you see him."

The night manager looked at Doss, confused. "Beg pardon, sir? Who?"

Doss offered a polite smile and shook his head. "Never mind."

He saw an empty booth in a quiet corner of the restaurant, took a seat with his back against the wall, and powered up his laptop. When he connected the DVD player to his laptop, he noticed the adhesive tape along the top of the player with the words *Property of Ocean Club, Nassau*, smiled to himself and discreetly peeled the label off.

"Mother, Max calling. I've just emailed you a picture of the brunette."

"Good morning, Max. I have it."

But before Mother could run a facial recognition search, Doss glanced up to find the stunning brunette from the bar staring down at him. Dressed in white slacks with a white, crisscross belted blazer, without the benefit of a blouse or a bra, exposing a good bit of skin from her neck down to her navel, she smiled sweetly at Doss.

"Mother, let me call you back..."

"*Bonjour, monsieur*," the brunette said in a friendly tone with a French accent. "May I sit?"

"By all means, please do," Doss replied, intrigued, motioned her to take a seat across from him and stood out of good old-fashioned etiquette. "Coffee?"

"*Oui, merci.*"

"Are any of your henchmen joining us?" Doss asked as he glanced around the restaurant for trouble. "Do I need to call the police for protection?"

"Clearly, you don't need protection, Mr. Doss. I saw you break the big man's jaw and crush the other man's larynx. As for the third fellow, well, I doubt he will be in the mood to make love to his woman anytime soon."

"Yes, about that -."

"No need to apologize."

"Apologize, you can't be serious?"

"Two of those men will be in the hospital for some time."

"We can only hope your employer provides good medical and dental coverage."

"We merely wanted to talk with you."

"You and I could have had a pleasant chat at the bar yesterday afternoon without the muscle."

"We made a mistake."

"Who is *we* and how do you know my name?"

"I am with DGES."

"You're French Directorate-General for External Security?"

"Yes. Why so surprised? You don't have female agents in America?"

"Of course we do. What was the mistake?"

"We, that is to say, someone within my agency, mistakenly interpreted your actions in New Orleans."

"I was in New Orleans?"

"Please, Mr. Doss. The wild west shootout on U.S. I-10? Though you managed to evade public scrutiny by hiding in a swamp, one of our agents was able to get close enough to take your picture. You have a rather photogenic, distinguished face, I must say. Not a face one soon forgets. My assignment was to bring you in for questioning."

"Why?"

"In all the confusion in New Orleans, we thought you were working with, not against, Jack Conrad."

"Why would a thug like Conrad interest the DGES?"

"He was no common thug. Conrad was an operative for the Council. Ah, you Americans can be, how do you say, so easy to read. I see my mention of Conrad and the Council has piqued your curiosity."

"The three Musketeers who jumped me last night, they work for DGES?"

"Of course not, they are local blunt tools for hire."

"You hired them?"

"No. Paris chose them."

Doss fell silent as a waitress brought them hot coffee. "Thank you," Doss said as she set two mugs on the table. "No breakfast for me. Darling, what about you? No? Still upset about last night? I'm sorry if I embarrassed you in front of your friends. Just the coffee then Miss, thank you."

Doss waited for the waitress to walk off before resuming their conversation. "Something doesn't add up."

"What does this mean?"

Doss subtly removed a pocketknife from his trousers, a knife he had found on the pavement next to the giant, and pressed the blade against her upper thigh, against her femoral artery. "Something is amiss. Either you're lying to me or you are being used."

"Yes, I think the men last night were hired to kill you," she said with no anxiety in her tone. "I'm certain now they would have killed me too. I think we have a rat inside DGES who used me to get to you. This is why I come to you now - in peace and unarmed."

Doss folded the blade into the handle and slipped the pocket knife back into his trousers. "I pity the fool who thinks you're unarmed. *Plus de jeux*, no more games. Why risk coming here to talk to me if I might be associated with the Council?"

"Last night, I made a few calls to people I trust, and then they made some calls. You are an independent contractor for various American intelligence agencies. You were a close friend of President Calhoun."

"How did you track me to Nassau?"

"I didn't. And I doubt DGES did. DGES does not have those kinds of resources outside of France. But Interpol does."

"Huh, interesting."

"What is interesting?"

"DGES and Interpol, collaborating together on this particular matter. What is your name?"

"Madeline Beauvilliers."

"The man you were with at the bar, a husband, a friend?"

"No."

"A problem?"

"No, just a stranger, a guest at this hotel. He introduced himself and offered to buy me dinner."

"Where were you supposed to take me last night?"

"To a safe house - but that was another red flag for me. Before I left Paris, my department chief never informed me that we had a safe house in Nassau. I confirmed last night that we have no such place."

"Well Mademoiselle Beauvilliers, I suggest we not linger here. Let's take our coffees to go."

Doss led Beauvilliers to his room to collect his things and then called Mother.

"Max, your brunette is DGES."

"So, she said."

"You spoke with her?"

"She joined me for breakfast. She is with me now."

"What? At times I worry about you, Max. Her name is Madeline Beauvilliers. She was formerly with *Groupe d'intervention de la Gendarmerie nationale* before DGES lured her away. She was no French pastry tart working in human resources either. She is a highly trained field operative assigned to Force Intervention, the tactical operations arm of the GIGN, because of her superior skills. She has been credited with three confirmed kills."

Doss looked over at Beauvilliers and smiled, pleased that she was who she claimed to be. "Impressive."

"You sound smitten. I can see from her photos that she's pretty. She's dangerous Max."

"No need to worry, Mother. I'll be in touch soon."

"That was your mother on the phone?" Beauvilliers asked with surprise when Doss ended the call.

Doss laughed. "No, she just thinks she is."

Doss convinced Beauvilliers to return with him to Washington. They both agreed that jumping on a commercial flight was too risky. Doss considered hiring or stealing a boat, but the distance from Nassau to Miami is 185 miles, a long trip in a small boat on a big ocean with nowhere to hide. He did not like their other options either and finally decided to call Mother back and had her charter a private jet out of Miami to pick them up. Section M3 had the cash.

When they landed at Regan National Airport a few hours later, they saw a dark SUV with government plates waiting for them on the tarmac. The driver drove them directly to Adelman.

"The Director of the DGES and I go way back," Adelman said as his assistant Brianna stepped into his office with a tray of blueberry scones and a fresh pot of hot tea.

"You know Henri Murat?" Beauvilliers asked.

"Yes, Henri and I worked several operations together when I was with BND in Berlin."

"Director Murat and my father are good friends."

"I am aware, Madeline. May I call you Madeline? My first call was to your father to let him know that you are safe and under my protection."

"Please, call me Maddie. You know my father?"

"Only casually. Your family has a long and distinguished history and still carries weight in some circles."

"What is," Doss asked," DGES's assessment of Nassau, Herr Direktor?"

"Unfortunately, Max, the man who sent Maddie off to Nassau to apprehend you vanished before DGES could question him, but they do have his computer. His name is Richard Rubenfeld. The evidence seems to implicate Rubenfeld moonlighting for the Council while an employee of DGES. Some might call that a conflict of interest or worse, working as a double agent. Maddie, would you consider working for me for a spell? DGSE has been compromised. Murat has provided me with a copy of your file. We could use someone with your skill sets and Murat has given the idea his blessing until he gets his own house in order - before any good people are killed."

Chapter Fourteen

Excerpts from Hermann Adelman's private journal:
The Great Turmoil

The world watches the meteoric rise of the man cloaked in mystery in awe, the man many call Temüjin the Blessed, a man who claims to be a direct descendent of Genghis Khan - or is his claim that he, in fact, is Genghis Khan reincarnated? No one seems quite certain. The world stands helplessly on the sidelines as overnight the ancient lands of the Golden Horde - Kazakhstan, Uzbekistan, Tajikistan, Turkmenistan and Kyrgyzstan - one by one join Mongolia, not as allies but as one mighty nation under the benevolent autocracy of Temüjin, willingly anointed by the people as the Khan of Khans and the rightful heir to the empire and the legacy of the great Genghis Khan.

A savior or a liberator, a false prophet or a usurper, or, as proclaimed by the newly elected Pope Joseph I, simply the Great Deceiver? No one really knows. But, besides the extraordinarily charismatic leader, the brilliant orator, and budding military genius himself, Temüjin's fanatical followers have one remarkable holy relic to win over the hearts and minds of men. They have in their possession the lost *Book of Prophesies* as written by Al-Zubayr ibn al-Awwam ibn Khuwaylid al-Asadi, one of Prophet Muhammad's closest Companions and proclaimed by the Prophet himself to be the Disciple of the Messenger of God. This ancient book was discovered by sheer accident nearly a year before Temüjin's rise to greatness during a routine building excavation outside of Faiyum in Egypt, a city Zubayr had captured from the Byzantines over 1,400 years ago.

Temüjin invites experts from around the globe to examine the book for themselves, to validate its authenticity, or to prove it is a hoax. World-renowned scholars, historians and scientists make the pilgrimage to Mongolia to inspect and rigorously test the book and all agree, even the papal delegation dispatched by Rome, that the book is indeed authentic.

The accuracy or meaning of Zubayr's prophesies, however, is a different matter. Only a few dozen Muslim clergymen, from all the major sects within the Islamic faith, are permitted to read and study the book. And though there is disagreement, even heated bickering amongst the Select Few - as they have proclaimed themselves - on how various passages in the book, some only fragments, should be interpreted, all were in unanimous agreement that Zubayr had accurately prophesied the rise of Genghis Khan, the man Muslims would call the Scourge of God, and the coming of his true heir centuries later: Temüjin.

Zubayr had written, in part: *the Great Unifier and Giver of Light ... a direct descendant of the Scourge of God, that mighty horse king from beyond the Urals yet to come who will rule over the many Nomad Tribes and nearly devour the world ... will himself ascend to power and glory many generations later ... he shall raise a mighty host from the oppressed multitudes of many nations and you shall know his time is at hand when the twelve great tribes of the Slavic people fall; when the white castle of the mightiest of Christian strongholds across the sea, the place true believers will come to know as the Great Satan, is split asunder and crumbles into dust from centuries of perversions and rot; and when the lands in the East, the lands of silk, of the long walls and the mulhidun, finds her coffers of gold unfilled, her granaries of food empty ... then shall Allah's messenger descend from the heavens upon the Earth with his vast legions in ships breathing serpent's fire, in ships that can float across the skies ... this and more I, Allah's faithful messenger, have foreseen ...*

All these strange events and ominous signs of tribulations seem to be unfolding as the Twelve Great Houses of Mother Russia are collapsing into ruin, one upon the other, as the cold civil war facing America, known by many as the Great Satan, is a hair trigger away from mushrooming into a hot civil war and as China continues her slide into chaos following her catastrophic financial meltdown. The *oppressed multitudes of many nations* - the Russian people, no longer willing to live under the yoke of tyranny, unwilling to live under the whip of crooked, power-hungry tsars and oligarchs, and the Chinese, desperate to be free from plagues and famine - find hope, comfort and inspiration in Temüjin's words and deeds They are flocking to his banner by the millions.

Ah, and then there is the mysterious society that calls themselves the Council, a force Zubayr seems to make no mention of. With the exquisite deftness of a magician's misdirection while performing on stage, drawing the audience's attention to one thing to distract it from another, the Council keeps to the shadows, growing in wealth and power with each passing day while the world focuses its attention on Temüjin. But before the Council can step into the light and proclaim a single world government, the upstart Mongol and his militant followers in the East need to be dealt with first and then the Americans in the West, with their toxic notions of individual freedoms, capitalism, and republicanism, cannot be allowed to heal the schism between them, cannot be permitted to return to the world stage and resume their place as first among nations, especially with an arsenal built on alien technology.

Duc had been a disappointing loss. But there are many brilliant scientists for sale around the globe and the Council's tentacles reach far and wide and deep, deep into the inner sanctums of governments and into the boardrooms of large industries of every nation. This is especially true in Great Germany, where the Germans keep a UFO hidden away inside a secret lab.

Adelman had only seen pictures of the *Blue Swan*. He stared at the ship, bathed in flood light and surrounded by scaffolding, sitting inside a sterile, white hangar, with childlike wonderment. The ship was bigger than he had expected. She was several times larger than the German vessel and far more elegant. The *Cigar* was just that, a long brownish tube, probably designed as a shuttlecraft Adelman figured, and capable of carrying a crew of only about six to ten beings, depending upon their gear and equipment. Adelman ran his fingers, almost lovingly, along *Swan's* hull. There were no seams, bolts, or panels, no scorch marks, no dents, scratches, or imperfections of any kind. The material appeared flawless to his eye.

"She's magnificent, isn't she, Herr Direktor?" Major General John

Pederson, the Director of Project Swan for the past six months, asked as he walked up behind Adelman.

"Ah, General," Adelman said, turned, and warmly grasped Pederson's hand; Pederson had been a tremendous improvement over his predecessors. "She is indeed."

"I understand you came bearing gifts," Pederson said with a wry grin.

"I did. Let us hope Billy Duc is as impressive as his reputation. I am also assigning a man named Ed Rice from CIA over to you."

"The one who worked the Papenfuss case, the one they call the Master of the Universe because of his achievements in AI?"

"That's the guy. Come, my jet is waiting to take us to Cheyenne, where I'll introduce you to the newest members of your team and then we must talk privately."

Though he served as more of a moderator than an interviewer as he had invited a small cadre of top-notch scientists and engineers at Cheyenne Mountain to pick Duc's brain, Adelman's first interview with Duc proved extraordinarily profitable. Some attended in person, others by videoconference, and for hours they grilled Duc. The consensus after the first conversation was unanimous. The world had not witnessed such an extraordinary intellect since Albert Einstein. Duc's thoughts and ideas - he rattled off promising new theories and complex equations as if he were plugged into some otherworldly, metaphysical plane of consciousness - infused a renewed energy and optimism into a team that had suffered far more setbacks than victories over the years. And Duc hadn't even dirtied his hands yet working on the spacecraft herself.

Regretfully, Adelman had no choice but to keep one of the world's greatest minds, possibly the greatest, cooped up like a prisoner at Cheyenne Mountain. The stakes were simply too high. Adelman would not risk losing Duc again. Duc was given full access to anything and everything at the Project and could travel, with extraordinary security, to Kings Bay to physically work on *Blue Swan*. He was also allowed to communicate with friends and family on a time delay, as everything had to be pre-screened and scrubbed by his censors beforehand. Under Adelman's watch, there would be no repeat of Robert Oppenheimer's Los Alamos facility where the lack of security had allowed precious national secrets regarding the atom bomb to end up in the hands of the Soviets, America's archrival at the time.

Adelman allowed himself to bask in the newfound optimism and confidence energizing the scientists and engineers working on Project Swan deep within Cheyenne Mountain - if only for the briefest of moments, for he knew such feelings were a luxury he could ill afford. In the world of intelligence, one had to be an obsessive pessimist to survive.

And then he learned that the silliest of spats, between the silliest of people, regarding an event so inconsequential it seemed laughable, had set off a domino-like chain reaction in Texas that threatened to trigger a hot war between the states. He hurried back to Washington.

The wife of an E-7 in the Marines, a man dedicated to the Resistance, had not so discretely entered into a torrid affair with an E-8 in the Army, a diehard Nationalist man. When the Marine first learned of his wife's infidelity, he confronted the Army sergeant at a local bar, blows were struck, Marines came to the aid of their man, soldiers came to the aid of their man and the bar turned into a bloody free-for-all. Military police from both services responded, but instead of breaking up the fight, they joined in.

Then a Marine Lieutenant Colonel stationed in Corpus Christi, who happened to be the uncle of the Marine sergeant, rushed to the bar after he was informed of the escalating melee - and took half of his battalion with him. When the Army learned of this, they too sent reinforcements down from San Antonio. With hotheads in charge on both sides, the situation rapidly spun out of control. Shots were fired, men were wounded and hospitalized. Mercifully, no one was killed.

"And what did Dreyfus want to do at her emergency meeting with her Cabinet and advisors?" Calhoun asked Adelman after Adelman left the White House and drove over to see him.

"She wanted to form a joint commission with representatives

from both the League and the Union to interview witnesses and provide recommendations on how to avoid such conflicts in the future."

"That sounds like Dreyfus, create a commission to study the issue. Peace at any cost."

"What would you have done, Mr. President?"

"I would have stood both sergeants up in front of a firing squad."

"Abe, that is what you would have liked to have done."

"Yes, you are right Hermann, perhaps I'm being a bit too melodramatic. Honestly, I don't know, but we are sitting on a ticking time bomb and this peaceful coexistence between the two halves of one nation isn't working. This spat in Texas isn't the only episode of political violence. I fear things will only get worse as time goes on. Forgive me my friend, how thoughtless of me. How is your daughter, Gretchen?"

"She is well, thank you. She is out of the hospital and is fully recovered, at least physically. She didn't want to return to school as her friends have all graduated and have moved on to various universities. I have had to hire private tutors for her. A teenage girl with no mother and no friends nearby is rough."

"Certainly understandable. Well, if she is anything like her father, she's strong and she'll find a way to overcome her emotional scars. She'll find her way back into the world again."

"I pray you are right, Abe. She has discovered the joys of writing and that seems to have had some cathartic benefits. Her work is quite good, I think. Of course, I'm biased. She certainly didn't acquire that talent from me."

"Wonderful. Perhaps she'd honor me with a sample of her writing. Let me know if I can help in any way. Now tell me about Billy Duc, tell me about this Genghis Khan fellow, Version 2.0, and tell me about the Council. And I want to know what mischief you have Doss involved in, too. Beer, Hermann? Not that watery swill we Americans are forced to drink. I had some of my boys bring the genuine article back from Munich for us."

Chapter Fifteen

Doss waved Bijeau over to the bar when she stepped into the tavern. She strolled into the room with swagger.

"Good to have you back, Bijeau," Doss said and handed her a margarita.

"Good to be back bossman, someone joining us?" she asked and pointed to a third margarita on the counter.

"Ah, here she comes now, back from powdering her nose. Alejandra, meet Madeline Beauvilliers with French DGSE. Maddie, Alejandra Bijeau, my Number Two."

"Pleasure, Alejandra," Beauvilliers said and sat down on a stool next to Doss.

"The pleasure is all mine," Bijeau replied as she took a seat next to her. "DGSE, eh? That's like being in the French Foreign Legion?"

"You are funny! Not quite. France lost her appetite for colonial expansionism long ago. Your family name, Bijeau, this is French, yes?"

"Creole French, born in New Orleans. You on loan to us?"

"I suppose you could say that."

And then one of the special ops guys who had been with Doss in New Orleans, and then had accompanied Bijeau to the Village as part of her security detail, walked into the tavern. He smiled at Bijeau in a familial sort of way and she returned his smile with the bashful grin of a high school freshman.

"A new friend?" Doss asked. "Kraft, right?"

"I suppose you could say that. Yeah, George Kraft."

"Ah, ha, I thought you preferred playing for the other team, Bijeau," Doss said teasingly.

"I'm a free agent, baby; I play for any team who will play with me, provided there's mutual interest, of course," Bijeau replied drolly, then turned and winked at Beauvilliers.

"Please forgive Alejandra, Maddie," Doss said. "I'd tell you to file a sexual harassment complaint with HR, but we don't have an HR."

Beauvilliers laughed. "We French invented the double entendre. We perfected foreplay. I certainly do not mind."

"Well, you'll find Alejandra's humor is an acquired taste."

"No, not really bossman," Bijeau interjected. "Asparagus, anchovies, or even scotch might be an acquired taste for some. With me one bite and you're hooked. This gal just tastes sooo good... How do you know Max, Maddie?"

"Our paths crossed in Nassau. Max saved my life."

Doss chuckled. "Not sure about that Maddie, but feel free to return the favor anytime. Alejandra, did you really send Pollard off to prison?"

"Only for a few days, until he and Brighton both cracked. You have my report."

"I do, and you did good. Some interesting names on that list. Well, drink up ladies. Herr Direktor wishes to see us - and I'd ditch the colorful humor for now. He's all business these days."

"Margaritas?" Bijeau asked, surprised.

"Maddie's first. You know how I like to provide my teammates with a fun and exciting work environment filled with new experiences."

"Herr Direktor."

"Doss, ladies, or if that offends, Captains Bijeau and Beauvilliers - you do hold the rank of captain in the *Troupes de Marine* of the French *Armée de terre* as I recall Beauvilliers, yes? Good. Please, step into my office and take a seat. Tea? Coffee? Something with a bit more kick?"

"Not for me, sir," Doss replied as he took his seat. Bijeau and Beauvilliers followed his lead.

"Suit yourselves. President Dreyfus sent over a bottle of this very fine Pappy Van Winkle Family Reserve, aged twenty years or so it says on the label."

"I thought Dreyfus disliked you?" Doss asked, grinning.

"Indeed, she does. I suspect this bottle is laced with hemlock poison. Thought I'd give one of you a try as my royal cupbearer. Maddie, smile, I'm joking. Alejandra, fine work up at the Village.

Mother has been busy trying to connect the dots between your list of names and other people, places, and things."

"Anything yet?" Doss asked and decided he had to try a four-thousand-dollar bottle of bourbon, He poured himself a small glass and poured another for Adelman when he nodded.

"Yes. We know the Council met in Vienna recently and in Zurich before that and in Stockholm before Zurich. Everyone on that list was in at least one of those three cities at the same time as the Council. No coincidence, I think."

Doss took a sip of his bourbon and smiled, some things in life are worth the price. "Do you need us to begin rounding up folks?"

"No, it's too soon to spook the Council. I have the individuals on that list under surveillance. I've tasked multiple teams to track their movements, etc."

"And Dreyfus approved of this?"

"Of course not. I never informed her. I did, however, go to see *the* President."

Adelman turned to Beauvilliers. "Maddie, before we proceed, I will need your oath, *the* oath. You may call Murat first. Like you, he is a good Frenchman and loyal to France, but he has taken this oath and has approved of you taking the oath. But I warn you, once you take the oath, the penalties for breaking the oath are severe. But you know this already."

Beauvilliers took a moment to consider the gravity of what she was about to do. "I could never betray France."

"I would never ask you to."

"Very well then, I will take the oath provided Director Murat approves."

"He is expecting your call. Call him now. Use the landline on my desk."

After Murat gave his consent over the speakerphone, Adelman swore Beauvilliers in. She decided to have a glass of bourbon after all and poured one for Bijeau, too.

"Doss, you are authorized to read Maddie in later on Calhoun."

"Will do. And what of Duc?"

"I do not understand how that man knows what he knows. Truly baffling. He delivered the goods on that neutron particle weapon. The brass over at the Pentagon are still pissing their trousers with glee. For better or worse, I believe this is only the beginning. Years from now, will humankind praise us, I wonder, or rue this day and curse us?"

"And our next assignment, sir?"

"The French, the Germans, and the Israelis, even our new Iranian allies, all have far better resources than we do in gathering intel on this Temüjin fellow. Too early to poke the Council in the eye yet as I have said. The investigation into Calhoun's matter has stalled. I didn't build M3 for Calhoun to be stumbling around in the dark. We have better talent, better resources, and a lot more money than the agencies investigating the assassination, and we don't need to worry about interference from the White House."

"I've always wondered," Doss asked as he refilled his and Adelman's glasses and then handed the bottle over to Bijeau, "why Dreyfus hasn't moved against you and dismantled the Section. You have been a real thorn in her side. You must have something on her? Ah, by the twinkle in your eye, I see that you do!"

Adelman rose from his chair to stretch his legs. "During the Cold War, you Americans coined the term MAD, Mutually Assured Destruction. Dreyfus likes to talk a big game, but she will not and cannot move against me. So, while we have a lull in the action, let's quietly look into the Calhoun investigation. But tread lightly. If the Council is involved, I don't want to tip our hand and expose who we are. Though I have no doubt they know of us generally from one source or another, perhaps from DGES or even from someone within Dreyfus's Cabinet, they won't know what we do precisely or what we're capable of doing. Not yet."

"Understood, sir. Interpol appears to have been infiltrated as Maddie suspected in Nassau. I would like to have a peek at their data on Calhoun, though I wouldn't trust what they provided."

"Nor would I."

"Then, with the limited resources at hand, we will start work at once."

"Very well Max. Ladies, do be careful out there; now if you will excuse us, I need Doss for a moment."

After Bijeau and Beauvilliers left Adelman's office, Adelman poured himself another glass of bourbon and offered Doss another, too.

"No thank you, sir. I felt guilty with every sip. That's a rich man's drink."

"Ha, you've done extraordinarily well with your investments, Max. You can afford a case of this stuff every week if you want it."

"I've been extremely fortunate, in part because of you, sir."

"You are too modest. While you are investigating the assassination attempt, I'd like you to quietly review the investigations into my daughter's accident and her mother's death."

"You suspect foul play?"

"Possibly. Probably. But I'm not sure."

"Your wife passed away from natural causes, I thought?"

"An aneurism was the official cause of death, but no, I have good reason to believe she may have been poisoned. If that is true, the poison was probably meant for me."

"I will, of course, reopen both investigations, Herr Direktor. Is there some reason you don't want me to involve my team?"

"As this is something of a private matter regarding my family, their priority must be focusing on the President's matter. I will introduce you to someone who may be of help, a fellow by the name of Jeremiah Stone. Do you know him?"

"I only know him by reputation."

"Well, it's time you both met."

After three tedious, nauseating months of reviewing FBI files and re-interviewing eyewitnesses - the part of the job Doss detested - witnesses at the town square in Virginia on the day Calhoun was shot and the witnesses at the White House when a missile took out the North Portico, he had nothing. Doss even interrogated the six men they had captured in New Orleans, but they were nothing more than hired guns from Germany, Russia and France. The names Brighton and Pollard had given up to Bijeau might have been interesting, more than interesting, but he knew Adelman was right to ignore those names for now. And then one evening, after a very long, monotonous day, he caught a lucky break on Adelman's private matter.

Doss and his modest team of two sat around a table piled high with files, transcripts, jump drives and thousands of photos in a small conference room, their war room, down the hall from Adelman's office. They were discussing next steps when Beauvilliers, perusing through the photos Stone had sent over of the car involved in Gretchen's matter, just for a change of pace from Calhoun's investigation, saw something of interest through a magnifying glass and handed the photo over to Doss.

"Jeremiah, Doss here. I have you on speaker."

"Max, ladies, good evening. I only dropped my files off two days ago. You found something?"

"Maddie may have. Do you know if the car Charles was driving on the night of the accident was demolished?"

"Once the Maryland State Troopers closed their investigation, the car was towed to a local salvage yard."

"So, the car was destroyed?"

"No. Adelman was understandably in great anguish with his daughter lying in a coma and his wife dead. I took the liberty of making a few decisions for him. One decision I made was to purchase that vehicle. Not sure why, just a hunch, I suppose. I figured someday someone might want to reopen the investigation. I have the car in a storage rental not far from your offices. Why?"

"Can you text me the address and unit number?"

"Sure."

"We're leaving now. Meet us there."

Doss waved to Stone as Stone pulled up to the rental unit thirty minutes later in an old Tacoma pickup, a truck that had plainly survived many years of abuse and punishment.

"As you can see," Stone said as he raised the unit's aluminum folding door and flipped on a light switch, "the car is in pretty bad shape. It's a miracle Gretchen survived."

The roof of the cherry-red Mazda Gazelle, a favorite among high school and college students, had been smashed into the cabin. The body was badly dented, cracked, bent and scratched, exposing a good bit of bare metal.

"Show Jeremiah the photo Maddie," Doss said.

"What am I looking at?" Stone asked when he saw nothing of

interest. The photo was one of many he had seen from the photos taken by the State Trooper investigators after working crews had recovered the car from the water.

"Oh, sorry, you'll need this," Beauvilliers replied, handed Stone a magnifying glass and placed her index finger on the driver's side headlight in the photo. "Look, see these blue streaks? They are very faint."

Stone nodded. "From the other vehicle?"

"Maybe, let's find out," Beauvilliers said and walked over to the front of the Mazda.

She removed a flashlight from her pocket and took a knee. "Interesting," she said. "What do you think?"

Stone knelt next to her and whistled. "The streaks are hard to see, but yes, they look like paint scuff marks. We have ourselves a possible clue. Could be from a different accident. Might not even be car paint. Watcha thinking Max, call the authorities in or keep this between us? You'll jeopardize chain of custody protocols regarding evidence if you alter this quarter panel in any way."

Doss smiled. "I forgot you went to law school. Boston College?"

"Yeah, but I never actually practiced law. Herr Direktor sank his fangs into me first. He made quite a recruiting pitch."

"Could the state investigators have been just sloppy, or did they intentionally ignore this clue?"

"Don't know. They don't teach you best practices for crime scene techniques in law school. The car was covered in mud and slime when I first saw it. I hosed it down before moving it in here."

"Maddie, call home and tell Mother we need an expert in auto paint pigments ASAP. Don't explain why, not yet. Too early in the game to get Adelman's hopes up. If the expert needs to alter the vehicle to get the sample, do it."

Two days later, Beauvilliers and Bijeau rushed into the Men's Room together.

"What the hell?" Doss asked with surprise while standing at a urinal. "If you're here to give me a piss test, you're a drop too late."

"We have a winner, bossman!" Bijeau exclaimed excitedly. "I canvassed every car rental within a hundred-mile radius of the accident as you suggested and found a Hertz Dream Collections Car Rental in Tysons Corner which not only offered Ford Mustang GTs in Metallic Cerulean Blue a clerk told me but had one returned the day after Gretchen's accident with some minor damage to the driver's side front quarter panel!"

Doss beamed with delight. "Do you mind if I zip and wash before I congratulate you both with a group hug?"

Doss and his team met Stone at the Hertz facility an hour later. They walked straight into the manager's office unannounced and found him sitting in a chair behind his desk.

Doss flashed his fake FBI credentials at the man and handed him a sheet of paper on FBI letterhead. "I need to see your files on a Mustang GT in Metallic Cerulean Blue rented to a customer on the date shown on that piece of paper."

"I'm sorry agent, ah, Agent Jenkins, but our rules for protecting the privacy of our customers do not allow me to hand over such information without a proper search warrant."

"Agent Jones, give the man his warrant."

Stone reached into his breast pocket and handed a forged warrant over to the manager.

"I'll need to call the home office first."

Doss reached across the manager's desk and grabbed him by his name badge. "Ah - Mr. Danny Dobrinka - this is a matter of national security, a matter of extreme urgency. Let me see the files now or face criminal charges later for interfering with an FBI investigation, or worse, with conspiring to assassinate the President of the United States."

The manager, a plump man sitting in a warm office, started squirming uncomfortably in his chair. Beads of sweat began popping up all along his upper lip. He was too afraid to move.

Doss turned to Bijeau. "Agent Sterling, read the man his rights, cuff him and take him downtown for interrogation. Agent Jones, bring in the other employees. One of them will do their patriotic duty and cooperate."

"No, no, that won't be necessary," the manager blurted out

nervously, and rolled his chair over to his computer. "Um, let me see, Mustang GT, on, eh, I see the date. Searching, come on. Still searching."

"Let's go, Mr. Dobrinka."

"Ah, got it," the manager finally declared triumphantly and swung his computer monitor around to show the four FBI agents staring down at him a photo of the driver's license of the man who had rented the car.

"Oh my God," Beauvilliers mumbled under her breath and grabbed Doss by the forearm.

Doss turned to Stone. "Agent Jones, get copies of everything. Impress upon Mr. Dobrinka that he is not to discuss this official FBI business with anyone. Agent Sterling, cover Jones. Agent Smith and I will be outside for a moment."

"Maddie?" Doss asked Beauvilliers after they stepped into the parking lot.

"I've seen this man before."

"Where, Maddie?"

"In France, at DGES."

"He's an agent for DGES? Are you certain?"

"Absolutely certain. I agreed to meet him for drinks one evening with some of his friends. I had one drink and left and never saw him socially again. He is not an agent. He's a freelance asset used by DGES on occasion. His father is French, his mother is Algerian. He was born in Algeria."

"Do you know what he does? What department at DGES uses him?"

"Ye, yes," Beauvilliers said softly and hesitated.

Doss thought she was about to cry and tried comforting her by caressing her shoulder. "Maddie, you don't need to say more to me but you will need to disclose everything you know, and I mean everything, to Adelman."

"I'm sorry Max. I am trying to understand, but this makes no sense. The name of the man in the photo is Marc Laurent. He reports directly to Richard Rubenfeld, my department chief, and Rubenfeld reports to Henri Murat. This is what I know."

Adelman fell back into his desk chair, visibly shaken after Doss and Stone reported what they had learned.

"Herr Direktor," Doss said softly, "Do you need a moment to process this? Should we come back a bit later?"

Adelman waved Doss's thoughtful offer aside. "No, no. That won't be necessary. Sit, gentlemen."

"We have," Stone said, "already, quietly, validated what Beauvilliers has told us is true."

"Why Gretchen?" Doss asked. "Why go after your teenage daughter?"

"Not her, me," Adelman answered wearily. "My wife, Natalie, at first refused to let Gretchen go to the prom with Charles. We both liked Charles, but he was almost nineteen and Gretchen had just turned sixteen. After some gnashing of teeth as mothers and teenage daughters are wont to do, Natalie finally relented, but only on the condition that I accompany Gretchen and Charles as a chaperone. I was supposed to be in that car with them that night. A last-minute crisis kept me here."

"Didn't you travel with a security detail, Herr Direktor?" Doss asked. "From what little we know so far, Laurent was working solo that night. Why wouldn't he bring more men with him to neutralize your security first?"

"I've rarely used a security detail, Max. Back then, even now, hardly anyone knows who I am or what I do or cares. Limos and security details only attract unnecessary attention, attention I don't want. This Section has over three thousand full and part-time employees now and half as many contractors. Of that number, all but about twenty men and women believe they are working for, and being paid by, Homeland Security. The only people who ever see my face are the souls working in the Command-and-Control Center on this level and you, Stone, and occasionally a few folks within your respective teams."

"Well, someone knew you would be in that car that night on that particular highway. Someone in this building, or perhaps a family friend, talked."

Adleman glanced up at Doss with a sudden fury in his eyes. "We shall find out who."

"Yes, indeed, we will. And your wife, does any of this reveal anything more about her death?"

"Possibly. After Gretchen's accident, Natalie was terribly distraught, as you might imagine. We had accepted some black-tie dinner, a low-key affair, followed by an auction for charity before the accident but after the accident, I sent our regrets. One evening, Natalie told me that she needed a distraction and had had a change of heart about attending the charity, so we went. She didn't like her cabernet during dinner and as I had chosen a pinot, we switched glasses before I took a sip. She died the following day, most likely from poison. I cannot say with one hundred percent certainty, however, that a glass of pinot killed her."

Stone turned to Doss. "Our fearless leader once told me not to believe in coincidences in the world of intelligence. You thinking what I'm thinking, Max?"

"Yep, we look for the security video Jeremiah and if they're gone, we interview everyone who worked for the caterer that night and anyone else we can find who might have seen something."

Stone nodded. "I'll wager the video, or at least one witness can place Mr. Laurent dressed in a waiter's suit at Herr Direktor's table serving drinks. Laurent would have known he had botched his first attempt on your life, Herr Direktor. He would have known he needed to finish the job before somebody finished him."

Three days later, Doss and Stone returned to Adelman's office. Adleman walked over to an elegant service trolley, poured Doss and Stone each a cup of black coffee, then returned to his desk, a wooden, complicated, austere piece of furniture, not unlike its owner.

"The security jump drives were misplaced, possibly stolen, according to the building manager," Doss reported as he savored the coffee's rich aroma. Brianna always made the best coffee. "No surprise there, but we found three people working that night and they all positively identified Marc Laurent. We have their sworn affidavits. He was there, Herr Direktor. They saw Laurent serving drinks. Others thought they remembered seeing him but weren't positive."

"And the catering company?" Adelman asked.

"Out of business," Stone answered. "We tracked the owner down. He remembers hiring Laurent for the evening after one of his employees called in sick. His employee recommended Laurent for the job who, he claimed, was his cousin. The man refused to sign an affidavit, though. He's scared. The employee who called in sick was found dead in an alley the next day from an apparent mugging. The owner never saw Laurent again, not even to collect his pay."

"And do we know where Laurent is now?"

Doss set his cup on a small accent table between himself and Stone. "We do. He still does odds and ends for DGES here and there."

"Anything else, gentlemen?"

"No, sir," Doss replied. "What do you want us to do?"

Adelman appeared lost in thought for a moment, staring absently at the wall as he drummed his fingers on the desktop. "Too soon, too soon," he mumbled to himself, then turned to Doss and Stone. "For now, gentlemen, do nothing, absolutely nothing. We bide our time."

Chapter Sixteen

Excerpts from Hermann Adelman's private journal:
The Great Turmoil

The President, fully dressed in youthful, casual clothing, looked healthy, fit and well-rested. His boyish good looks were back. All the high-tech, sensitive electronic equipment in his hospital room had been packed away in crates and boxes and stacked against the wall for transport.

"Hermann, thank you for stopping by."

"Of course, Mr. President. I understand the doctors are releasing you today."

"On the condition a physician checks on me once a week. No rugby, no tackle football, that sort of thing for a while. No mention was made of climbing mountains. Are the arrangements all in place?"

"Cheyenne Mountain awaits you, sir. You will have thirty thousand square feet to use as you see fit and the mountain is very much accustomed to personnel and equipment being moved secretly in and out. Transferring your flag, so to speak, will raise no eyebrows. I fear you have a windowless office - but it does have a well-stocked bar. I saw to that myself."

Calhoun placed a hand on Adelman's shoulder. "Our mutual friend has brought me up to speed on this and that. Your loyalty to this country and to me has cost you dearly. I want you to know that I am deeply saddened by all of it."

"Thank you, sir. I chose a dangerous profession as a young man. I was never naïve about the possible consequences of my decision. But my daughter, my wife, Abe!"

"We will settle all scores. Not for those we've lost, we can do nothing more for them, but for the ones we love still in this world, for the ones we must protect, there will be a reckoning. And yet, my friend, it is too soon, too soon."

"Yes. We have a mind-boggling number of moving pieces on the board. Perhaps a short briefing before you leave, Abe?"

"Please. Take a seat. Let's start with that Khan of Khans fellow in the black hat. What have your folks learned that the other agencies haven't?"

"I will have a comprehensive written report waiting for you in Cheyenne on all critical matters but, in broad brush strokes, we might know where he keeps his Chinese booty. We have reason to believe he has stashed the alien spacecraft away in a cave, not unlike your new home, in one of the mountains along the Azutau Mountain Range overlooking Lake Markakol in East Kazakhstan. The problem is the Mongolians keep moving the damn thing around in a game of whack-a-mole. As for Temüjin himself, we still know precious little about the man or his ambitions. He continues to expand and consolidate his power and rules over a territory nearly as large as Continental Europe if you exclude Scandinavia, Belarus and Ukraine. We believe it is more likely than not that he recently added Russian tactical nuclear weapons to his arsenal."

"I'm a bit surprised President Zhang hasn't dropped a nuclear bomb on his head."

"Even without strategic nuclear weapons, Temüjin could inflict unthinkable horrors on the Chinese people in retaliation. Zhang, if nothing else, is a pragmatist."

"This matter with DGSE is troubling. And I am concerned about you, Hermann."

"You need not be."

"This man, this assassin, ah…"

"Laurent, Marc Laurent."

"Yes. He murdered your wife and nearly killed your daughter. Can you proceed dispassionately, without emotion? I would understand completely if you couldn't."

"I can. Of course, I want my pound of flesh but I will not be satisfied with just Laurent, I want the puppet master too. Finding this person will require patient, cold, calculated intelligence gathering and careful planning."

"Good answer. You suspect the Council is somehow involved?"

"I do. In my matter as well as yours."

"I did review the list of names Bijeau obtained from Brighton and Pollard. We continue to show patience, yes?"

"Agreed, Mr. President. It seems that tensions in Texas and other places around the country have quieted down for now. That takes some pressure off of us."

"Yep, by doing nothing, Dreyfus has temporarily bought herself some time too, time she'll use to continue trying to push her stupendously idiotic agenda through Congress to dissolve the Union. I don't know if she is just ignorant, as dumb as a goat, or as sly as a fox, but she's dangerous. Hermann, we're fighting a third world war on multidimensional levels across multiple fronts. With my whole heart, with my entire being, I still believe that America, despite its flaws, at its core, is a good and noble country and that Americans, despite our flaws and foibles, are a good and noble people. God help the world if we lose this fight. I'm grateful you are one of my generals. I am grateful to Max and his team and for their sacrifices. I'd pin medals on all of you if I could."

"*Nishek cham, ani omer shuv nishek cham!*" an excited voice said in Hebrew.

"English!" a second voice demanded.

"Weapons hot, I say again weapons hot," the first voice repeated in English. "Red Team, boots on the ground now! Deploy the Jevit demining robots out front, launch tactical surveillance drones overhead. Move, move, move! Blue Team, hold position, support Red Team as they move inside the cavern!"

And then the President and her advisors, who were gathered in the Situation Room, heard a third voice, a woman's voice, that none could understand. "What is that?" the President asked. "Does anybody know?"

"That is, I believe," Adelman offered, "Persian, Iranian Farsi."

"Tom, get a translator in here now!"

The eyes of the President and all of her advisors were glued to one of the wall monitors as they watched a dark, grainy satellite video in real time with sound provided by the CIA, as they watched scores of boots on the ground and squadrons of helicopters hovering around a mountaintop like a swarm of angry wasps buzzing around their nest. Then one of the President's staffers entered the room and handed the President a note.

"Put him through on speaker, Sally," Dreyfus ordered harshly. "Prime Minister Sofer, you are on speaker. I am in the Situation Room with my senior advisors. What the fuck is going on?"

"Madam President, I wish to inform you that a joint Israeli and Iranian party of elite commandos is executing a mission inside Kazakhstan as we speak."

"Why do you think I'm sitting in my Situation Room, Avner?" the President asked angrily. "You thought to inform me now, not consult with us before you launched this absurd assault? You think Israel could pull this crap without the U.S. knowing? What the heck were you thinking and what the fuck are you up to over there?"

"We have good, hard intel confirmed by multiple sources that whatever new weaponry the Mongolians stole from the Chinese, in all probability a weapon of mass destruction, is hidden inside a mountain near Lake Markakol."

"So?"

"Israel and Iran will not permit a madman to have such a weapon, especially when it could be placed in Turkmenistan next to Iran. This weapon, whatever it is, threatens the security of both Israel and Iran. This is an unacceptable threat to both our countries."

"Avner, have you lost your mind? By launching this preemptive strike, you are declaring war on Mongolia!"

"Did the United States Madam President allow the Soviets to place nuclear missiles in Cuba in the last century?"

Dreyfus jumped out of her chair. "What does that have to do with anything Avner?" she demanded, and then turned to General Phillips. "What weapon did the Mongolians steal from China, General, and why was I never briefed?" she asked, then muted the phone before the general could answer. "For the Prime Minister's benefit, General, lie," she commanded and unmuted the phone.

"Ahem, Madam President," Phillips replied, "we simply don't know what the Mongolians took from the Chinese. It could be a nuclear device or some chemical or biological weapon. Perhaps the

Chinese have finally perfected a viable railgun system."

"Avner, you don't," Dreyfus said in a haughty tone, "even know what you are looking for. You are jeopardizing world peace with this foolishness and I will not forget that Israel failed to confer with its greatest friend and closest ally before going forward with this, this insane misadventure! You need to withdraw your forces and stand down now Avner or by God, I'll -."

"Madam President!" General Phillips interrupted. "Look at the monitor, ma'am."

The room fell silent as concentric rings of dust - shockwaves - expanded outward from the mouth of the cavern, followed by an impressive mushroom cloud rising above the mountain.

"President Dreyfus," the Prime Minister said slowly, gravely, a few moments later. "I've just received word our forces found the cavern empty of any weapons or personnel. The cavern was rigged with a tactical nuclear device. Our commandos had no time to withdraw. We've suffered catastrophic losses. I must leave you now. I must find what's left of our brave forces and bring them home. I must somehow console my people. Goodbye, Madam President."

"A trap," Adelman mumbled to himself. For the briefest of moments, he dared to think the unthinkable, that Israeli intelligence had been compromised, or perhaps the issue was on the Iranian side. Ever the pessimist, he considered the ugly possibility that someone within Dreyfus's inner circle, or even someone within his own organization, had tipped the Mongolians off. He immediately handed the problem over to Doss and told him to deal with the problem quickly.

Chapter Seventeen

You can always catch a mouse with a dab of peanut butter mixed with chocolate. Catching a rat is no different. At first, Doss had suspected Adelman's executive admin, Brianna, which had troubled him greatly. She was smart, efficient, cultured, attractive and, by all appearances, loyal. She had no access to Adelman's computer. She was not included in the small circle of people who were privy to what the Mongolians had stolen from the Chinese or where they might have taken it. She passed a polygraph test with flying colors.

Frustrated with having no leads, Doss borrowed a trick from World War II where American cryptanalysts had broken the secret coded messages of the Japanese military. In the Spring of '42, they knew the Japanese were planning a major offensive, an invasion, against something designated AF, but the cryptanalysts weren't sure what AF stood for so they had Midway Island, a likely target, transmit a routine, uncoded message to Hawaii to report that its water purification equipment was down - even though nothing was wrong with Midway's water purification equipment. Japanese intelligence took the bait, informed the Japanese Admiralty that AF's - that Midway's - water purification system was broken and, with this precious piece of intelligence in hand, an American carrier group promptly sailed for Midway to ambush the Japanese invasion fleet. In one of the most spectacular and decisive battles of the war, the U.S. Navy destroyed four Japanese carriers and their aircraft and killed hundreds of highly experienced, irreplaceable pilots.

Using Adleman's computer, Doss sent emails to various high-level staffers within the West Wing of the White House, to CIA, NSA, the Agency and DNI, an email embedded with a nearly undetectable tracker, an innovation by the Master of the Universe, Ed Rice, informing everyone that his Section had discovered that the Mongolians had relocated their secret weapon to the Siilkhem Mountains in northwest Mongolia. The rat took the bait and forwarded the email to her contact in Pakistan.

"Money, religion, politics, love, blackmail, what?" Adelman asked after Doss finished briefing him on the interrogation.

"Money," Doss answered.

"Has Dreyfus noticed she is missing one of her assistants?"

"I figured that was your prerogative, that you'd enjoy telling her."

"Can we turn this person? Can we use her?"

"No, she doesn't have the stomach or the brains for it. She is young, immature, and naïve. She likes the things money can buy. Clearly, she has no ethical compass. Poor girl didn't even grasp that what she did was seriously wrong until I showed her the video of the Israeli and Iranian soldiers she had a hand in killing. She broke down in tears after that."

"Who was her contact in Pakistan?"

"That's where things get interesting, Herr Direktor. She was not working for the Mongolians. A few months back, she had an affair with a British chap here in D.C. He offered to pay her for any interesting information crossing her desk at the White House. His name is Dan Perkins, and he is the Deputy High Commissioner for the British High Commission in Islamabad."

"You think the Council is somehow involved?"

"Unclear. Someone obviously shared this intel with the Israelis or with the Iranians. We should ask them who. And then someone must have tipped off the Mongolians, informed them that the Israelis and Iranians were coming. The Mongolians didn't leave a tactical nuke behind in an empty cave for shits-and-giggles."

"We've been hands-off with the Council, as those have been Calhoun's wishes. Still, I think you should introduce yourself to this British deputy commissioner and follow the trail wherever it leads. Is he in Pakistan now?"

"He is."

"Off you go then. I'll explain my reasoning to the President. And Doss, try to handle this matter discreetly, quietly."

"And the White House staffer?"

"She has blood on her hands. Let's hold her in isolation until you return, then we can toss the matter over to DOJ and let her burn. I'll inform Dreyfus that the White House's internal security measures are antiquated and have been compromised."

A private jet carrying Doss, Bijeau and Beauvilliers touched down at Islamabad International Airport 24 hours later during a heavy downpour in the midst of Pakistan's monsoon season. A man with a crewcut from the U.S. Embassy in Islamabad, dressed in a preppy, blue sports coat with a green tie and tan slacks, met them once they cleared customs.

"Mr. Doss, Blake Watkins, welcome to Pakistan," the man said with a heavy southern drawl and extended his hand.

"Pleasure," Doss replied as the two men shook hands. "My associates Alejandra Bijeau and Madeline Beauvilliers. Good of you to meet us."

"Nice to meet y'all," Watkins said as they started walking towards the terminal exits. "My orders are to see you safely to the hotel and get you whatever you need."

"What is your official position here, Watkins?"

"I'm the Embassy's Detachment Commander. Master Gunnery Sergeant Watkins, United States Marine Corps, at your service, sir."

"How large is your detachment?"

"Fifty-four Marines, sir."

"Isn't that an unusually large detachment for an embassy?"

"Pakistan is cascadin' into a hotbed of turmoil, sir. You'll be havin' breakfast tomorrow with Mike Meyers, Chief of Mission. He can explain the situation in greater detail than I can. Rumor is we'll be pullin' all embassy personnel out of Pakistan shortly. Whatever you are here to do, sir, I'd be damn quick about it and then get the hell out."

"The entire world is cascading into a hotbed of turmoil, Master Gunnery Sergeant. Soon there may be nowhere to get the hell out to, nowhere to run, but I'll try to heed your sound advice."

Before they jumped into a Black Yukon Denali XL with diplomatic plates, Watkins opened the rear hatch, reached into the back to grab an olive drab duffle bag and handed it over to Doss. "As I said sir, whatever you need. VIP treatment."

As the ladies piled into the back seat, Doss took the front

passenger seat and peeked inside the bag while Watkins eased the big SUV onto a two-lane highway leading away from the airport.

"Ladies, one Sig 229 for each of us with shoulder holsters, plenty of mags, ammo, knives, gloves, tactical commo kits, etc. Thank you, Watkins."

After Watkins checked the rearview mirror for any tails, he nodded. "For self-protection. There are more serious accessories stored at the Embassy. Islamabad is a dangerous place right now, especially for us dang foreigners."

"Where to next?"

"Y'all will be stayin' at the Islamabad Serena Hotel, within easy walkin' distance of the Embassy. You'll be more comfortable there than at the Embassy as we're short on quarters. Meyers will meet you at the hotel restaurant tomorrow mornin' for breakfast."

"Good. Were you able to confirm our person of interest is still in Islamabad?"

"Affirmative, sir. He's not left the country. He resides within the British High Commission."

"The High Commission?" Bijeau asked.

"The name is a relic from the old days of the British Empire, when Pakistan was part of the British Commonwealth, ma'am," Watkins explained. "It is, in fact, their embassy."

In the morning a distinguished-looking middle-aged man with a distinct limp that comes with a prosthetic leg, dressed in a khaki-tailored suit with a garish, purple paisley tie, walked over to the table where Doss and his team were sitting. "Mr. Doss, Max Doss?"

"Meyers?"

"Yes, Mike Meyers, Chief of Mission."

"Pleasure," Doss said and stood to pull a chair out for Meyers. "My business associates Alejandra Bijeau and Madeline Beauvilliers."

"Alejandra, Madeline, welcome to Pakistan," Meyers said, smiling appreciatively at the two women as he plopped down in his chair. "I didn't realize that beauty was one of the company's skill requirements. And Doss, you're looking fit, how have you been?"

"Beg pardon, have we met?"

"No, you wouldn't remember. I was an instructor once, though not for your class. I recall the day some fool dropped a live grenade on the firing range. Everyone in the pit panicked, ran, or froze. Not you. You calmly picked the damn thing up and tossed it over a dirt berm, in the nick of time, I might add."

"You were with the Project?"

"What project we talkin' about?" Bijeau asked.

"The X-Max Project," Meyers offered. "I read your files ladies, files embassy personnel normally wouldn't have access to. I know your clearance levels and I know who you work for. Well, I'll let Max explain the Project to you some other time if he is so inclined. Doss was one of Adelman's most promising students. I'd still be in the field but for," he explained, pausing to pat his right leg, "this old wound from a mission gone wrong."

"Perhaps we should," Doss said, clearly annoyed, "take this conversation somewhere more private Meyers."

Meyers smiled playfully and subtly pointed at the chandelier above them with his index finger. Around the chandelier's baseplate was a thin metal band with tiny, blinking red lights.

"An invention by one of Mother's minions. I had one of my men install it last night and then paid the maître d to seat you at this table. We are inside an invisible, soundproof cone of silence, so to speak. Don't ask me how it works because I haven't a clue."

"You seem to know a lot," Doss said gruffly, unimpressed by the man's gadgets and still annoyed. "Do you know why we're in Pakistan?"

"Of course I do."

"The Ambassador knows?"

"Of course not."

"What do you know?"

"Dan Perkins is my British counterpart. You need to speak with him. I suspect he's bent and has something important to say or Adelman wouldn't have sent you."

"And why did you insist on meeting us?"

"Because I can get you Perkins, and I can get all of you out of Pakistan. But for me, you wouldn't have gotten into Pakistan in the first place. The whole damn country is a tinderbox and is coming apart at the seams. Of the four principal provinces, the majority of the people want change - and by people, it is important to understand that the median age of the Pakistani population is only twenty years old compared to the median age of the ruling class which is seventy years plus, quite a disparity. Now where was I, oh yes, the folks in Khyber Pakhtunkhwa and Punjab are on the brink of open rebellion. They believe Temüjin the Blessed is the Messenger of Allah and are eager to join his Mongolian confederation, now calling itself Greater Mongolia. The Islamabad Capital Territory and the disputed territories, Azad Jammu, Kashmir, and Gilgit-Baltistan, will certainly follow. The people of Balochistan and Sindh believe Temüjin is a false prophet. They are staunchly opposed to any union with Mongolia and will look to Iran and India for support if the other provinces secede."

"Who's in charge?"

"The three major political parties, the Pakistan Muslim League-Nawaz, the Pakistan People's Party, and the Pakistan Tehreek-e-Insaf are in shambles. Pakistan's powerful military is as divided as the people. And - spoiler alert - General Ashan Talpur, who has been the real power here for the past seven years, was found shot dead in his bathtub last night. That tsunami will roll over the country within hours. For days now, Pakistanis have been deliriously chanting in the streets of Islamabad in Urdu and in English: *Timojan aa raha hay! Temüjin is coming! Timojan aa raha hay! Temüjin is coming!* No one is in charge. Pakistan, I fear, is lost."

"How," Beauvilliers asked, "could Washington, Paris, London, Berlin, how could the West be so ignorant about what is happening in Pakistan?"

"I cannot speak for the entire West, Madeline, but Washington has known for some time that Pakistan was deteriorating as a nation. But what could Washington do? America has slammed itself into an iceberg, an iceberg made of festering old wounds, and is in danger of breaking apart and sinking. She can hardly be bothered with a leaky faucet down in steerage."

"We are wasting time," Doss said with growing impatience. "How do we get to Perkins before all hell breaks loose and the mobs now rioting in the streets turn to violence?"

"I took the liberty of calling him this morning to tell him that the

U.S. Government has graciously offered to pick him up in Peshawar and fly him out of the country later today."

"Why would we do that? And why would he leave Islamabad for Peshawar?"

"We will do it because you want to illegally take a British subject into custody. I have lured him out of the High Commission and into the open for you. He is already on the road to Peshawar. He is doing it because the fool has taken on a mistress, a young Afghan woman. Worse, he has fallen in love with her, though I must say, she is quite lovely. She's in Peshawar. He will want to get her safely out of the country. He can hardly bring her back to Islamabad and ask his superiors to help him."

"Can you authorize a helo flight to Peshawar?"

"No, but with your highest priority mission designation, you can."

Thirty minutes after checking out of the hotel, Doss and his team met Watkins, now suited up in his desert camouflage battle dress uniform with a 9mm strapped to his side, at the arms locker in the basement of the embassy. Doss and the ladies had changed into their combat fatigues after reaching the Embassy as well.

"Good morning, Master Gunnery Sergeant," Doss offered cheerfully. "Meyers texted me, said you have a chopper on the way?"

"Yes, sir," the Marine answered crisply, as he set a brown leather gym bag down by his side. "She's a Marine twin engine UH-1Y Venom armed with one 7.62mm door gun. She's at the airport and should be ready to fly within the hour. I can spare the chopper and the pilot, but not a gunner."

"I understand. We heard isolated shootings in the streets as we walked from the hotel to the Embassy. We saw looting and cars being set on fire. Do you have orders to evacuate the Embassy yet?"

"No, sir."

"Won't be long before you do. You sure you can spare the chopper?"

"Yes, sir. We have six Sea Kings sitting in Jalandhar on standby and Fifth Fleet is steaming off the coast of Iran to support any evac of embassy personnel."

"Good. What's the max range of a Huey Venom? How do we refuel in Peshawar?"

"The Venom has a combat range of one-hundred-fifty miles and a max speed of one-hundred-eighty-nine miles per hour, but you can push her up to two hundred in a crisis. You pay for fuel and any bribes with cash, sir. This bag is for you. There's one hundred thousand U. S. Dollars inside."

"Think I'll just have to trust you on the amount," Doss said and winked. "Can you spare three assault weapons, two sniper rifles, some grenades, ammo, and body armor?"

"Can do. Help yourself."

"You're a good man, Master Gunnery Sergeant. Get home safe."

Watkins nodded as he looked down at his phone. "Excuse me, sir, I see I'm needed upstairs. Folks are sayin' General Talpur has been assassinated. Things are really goin' to turn to liquid shit now. I'd tell you to call the Marines if you run into trouble out there, but considerin' present circumstances, I'm afraid y'all are goin' to be on your own. Good huntin', sir."

"Sniper rifles?" Bijeau asked.

"Yeah, something with Meyers's story seems off. Maddie, are you qualified for sniper duty?"

Beauvilliers grinned. "For the Olympics, no. But I can handle anything up to a thousand meters in fair weather."

"Good. Grab some duffle bags and load up ladies."

"And where you off to, bossman?" Bijeau asked.

"To find Meyers and some maps. Pack a bag for me and meet me up on the helipad."

As the chopper lifted off in a light downpour, Doss plopped down between Bijeau and Beauvilliers on the rear bench and buckled in. As they gained altitude, with the cabin doors open, they had a bird's-eye view of Islamabad. Her streets were overflowing with angry mobs bent on anarchy and destruction. No police or military were around to stop them.

"Alright Alejandra, Maddie," Doss said as he spread a map across their laps. "I couldn't find Meyers, but he left me these notes. See this small compound on Kass Maira Road surrounded by these fields? If he is right, Perkins will be waiting for us there. Alejandra, I'll drop you here by this rise, and Maddie, you'll set up over here by these boulders to cover me. If all goes well, Perkins won't suspect anything and he'll board the chopper voluntarily. If something does go wrong and I can't reach the chopper for whatever reason, have the pilot circle back to pick you both up. If you can grab Perkins, do it. You should be able to refuel at Bacha Khan Airport and then from there you can either fly east and make for Jalandhar or fly south and head for the Iranian coast and the Fifth Fleet. Either way, you'll need to stop somewhere in between to refuel. If you don't have Perkins, I'd return to the Embassy, evac with everyone else, but you do whatever you think best under the circumstances. Questions? Good. Let's check commo, weapons and gear."

After 60 minutes of flying, the pilot spotted a large house made of sand stone, a smaller cinder-block building and one metal utility shed all surrounded by a high, concrete wall crowned in rings of coiled razor wire. The skies were clear over western Pakistan. The day had turned uncomfortably warm and sticky.

Doss had the pilot hover a few feet off the ground and pointed to Bijeau. The chopper's blades started kicking up a cloud of dust and sand when she jumped. Then Doss had the pilot move north 500 yards and after Beauvilliers jumped, he had the pilot set the Venom down in front of a pair of wrought-iron gates outside the compound. He ducked his head under the whirling rotor blades as he started moving towards the compound and was surprised when Meyers walked through the gates with Perkins and a young woman at his side to meet him. A dozen men dressed in customary Afghani desert clothing with chitrali caps and armed with Russian AK-12s followed close behind.

"Meyers."

"Doss."

"You and Perkins must have driven here in a hurry after breakfast."

"We did."

"These some of your friends?"

"Afraid so Doss. I'll be needing that chopper."

"Why?"

"Obviously, there's been a change of plans."

"What change?"

"I need to get the girl safely back to her father."

"Not my problem. Give me Perkins."

"No can do. The girl is the daughter of a Pashtun warlord, one of the three Afghan Opium Kings. Perkins and I have a little side action going on with her father. The borders are closed, and I need that chopper."

"Side action? Some might call that treason Meyers."

"Wake up Doss. You always did have a reputation for being naïve. Treason against whom? Soon there will be no countries and no borders. Civilization is crashing down all around us. Opium. Opium will become the universal currency then. Now step aside and you might make it out of Pakistan alive. Have those two G.I. Jane beauties you flew in with step out of the chopper."

"Ladies," Doss whispered into his mic. "Do you copy those last instructions?"

"Loud and clear, Doss," Beauvilliers answered.

"Loud and clear bossman," Bijeau said.

"On three, take out the hired help - one, two, *THREE!*" Doss shouted and dropped to the ground.

Within a few heartbeats, Bijeau and Beauvilliers picked off ten armed men from 500 yards away. Child's play. Doss took out the last two just as Perkins grabbed the girl and ran back into the compound, with Meyers hobbling a few steps behind him. They didn't stop to close or lock the gates.

"Team, on me!" Doss ordered.

Bijeau and Beauvilliers grabbed their gear and raced across the field towards the compound while Doss stripped the weapons off of the dead and wounded. "Front door," he said when Bijeau and Beauvilliers reached him. "I'll try kicking it in. Bijeau, flash and bang, Beauvilliers behind me!"

But when Doss reached the door, he saw that it was heavy steel plate. He glanced over at the windows and saw that they were protected by wrought iron bars bolted into walls of solid stone. The compound was a mini fortress.

"Doss!" Meyers called out. "I wanted to do this the easy way. Now you've made a certain Afghani warlord extremely angry. He's sending men this way as I speak, men who won't show you or the women any kindness."

Doss ignored Meyers and did a quick survey of the main house and the metal utility shed. He saw one motorcycle and a vintage yellow sedan that appeared fully restored parked inside the shed. And then he noticed a large generator sitting against the shed with jerry cans stacked behind it.

He turned to Bijeau and Beauvilliers. "Check the jerry cans for fuel. I'll cover you."

"They're filled with gasoline, Doss," Bijeau shouted back.

"Good. Place them against the door."

Bijeau and Beauvilliers stacked six jerry cans against the door while Doss placed four packs of C-4 against the cans and two against the door, and then they all took cover. Doss shouted to Myers to move away from the door and *BOOM!*

Doss bolted through a burning wooden doorframe with Bijeau and Beauvilliers a step behind him. They stepped inside a compound filled with dust and smoke, then went from room to room but found nothing.

"Tunnel," Beauvilliers said. "There must be an escape tunnel."

"Quick, the chopper," Doss said when he heard the Huey's engines increasing power.

Once outside, Doss saw an open trapdoor in the dirt near the chopper. He could see the pilot struggling with Meyers inside the main cabin. Then he heard someone cranking up the motorcycle, turned, and watched Perkins and the girl speed off on the bike.

"You two take the sedan; I want Perkins alive," he shouted and tossed a set of car keys he had taken off the kitchen wall to Bijeau. Then he ran towards the Venom. He jumped aboard just as a single shot rang out. The pilot, still struggling with Meyers, dropped to his knees, clutching at his chest.

Unaware Doss was on the chopper, Meyers was about to slide into the pilot's seat when Doss grabbed him from behind. Meyers turned and pulled a handgun from his belt, but Doss grabbed his wrist and twisted, forcing Meyers to drop the weapon. Then Meyers tried to crush Doss's foot with his prosthetic leg, but he was too slow. When Doss reached for the handgun lying on the floorboard, Meyers also saw the gun, pulled a karambit knife and sliced him open just below his body armor. Doss grimaced. He ignored the pain and threw an uppercut, barely grazing Meyers on the chin. Meyers then swung his knife at Doss's throat, but Doss was surprisingly quick and blocked the blow with his left forearm as he landed a devastating punch to the nose with his right fist. Meyers shrieked in pain and staggered backward. He dropped his knife to hold his shattered nose. Spurts of blood sprayed across the cabin as the two men, like wrestlers in the ring, locked arm-in-arm together, danced around for a bit until Doss dropped to one knee and ripped Meyers's metal leg off. Meyers lost his balance, fell and hit his forehead hard against a fire extinguisher mounted against the fuselage. The blow knocked him out cold.

Doss sat the pilot up against the bulkhead. "Can you fly?"

"No. Feeling a bit woozy, sir."

Doss looked at the wound and checked the man's nametag. "You're losing a lot of blood, Dawson," he said, reached for a first aid kit and found a roll of gauze. "Keep this compressed against the wound. I'll get you to a hospital ASAP."

"You can fly a helo, sir?"

"Not well," Doss replied with a comforting smile, and gently patted the pilot reassuringly on the shoulder.

Doss plopped himself down in the pilot's seat, took a quick look at the instruments, the gauges and the controls and grabbed the collective. He had never flown a Venom before. He was not certified to fly any type of rotor wing, but managed to get the helo up in the air. When he saw a plume of dust trailing behind a motorcycle racing across the desert with a vintage yellow sedan chasing after it, he increased power to the main rotors and quickly overtook both vehicles. He eased the Huey up alongside the bike and, with one clumsy, lucky pass, he used the chopper's skids to nudge Perkins and the girl off the bike. Doss quickly set the Venom down, hoping he hadn't killed them.

"What do we do with the girl?" Bijeau asked as she stood over the couple, with Beauvilliers standing at her side.

"Bring her along," Doss replied.

Bijeau and Beauvilliers lifted the dazed couple to their feet, secured their hands with zip ties, and hustled them into the chopper.

"We've got company," Doss shouted over the noise of the rotors and engines as he watched a long column of cars and pickup trucks crowded with armed men racing towards them - men loyal to the girl's warlord father, Doss assumed.

The airport at Peshawar was only minutes away, but that now seemed too risky to Doss. "Alejandra, find us an alternate airport. What's close?"

Bijeau unfolded her map. "Kohat, about fifty kilometers due south. It's a Pakistani military airbase."

"Nothing closer?"

"No."

"Keep your fingers crossed ladies," Doss said gravely as he pointed the chopper south and gained altitude.

When Bijeau saw blood seeping through Doss's fatigue jacket, she took her knife and cut away the bottom part of the jacket. "You've got a deep gash along your ribcage, bossman."

"Yeah, silly me. I brought my fists to a knife fight."

Bijeau reached over to grab the first aid kit, stopped to check the pilot's pulse, and felt nothing. "Dawson's dead Max."

Doss nodded. "What about Meyers?"

"He's still breathing," Beauvilliers replied.

Bijeau dressed Doss's wound as best she could while he focused on piloting the Venom. She offered him morphine, but he refused and swallowed a couple of Advil instead.

When they reached Kohat fifteen minutes later, Doss landed the Huey with the fuel gauge needle on empty and the fuel warning alerts flashing and beeping. He set the chopper down close to a fuel dump and had Bijeau man the 7.62mm door gun when two camouflaged Land Rovers drove up to meet them. After eight Pakistani soldiers jumped out of the vehicles with weapons at the ready, a major in the Pakistani Air Force stepped out onto the tarmac with them. He casually strolled up to the Huey as Doss powered her down.

"American?" the major asked.

"Yes," Doss answered and opened the pilot's door.

"State your business."

"We need fuel."

"Do you have the proper authorizations?"

"No, there was no time. But we can pay."

"We don't give credit here. Are you aware of what is happening across our country?"

"I am, and I am deeply saddened by it."

"Apart from fuel, what is your business in Kohat?"

"We are from the U.S. Embassy in Islamabad. We are on a diplomatic mission. Check the aircraft's registry if you have any doubts. And we can pay cash for the fuel with U.S. Dollars."

"We usually do not see diplomats visit our base, especially diplomats who are bleeding all over themselves. Will your President send American soldiers to Pakistan, or will she allow the Khan of Khans to ravage our proud country?"

"I cannot say because I honestly do not know. Have Mongolian forces crossed the border?"

"No, but it is only a matter of time before they do."

"Will you help us or not?"

"Can you prove you are with the U.S. Embassy?"

"Beauvilliers, I left my wallet on the seat over there with my other things. Would you be so kind?"

Beauvilliers patted Meyers down, grabbed his wallet and embassy credentials, and handed them over to Doss. Doss gingerly eased himself out of the chopper and handed the major the identifications. Doss looked nothing like Meyers and held his breath.

"You've lost some weight and have colored your hair, Mr. Meyers. I think you need a more recent photo. What is the fuel capacity of your helicopter?"

Doss did not know and guessed. "Over two hundred U.S. gallons."

"You, I think, are a soldier. Did you serve in Iran?"

"I did."

"Ah, as did I. Combat? What unit?"

"I served with the armored cav."

"Truly? The 11th?"

"Yep, Eagle Squadron."

"Small world. I was the tactical air support liaison officer between your regiment's command and the PAF. Regrettably, I did not see much action. I would hand the fuel over to a brother-in-arms for free considering the circumstances, but I fear I'd be shot by my superiors if

I did. Say twenty U.S. Dollars per gallon plus another one thousand for my men?"

"Done."

The major barked out orders to his detachment and his men hustled when he told them the Americans would pay them handsomely in U.S. dollars for their time. "Shall I summon a medic for you while we wait?"

"I'd be most grateful, Major, please."

While a Pakistani medic cleaned Doss's wound and stitched him back together, a fuel truck started pumping 242 gallons of aviation fuel into the Huey. And then the major had his men stow 25 gallons of spare fuel in five jerry cans onboard. Doss handed the major $10,000 U.S. Dollars and told him to keep the change.

"Most generous, thank you," the major said and showed his men the money. "You wish to leave the country, yes?"

"Yes."

"I strongly urge you to avoid Islamabad, Mr. Meyers. You can easily make the airbase at Mianwala, about one-hundred-fifty kilometers southeast from here. My brother-in-law is the commanding officer in Mianwala. From Mianwala, you will head east to Lahore, another three-hundred kilometers of flying. Weather is poor in eastern Pakistan. You will be pushing your maximum operating range to the limit, so fly smart and conserve fuel. The commander of the airbase in Lahore is my uncle. I will call both men and tell them to expect you. From Lahore, it is an easy flight into India."

"*Allah Hafiz*, Major."

"And may God be with you, American."

After the two men exchanged salutes, Doss eased himself back into the pilot seat, conducted his preflight checks and powered up the Huey. The flight to Mianwala was mercifully uneventful. At the cost of another $10,000, they refueled, happily accepted rations and water from the Pakistani soldiers and immediately departed for Lahore, reaching the city at dusk with just enough fuel in the Huey's interconnected tanks, having landed earlier to add the extra 25 gallons from the jerry cans. They saw scores of small fires raging across the city. They saw red tracers from machine gun rounds arching across the night sky. When they approached the airbase, the facility was dark and appeared deserted. But after Doss set the Venom down on the main runway, six pairs of headlights popped on.

"Meyers?"

"Yes, sir," Doss replied as he slowly stepped down from the cockpit.

"I am Colonel Farooq, base commander. We will start refueling your Huey immediately and then you must leave. Islamabad has fallen to radical groups. Lahore is next. Your aircraft will be the last to leave this base. After you depart, my men will burn every liter of petrol and burn the hangars too."

"May I ask where you sent your aircraft?"

"South. We Pakistani patriots intend to fight and hold the south. A provisional government has declared that Karachi will be our new capital."

"Thank you for the fuel, Colonel. What do we owe you?"

Farooq burst out laughing. "Today we are having a fire sale - everything is free, my friend!"

After the Pakistanis finished refueling the Venom, Doss wished the colonel well and handed him a stack of money to distribute to his men. He eased the chopper into the air with a fresh wave of explosions rocking Lahore and headed east. When they reached the Pakistani-Indian border, Doss and his two warrioresses breathed a collective sigh of relief. The day had been long and hard, and they had each doubted whether they would make it. And then someone slid the side cabin door open and Meyers, standing at the doorway on his good leg, turned and smiled and stepped out into oblivion.

Two Indian Sukhoi Su-30MKI fighters suddenly appeared, one on each side of the Huey, after Doss crossed over into Indian airspace. The lead pilot instructed Doss to set down at Adampur Air Force Station in Jalandhar. Doss needed the fuel anyway and nodded. The next morning, after some calls were made, the Indians agreed to refuel and release the Venom and Doss wasted no time flying straight for the U.S. Embassy in New Delhi. He was pleasantly surprised to find Watkins standing on the helipad waiting for them.

"Wasn't sure I'd ever see y'all again, sir," the Master Gunnery Sergeant said with a broad smile and a wad of chewing tobacco tucked inside his cheek.

"Glad you made it out, Watkins. Did everyone get out?"

"We received orders from Washington to evacuate Islamabad not long after you took off. We got everyone out but Meyers. He musta' left the Embassy on an errand of some sort. We searched every room but never found him."

"That's curious. Hopefully, he'll turn up in one piece. I met a Pakistani Air Force colonel in Lahore before we crossed the border last night. It would seem all northern Pakistan is in revolt."

"Pakistan's a mess, sir, sure is. Appreciate you returnin' the chopper in one piece. Saves me a lot of paperwork. I don't see Warrant Officer Dawson."

Doss rested a hand on the Marine's shoulder. "KIA I'm sorry to inform you. I'm not at liberty to say more. His body is in the back. Please inform his family that he died bravely fighting for his country. He risked his life to save the mission. He died a hero."

"I understand, sir. Those two steppin' off the chopper with zip ties, you need me to secure 'em?"

"Yes. No one is to talk to them or visit them but me, not even the ambassador himself. Are we clear Master Gunnery Sergeant?"

"Crystal, sir. I'll have two guards posted outside their cell around the clock with strict orders. Speakin' of the ambassador, he's asked to see you."

"Now?"

"Affirmative, sir," Watkins replied, then pointed to Doss's side. "You require medical attention first?"

"No. A Pakistani medic patched me up. Where's a decent hotel, something not too far away?"

"VIP types stay at the Leela Palace. It's close."

"Bijeau, Beauvilliers, return the weapons and gear we borrowed from the Master Gunnery Sergeant, then get us rooms at the Leela Palace. Clean up and relax. I'll join you when I can. Watkins, can you have a car take the ladies to the Palace? Excellent, thank you."

The ambassador, a retired CEO of one large tech company or another, peppered Doss with questions and showed his displeasure when he didn't get any meaningful answers. He made subtle threats that he might need to call the President but decided not to make that call when Doss shrugged his shoulders and more or less dared him to do it. After the ambassador angrily dismissed him, Doss walked down to the basement to check on Perkins and the girl.

"Perkins, Dan Perkins, my name is Doss, Max Doss."

"No, you are just screwed," Perkins replied, sitting tied to a chair with his girl sitting tied to a chair across from him. "I'm a British subject and a British diplomat. You have no jurisdiction over me. You've got yourself in the middle of an international incident."

"Nah, you heard what your buddy Meyers said. You're just an international drug dealer, a disgrace, the lowest of the low."

Doss turned to the girl. "And what's your name?"

The girl leaned closer to Doss and spit in his face.

"Well, that's just rude," Doss replied calmly as he wiped the spittle off his cheek. "I'll need to break you of that filthy habit. We have lots to talk about and plenty of time to enjoy it. I tried to get you separate cells, but this place is booming with business so, we'll just have to make do. Well, it's a hot bath and a good stiff cocktail for me before I have an expensive dinner with a bottle of fine wine at some swank restaurant in town. I'll check on you crazy kids in the morning."

"I'll never talk to you," the girl replied defiantly.

"Oh, I almost forgot," Doss said absently as he stood to leave, then reached into his pocket. "Wouldn't want you to feel unclean or ashamed," he said as he tossed a brown hijab headscarf into the girl's lap. "Sweet dreams."

After Doss left the cell, he called home. "Mother."

"Max, you had me worried. You've been jumping from town to town across a country in rebellion."

"No need to concern yourself. I'm on holiday in New Delhi. I'll send you a postcard. Let the big man know where we are and tell him I have Perkins and his gal. Can you send me everything you have on Perkins? I need to know his pressure points. I'll text you what little I know about the girl, which is almost nothing. I don't even know her name."

"Her name is Zuhayra. She is Pashtun."

"I won't even ask how you know that. Family?"

"I'll send the file we have on her father to the Embassy for your eyes only. Sociopathic drug lord with a cold, narcissistic, spoiled brat for a daughter about sums it up."

"I met Meyers."

"Be careful of that one."

"No worries, you can cross him off your Christmas list."

"Happily."

"He told me that he was an instructor in the X-Max Project. I never saw him."

"He was never an instructor and was never in the Project. He washed out during orientation week."

"Huh, he seemed to know me."

"He heard something, saw something, nothing more. It sounds like he used what little he knew about you to get on your sweet side. How are your lovely teammates? The sexy, playful Alejandra, the French beauty Maddie and let's not forget the blonde with the Scandinavian glow, Heidi. My, my, you've surrounded yourself with a lot of temptation, Max. I worry about you. You're no match for that pack of ravenous maneaters."

"Good night, Mother."

Exhausted and in pain, Doss took a taxi from the Embassy to the Palace and met Bijeau and Beauvilliers at the hotel's nightclub. He bought them each a round and thanked them for a job well done. Then he excused himself and went up to his room where he collapsed on the bed and fell fast asleep in his filthy, bloodstained fatigues. He didn't stir until late morning. He didn't wake until a shaft of golden sunlight slipped between the curtains and settled quietly on his face.

Chapter Eighteen

Excerpts from Hermann Adelman's private journal:
The Great Turmoil

A man, dressed in the white flowing robes of a king, or perhaps a saint, emerged from a magnificent white mosque with four gleaming towers to the chants and praises of the multitudes. He is a tall, broad-shouldered fellow in his mid-thirties. He appears trim and fit. He wears no hat, no turban or headscarf. He wears nothing that would otherwise obscure a thick head of hair with glistening curls the color of autumn. He keeps his beard cut short and neat, complimenting a prominent yet noble nose. His face is neither cruel nor kind but with his smooth, caramel skin and a strong jaw, he is decidedly a handsome man. He stares into the sea of people gathering around him with piercing blue eyes and a fetching broad smile. Men and women, dressed mostly in black, black tagelmusts, black tunics, black baggy trousers with black boots - many holding the Khan's sacred, white banner with its nine blue ribbons fluttering in the breeze - reach out, desperately trying to touch him.

He carries himself like royalty as the throngs of people, numbering in the tens of thousands, part before him, as he walks up to a wooden stage erected in the middle of a large, city square. There is power in his voice when he begins speaking. And yet his tone is somehow comforting, even disarming. He strings his words together with the melodic cadence of a poet, without the help of any notes, without the aid of a teleprompter.

"I assume," the President asked with obvious boredom as she watched the Khan of Khans speaking on a large screen TV her staff had wheeled into the Oval Office only moments before. "That someone is working on a translation for me?"

The Khan's first public appearance on the world stage had been unannounced, at least to the West. His speech had caught everyone by surprise.

"Yes, Madam President," CIA Director Nestle answered.

"So that's what the great and powerful wizard behind the curtain looks like. I've only seen fuzzy, poor-quality photos of the man before."

"Because that's all we had until now, Madam President."

"Well, he's certainly a pretty boy, looks like a magazine model to me. Hard to take a man like that seriously. Why now? Why does he show himself to the world now?"

"An excellent question, Madam. We don't know. I assume he'll give us some clue during his speech. Perhaps he's celebrating the addition of half of Pakistan and the disputed territories between India, China and Pakistan to his empire, an area roughly the size of Texas. A feat he accomplished with little bloodshed. We think Georgia, Armenia, and Azerbaijan will open their borders to his soldiers and declare their loyalty to him next."

"Will he move on Afghanistan or India?"

"We don't know. India might be tempting but his ancestors were never able to subdue India and history appears to influence this man. As for Afghanistan well, if we Americans, the Soviets and Alexander the Great couldn't bring the Afghanis to heel, he might just decide to bypass the country. Afghanistan has no strategic value for him that we know of."

"What's the time over there?"

"We believe he is broadcasting from Kazakhstan, which is ten hours ahead of D.C., so it is 6:30 p.m. over there."

As the Khan of Khans continued speaking extemporaneously, as the President and her advisors went back and forth debating what to do, Adelman quietly slipped out of the Oval Office to call Mother.

"How soon can we have a translation of Temüjin's speech?"

"We are translating his words in real time Herr Direktor."

"Damn. I wish I had stayed at the office. I'll get back as soon as I can. What's the gist of his message so far?"

"He reminds me of the films I've seen of Adolf Hitler, but without the theatrics, without the obvious evil, without the hatred towards the

Jews or any people. Still, he has the power to whip the mob into a frenzy with promises of peace and a good life for all. Still, in so many words, he intends to rule the world. He claims Allah has shown him the way to accomplish his holy mission here on earth and has showered him with gifts from the heavens. Unlike Hitler, he appears rational and sane. He's quite good-looking. He comes across as likable and charming."

"Does he disclose why he is making his grand debut on the world stage at this particular moment?"

"Unclear. We'll need to analyze and digest the transcript of course."

"Does he say why he wants to conquer the world? Egomania? Religion? Revenge perhaps? Does he talk to Allah? Apparently from what you've said Allah talks to him. I wonder if the Prophet Muhammad whispers commands into his ear?"

"He has not said."

"He's a cocky son-of-a-bitch, I'll give him that."

"He appears supremely confident."

"Yes, yes, indeed he does. *Gross Gott!* Yes, he is supremely confident! I think I may know why."

"Oh? Perhaps Herr Direktor you should prepare for your call with Doss first."

"What time is it in New Delhi?"

"New Delhi is ten hours and thirty minutes ahead of Washington. Your call with Max is in ten minutes."

Two imposing female Marines with stone-cold expressions escorted Zuhayra to a room with a shower. They made her strip, scanned her for trackers, found one, removed it, and bagged her clothing. After she finished washing, they handed her fresh clothing, a mechanic's navy-blue coverall with a pair of white Docksiders, and then returned her to the cell. Two male Marines did the same with Perkins, though they found no tracker on him. In the early evening, Doss entered the cell with two large Cokes and a pair of Big Macs. The Marines followed him in, set up a camera on one tripod and a microphone with speakers on another tripod and then left.

"Anyone hungry?" Doss asked. "No? I'll just leave these burgers and sodas here on the floor in case one of you changes your mind later. We have a wonderful guest today who would like to ask you a few easy questions. Sir?"

"Thank you, Doss," the voice of an older man with a German accent said over the speaker. "My name is unimportant. What is important is that I hold your futures in the palm of my hand. You can cooperate or not. We will get the information we want with or without you. But if we do it without you, I promise it will cost you dearly. Think on that for a moment. Ms. Zuhayra, I'll begin with you. Who implanted the tracking device on you?"

"Piss off," Zuhayra replied defiantly. "I do not need to answer your questions."

"This is true, and yet you really should. Who implanted the tracking device on you?"

"Let me out of here, you stinking pig!"

"There is a future where you may leave. Who implanted a tracking device on you? Come now, it is a harmless question."

"Go fuck yourself."

"Who implanted a tracking device on you?"

"Aren't you listening? Are you deaf?"

"Who implanted a tracking device on you?"

"For fuck's sake, shut up!"

"Who implanted a tracking device on you?"

"Fine, you idiot. What does it matter? My father, my father did."

"Ah, that wasn't so hard, was it? Your father is Abdul-Khaleq Kohistani, correct?"

"Yes. This is common knowledge."

"And you would like to return to him, yes?"

"He is a powerful warlord. You'd be wise to return me to him."

"This is possible. Who is Daniel Perkins to you?"

"He is my friend."

"A friend, you say? How good a friend is he to you?"

"We hang out together."

"You first met in London, yes? How good a friend is Daniel?"

"You are an annoying person. We are lovers. This too is common knowledge. You happy now, pervert?"

"I see. I bet your father is unaware of your intimate relationship with Daniel, correct?"

"That's none of your concern."

"Would your father approve of Daniel if I told him you are lovers?"

"What does that matter?"

"We both know he would not approve."

"No."

"What business does Daniel have with your father?"

"Shut up Zuhayra!" Perkins suddenly burst out. "Stop talking. These men are not your friends. They will lie to you, make false promises to you, abuse you and twist your words against you later."

"Zuhayra," the voice over the speaker said calmly. "You should trust me when I tell you: Perkins cannot help you return home. But I can. Please answer my last question. I already know the answer, but want to hear it from you."

Zuhayra glanced down at the floor. The daughter of one of the great Opium Kings did not frighten easily, but she felt alone and frightened now.

"Ye, yes. He works with my father."

"Embassy business, farming business, investing in some fish and chips fast-food franchise together? A hair salon? No? Perhaps the heroin business?"

"I, I don't know."

"Of course you do. Do you wish to go home or not?"

"Ah, her, heroin."

"Lying bitch," Perkins muttered and looked away.

"Excellent," the voice said, ignoring Perkins. "Zuhayra, we are not finished yet, but you have taken the first step on a path to freedom. The Marines will now take you to a private room. The two women you met on the helicopter have more questions for you. Do not be deceitful with them or you will suddenly find the path home closed to you. If that happens, you will be put on a military transport plane alongside Perkins and flown to the U.S. Either way, I doubt we ever chat again. Doss..."

Doss had the two Marines standing outside the door step inside and escort Zuhayra to another room. She reached down and grabbed one of the Cokes and a Big Mac off the floor on the way out and never looked back at Perkins.

"Just you, me and Doss now, Perkins."

"And who the fuck are you?"

"Why, I thought you would have figured that out by now. Surely the German accent gave me away? I am Herr Direktor."

Adelman and Doss took turns in their relentless and psychologically merciless questioning of Perkins. With men and women who fervently believe in something, who are ready to give their lives for something they believe is noble, interrogation, even physical torture, is often ineffective. It is the men and women who have sold their souls, who are desperate to salvage something of their miserable lives after they are caught, that crack without too much effort. Perkins was no true believer in anything but himself. A trainee could have done the job and Doss told Perkins as much when Perkins finally broke. But, unlike Pollard before him, he did not sob. He burst out laughing once he collected himself and had a lot to say about the Council.

Kurt Stromquist. Perkins eagerly educated Adelman and Doss on Kurt Stromquist. He spoke about Stromquist with pride, almost reverence. Stromquist's ascendency to the throne was far more subtle, far more nuanced than that of his rival to the East. Where Temüjin seemed to be in a hurry to seize his destiny and relished the public adulation of his followers, Stromquist was patient, methodical and precise and liked to work in the shadows. He avoided the limelight and the masses. If Temüjin was the reincarnation of Genghis Khan, Stromquist, according to Perkins, was the reincarnation of Niccolò di Bernardo dei Machiavelli. Though the two men were very different, they shared the same goal: they both dreamt of creating a single world order.

"Max, let the ladies enjoy themselves in New Delhi," Adelman said after two Marines took Perkins out of the room. "Give them a few days off - compliments of the Section. I need you back in the U.S., immediately."

"Another mission, sir?"

"There is always another mission. Bring Perkins with you. That disgrace has more to tell us. I'm certain of it."

"D.C.?"

"Yes, drop Perkins off in D.C. But Mother can assign an interrogation team to squeeze him, to keep him talking. You get yourself to Cheyenne Mountain. I'll meet you there. I think I might know why Temüjin made his first public appearance to the world the other day."

"Oh?"

"A supremely confident fellow like that has a secret, a huge secret. He may not be ready to share his secret with the world, but he wants the world to know he has one. I think his folks may have unlocked the mysteries of their alien craft. If that is true, God help us all."

As the Blue-Eyed Mongrel - yes, this is the title nonbelievers have bestowed upon Temüjin following his remarkable appearance in front of the Hazrat Sultan Mosque on Independence Square in Astana, the capital city of Kazakhstan - continues consolidating his gains and resumes his march west with impunity, the countries of Europe do not sit idly by. Nor does the Council.

Throughout Europe, new alliances are being forged, and old ones reaffirmed. Factories are kept open night and day, never closing, and begin churning out terrifying new weapons of war in daunting numbers. The young men and women, 18 years and older, are summoned for duty. They are issued smart-looking uniforms, conditioned, and given intensive training in weaponry, individual combat techniques and small-unit tactics. Europe also assembles an army of civilian laborers to begin construction on a massive fortification line dubbed the Zhukov Line after the famous Russian general who never lost a battle in World War II. The line, when finished, will stretch from St. Petersburg on the Baltic Sea in the north to Rostov-on-Don on the Sea of Azov in the south. In critical, strategic areas like Moscow, the West begins erecting towering, concrete walls reinforced with enormous stones and massive steel I-beams. And the guiding architect behind all of it? The illusive fellow named Stromquist.

Chapter Nineteen

It was late when Doss returned to his hotel room, but he was wired after the long interrogation session with Perkins and decided to go down to the hotel bar and have a drink or two, hoping to find the right switch to turn off his brain. The lounge was nearly empty, and he took a seat at the bar. He thought of asking Bijeau and Beauvilliers to join him, but decided it would be selfish of him to wake them.

Doss thought of himself as exceptionally good at what he did, but never thought of himself as the best of agents. Even so, he had three advantages that kept him in the game. First, he was, he knew, very bright. Not in a highbrow, Ivy League sense. He possessed a refined native intelligence enhanced with an abundance of common sense few have. Second, he was a natural with firearms. He pointed, he pulled the trigger and damn near always hit his target, even when the target was moving and shooting back; he was faster and more poised under fire than most. Finally, he had been born with a wonderful intuitive sense, often eerily prophetic, what the military might call situational awareness, but his gift was far more than that. These three qualities had kept him alive over the years - at the expense of numerous others despite their often overall superior skills.

When he started on his second drink, he knew something was amiss. He sensed it. The bartender suddenly disappeared. A young couple sitting in a corner, the only other patrons in the lounge, abruptly hurried off without paying their tab. Everything was too quiet.

He carefully reached inside his jacket, grabbed his Embassy Sig, turned and dropped to one knee just as two young killers stormed into the lounge with automatics. Doss breathed in and out with steady, measured breaths, aimed and shot both men dead. Then someone behind him tried to club him with a baseball bat, but the club grazed his scalp and hit the bar stool instead. When Doss stood and turned, the bartender, a large beefy man, used the bat to slap the Sig out of his hand and then lunged at him.

The two men wrestled for a bit and though big, the bartender was more fat than muscle and he soon realized Doss was the stronger, quicker man. He suddenly understood, with a sickening feeling growing in the pit of his stomach, that he was fighting for his life. When Doss managed to slip behind him and put him in a headlock, the bartender foolishly tried reaching for the Sig lying on the floor - but Doss saw the move, had no choice, and snapped the man's neck in two.

Doss dragged the three bodies behind the bar and tossed a tablecloth over them. He checked the cameras next, but someone had switched them off. As he left the lounge, he realized he had popped some of his stitches and thought of asking one of the ladies for help but again decided not to wake them.

In the morning Doss went straight to Bijeau's room and rapped firmly on the door. To his surprise, Beauvilliers, dressed in a white hotel bathrobe with a white towel wrapped around her hair, opened the door instead. She stood silently gawking at him, looking slightly embarrassed.

"Oh, pardon me, Maddie. I thought this was Alejandra's room. I wanted to tell you both to have some fun for a few days while I return to the States - expenses are on the Section."

"Bossman?" Bijeau said and opened the door wider. She was dressed in an identical bathrobe and greeted Doss with a huge shit-eating grin. "I heard you say something about having fun?"

"Ahem. Ladies, I do apologize for the intrusion."

"Are you blushing, Max?" Bijeau asked and laughed.

Doss managed to smile despite the pain. "My German Puritan roots run deep. You may have permanently damaged my psyche. But do have fun. Just not here. I was attacked in the hotel lounge last night by three men. Two had automatics. The bartender had a baseball bat."

"But why, who?" Beauvilliers asked.

"Good questions. Had the night to think about it."

"You're bleeding again Max," Beauvilliers said as she pulled Doss inside while Bijeau disappeared into the bathroom.

"I'll call the Embassy and have a doctor sent over," Bijeau said after she returned with a bottle of hydrogen peroxide, cotton balls and a washcloth. "Sit down on the sofa - now."

"Yes ma'am, thanks, whew, I think I will take a seat. Good lesson ladies, never let your guard down. We're surrounded by some nasty people who will hurt us if they can, and we've hardly kept ourselves invisible. As for the why and the who, I'd place my chips on Zuhayra's father, Kohistani. I didn't give much thought to the tracker on her. Stupid. No doubt there were cameras back at the compound too. They saw our faces and the helicopter probably traced the tail number back to the U.S. Embassy in Islamabad, and then tracked us all the way here to New Delhi. I think my assailants meant to take me alive, trade me for the girl. They never took the safeties off their weapons and made themselves easy kills. I ended the lives of three men who probably didn't need to die. Sloppy work on my part and I put both of your lives at risk. For that I am sorry. Ouch!"

"Sit still, tough guy," Bijeau ordered as she cleaned and disinfected his wound. "We're trained, experienced professionals, Max. Maddie and I should have paid more attention to that tracker as well. We did this mission on the fly. Shit happens. If you don't let this wound heal, if you don't recharge your own batteries, you are going to make mistakes, bossman. You said you are returning to the States?"

"Yes, Adelman needs me. A plane is waiting. I'll be taking Perkins with me. We keep the girl in custody for now but make her reasonably comfortable. I think Adelman will release her soon. Hopefully, that will satisfy her father from any future retaliation."

"Has Perkins told you yet what he did with the intel he bought from the White House staffer?"

"He did. I think he wanted to impress me. He sold the intel to the Council, and the Council passed the location of the mysterious weapon on to the Israelis, knowing full well that the Israelis would try to destroy the damn thing. But Perkins also sold the intel to Zuhayra's father, who in turn tipped the Mongolians off to, my guess is, curry favor with them in the event Temüjin decides to gobble up Afghanistan."

"What a worthless sack of shit. When do you want us back?"

"Leave India, go somewhere fun - no wild spending sprees on expensive clothing or jewelry or the like or Herr Direktor will have my head. Take a week, then get yourselves back to Washington."

"Mr. Duc, or should I call you Dr. Duc?" Adelman asked as he, Duc and Doss sat down in Duc's office within the *Cosmos Cavern*, the name of the facility deep within Cheyenne Mountain where Duc and his scientists worked on Project Swan. "You've more than earned the title."

"Ah, *Dr. Duc*," Duc mused. "How proud my parents to hear this if they alive, but no Herr Direktor, I simple man. Big title, eh, I learn new word *lofty* yesterday, ha-ha, lofty title will not improve my work. Please, I just Billy."

"Billy it is."

"Tea Herr Direktor, Mr. Max?"

Adelman nodded.

"No tea for me thank you," Doss answered. "Please, just call me Max."

"Max, you have knowledge in mathematics, physics, engineering?" Duc asked as he placed two tea cups on his desk with teabags.

"Afraid not, Billy. You caught a glimpse of what I do back in Seattle and then again in New Orleans."

"Ah, you Herr Direktor's number one soldier?"

Doss smiled. "Something like that."

"Max," Adelman interjected, "had some surgery recently and is taking it easy while his body heals. I brought him with me to make certain he takes it easy, as he's a terrible patient."

Duc smiled, reached behind his chair and opened a cabinet on the wall to remove a small box. "I make you special tea, Calendula Tea, good for healing, you drink, yes?"

Doss chuckled and nodded. "You win Billy. Ok."

"Do you know who Temüjin is?" Adelman asked. "Have you seen him on TV or the internet?"

"Yes, yes. Fascinating fellow."

"He is that, Billy."

"Everyone talk about Khan. I watch his speech, read translation later. Is this why you here? I know nothing about this man."

"Do you have any idea why he gave that speech? Before that speech, the world had never really seen much of him or heard his words."

"No, I tell the truth," Duc replied defensively, with some agitation in his voice. "I not know this man."

"I believe you. I didn't come here to accuse you of anything. Please relax. Your work here has been superb. We are friends now. I just wanted to pick your brain."

"What this mean, *pick brain?*"

Adelman chuckled good-naturedly, something he rarely did, then reached across Duc's desk and patted Duc reassuringly on the shoulder. "The phrase means to get your thoughts on a matter."

"Oh, I see. I tell truth. I think you have madman on your hands. But I no expert on such matters. Please continue as me brew tea for us."

"You may be right, Billy. The timing of Temüjin's speech is what brings me here to see you. I read the status reports you and your team provide daily, of course. Your progress is truly remarkable, extraordinary."

"Thank you, sir."

"What I'm about to tell you is highly classified, very, very, top secret stuff. Do you understand?"

"I do."

"You cannot discuss this with anyone except for a few members on your team, people who you trust and who you believe should have this information. Their names must be approved by me first before you say anything. Agreed?"

"I say yes."

"Temüjin has his own alien craft. He stole it from the Chinese."

Duc, who had stood up to reach for a pot of hot water sitting on a hotplate on a credenza behind his desk, turned and stared at Adelman, dumbfounded. "Is like what Germans have or like *Blue Swan?*"

"We have no clue what kind of craft it is or what condition it is in. Maybe it is like what the Germans found, maybe it is like the *Swan* or maybe it is altogether different. We think, well, I think, Temüjin introduced himself to the world when he did because I think his scientists may have figured out how to turn the damn thing on. Worse, they may understand its capabilities, at least in part, and I bet they know how to use them. Temüjin certainly knows the Germans have a spaceship and probably suspects we do too. I think his message was meant more for us than for the masses."

Duc sat back in his chair with the pot and poured boiling water into three cups. "I understand Herr Direktor's purpose here now," he said solemnly. "We in arms race, messy, terrifying arms race. Maybe winner take all, yes?"

"That sums things up nicely, Billy. I don't know what your politics are. I don't know what your religion is. I know that we have kept you here against your will. Truly, I am sorry about that but -."

Duc cut Adleman off with the wave of his hand. "Please, Herr Direktor. Me, I, do same in your position. Vietnamese always admire America, even during ugly war. My great-grandparents blamed American government for bad war, not America people. Vietnam and U.S. now good friends. I think I bring my family here, stay in America, except for nasty civil war. You want me help you win race, yes?"

"Yes."

"I no want to live in world of Khan. I no want to serve him, help him with his plans. I get you list of my best. We behind Mongolians maybe, ah, we are maybe behind the Mongolians. We must work harder, faster, better. I do all in my power to help America, help Vietnam. Please drink tea. And then you excuse me, I get back to work. We might be closer than you think."

"I can ask no more of you, Billy. The stakes, that is the dangers, are exceedingly high. We cannot, we must not fail."

"Yes, yes. May I tell you what frighten me most?"

"Certainly."

"Our enemies frighten me, sure. Alien technology in hands of mankind frighten me. But what frighten me more - who bring down our poor *Blue Swan* and others? Who, I wonder, has such terrible power? Hmmm..."

Chapter Twenty

Excerpts from Hermann Adelman's private journal:
The Great Turmoil

As the days and weeks and months slipped by, the momentous events threatening civilization across the world went from bad to worse. The great House of Sakha, the Russians of the frozen tundra - with lands stretching from Yakutsk in the west to the Seas of Bearing, Okhotsk and Japan to the east - determines that an alliance with the Chinese and the North Koreans is in its best interests. The three allies field a combined army of millions to march on Mongolia while the Khan of Khans is away, leading his armies farther and farther west towards Europe.

And when the three nations launch their joint offensive from the north, the east, and the south in a three-pronged pincer movement, the allied armies jump from one easy victory to another and drive deep into the heart of Mongolia. After the allies converge on, capture and level Chinggis to the ground, a city less than 400 kilometers from Ulaanbaatar, the sacred capital city of Mongolia, spirits soar and hopes are high as the allies prepare to deliver the final blow.

But then disaster raises her ugly head. With armies that seemingly appear out of thin air, Mongolian hordes return to defend the motherland. They come from the west, from the north and south. They strike back fast and hard and come oh so close to encircling and totally annihilating all three allied armies.

The ferocity and swiftness of the Mongolian counteroffensive shocks the world. Unburdened by conventional heavy tanks, slow-moving armored personnel carriers and self-propelled artillery, equipped instead with all manner of ATVs, dirt bikes, motorcycles, lightly armored vehicles of every kind and description, including thousands of faithfully reproduced American robotic twelve-ton RACER Heavy Platform autonomous tanks, and augmented with swarms of drones, tens of thousands of drones of all types, Temüjin's forces move incredibly fast over all kinds of difficult terrain.

Panic spreads like wildfire throughout the allied ranks of inexperienced, poorly trained soldiers when Temüjin's magnificent warriors magically appear and close in on them on all sides. After the Mongolians target and destroy the long convoys of the enemy's refueling trucks, gas tanks run dry and allied soldiers are forced to abandon their armor, leaving thousands of undamaged tanks, APCs and self-propelled artillery behind. Whole divisions melt away as soldiers flee on foot. Temüjin's forces slaughter countless numbers on the run and conscript any who surrender to replenish their ranks. But at the very height of his astonishing victory, Temüjin, reluctantly, is forced to agree to a truce with the Chinese and the North Koreans after the President of China threatens all-out nuclear war if Temüjin's armies do not remove themselves from Chinese territory and return across the border.

The House of Sakha has no such leverage. Before the rise of Temüjin, Sakha had plenty of Siberian oil and gas to sell, but few farms or ranches to produce food. When the Americans, desperate for cash, opened their spigots to oil and natural gas, flooding the markets with cheap energy, the Siberian energy markets collapsed, the country's economy imploded and unemployment and famine set in. In desperation, the House of Sakha sold off its modest nuclear arsenal for food.

Temüjin's fast and nimble tümens - regiments of ten thousand warriors operating independently from each other as in the days of Genghis - ruthlessly pursue the Russians, all the way to the rocky, eastern shores of the salt seas, butchering tens of thousands along the way. The House of Sakha, the last of the great houses of Mother Russia in Asia, falls, and Temüjin adds vast new, energy-rich territories to his empire.

After the battle, Temüjin declares he had seen the invasion of Mongolia in a dream and that he had secretly brought his armies back from the west before the allied armies had even stepped foot into Mongolia. Inspired by Hannibal's tactics at Cannae where the famous Carthaginian feigned a retreat, luring eight Roman legions into a trap and destroying them in one of the greatest military feats of all time,

THE SAVAGERY OF MAN

Temüjin had lured the allied armies deep into Mongolia with a false sense of victory before he sprung his trap. Like his brilliant forefather and namesake, he has shown the world that he is a gifted military commander, a master of strategy, and a shrewd politician of the first order.

Dreyfus gathered her closest advisors around her in the Situation Room. Crisis meetings at the White House were becoming increasingly routine.

The President looked around the crowded room and smiled. "I should send this Temüjin fellow a box of chocolates," she quipped, "inasmuch he has accomplished what we could not. He's taken the Chinese down a peg or two."

"The Chinese will be licking their wounds for some time," Nestle agreed to the sounds of hands thumping against the table.

"What happened to the vaunted Chinese air force?" Dreyfus asked.

"Unclear," General Phillips answered. "Aircraft killer drones, electronic warfare weapons of some kind. We just don't know. It is possible the Chinese grounded their fighters and bombers after they witnessed two of our F-51s being vaporized from space."

Dreyfus turned to Adelman. "Why so grim, Herr Direktor?" she asked when she noticed Adelman wasn't smiling or applauding.

"I for one Madam President, feel less secure with this Mongolian victory," Adelman replied.

"Why?" the President asked. "The Chinese have been our mortal enemy for decades. They have a huge, modern military and an impressive arsenal of strategic nuclear weapons. The Mongolians haven't threatened us. They have no strategic nukes."

"They have access to alien technology."

"Last I heard, so do we. But what good is our alien spaceship? Seems like a piece of junk to me. Your team has failed to do anything with it - why shouldn't I turn the Project over to the Space Force? In fact, why do we even need your Section? I should merge your Section into the Agency or CIA - you know, to remove some of those irksome redundances and save the taxpayers a little cash."

Unruffled, Adelman shrugged his shoulders, couldn't help himself, and went on the offensive. "So why don't you Madam President? Ah, that is because, forgive me for being blunt, you can't under the law. President Calhoun handed Project Swan over to us. The Gang of Five on Capitol Hill created Section M3. I report to them, not you."

Dreyfus threw her coffee mug against the wall in a sudden flash of rage, then jumped to her feet while violently shaking her head. "Ohhh, that German arrogance of yours, Adelman, that impertinence, that smug sense of superiority - someday it will cost you dearly. Laws can be changed. The careers of little men like you can easily be broken."

"I see that I've agitated you, Madam. I do apologize. That was not my intent. Perhaps I should excuse myself?"

"You'll know when I've excused you, Herr Direktor. Midterms are around the corner. The polls are looking good for my side. We will see if any of the Gang of Five survives November. If they don't, your ass is mine. And if by some miracle the entire Gang is reelected, my attorneys are already preparing to petition the Supreme Court to declare the laws creating your Section unconstitutional, null and void. I am the sole Commander-in-Chief of the military under the Constitution. Now Adelman, now you are excused. Leave, go do whatever it is mad German spymasters do."

"Happily, thank you, Madam President," Adelman said in a respectful tone, and left. He had to agree the President was right about one thing, though he'd never give her the satisfaction. *Blue Swan*, despite the brightest minds and the billions spent, was little more than junk.

Temüjin wastes no time on parades, fireworks, or victory celebrations of any kind. Repelling China's invasion is little more than a distraction, a nuisance for Temüjin. His destiny demands he resume his march on the West. And the Khan of Khans is no longer a patient man. He confides to his inner circle that he feels the heavy hand of time resting upon his shoulders. Time, he tells them, is the only enemy he dreads, the only enemy that can defeat him.

After resting his men and reequipping his armies with their vast booty of war machines taken from the allied armies, Temüjin gives the order to march. But before leaving Ulaanbaatar - as captured on video and released anonymously for all the world to see - Temüjin has hundreds of deserters, criminals, perverts of all kinds, war profiteers, political rivals, instigators and dissenters, incompetent bureaucrats and high-ranking military officers - including one Field Marshal Muunokhoi Altanbaatariin, the head of the Department of Advanced Weaponry Development - taken in chains to Sükhbaatar Square before throngs of onlookers where they are executed en masse to the sounds of bagpipes, fife and drum. The beheadings go on for hours. The street gutters run red with blood.

The undefeated armies of the Khan of Khans, now officially the Armies of the Second Mongol Empire, sweep across the vast steppes of Russia next, lands of immense beauty seemingly stretching into the horizon forever. The light divisions in the vanguard move with incredible speed. Temüjin pushes his warriors hard, males and females alike, to the breaking point, but pushes himself even harder. His armies don't pause until they reach the majestic Ural Mountains, the demarcation line between East and West, between Asia and Europe. Once he brings his mighty hordes over the mountains and steps foot in Europe, with supply lines stretched thin, with soldiers and machines overwhelmed with exhaustion, Temüjin orders his armies to halt and make camp.

When his armies are again rested and resupplied, after worn and broken machines are repaired or replaced, Temüjin crosses the Volga River and rolls through Saratov next - at one time a city of the Golden Horde known as Uvek - without a fight. From Saratov, Temüjin sends one-third of his forces south towards Volgograd, the place where the Third Reich died in a wintery hell over 100 years ago, and sends another third north to march on Kazan, the fifth largest city of old Russia, while he leads the cream of his forces straight at Moscow.

By the tens of thousands, Russian refugees flee in fear as the Mongolians and their allies approach. Others stubbornly remain behind in their homes, praying for the best. As the invaders roll past them, word spreads like wildfire across the land that Temüjin the Blessed, the Khan of Kahns and their new sovereign, is merciful, benevolent and kind. Under penalty of death, Temüjin's soldiers do not seize or destroy property, they do not arrest, abuse, or violate Russians. The churches, mosques, temples and synagogues, the schools, hospitals, shops, restaurants and parks, and even the factories and other places of work, are left undisturbed and are permitted to remain open.

Upon hearing of this, the people of both Kazan and Volgograd choose to stay and welcome the Khan's vast columns of soldiers - numbers beyond reckoning - with open arms, with cheers and praise and flowers. Then Georgia, Armenia, and Azerbaijan all declare their loyalty to Temüjin and open their cities to his armies as well.

The West answers Temüjin's provocations by mobilizing, by calling up reservists and rushing their own massive armies, with tanks, armored personnel carriers and artillery, with fighter jets, bombers and countless drones, to man the Zhukov Line, more commonly known as the Z Line, while Temüjin's three army groups advance methodically across a broad 1,000-mile front. Men on both sides prepare themselves as best they can for a titanic bloodletting of biblical proportions. But 40 miles short of Moscow, and all along the Z Line, the Khan of Khans inexplicably stops his armies and orders his troops to dig in.

A world away, President Dreyfus responds to these dire events by asking Congress to declare war on Temüjin and his followers, to come to the aid of old friends and allies. But Congress balks. As the League wants no part of any intervention in a foreign war and refuses to participate, Congress wasn't about to send Union military might overseas and hand the League a decisive military advantage at home.

Dreyfus has no power to declare war but as Commander-in-Chief, she does have the power to move units and material around. She orders five full divisions: the 1st Infantry Division, the 1st Air Cavalry Division, the 82nd Airborne Division, the 10th Mountain Division and the 1st Armored Division, augmented with one squadron from the 11th Armored Cavalry Regiment to Poland, ostensibly to participate in war games - war games that are on nobody's calendar.

Not long after they had sat down with Duc in Colorado, Adelman took Doss with him to Georgia. After they passed through the rigorous security checks at Kings Bay and entered an underground hangar deep below the earth, the most secret, secure facility in the nation, perhaps in the world, Doss, who had never seen the ship before, stood transfixed, too stunned to speak. Amused by Doss's reaction, Adelman couldn't help himself and chuckled.

"Beautiful, isn't she Max?"

"Yes. She's larger than I expected. Large enough for a complement of twenty, perhaps?"

"Depending on how much space her engines take up, at least. Maybe she's a drone and carried no crew. Hopefully, Duc and his team will figure a way to open her up and find out."

"And you say her outer skin has no seams or imperfections of any kind?"

"None that I could discern, not to the naked eye. Maybe the boys and girls wearing the white coats crawling all over the ship have found something."

Adelman led Doss through a glass door and into Duc's office, the largest office on the base and just a few yards away from *Blue Swan*. Duc was working his way through an elaborate equation on one of his many whiteboards hung up along the walls as they stepped inside.

"Billy, what do you have, what is so important that you dragged me down to Georgia? We have secure communications. You have my number. You could have just called."

Duc removed his round glasses and smiled. "Herr Direktor, hello. Max, welcome. Please sit. Tea?"

"Perhaps later, Billy," Adelman said testily as he wiped his runny nose with a handkerchief before he took a seat. He had been fighting a nasty, head cold since leaving D.C. and was in a foul mood. "So, Billy, tell us why are we here?"

"Nothing we do make *Swan* turn on. We can power certain instruments inside remotely with highly charged electromagnetic particle waves enhanced with strong pulsating microwaves. But no open doors, no awaken primary power, no do much of anything. I have idea. Admiral Martin no do unless big boss say yes."

"Ok, let's hear it."

"Dr. Simpson, he take me out for fun in his new Toyota Running. Ah, Toyota! High, high quality. Primo good. Japanese make good autos. You know it?"

"You mean a Toyota 4Runner, Billy?" Doss asked.

"Yes, yes, 4Runner, Mr. Max, I mean Max. Admiral say ok, one day you spend in backcountry but you take thirty soldiers and six helicopters or no deal. We say ok, Admiral, sir."

"We follow Billy," Alderman said testily but really didn't and began wondering if someone had slipped Billy a baggie of peyote back in Cheyenne.

Doss cleared his throat. "You and Dr. Simpson went off-road," he explained. "You went out on the dirt trails. A 4Runner is an excellent vehicle to go off-roading. Is that what you mean, Billy?"

"Bingo, Max! Much fun in Toyota 4Runner. I learn drive old U.S. Army Jeep in Saigon as boy, go in water, mud, rocks. Change gears with lever shift. Much fun!"

"Jeeps are fun Billy," Doss agreed. "You mean a stick shift."

"Stick shift. Ok, ok, good for you!"

"And?" Adelman asked, obviously growing impatient as he slumped back in his chair, feeling achy, tired and bored.

"Ok, so sorry I speak bad English. We get stuck in wet Georgia dirt, ah, clay, red, rotten goo, bad, bad stuff. Like superglue. I tell Dr. Simpson I get soldiers to dig out. Dr. Simpson laugh, say to me, no, watch Billy. He put Toyota in four gear low. He reach to roof with buttons. One button for sand, one for mud, one for water, one for gravel, one for ice and snow. He press mud button with finger, tires grab earth and we go out! Wonderful fun! Me laugh so hard I cry!"

"Billy, I'm glad you had fun," Adelman said impatiently. "What does any of this have to do with your work?"

"Modes," Doss offered softly.

Adelman turned to Doss. "What?" he asked, confused.

"Billy has just given us an analogy related to switching control modes to react to the surrounding environment."

"Modes!" Billy said excitedly. "Yes, yes, modes! You get it, Max! You scientist now! We find *Swan* deep in ocean, yes Herr Direktor?"

"Yes, Billy, that is correct."

"We have *Swan* in hangar on dry earth. Maybe *Swan* no do

anything, no ah, no react, because it in wrong mode! It in sea mode maybe. If Dr. Simpson take Toyota on highway in four high and press mud mode, Toyota no respond. Must be in four low. If you try start Toyota in drive, it no work, must be in park or neutral mode. Yes?"

Adelman suddenly sat upright in his chair. "Huh. What a fascinating connection. An interesting theory, Billy. How do we test your theory?"

"I want to build big, big fish tank around *Swan*, fill tank with seawater. Maybe something start. Maybe not. We try. No harm."

"Assuming your plan works, won't the doors remain closed? The doors, I would think, will have safety locks to prevent an accidental opening while underwater, or in space for that matter."

"Quite so, Herr Direktor. Bingo! We attach air tunnel with vacuum seal where we think access door located, like when men need to get inside broken submarine. We trick door safeties. Admiral no approve big expense unless big boss say yes."

"Big boss says yes, Billy."

"Wonderful!"

"Why seawater, Billy?" Doss asked. "Wouldn't fresh water work just as well? Be a lot easier to fill the tank with freshwater. After all, we're a few miles from the ocean."

"I think seawater because it denser, has other different properties than freshwater. Seawater closer to environment we find *Blue Swan* in."

"Our submarines operate in freshwater, brackish water, or seawater."

"True, true. Very logical Max. Ok, we try freshwater first. Not lose much time if no work."

But Duc's trickery did work. Five days later Adelman and Doss returned to Kings Bay with *Blue Swan* sitting inside a clear, plexiglass tank filled with water, with scientists and engineers moving in and out of the alien ship through a ribbed, accordion-like white tube. Twenty-four black body bags, eight-foot-long bags, were laid out in a neat row against a far wall.

Adelman hurried through the tube and stepped into *Blue Swan* for the first time with Doss a leg behind him. The interior was awash in scores of bright lights, lights affixed to tripods set up by Duc's technicians. Duc looked down on them from the *Swan's* neck, a conning tower or command deck of sorts, offered a triumphant grin and rushed down a spiral staircase to greet them.

"Well done, Billy!" Adelman said excitedly and vigorously shook Duc's hand. "The body bags outside contain alien remains?"

"Yes, just bones, clothing, hair. Except one child with necklace."

"A child and a necklace, interesting; what else have you discovered?" Adelman asked as he took in his surroundings. Hollywood's sci-fi imagineers weren't far off the mark he thought to himself.

"Bad news, good news, Herr Direktor."

"Well, let's have it."

"Good news, we inside. We analyzing, testing and learning."

"But?"

"Bad news. One key component damaged," Duc said and pointed to a gray box about the size of a car battery sitting on top of a control panel. "We think it something like a motherboard, or maybe something simpler, like transformer or junction box. Whatever is it, ah, I mean whatever it is, this critical component. It fried."

"This vessel," Doss asked, "runs on electrical circuitry?"

"No. Aliens be masters of light."

"Laser power?" Doss asked.

"No, no. Laser technology to them like bow and arrow technology to us. Too crude."

"Can the box be repaired?" Adelman asked.

Duc shrugged his shoulders. "No one know. Probably, but maybe take months, maybe years to understand and fix."

"We have nothing?" Adelman asked, suddenly feeling very dejected and old. "Billy, we don't have years. We may not have months. The President of the United States will ship you and me back to Germany if we don't produce results soon. And if she does, the Germans will most likely shoot us both."

Duc smiled. "Good news, good news, Herr Direktor. *Cigar* has component onboard, look same. Maybe compatible. I see no damage when I working alongside Germans. Very bright, Germans. But little imagination. We need *Cigar* box. No good to Germans. Make trade, yes? All good?"

"We'll see, Billy," Adelman said absently, lost in thought. "May Max and I borrow your office for a few minutes? Thank you."

"Two steps forward and one step back," Adelman said wistfully as he took a seat behind Duc's desk, shaking his head in frustration. "Max, the Germans don't really have the *Cigar*, leastwise, not the legitimate German authorities."

"I assumed as much, sir. The Council has taken possession of *Cigar*?"

"Yes. Even if the legitimate German authorities were still in control, I doubt very much they'd just hand over this mysterious box to us, certainly not without some form of quid pro quo. Now it doesn't matter who has it. What matters is that I know where the *Cigar* is and you are going to get that damn box for Duc."

"And where is *Cigar*?"

"Oh, you're going to love this, Max. During World War II, the Nazis, employing slave labor from nearby concentration camps, built a number of underground war production factories to avoid Allied bombers. One - designated B-8 Bergkristall - is a large underground complex covering seventy-five acres close to the town of Sankt Georgen an der Gusen in Upper Austria. Apparently, the Nazis built fuselages there for their Messerschmitt Me-262s, the world's first operational jet fighter. Saint George is a small market town and while little of the B-8 facility remains intact today, in 2014, another huge Nazi underground factory, probably meant for production of WMDs, was discovered adjacent to B-8. This is where the Council has moved the *Cigar*."

"How do you know this Herr Direktor?"

"The Council has their spies and I have mine."

"Why Austria?"

"Saint George isn't far from Munich and is a tad more secluded, for starters. More importantly, the Council has a very tight grip on Austria. Many key government officials in Austria, even though Austria has been subsumed into Germany, are, in fact, Council loyalists."

"Austria is lovely this time of year."

"True, Max. Ordinarily, I'd ask for a risk assessment and

feasibility study on breaching such a facility prepared - but we have no time for that. Do you understand?"

"I do," Doss replied as he Googled Sankt Georgen an der Gusen on his phone. "We wouldn't want the job to be too easy now, would we? Do we have blueprints of the facility?"

"No. They didn't survive the war."

"Do we know how large the facility is?"

"B-8 was seventy-five acres. This other facility was built later in the war and with Germany's dwindling resources, my guess is this facility is smaller. But, for all I know, it could be larger."

"Pictures?"

"A few, but not particularly useful."

"Number of foot soldiers at the facility?"

"Unknown, but you know the site will be heavily guarded with no easy entranceways in or get-a-way routes out. You know security will be first tier and we won't be able to do any on-the-ground reconnaissance lest we trigger some hidden warning system and tip off the Council."

"We go in blind?"

"I'm sorry Max, but yes."

"Closest military bases?"

"Vogler Air Base next to Hörsching Airport in Linz, roughly fifteen kilometers west of Saint George. It's primarily a repair facility for C-130s and helos, but typically there is a regiment or two of attack helicopters stationed there. No army bases nearby. Forty-three kilometers west of Saint George is Flugplatz Wels, a small, private airport with a forty-five-hundred-foot runway that might prove useful."

"You've thought this through."

"I wouldn't be very good at my job if I hadn't."

Doss squinted his eyes at Adelman. "You knew we might need this mission someday."

"I wasn't certain, but I suspected we might. In my position, Max, you try to anticipate every contingency. I've had surveillance teams watching *Cigar* for some time. I wanted to relieve the Germans of *Cigar* a few months back before the vessel was moved out of Great Germany, as I didn't want to risk losing her location - in the event *Blue Swan* was a bust - but I was overruled."

Chapter Twenty-One

Within 24 hours after leaving Kings Bay, Doss had a plan. Within 36 hours after that, he had assembled an assault team, an extraction team and a technical support team made up of six Project Swan scientists handpicked by Duc. Doss had everyone gather at a modest hangar occasionally used by the CIA near Andrews Air Force Base in Maryland.

"People," Doss said with a laser light pointer in his hand as he began to address over 100 men and women standing around a vast map of Austria stretched out across the hangar floor. Adelman, who had already blessed Doss's plan, stood off in a corner as an observer with Duc at his side.

"We are going here," he continued as he pointed his laser at the map, "to this small town in Austria called Sankt Georgen an der Gusen - Saint George. Our mission is to recover several critical components from a highly secret object dubbed the *Cigar* by the Germans because that is what it looks like. Don't ask me what the *Cigar* is because I don't know, but the *Cigar* was recently stolen from the Germans by a fanatical political fringe group and taken to an old underground facility built by the Nazis during World War Two. The *Cigar* is about twenty feet in diameter and over one hundred feet in length, making the object too big for us to recover, at least not within our limited time window. This mission is vital to our national security. It has been given an Alpha-1-Xray Top Priority Mission designation. Yeah, that's right, serious stuff. Failure is not an option.

"We know almost nothing about the facility or the facility's security but rest assured people, the facility will be extremely well-protected with all the latest high-tech gadgets and the elite security forces guarding the *Cigar* will shoot to kill without warning, without hesitation. First order of the day, rules of engagement: we go in hot. We shoot to kill. Treat this exercise like any highly dangerous combat mission of extreme importance. Understood? Good. Lieutenant

Wagner, welcome back."

"Thank you, sir."

"You and your pilots ready for this?"

"Aye, aye, sir!"

"Good. Navy Lieutenant Wagner and her pilots will be flying out tonight for the Med to hook up with *Iwo Jima*, a Wasp Class LHD carrier operating off the coast of Italy. *Iwo Jima* is carrying a dozen newly minted V-280A2 Valor tiltrotors the Navy has graciously agreed to loan us. Each Valor is configured for assault missions and can transport fourteen fully equipped combat troops, that's one hundred sixty personnel total, more than we should need, but it's always good to have a spare. Isn't that right, Wagner?"

"Roger that, sir!"

"From *Iwo Jima*, Lieutenant Wagner will lead her squadron here, to Flugplatz Wels, a small private airport forty-three klicks west of Saint George. The rest of us will fly in on two C-130-J Super Hercules, refitted with the latest in stealth technology. The Army is leasing the entire airfield just for us. Wels will be our staging area and primary rendezvous point after we complete the mission. As you know, President Dreyfuss has ordered five divisions into Europe to participate in war games with our European friends. We use that as our cover. We will be arriving as an advance party for 1st Air Cav. Word will spread among the locals through the 1st Cav public relations officer that Wagner's tiltrotors will be practicing SAR drills and recon missions day and night around the countryside between Linz and Saint George. The Valors shouldn't set off any alarm bells.

"We already have a team on the ground in place. These folks will be dressed in Military Police uniforms on mission day. They will preposition various trucks and Humvees near the target, along with one barge on the Danube anchored here and three go-fast boats tied to the barge. Once the assault begins, the MPs will direct the town folk to leave. The trucks, the barge and the go-fast boats are all decoys and once we have what we came for, and the Tech Team has replaced any components they remove from the *Cigar* with fake duplicates, three of Lieutenant Wagner's tiltrotors will recover the Extraction team and the Tech team at this large farm field here, just north of Saint George, with alternate LZ recovery points here and here. The MPs will simultaneously move out with the vehicles and disperse. The bad guys will need to decide which vehicles to chase, if they decide to chase anything at all, because we will make it look as if we were trying to steal the *Cigar* itself and failed. Their first priority will be to protect the asset, not chase us. The Assault Team will take the barge and the go-fast boats over to the west side of the Danube and from there move on foot to this quarry on Kronau Road, where nine of Wagner's tiltrotors will be waiting. With luck, the hostiles will decide to secure the *Cigar* and the facility not realizing we took the components, and leave any pursuit of us to other resources, which will be too late by then as we'll be long gone. Questions so far? Good.

"I will be leading the Assault Team of one hundred personnel. Assault Team will secure the outer perimeter, breach the entrance and neutralize all hostiles we encounter inside. Major Murry, who some of you have served with before, will lead the Extraction Team of twenty along with the Tech Team of six scientists. When all is clear, the Extraction Team will escort the Tech Team into the facility to do their thing. The Extraction Team will protect the scientists and the components at all costs. We'll all rendezvous back at Flugplatz Wels. The two C-130s we flew in with will be standing by, one to transport the Extraction Team, the scientists, and the components out of Austria, and the other to transport the rest of us. Lieutenant Wagner will return the tiltrotors to *Iwo Jima*. Anyone left behind will scatter and catch different civilian flights back to the U.S. Just to be clear: the mission doesn't end until the components we came for are in our possession and are secured.

"Well, that's the good if everything goes according to plan. Now for the bad and the ugly. You all volunteered for this, so buckle in. We have no blueprints. We have only a few old pictures of small portions of the facility. It's not much. Copies of those pics and an artist's rendering of the *Cigar* are included in your folders, along with maps, travel cash, forged IDs, passports, and burner phones with emergency contact numbers should you get separated and trouble finds you. Our intel is only aware of one way in and one way out of the facility. There must be alternate entrances, ventilation shafts, HVAC equipment, access plates and the like somewhere on the grounds above the facility, but we haven't located any by satellite and we don't have time to take a closer look via air or ground recon. We know that the entrance doors are not blast-rated bunker doors. They're one-inch steel. In a week or two they'll be replaced with blast-rated doors - thus the urgency of the mission. We'll be going in and out of the front door. We'll need to hit the facility fast and hard. We don't know the quality of our opponent, his weaponry, or his numbers. We don't know what air or ground support capabilities he might have. We are going in blind.

"Deception. Deception ladies and gentlemen is the key to the success of this mission, along with surprise of course, speed and good aim. We will be fighting at night within an area populated with civilians who, no doubt, will be terrified when they hear explosions and gunfire close by. If the Austrians scramble their security forces to intervene, Washington will instruct the Austrians to stand down and declare that chemical weapons have been deployed by terrorists in Saint George. That ruse won't hold up for long, so we need to work quickly and leave quietly.

"We are now in total lockdown. Nothing you've heard or seen here tonight can ever be discussed with anyone outside this hangar. Apart from the people in this room, you don't take orders from anyone during this mission and I mean anyone unless it is the President of the United States speaking to you in person. Questions?"

After a lot of questions, suggestions and a few minor tweaks to the plan, Adelman walked over and pulled Doss aside. "Simple plans are best," he said reassuringly, then handed Doss a flask.

"Yes, sir. I hope we haven't missed something. The missions that go sideways are the ones with little, bad, or no intel or rushed like this one. And the Austrian government may be a problem if some of their key decision-makers are compromised, as we suspect."

"People, even the best of us, Max, make mistakes, equipment unexpectedly fails, maps or intel is wrong, something, an obstacle, suddenly appears where it shouldn't be, occasionally we even need to deal with betrayal - we do the best we can with what we have and improvise as needed. It is a good plan, Max, and you've assembled an outstanding group of men and women to execute it."

Doss nodded his appreciation and took a sip of scotch from Adelman's flask. "How the devil did you get the captain of *Iwo Jima* to hand over twelve Valors to us with no written orders from his fleet commander?"

"I convinced the President, and I do mean *the* President, to expand his inner circle with a few more military types. Captain Leslie Jackson of *Iwo Jima* is a first-rate commander, a patriot, and is now happily ensconced as a part of President Calhoun's inner circle."

"Same with convincing the Army to lease Flugplatz Wels for us?"

Adelman smiled and patted Doss on the chest. "Always good to have friends in high places, my boy. Remember that, you may be me someday."

"And if we fail? You have a contingency plan, don't you?"

"You won't fail. But if you do, I have a second team standing by. They'll bury *Cigar* in hundreds of tons of radioactive rubble, and then we'll go back and try again with a different plan. As you so astutely noted: this mission doesn't end until we have the components."

Two days following Doss's mission briefing at Andrews, a pair of C-130-J Super Hercules aircraft carrying a half dozen scientists, 120 special ops personnel and a couple of tiltrotor maintenance technicians set down at night at Flugplatz Wels in Austria and taxied over to 12 Valor tiltrotors parked in a neat row off to the side of the runway. A Lieutenant Colonel of the 1st Air Cav met Doss outside the airport's small one-story terminal and, in accordance with the strict orders given to him by his commanding officer, he made no statements and asked no questions. He saluted, promptly evacuated his men from the area in the Army's new JLTV Raptors and left behind ten FMTV A-2 cargo trucks and 12, 3,000-gallon capacity aviation refuelers.

Doss wasted no time. With the MP ground team already in place, scattered in and around Saint George, he had his team load into the ten cargo trucks with their gear and led the convoy from the airfield to the City of Linz and then headed south until they turned off onto a forest service road alongside the Danube near Abwinden, a small village adjacent to Saint George and less than a mile away from the facility. Doss stopped the convoy when he saw the barge and three go-fast boats anchored in a small inlet a short distance away.

He stepped off the passenger side of the lead truck, took a

moment to savor the crisp, clean air and glanced up at the brilliant stars, the Milky Way, scattered across black heavens stretching far into infinity. He weighed his peek into eternity against his own insignificant mortality, accepted the fact that he might die before morning and passed the word to check commo, weapons and gear.

"Twenty-three hundred hours and ten minutes, mark," he said after he called his team leaders to his side. Everyone synchronized their watches to his - old-school stuff - and then he turned to Bijeau. "Alejandra, you're up."

"Roger that!" she replied enthusiastically with a wide grin, as if she was about to embark upon an enjoyable hike through the Alps. She led her scouting party of 20, dressed in green camouflage BDUs, combat boots, black watch caps and carrying tactical rucksacks, up the forest road towards Saint George. Beauvilliers, with her platoon of 30, fell in behind Bijeau, then Doss fell in behind Beauvilliers with his main assault force of 50 while Murry and the rest brought up the rear.

Bijeau split her team into five squads, marching in four-man columns spaced 20 yards apart, and led them through farm fields on the east side of Abwinden while Beauvilliers slipped over to the right flank and deployed her platoon into a skirmish line. Doss fell in behind Beauvilliers and Murry fell in behind Doss. When they reached the outskirts of Saint George, they found a sleepy, little county town well-lit by street lamps and outdoor house lights. Except for a barking dog or two, one stray cat and a gentle breeze rustling through the trees, all was quiet. Within 150 yards of the facility's entrance, Doss had everyone drop to the ground, and they crawled the rest of the way on their bellies - avoiding several cleverly placed sensors - over to a long grove of tall evergreens.

"Bravo One," Doss whispered into his mic to Bijeau while he waved Beauvilliers and Murry to his side. "Hold your position, you are the anchor on the left flank. Do you have good fields of fire on the hostiles in front of the entrance?"

"That's affirmative, Mission Leader."

"Prepare to neutralize," he said as he scanned the area with his night vision binoculars one last time and then looked over at Beauvilliers. "Maddie, move Charlie Team to the north, skirt over to the west, create a defensive perimeter around the general vicinity. You hold our right flank. Prevent any reinforcements from reaching the entrance. Go now. Murry, once I give you the all clear, you know what to do."

Twelve men dressed in black fatigues and black berets, with a pair of German Army sixteen-wheeled ARTEC Boxers armed with heavy machine guns parked close by, stood guard in front of two steel doors set at an angle against an earthen berm. With submachine guns slung casually over their shoulders, the men, chatting, laughing and smoking cigarettes, seemed to be in a mellow mood.

Doss called Adelman on his satellite phone. "Hotel-Delta, we're in position," he whispered. "Two Boxers, a dozen mercs, guard the entrance. Permission to engage?"

"Facility security confirmed to be hostiles," Adelman replied. "Mission is a go, I repeat, mission is a go. Good hunting Mission Leader."

A few moments later, two terrifying explosions and multiple gunshots rocked the sleepy town of Saint George. The twin Boxers went up in flames after being hit by a pair of 110 mm rocket-propelled HEAT grenades launched from two handheld German Panzerfausts, while Bijeau and the rest of her squad simultaneously took out the twelve guards. Their listless bodies dropped gracefully in unison like a troupe of marionettes severed from their strings.

"Demolitions with me!" Doss cried out as he jumped to his feet and rushed towards the entrance. He could feel his heart racing, could feel the raw adrenaline pumping through his body and used both to his advantage. His mind was keen, alert and laser focused. He relished the joy of the hunt. He was born to lead men into action and felt no guilt about it.

"Shape charges set, sir!" the lead demolition man exclaimed excitedly.

"Fallback, take cover!" Doss shouted.

The demolition team did its job. The explosions were enough to bring down the double steel doors, but not powerful enough to cause a cave-in. Doss led his team of 50 forward and was the first to step through the breach. He entered a long, narrow tunnel filled with smoke and dust and started walking. A string of lights hanging along the walls started flickering and then went dark. Doss stumbled over rubble and bodies before he could slip his helmet over his head and switch on his night vision goggles.

Then a man beside him raised a handheld radar device to show Doss the green images on a screen. "Fifty feet, next right sir, looks like a large bay area with folks frantically moving about a large cylindrical object. I count about twenty-plus souls inside."

Doss repeated what his radarman had told him over his mic to his team leaders. When they reached a steel hatch door with a locking wheel blocking their way, Doss's demolitions team set three small breaching charges against the hatch, one on each hinge and one on the wheel and blew the door clean off.

Doss removed his helmet and goggles, stepped into the opening, caught his first glimpse of the *Cigar* but immediately stepped back into the tunnel when he was met with a barrage of automatic weapons fire. "Two men, flashbang grenades, now!" he ordered.

A pair of men with grenades in each hand stepped forward and simultaneously tossed four grenades into the bay. One man stepped back into the tunnel unharmed. The other toppled over, clutching at his throat. His body tumbled down a short, grate metal staircase into the bay. After the grenades exploded, Doss rushed inside, spraying the area with bullets, with his team following close behind. The *Cigar*, bathed in floodlight and resting up on pedestals and attached to cables and pulleys hanging down from a retractable roof, sat in the middle of the bay. Technicians in white coats started fleeing towards a second door across the bay as a handful of mercs hastily formed a semi-circle and took a knee to provide them cover. Doss and his men fanned out, circled around both ends of the *Cigar* and overwhelmed the last of the mercs with a brutal barrage of hollow-points tipped in ruthless copper.

When the shooting stopped, Doss took a moment to survey the bay and reload. The technicians who had fled through the back locked the door behind them. A heap of dead and wounded bodies lay scattered across a concrete floor. Four of the dead were his. When a control panel sitting on a wheeled cart with power cables running into the *Cigar* suddenly hissed at him and exploded into flame, he yanked the cables out of the panel and kicked the cart aside. And then he had his men move their dead and wounded outside and ordered the Extraction Team inside.

"Dr. Fuller," Doss called out to the lead scientist as Murry and his team stepped into the bay a few minutes later. "There's *Cigar*. Get what you need and be quick about it!"

"Mission Leader, this is Charlie One, over," Doss heard Beauvilliers say anxiously into his earpiece over the command channel.

"Charlie One, Mission Leader, over."

"Beaucoup activity up here, Mission Leader. Civilians running wild in the streets in panic. Mike-Papas have their hands full directing them out of town. Four black SUVs moving fast to your position, probable hostiles, over."

"Bravo One, you copy last from Charlie One?" Doss asked.

"Roger that," Bijeau answered. "Permission to neutralize SUVs if they approach our position."

"Affirmative," Doss replied. And then he heard shooting close to the entrance of the facility. He poked his head inside the *Cigar*. "Doc, you have maybe ten minutes tops, move faster."

Fuller nodded nervously as he and his five colleagues continued removing tools and instruments from their duffle bags and hastily went to work.

"Charlie One, sit rep," Doss asked.

"Taking heavy fire, Mission Leader," Beauvilliers replied. "Twenty, maybe thirty hostiles from the town, attacking our position. *Putain!* We are fighting *Groupe d'intervention de la Gendarmerie nationale* - GIGN!"

"You certain of that, Charlie One?"

"They're speaking French and carrying Heckler and Koch MP-5s favored by GIGN. They're dressed in the special ops intervention uniforms worn by GIGN, a one-piece black overall. Wait, I hear diesel motors cranking over. Two, no, three Boxers approaching my position with infantry support. Say again three Boxers approaching my position with infantry support, platoon strength!"

"Fall back to the entrance now," Doss ordered. He knew Beauvilliers's team was spread out too thin, was too exposed to hold off that many mercs, especially professionals with armor. "Bravo One, move forward, support Charlie Team with covering fire to the east and west. Avoid friendlies."

"Gotcha covered Charlie Leader," Bijeau replied. "Turning into a shitshow up here, Mission Leader. Hostiles are laying down suppressive fire at civilians and their homes as they move forward towards us. Fuckers are indiscriminately killing everyone in sight."

Doss grabbed one of the sergeants by the shoulder. "Gleason, right?"

"Good memory, sir."

"You're Alpha One now. Take your team and reinforce Bravo and Charlie. Deploy your team however you think best. It's turning ugly fast up there. I'll stay behind with the Extraction Team. You need to buy us more time."

"Roger that sir," Gleason said, then turned and waved an arm forward. "Alpha Team on me! Outside, now!"

"Air One, Mission Leader," Doss called out to Wagner, who was flying combat air patrol over the town with her squadron.

"Air One, over," Wagner answered.

"Anything coming down the pike outside of town towards us?"

"Negative."

"Peel off a couple of birds, take out the hostile SUVs and the Boxers."

"On the way Mission Leader."

Long minutes passed as Doss listened to the intense fighting raging above the facility. He knew the fight was deteriorating into a bloodbath. He heard automatic weapons fire, heavy machine gun fire and explosions from fragmentation grenades. Then he heard the initial explosions, three in all, made by AGM-114 Hellfire missiles - by air-to-ground anti-armor missiles - and the secondary explosions that follow a direct hit on armor.

He desperately wanted to go outside and join the fight but knew his place was with the *Cigar*. "Fuller," he barked as he stepped inside the alien ship. "How much more time?"

"We're wrapping up."

"Do you have the box?"

"This is the grand prize," Fuller replied proudly as he pulled the box out of his bag to show Doss. "And we found three other interesting items."

"Excellent work," a deep, gravelly voice behind Doss, a heavy smoker's voice, called out. "I'll take those."

Doss felt a muzzle pressing against his spine and raised his hands above his head. He slowly turned around to find Murry smiling up at him with his handgun pointing at his chest.

"How far do you think you'll get Murry?" Doss asked as he slowly stepped down from the *Cigar* and saw they were alone. Murry had ordered his entire team out of the bay and appeared to be working solo.

Then a single shot rang out. "Too slow," Murry said and chuckled as Fuller fell over dead. "You there, Doctor, whatever the fuck your name is, hand me those two duffle bags with the goods, and then, Doss, you are going to order your teams to fall back to the river."

"Spies within spies within spies," Doss said softly. "Like those Russian Matryoshka dolls."

"What the fuck does that mean, Doss?" Murry asked and pointed his handgun at Doss's head. "You, Herr Direktor, what's left of the country, you're all relics of a broken past. The New World Order is here and no one can stop it. The old order is dead, just doesn't know it yet."

"How much are they paying you, Murry?"

"More than you could make in a hundred lifetimes. Now hand me the fucking bags and give the order for everyone to retreat."

"How will you leave here alive with no one to help you?" Doss asked, baiting Murry to see if he'd disclose whether there were others in his team who were working with him.

"You let me worry about that, Doss," Murry replied, then turned his handgun on the scientist holding the two duffle bags. "If I have to ask for those bags one more fucking time, you die."

The man quickly handed the bags over to Doss and Doss, in turn, was about to hand the bags over to Murry - as he thought how best to kill him. Instead, he only needed to nod.

Murry reflexively spun around to see if someone was sneaking up behind him and caught a bullet in the forehead for his effort. His body hit the concrete floor hard.

"Whew, good timing Sanchez," Doss said with a wide grin, relieved he didn't need to test his speed against Murry's. "Thank you."

"No worries, sir."

"Adelman added you to the team at the last minute. You working for him? This was your assignment?"

"Best ask him, sir."

"Right. You're Echo One now and in command of the Extraction Team. Find me a way to the primary LZ, Sergeant."

"On it, sir."

"And have Demolitions blow whatever this *Cigar* thing is off its blocks. Leave the winching cables and winching equipment behind. Make it look like we failed to take the odd contraption with us."

"Straight away, sir."

"Alpha One, Bravo One, Charlie One, Air One, this is Mission Leader," Doss shouted into his mic over the command channel. "Prepare to disengage and evac. Extraction Team is on the move. Rendezvous at Foxtrot-Whiskey, I say again, rendezvous Foxtrot-Whiskey!"

"Alpha One acknowledges last transmission to evac to Foxtrot-Whiskey."

"Bravo One, copy same."

"Charlie One acknowledges."

"Air One, on the way to designated extraction points."

"This is Mission Leader. I'm staying with the Extraction Team. Stay sharp. We're not home free yet."

"Mission Leader, this is Mike-Papa Leader, we're hauling ass out of here too. We're taking your dead and wounded with us. Godspeed."

"Appreciate what you and your men did," Doss replied. "Fine work, thank you. Mission Leader out."

And then Doss's satellite phone vibrated. "Mission Leader, Hotel-Delta here. Do you have the package?"

"Affirmative Hotel-Delta."

"Well done. Any complications?"

"Extraction Team Leader won't be celebrating with us."

Adelman let out a long sigh. "A certain Master Sergeant Sanchez had your back?"

"Affirmative."

"Safe travels home, Mission Leader."

When Doss emerged from the main tunnel, he saw an entire town engulfed in flames, along with many burning civilian and military vehicles. He saw dozens of bodies lying on the ground too, most were dressed in black overalls but there were plenty of civilian bodies too. He paused to search the pockets of one of the dead hostiles, but found nothing. Then he started looking for tattoos and found one. He recognized the words *Ils s'instruisent pour vaincre* tattooed over a sword and shield on one man's right shoulder, the motto and insignia of the *École spéciale militaire de Saint-Cyr*, France's equivalent of West Point.

After they returned to Flugplatz Wels in the tiltrotors, with Murry's treachery fresh on his mind, Doss decided against using the two C-130-J Super Hercules sitting on the runway to transport everyone out of Austria. He decided to mix things up instead. He sent most of the team back home on the C-130s but once Wagner's tiltrotors had been refueled, he took the scientists, the duffle bags, Bijeau, Beauvilliers, and 20 men who had served with him before, and flew back to Iwo Jima with Wagner and her team.

Iwo Jima had been steaming at flank speed up the Adriatic Sea along the east coast of Italy for several hours towards Trieste, to make Wagner's return flight short and easy. Doss sat back and reviewed a list of casualties during the brief flight. The mission had cost him 27 dead, including Fuller and Murry, and 35 wounded. His unit had suffered nearly 50% casualties. Bijeau, with a flesh wound to her right thigh, and Beauvilliers with a deep bruise and a fractured collarbone caused by a ricochet from a 7.62mm armor piercing round, that might have been lethal had the round not imbedded itself in her thick shoulder harness and body armor first, were among the wounded. Doss had been on costlier missions, but he couldn't remember when and that had been in wartime.

Twenty-four hours after touching down aboard *Iwo Jima*, Doss's 20-man security detail was sitting comfortably aboard a private jet in Trieste sent over by Adelman, taking full advantage of an open bar, while Doss and his lionesses, the five scientists and the alien components, were transferred over to a vessel nobody could track, the Virginia class, nuclear-powered submarine SSN-803 *Arizona*. Within minutes after her guests step aboard, the sub slips beneath the waves and her captain, a seasoned pro, a diehard Union man with a loyal crew, instructs the officer of the watch to plot a course, the fastest route, to their secret destination: Kings Bay.

Chapter Twenty-Two

Excerpts from Hermann Adelman's private journal:
The Great Turmoil

Oh what cruel sorrows mankind reaps when the lessons of the past are ignored, forgotten, or tossed into the gutter like trash. Even the innocent, even the little children, must suffer.

Just as the coming of Genghis Khan over 800 years earlier had filled their ancestors with foreboding and dread, the coming of Temüjin now paralyzes Europeans and their governments with sheer terror. Temüjin and his vast legions are standing at the gates of Europe and Europeans, except for a token American expeditionary force, standalone on the ramparts to face him and no one is coming to help them.

Stromquist uses this fear and paralysis to great advantage. Unlike Hitler, Stalin, or Mussolini in the last century, Stromquist doesn't waste his extraordinary powers of persuasion on seducing the masses. He continues to beguile the elites instead with his charm and impeccable intellect. With promises of a peaceful, enlightened world united once the Mongolian threat is dealt with, he rallies the influential, the rich and the powerful to his banner. As Temüjin bides his time and fine-tunes his battle plans, the Council's influence over governments all across the globe increases exponentially.

Great Germany was understandably livid at the attack on her soil. The newly elected German Chancellor expressed outrage but did little more than that. Austrians were confused and appalled by the slaughter. The lack of any meaningful response by the government angered everyone. Then the Chancellor of Great Germany, together with the President of France, issued a joint statement claiming that a terrorist cell loyal to Temüjin had been discovered making bombs at the old Nazi underground factory in Saint George and that a joint task force of elite counter-terrorist teams from both countries had killed the terrorists and had destroyed all the bombs.

But there were many eyewitnesses to the attack, and this explanation confused and infuriated people even more. Austrians began asking questions. Why weren't the town folk of Saint George given any forewarning of an imminent terrorist threat? Why weren't they evacuated before the assault? Why had the terrorists left the protection of the facility to fight in the streets? Why had they not set off any bombs? How did the terrorists acquire five German Bundeswehr armored vehicles? Why did the counter-terrorist task force remove their dead and wounded and not help treat civilian wounded? Who had abandoned ten American Army cargo trucks along the Danube? And why had French security forces prevented the Austrian federal police from entering the facility, a crime scene, for nearly forty-eight hours? And when the police finally were permitted inside, why was the old Nazi facility empty? Rumors sprouted up like wild mushrooms all across Europe and no one seemed satisfied by the official explanations offered by France or Great Germany.

The men and women sitting around the table in one of the White House's Situation Rooms engaged in small chitchat while munching on snacks as they waited for the President. Dreyfus had called an emergency meeting to begin at noon. When she burst into the room at 12:45, with eyes full of fury and an armful of folders, she glanced around the table, looking for a victim.

"Who can explain this cluster-fuck of an operation in Austria to me?" She asked angrily and took her seat. "Who the hell authorized this abortion? I certainly didn't. The Austrians claim American soldiers may have participated. Really? By God, if true, I'll root out these traitorous rogues by any means necessary. Heads will roll!"

When no one dared to speak, Dreyfus took a moment to consider the faces around the table and stopped at Adelman. "Herr Direktor, you are never shy about sharing your opinions. You always have something to say. What say you now?"

"I'm confused Madam President. You didn't authorize this counter-insurgency? Are you suggesting this was a rogue operation by U.S. forces in league with France and Germany? Unthinkable!"

"Do you know anything or not, Adelman?"

"I only know what Germany and France have told the world. A major terrorist threat was neutralized in Austria. Though I have no credible intel that this was the work of the Mongolians, I suppose it's possible. But why a small town in Austria, of all places, I wonder? Why now? Were there any nuclear, chemical, or biological weapons recovered from the site, or even any trace residue of any such weapons found?"

"Remind me, Adelman, what is your title?"

"I am the head of Section M3."

"Ah-ha. And what is my title?"

"You are the President of the United States."

"Which of us has the higher rank, the greater authority?"

"Why, you do Madam President."

"Good Herr Direktor, good. *THEN I WILL ASK THE FUCKING QUESTIONS!*"

"As you wish Madam President. What I know is what the Germans and French have stated publicly. I may have been born in Germany, but I am an American, have been for years now. My loyalties are unequivocally with America. I want to learn the truth about this matter as much as anyone in this room."

"The truth Adelman? Wouldn't that be refreshing? But what is the truth? I'll tell you. The truth is nineteen Austrian civilians were killed during the raid on this mysterious facility, five of them children, and thirty-nine others were seriously wounded, many are in critical condition. More will die. American soldiers may have been involved. American military helicopters were seen flying in the vicinity. American military vehicles were found abandoned near Saint George. And, if you can believe anything the French are saying, nothing was found inside the facility. The truth is the Mongolians deny any involvement and I've seen no evidence to the contrary that would implicate them. The truth is no one around this table seems to know anything about any of this. The truth is, I goddamn hate - with a goddamn passion - being in the dark. General Phillips, any updates on these ten U.S. Army trucks the Austrians found?"

"Yes, Madam President. These A-2s belong to the 1st Air Cav Division. The trucks disappeared off the docks at Marseilles sometime after being offloaded. That is to say, they were stolen."

"Did we have any troops on the ground at Saint George?"

"No, Madam President. Not to my knowledge, and I've made all the appropriate inquiries."

"Well, I want a full investigation. The Agency, CIA and NSA are stretched to the limit. Herr Direktor, things at your Section appear slow. I want you to conduct the investigation."

"But Madam President -."

"But nothing. For once, just do what your President tells you to do."

"As you command Madam President, so shall it be done."

Two weeks after meeting with the President, Adelman returned to Kings Bay. Doss, back from Austria, and Duc were there to greet him when his small private jet landed at a small private airfield operated by the Navy.

"You have the ship working under her own power, I understand," Adelman stated excitedly as he stepped off the plane with an obvious bounce in his step.

"Yes, yes," Duc replied enthusiastically with a broad, proud smile as they walked towards the hangar. "The *Cigar* box Max return with work perfectly. Still much to learn."

"Show me."

The plexiglass water tank and air tunnel had been removed. All around the vessel, access panels, hatches, and doors had been opened, and the ship was generating her own power. Duc and Doss led Adelman into an inner hull awash in soft, blue light, coming from no discernable source, light teeming with curious, tiny white sparkles slowly twirling and bouncing through the air like dancing snowflakes on a calm winter's night. Consoles and panels around the ship were alive with various solid, flashing, and sequential lights of assorted colors. Floating above one console, resembling a dashboard, multiple pulsating halos were spinning around in circles as they passed through one another. A low humming noise, coupled with soft thumping sounds, echoed throughout the ship.

But Adelman was disappointed that Duc and his team understood very little beyond how to power the ship up, power the ship down and how to open the doors, panels, and hatches, though earlier that day the team had at least learned how to operate the ship's environmental and climate regulator system. "The air is safe?" Adelman asked.

"Oh, yes. Refreshing to breathe, yes? All clean. No hazards. We still understanding white particles, some kind of enriched oxygen crystal for good health, we think."

"This is all well and good Billy," Adelman said as he and Doss followed Duc back to his office. "Men paid dearly with their lives for the components we brought back, including one of yours, Dr. Fuller. Regrettably, innocent civilians, children too, died. But far more will die if we fail to learn the secrets of *Blue Swan* and master those secrets quickly. You have brought her back to life Billy, this is a huge accomplishment, a momentous breakthrough. But now we must get her up and out of this hospital."

"Soon, soon, I think Herr Direktor," Duc replied with a hint of disappointment in his face.

Adelman caught the look and patted Duc reassuringly on the shoulder. "You've done fine, fine work, Billy. Remarkable work. I'm sorry if I sound ungrateful. I'm not. As you know, Temüjin has stopped his armies just miles outside the Zhukov Line. This is a man on a mission and yet he hasn't moved for nearly three months. The obvious question is why? I think it is because he is waiting. I believe he is waiting for his people to deliver a fully operational alien vessel. Perhaps the Mongolian vessel is like *Blue Swan*, perhaps not. But we must - at all costs Billy - beat him to it or all may be lost. Do you understand Billy?"

Duc grit his teeth and nodded. "I understand, Herr Direktor, we not finish in second place me, um, I promise," Duc proclaimed boldly while reaching into his desk drawer and handed Adelman a jump drive. "A gift."

"What is this, Billy?"

"A copy, we think, of part of ship's log by ship's commander. You see your first living, breathing alien. We very close, days away I think, from deciphering their language with help of Mother and Dr. Rice's AI."

"How close do you think the Mongolians are to a fully operational spacecraft?"

"The Chinese scientists, brilliant people. China's AI almost on par with America's AI. In ten years, your genius, my genius, will be obsolete. Children who master AI me, I think, will do what we do and do it better and faster. But now, we master alien language before Mongolians and when we do, everything possible for us. Enjoy gift."

After Adelman and Doss boarded the private jet together, after they each grabbed a beer from a mini refrigerator and took their seats, Adelman raised his bottle. "A toast to past and future triumphs."

"To triumphs past and future, sir," Doss replied somberly as he clinked his bottle against Adelman's.

"Max, I know you've been in the doldrums since Austria. The civilian casualties have troubled you. But you didn't kill those people. What we did in Austria was necessary, critical. What happened at Saint George most likely has changed the future of the world."

"Do you have another mission for me, sir?"

"Alright Max, alright. We don't need to talk about Austria for now. The Council's insidious infiltration into governments and organizations around the world, including ours, is far worse, far more serious than what we thought before Saint George. The time has come for us to introduce ourselves, up close and personal. Maybe we can't save the world, but perhaps we can get our own house in order. Yes, I have a new mission for you, Max, if you'll take it."

After months of tranquility all along the Z Line, Temüjin decides once again to unleash his mighty hordes of devastation. During those months he had carefully, secretly, moved staggering numbers of men and enormous amounts of material into Georgia, Armenia, and Azerbaijan. From the Black Sea to the Caspian Sea, he launches a brutal surprise attack, a massive offensive, into eastern Turkey and northern Iran.

Temüjin's forces sweep through Iran's three northern provinces - East Azerbaijan, West Azerbaijan, and Ardabil - with ease. His tumens roll through the streets of Tabriz as if on parade and then head due west with lightning speed, moving through northern Iraq and Syria with little resistance. They don't stop until they reach the Mediterranean Sea. Curiously, Temüjin leaves Israel, Israeli-controlled Lebanon and Jordan unscathed.

In Turkey, however, the Khan of Khan's forces are met with fierce resistance. The Turkish army is superbly led, well-trained, disciplined and equipped with the very best weaponry. The Turks make the Mongolians pay dearly in blood for every square mile of Turkish soil they take. But when Temüjin's armies in Syria turn and march north to outflank the Turks, the Turks have no choice but to abandon all their eastern provinces and fall back. They retreat in good order and form a strong defensive line from Trabzon on the Black Sea in the north to Iskenderun on the Mediterranean Sea in the south. Seemingly satisfied with this arrangement, Temüjin stops his armies from advancing further into Turkey and again orders his men to stand down and dig in.

"Why this offensive at this time, General, what will he do next?" Dreyfus asked with all her National Security Council gathered in the Oval Office. The NSC included the Vice President, the Secretary of State, the Secretary of the Treasury, the Secretary of Defense, the Assistant to the President for National Security Affairs, the Deputy Chairman of the Joint Chiefs of Staff, the Director of National Intelligence, the President's Chief of Staff, the White House Legal Counsel and the Assistant to the President for Economic Policy. Adelman, to his surprise, was invited as a guest.

"We don't know Madam President," Phillips answered. "This adventure into Turkey, Syria and Iran may have cost Temüjin close to a million casualties, that's a rough estimate of course as we have limited intelligence on the ground in the Middle East but whatever the true number is, we know he suffered what, in our world, would be considered catastrophic losses. If he wanted to secure his southern flank before driving deeper into Europe, he would have taken all of Turkey, the Arabian Peninsula, Iraq, Iran, and southern Pakistan. Afghanistan is no threat to him and India and Southeast Asia are doing their best to remain neutral on the sidelines. Had he taken Turkey, perhaps he planned to cross the Bosporus and the Dardanelles to outflank the Z Line. As for what he plans to do next, we simply do not know."

The President nodded. "If nothing else, General, we know this man has an insatiable appetite for war and conquest. Casualties don't seem to upset him. How did the Mongolians amass such a huge invasion force on Turkey's eastern border without our surveillance satellites noticing? Do we need more satellites?"

"There are about," the Director of National Intelligence explained, "twenty thousand active satellites orbiting the planet. Nearly nine thousand of those satellites belong to us. We have the satellites we need, Madam President. The problem is that our satellites, and the satellites of other nations, are experiencing brief periods of electromagnetic interference, or sometimes they vanish without a trace."

"Someone is targeting and jamming all the world's satellites?"

"Not all at once, no, but for certain short periods at selected locations, yes. This is how, in part, Temüjin surprised and beat the Chinese and how he managed to surprise Turkey - and us."

"Herr Direktor, do you have any thoughts on any of this? And how goes your investigation into the Austrian matter?"

"I have nothing to report on the Austrian matter, Madam President. The perpetrators have covered their tracks well. The French and the Germans have been uncooperative. Regarding your question to the General, just a thought, perhaps Temüjin wants to reestablish the Mongol Empire when it was at its zenith in the year 1259. If he takes the rest of western Russia, Belarus, and Ukraine, and returns east to finish off China and North Korea, he will have accomplished his goal and then some. We may know more after the meeting between Temüjin and Pope Joseph."

"What meeting between the Mongol and the Pope?" Dreyfus asked, clearly annoyed that she had to ask.

"My Section only learned of this summit a few hours ago Madam President. Pope Joseph had invited Temüjin to Rome for a private meeting in person and without publicity not long ago as you may recall. Temüjin agreed to meet, but proposed Moscow as the venue. The Pope, to the horror of all those around him, no doubt, apparently accepted. They are meeting at the Kremlin tomorrow at noon under a flag of truce."

"Jesus! We should take this opportunity to kill the bastard with a missile or with one of those new long-range Devastator drones the Pentagon is bragging about while we have the chance."

"Violate a cease-fire and risk killing the Pope? Even if we succeeded in killing Temüjin without harming the Pope, we'd almost certainly trigger all-out jihad with the entire Muslim world."

"Not my truce, Adelman. Not our war. Some say Temüjin isn't even Muslim but, for once, I must agree with you. In any event, I don't see His Holiness returning from Moscow with world peace. So, does anyone else around the table have anything to contribute to this matter? No? Well, I have one more piece of business to discuss.

"I wanted to let you all hear it from me before you see it in the news later today. As you know, certain members of Congress have gone to extraordinary lengths to keep my proposed bill to recognize the sovereignty of the League of North American States in a continuous state of limbo. We don't have the military or financial strength - or the time - to force reunification through years of bloody conflict. If we don't soon find a way to coexist and combine our military and financial resources to restore balance in the world, we won't have a house, divided or otherwise, much longer. We must help Europe defend itself. Therefore, the President of the League and I have reached an agreement on the basic terms of a Treaty of Perpetual Cooperation between our two nations. Under Article II, Section Two of the Constitution, I have the power to sign such a treaty, subject to ratification by two-thirds of the Senate. I am confident we have secured the votes needed."

Adelman shook his head. "Madam President, I am not an attorney. I am certainly no expert on the Constitution. But isn't the provision in the Constitution you are referring to only applicable to treaties between the U.S. and foreign nations?"

"As you say, Herr Direktor, you are not an attorney."

"Mr. President, please forgive the late hour."

"Hermann, you know better than to apologize to me for calling, regardless of the hour."

"Are you aware of Dreyfus's new scheme to recognize the League as a sovereign nation?"

"General Phillips beat you to the punch by about five minutes, my friend. Army one. Spies zero."

"What will you do? What can I do to help?"

"I've already taken steps to ensure that woman will never get the votes she needs in the Senate. But if by some miracle she does, we have our pick of U.S. District Court judges who are ready, willing, and able to grant us an immediate injunction until the Supreme Court can decide the matter. The Supreme Court will rule in our favor but, if I'm wrong about that, I'll step in and remove her from office first. And as for you? You keep doing what you are doing. Get that damn blue bird thing up and flying and find a way to weaken this Stromquist fellow and his lackeys before they can consolidate their power and make real trouble for us."

"Yes, Mr. President."

"You and Doss certainly know how to make a big splash on the international stage. The collateral damage in Austria was most unfortunate. But the mission was an absolute necessity, and I'd authorize the whole damn thing again, even if I knew the losses would be ten times as bad. I am grateful for what you and Doss have done."

"Thank you, Mr. President. I'll convey your compliments to Doss later, unless you've both already spoken. I believe, sir, the time is nearly upon us."

"Patience Herr Direktor. Nigh is the hour, but not yet. We need all the pieces on the board in play before we make our move."

Adelman had been raised in the Catholic faith many years ago as a young boy, though it never really took. But he was never anti-Catholic nor anti-religious. Neither was he an agnostic or an atheist. He simply was a pragmatist and assumed all would be made clear in the next life, or not.

Despite the vast intelligence-gathering resources at his disposal, he didn't know much more about the new Vicar of Christ than the public. Except for Pope Benedictus IX, Pope Joseph I, at thirty-one years of age, was the youngest pope in the history of popes. He had a natural, some would say spiritual grace about him that was immediately evident to all who met him. His kindness towards, and interest in, everyone he touched was genuine and sincere. Children and dogs especially adored him. He was intelligent, fit and photogenic. He had a laidback, homespun sense of humor and carried himself with an easy confidence. More importantly for the College of Cardinals, he had, singlehandedly, inspired vast numbers of people, especially the young, to return to the Church.

The Kremlin was not Adelman's proudest moment. After Russia, as a nation-state, disintegrated into twelve medieval-like fiefdoms, it was easy for Section M3 to recruit a respectable cadre of spies throughout Russia. Adelman had a dozen spies inside the Kremlin alone and one of those spies was able to plant a microphone with a high-resolution camera, not much larger than a button battery, in the ceiling of the room where the Pope and Temüjin were to meet. Inexplicably, she was able to accomplish this feat of daring after the room had already been swept for bugs and sealed off.

The two great men, each with a large entourage of advisors and security in tow, met in the glittering golden corridors of the Hall of the Order of St. Andrew within the Grand Kremlin. Both men came dressed in simple attire, with none of the trappings of wealth or power. The Pope wore a simple beige cassock with tan loafers. A wooden crucifix on a plain, rawhide cord hung around his neck. The Khan of Khans wore his signature white robes and common sandals without any jewelry.

After the two men shook hands for the cameras and exchanged pleasantries, they retired to a nearby private room with no staff or interpreters as the two men spoke fluent Mandarin Chinese, the Pope having learned the language during his three-year stint in Macau as a novice priest. They took seats across from one another at a sumptuous 19th-century Cossack marquetry Gueridon table with an elegant Imperial Romanov sterling silver tea service and two delicate bone china cups in the center. Hand-painted Russian forests, mountains and wildlife decorated the cups.

"May I pour you a cup of tea, Your Holiness?" Temüjin asked.

"Please, and how do you wish to be addressed, sir?"

The Mongolian smiled politely as he poured tea into one cup for the Pope and one for himself. "Something other than the Great Deceiver, perhaps?"

"Ah, yes. Perhaps I should have been more tactful when I uttered those words. Prove me wrong and I'll gladly think of a more appropriate title."

"Fair enough. Others have bestowed various haughty titles upon me but I am simply Temüjin."

"If I may share a secret with you, Temüjin, I actually prefer Joe."

Temüjin smiled. "Joe, your tea," the Khan of Khans said as he handed the Pope a cup and saucer. Then he reached into his robe and handed the Pope a roll of cream-colored parchment wrapped in a red silk ribbon. "A small gift, a token I pray of a budding friendship between us."

Pope Joseph grinned after unrolling the parchment. "Oh my, this is most exquisite," he said as he took a moment to admire a magnificent sketch in black ink, in the calligraphy style, with subtle red, green and brown highlights in watercolor of a proud Mongolian knight from the days of Genghis Khan galloping across grassy plains on a stocky, Mongolian stallion with his bannered lance held high.

"Thank you, Temüjin. The artist is quite gifted, and I will treasure this fine work." The Pope then paused to remove a small bronze medallion with an animal mask from his cassock and handed the medallion over to Temüjin. "I too come bearing gifts. I'm told this is a safe-conduct pass, known as a *Paiza*, with an inscription in Phakpa Script from the days of Kublai Khan. Although the Church seems to have misplaced the medallion's provenance, we believe this is the very safe-conduct pass Kublai Khan gave to Marco Polo."

Temüjin beamed with delight. "An equally exquisite gift!" he declared with genuine excitement. "Phakpa was a Tibetan monk who served in Kublai's imperial court as a royal preceptor. Let me see, the inscription reads: *By the strength of Eternal Heaven, an edict of the Khan. He who has not respect shall be guilty.*"

"I'm pleased you like this bit of history between East and West, at a time when commerce was much preferred over war between our two great cultures."

"Most thoughtful, Joe. And the symbolism is not lost upon me."

"I wish to understand you better, Temüjin."

"I assume you read Al-Zubayr ibn al-Awwam ibn Khuwaylid al-Asadi's *Book of Prophesies*, at least those verses pertaining to me, once your Vatican scholars confirmed the book's authenticity?"

"I can no more divine the meaning of those prophesies than I can divine the prophesies revealed in John the Apostle's *Book of Revelations*."

"Fair enough."

"Temüjin, I'm delighted you agreed to meet with me."

"Who would ever refuse an audience with the Pope?"

"Ah, a few names come to mind," the Pope replied and chuckled. "We in the West know precious little about you. Your past is a great mystery and Zubayr's *Book of Prophesies* provides little insight. The exact purpose of your mission is also a great mystery. Some believe you are a prophet of Mohammad, others that you are Genghis Khan reincarnated. Some say you are a secular man, a great military leader who simply wishes to fulfill the ambitions of Genghis. Who is this man, Temüjin? What does he hope to achieve?"

Temüjin laughed in a disarming, friendly manner. "Ah, I thought perhaps you came to Moscow to convert me, to baptize me. Now I see you have come to learn my battle plans."

"No baptism today, Temüjin. I offer the Gospel to those who wish to hear as best I can wherever I can. I've never believed in the hard sell. As for battle plans, I am ignorant in the ways of war. But war is why I am here. We are on the brink of total annihilation. You have assembled the largest army in the history of humankind and have shown the world that you have no qualms about using it. I ask you frankly, with an honest heart, can such a hideous war, certainly an abomination in the eyes of Allah, be avoided between Muslims and Christians?"

"Ah, my dear Joseph, you misunderstand. I do not prosecute a religious crusade. True, among my followers are many Muslims. But I have many Buddhists, Christians, Jews, Hindus and even nonbelievers among my flock. I do not judge a man by what God he prays or doesn't pray to. I am indifferent to such matters. The Eternal Blue Sky holds no sway over me, either. Where you strive to comprehend God's will and look forward to ascending into the spiritual world, my feet are planted firmly in this, the material world. I come to give succor to the discontented masses, to free the downtrodden from the masters who enslave them, to free them all from their meaningless, sad and unfulfilled lives. I come to end all wars and bring lasting peace. I am happy to leave the afterworld to you."

"You speak of utopia. A noble dream perhaps, Temüjin, but how do you accomplish such a thing on this Earth when people of every faith and race, and every nationality, have different views on what utopia should look like?"

"We must unite as one people or face extinction. I have seen it."

"Seen what?"

"The future Joe. I have seen three possible futures for mankind in my dreams."

"Where do these dreams come from? From Allah, from the Prophet Mohammad?"

"Truly, I cannot say because I do not know."

"Will you share these dreams with me?"

"I will. As I have said, in one dream, I have seen the extinction of men. I interpret this dream to mean that I have failed in my quest. In another dream, the world rallies to my banner with little blood being spilled and so begins the greatest of golden ages, an age of peace, prosperity and harmony with unimaginable advances in technology and medicine. In yet a third dream, the world kneels before me, but only after my banners are soaked in blood and countless millions, perhaps billions, have perished. In this dream, the world is grim and dark, a planet of desolation with little hope or joy."

"You claim to be the savior, the messiah?"

"I make no such claim. I am not some cheap, religious huckster or a false prophet. I am a simple man. I tell you truly, this path was thrust upon me. I was given no choice in the matter. You came here today to find peace in a fractured world. I am here to fulfill my destiny, and out of curiosity, if I am being honest."

"Curiosity, about what?"

"You are also a great mystery to the world. I am curious to know who you are. I am curious to know if you have the power and the courage to bring peace, true peace, between our peoples, between East and West. Are you the good shepherd here to protect your flock? I wish no harm to you or your Catholic Church. Under my reign, your Church will remain unsullied. You will be permitted to spread the Gospel as you see fit. This, I swear. But the nations of Europe must surrender the House of Moscow, the Ukraine, and the Belarus to me."

"I fear the worst if you pursue this dream of conquest."

"My dearest Joseph, I see an aura of goodness about you. I respect who you are. I respect your faith. But without me, all will perish."

"Again, you speak of conquest and war, Temüjin. Is there no alternative we can explore, no middle ground where honest men can meet to resolve their differences in peace and harmony and, together, build a better world for all?"

"As you can see, Mr. President," Adelman said as he set the remote down on the President's desk in his office at Cheyenne Mountain after the video abruptly went blank. "The explosion is triggered ten minutes and eleven seconds after the two men enter the room."

"What is the latest on the Pope?" Calhoun asked.

"He is back in Rome. He is in critical condition and has been placed on life support. The medical experts tell me that, barring some miracle, Pope Joseph won't survive the week."

"And Temüjin?"

"He was flown to Saratov and is expected to survive. He lost his left leg up to the knee and his left arm is partially paralyzed."

"Any theories on who planted the bomb?"

"I have no proof, but the man who has the most to gain is Kurt Stromquist. I wish I had proceeded with more care in Moscow."

"Nonsense. There is no way you could have prevented this

Hermann. Let's keep this video just between the two of us for now."

"Very well, Mr. President."

"I am reminded of what Ben Franklin once wrote. *Make yourselves sheep and the wolves will eat you.*"

"How true, sir, how true."

While the world's attention is focused on the shocking, tragic events in Moscow, Stromquist makes his move. The Chancellor of Great Germany suddenly, unexpectedly resigns, followed in rapid succession by the leaders, and certain key members of their respective parliaments, of France, Belgium, the Netherlands, Italy, Spain, Portugal, Norway, Sweden, Finland, Romania, Bulgaria Slovakia, Croatia and Greece. These governments are replaced by Stromquist's people, steadfast loyalists all to the New World Order.

Within days, the new leaders make a pilgrimage to Italy and gather in Turin for secret meetings. When they emerge the next day, they announce they have anointed Stromquist their supreme leader and bestow the title of Imperator upon him. Within weeks of Stromquist's coronation the remaining countries of Europe - except for the staunchly independent nations of Poland, Great Britain, Denmark, Switzerland, Luxembourg, Malta, Monaco and the Baltic States - all pledge themselves to Stromquist and his vision of the future.

Chapter Twenty-Three

Beauvilliers, fully recovered from her wounds, was barely half awake when she felt Doss snuggle up against her back. He nibbled on her ear, tenderly kissed her on the neck, kissed her bare shoulder, her hip and then stepped out of the bed. She admired his naked, muscular body, even his scars, as he walked away towards the shower. Content and happy, she pulled the covers over her head and soon slipped back into a deep and blissful sleep.

Doss had Brighton, Pollard and a few lesser Stromquist followers in custody. He had the list of names Bijeau had squeezed out of Brighton and Pollard. The President, his President, had finally given him his blessing to take the folks named on the list in for questioning. Calhoun knew he needed to do something about Stromquist's rising influence within the U.S. before he could move against the League.

Two beefy prison guards led the prisoner into a small room with a desk and two chairs used for privileged, attorney-client consultations. Doss instructed the guards to remove Brighton's shackles and leave as he stood to pull a chair out for her.

"Hello Lucy," he offered cheerfully as they both sat down. He slid a pack of her favorite brand of cigarillos across the table, along with a book of matches. Even in a gray jumpsuit with no makeup, and a truly bad haircut, she was still a real beauty, Doss thought.

"You double-crossed me, I have nothing to say to you," she replied bitterly.

"How so?"

"You promised me that I could serve my time at the Village, but here I am. Locked up in a federal maximum-security facility like an animal somewhere in bumfuck USA, compliments of that gnarly Marine pit bull of yours."

"You withheld information, Lucy. I warned you. And for the record, Bijeau didn't put you in this place, I did."

"Why are you here, to gloat?"

"No. I have no time for gloating. I'm here to see if you've learned your lesson."

Brighton's eyes betrayed her sudden hopefulness, her interest in what Doss had to say next.

"Have a smoke, relax. Your apartment in the Village hasn't been reassigned, not yet. You've only been in this facility for what, three months?"

"One hundred and eleven days," Brighton replied smugly as she lit a cigarillo. "But who's counting?"

"I'm here because I'd like your help on a certain matter. Take heed: I didn't say that I needed your help. Don't make the mistake of thinking you have any leverage because you don't."

Brighton nonchalantly blew a smoke ring at the ceiling as she narrowed her eyes at him. "Even in this wretched place, we do get news. The world is eating itself alive. We are on the brink of a world war that will most likely kill us all, and yet you have come to visit me in this cesspool in the middle of nowhere. Ohhh, I think I might have some leverage, Mr. Doss."

Doss scratched the stubble on his chin and smiled; he couldn't help but admire her bravado. "You've seen the rise of this Stromquist fellow and the New World Order in Europe?"

"I have."

"Well, if you agree to work for me, if you do everything that is asked of you - and I do mean everything - I can arrange to give you back your freedom."

"You mean you'll return me to the Village?"

"No, I mean a full pardon."

"A full pardon, my real freedom?"

"Yes."

"What about Pollard?"

"Sorry to be the bearer of bad news, Lucy. Pollard is dead. Nothing sinister. He died from natural causes, a massive coronary."

"Oh... When?"

"A few weeks back. He died peacefully in his sleep."

"I see. Um, ok. I was aware he survived two prior heart attacks. He was not a bad fellow you know. He had his qualities. I imagine you're going after the Order?"

"We can discuss the operation later once you've agreed to help me. If you do agree and later betray my trust, in even the slightest way, there will be nowhere you can hide. I'll leave the consequences of such a betrayal to your imagination. You will have squandered the last of your nine lives. I trust you haven't lost the parting gift I gave you during our last meeting at Fort Knox?"

"The Neanderthals here confiscated it from me during my intake processing," she said with a sly smile as she snuffed out her cigarillo on the table. "Guess they saw me as a real threat carrying around a 9mm bullet in my pocket."

Doss didn't have the resources to take Stromquist down, not in Europe. But Adelman had given him whatever resources he needed to take on Stromquist's senior, highest-ranking minions imbedded within the U.S. and Brighton was one of those resources, one potentially of high quality.

Bijeau glared at Brighton with a mix of surprise and contempt as she walked into an apartment Doss had rented in Las Vegas. "What the fuck bossman?"

"Missed you too, Bijeau," Doss replied. "Lucy is our way inside."

"Shiiit, somebody's gotten inside your frickin' head."

"Ladies," Doss said when Beauvilliers and Wagner entered the apartment behind Bijeau, "welcome to Operation Round 'Em Up. Before you make jokes, know that Mother chose the name. I'd risk offending the devil before I offended Mother. You ladies already know the thirty special ops guys and gals around the room. You can all get reacquainted later. Our mission is to expose and take down as many key New World Order operatives in the U.S. as we can. With former Senator Brighton's help, I intend to lure the higher-level folks here to Vegas, the capital city of conventions, where we will have ourselves a good old-fashioned Stromquist rally."

Bijeau grabbed Doss's beer off a cocktail table. "*Sic semper tyrannis*," she declared, drained the bottle and turned to Brighton. "You've only seen my sweet side, baby. Play us and, well..."

Using the list Brighton and Pollard had produced for Bijeau a lifetime ago, Brighton began making calls. Brighton's mysterious disappearance would raise suspicions, of course, but she had a good alibi. She was the third highest ranking New World Order recruit in the States and Mother had already hacked into several NWO servers to obtain thirty days' worth of verification codes they would need for each person on the list, codes that changed daily.

"Nighthorse, this is Sabre, good evening," Brighton said.

"Sabre? Where have you been? We thought you were dead, arrested, or compromised. You just disappeared."

"I've been handling a delicate issue for HQ. Took longer than expected."

"Oh? What kind of issue?"

"Nighthorse, do not question me. It is imperative you meet me at the Wynn Hotel in Las Vegas in three days. Your room has already been reserved. Flight arrangements have already been made. We will cover all of your out-of-pocket expenses, of course. Bring your golf clubs if you like or you can rent them here. There will be playtime."

"I, I can't. I have other business on that day. Important business."

"You will attend or you will pay the price, Nighthorse."

"Um, yes, yes, very well. Must be important. Verification?"

"Today's unique verification code is XL-five-eight-nine-forty-five-Salute."

"Um, yes, ok, I confirm verification is correct, Sabre. Will others be there? We've never had a gathering in the U.S. before."

"Nighthorse, Nighthorse, Nighthorse. You disappoint me. Ask me another question and I'll be forced to file a report with Berlin."

"No, no. No need Sabre. I'll be at the Wynn as instructed."

"Good. I shouldn't have to remind you, but it is strictly forbidden for you to tell anyone anything about this conference. By the way, you should feel honored by this invitation."

Brighton called everyone on the list, 35 calls in all, and then Doss gave her two more names on little more than a hunch he and Adelman both shared. General Barbara Ritter-Starling and President Dreyfus's Chief of Staff, Tom MacAfee, accepted Brighton's invitation without objection after Brighton provided them with the correct call signs and verification codes.

Doss had Mother book rooms for Brighton's guests at hotels scattered across Las Vegas. She purchased VIP suites for the general and MacAfee and booked a conference room at the Wynn.

Next Doss had Wagner preposition a squadron of six Apaches and six Sikorsky Black Hawks, the battle tank of helicopters, at Echo Bay Airport, a small private airport in the middle of nowhere just east of Vegas. He had no specific mission for Wagner, but enjoyed having six attack helicopters in his hip pocket on standby. He had Wagner bring the Black Hawks, borrowed from the 1st Air Cav Division, in case they needed to transport any prisoners or themselves by air. The Black Hawks, stripped of armament, could carry up to 11 passengers each and two were equipped with rescue hoists.

Three days later, all but two of Brighton's invitees had arrived in Vegas as instructed. With everyone dressed in loose-fitting, touristy type clothing over light-weight, body armor, and armed with concealed handguns, Doss and ten men parked ten rental vans close to the Wynn with duffle bags stuffed with assault weapons, magazines, and magazine belts stored aboard each van. Bijeau and Beauvilliers, each leading a team of ten, subtly established a perimeter around the Wynn to watch the exits.

The plan was simple. The guests were instructed to arrive at the conference room at ten on the Friday morning after they flew into Vegas. Brighton would personally greet each guest and exchange idle chit-chat before they took their seats and, after she took the podium to start the conference, Doss would lead his team into the room and make arrests. Then Doss would use the vans to transport his prisoners to Nellis Air Force Base, less than eight miles away, off I-15 to the north. Though they were operating in League territory, Nellis was a Union stronghold and Adelman was on good terms with the base's commanding general.

Thirty minutes before everyone was to arrive at the Margaux Room, however, Wynn's manager informed Brighton that the hotel had been forced to close the room because of a serious water leak. The manager apologized profusely. But, as the Wynn's remaining meeting rooms were already taken, she took the liberty of booking a meeting room at the Bellagio just a few blocks away at no cost to Brighton.

"Bravo, Charlie, Delta leaders, this is Alpha Leader. A change of venue has been forced upon us. Hotel blames a water leak. Our VIP speaker is texting each conference attendee now. New venue is the Bellagio, the Di Vinci One Room on the Renaissance Foyer."

"Don't like last-minute changes, bossman," Bijeau said and popped a bubblegum bubble into her mic. "Has our speaker played us?"

"Don't think so. Mother confirmed through airport security cameras and hotel check-ins that every invitee but two arrived. Why would they fly into Vegas as instructed and expose themselves to a trap?"

"Let me take care of the duplicitous bitch, anyway."

"No, Bravo Leader. Focus. Behave yourself. Calling Mother, Mother?"

"Alpha Leader, Mother."

"Mother, rerun analysis on all Brighton's calls for voice modulation, tone, speech pattern changes, out-of-place words or phrases, etc., for anything that could have been a coded warning."

"Understood. Will expand search parameters. Wait. Nearly there. Finished. Nothing of note from reanalysis."

"Bravo Leader, Alpha Leader, relocate to Bellagio."

"Big place Alpha Leader," Bijeau said. "Impossible to cover."

"Understood Bravo. Mission is still a go. Stay sharp."

"And the vans?" Beauvilliers asked.

"You and your team remain in place and be prepared to move the vans when I give the order," Doss replied.

When Brighton texted Doss twenty minutes later that all the invitees had arrived at the Di Vinci Room, Doss, Bijeau and their teams were casually walking around the front of the Bellagio in small groups of twos and threes. Doss instructed Beauvilliers to move the vans into the Bellagio's garage and then Mother called.

"Alpha Leader, Mother. Texting photos. You may have company. Four vans just pulled into the lobby driveway. Twelve men dressed in medium-blue coveralls are now exiting the vans and walking into the Bellagio front lobby. They're carrying ladders, paint cans, and three duffle bags."

"I see them," Doss acknowledged. "Something else caught your attention, Mother?"

"Their coveralls are new, not a spot on them. They're wearing government-issue combat boots. I may be able to retrace their steps from satellite video feed, but that will take time."

"Bravo, Charlie, Delta, we may have trouble, you copy Mother's last?"

"Bravo, affirmative."

"Charlie, affirmative."

"Delta, Roger that."

"Mission is still a go, Alpha Leader, out."

Bijeau scattered her team around the resort hotel's grand fountains while Beauvilliers and her team parked the vans in the garage and waited just as Doss went through the main lobby with his team in staggered groups to avoid attention. He had his team remain in the lobby while he followed the blue coveralls up to the Renaissance Foyer.

"Sorry sir," one of the workmen said as Doss tried to approach the Di Vinci Room. "This area is now restricted. Water leak."

"You intend to fix a water leak with paint?" Doss asked glibly.

The man, unamused, took an aggressive step towards Doss with an outstretched arm and his palm up. "For your safety sir stop and back away now."

Doss shrugged his shoulders, turned and walked away. "Bravo Leader, come to my position in the lobby with your team entering in small groups. Charlie Leader, hold in place."

"Charlie Team Leader, I acknowledge."

"Alejandra," Doss said as Bijeau straddled up next to him. "I only saw two men outside the Di Vinci Room. One of them told me to get lost. My guess is that the other ten have already gone inside the room. My guess is these are General Ritter-Starling's men."

"The General brought her own security detail? Either she doesn't trust Brighton, or maybe she doesn't trust her masters in Europe, or both."

"My thoughts exactly. They've seen me. Take two men with you, quietly subdue the lookouts. Draw your weapon, flash your ATF credentials. Try to take them into custody without a raucous. They may be innocent men just following the orders of a rogue general."

"And if I can't do it peacefully?"

"Then call me up. I'll try to reason with them with your team and my team behind me."

Bijeau stepped into the Ladies' Room, removed her body armor and handed the vest to Doss before walking upstairs. She unfastened the top buttons of her blouse, exposing a good bit of cleavage, as she sauntered up to a man with the weatherbeaten face of a grizzled veteran and gave him a big, friendly smile. Bijeau had no trouble turning heads. The man grinned back until her fist smashed into his face. As he fell backward, she pulled her 9mm out before the second man could intervene.

"ATF baby," she said as she removed the badge chained around her neck out from under her blouse. "Don't make a sound or I will shoot you in the face. On your knees now."

The second man, a thin, fresh-faced boy with ruddy cheeks and freckles, nodded vigorously and dropped to his knees next to the first man.

"What are you doing here?" she asked, then waved her two men over to zip-tie hands and feet.

"You're in a world of shit sweet cheeks," the man she had sucker punched said after he caught his breath. "This is a military op."

"Dang, no shit," Bijeau said nonchalantly and popped one of her bubblegum bubbles while she knelt next to the man and unbuttoned his coverall. Underneath he wore BDUs but had no nametag, rank, or unit insignias. Strapped to his belt were a Glock and a six-inch serrated hunting knife.

"What do we have here?" Doss asked with his team and the rest of Bijeau's team behind him and handed Bijeau her vest.

"Claims he's military. No ID on him. Weapons aren't military-issue."

"Who do you work for?" Doss asked in an unfriendly tone.

"Piss off," the older man said defiantly.

"I'm going to fuck your day up soldier if you don't start talking," Doss said and flashed his ATF ID at the man.

The man laughed and said nothing.

"That just bought you a lot of pain. I'm not ATF. I work for an organization far worse. We make tough guys like you cry."

Doss turned to Bijeau. "We're wasting time. Put one man on these two and have another watch the foyer. We'll rush the room with our badges displayed, guns drawn, and disarm the other ten. We zip-tie everyone, including Brighton, and take them out the front door and to the vans. Good?"

"Good."

"Charlie Leader, you copy all that?"

"Charlie Leader, copy."

"Ok. Grab our hardware, Charlie Leader, move your team into the lobby. Badges out, weapons hot, ski masks on."

"On the way."

"Alpha and Bravo Team on me," Doss bellowed and bolted into the Di Vince room with his ATF ID displayed, his 9mm in his hand and a ski mask pulled down over his face. Bijeau and the rest rushed in behind him.

Doss saw Brighton standing up at the podium, telling a joke. The attendees were in their seats with morning beverages and snacks in hand. The ten men in coveralls were standing rigidly at parade rest against the back wall. Everyone froze, even the soldiers in blue.

"ATF raid, no one move!" Doss commanded loudly. "Remain in your seats. Keep your hands out of your pockets. Do not touch your phones. Bravo Team, disarm the blues. Alpha Team, cover the room."

As Bijeau and her team quickly disarmed the soldiers, the general, dressed in a flattering, dark tan pants suit, stood away from her seat. She should have been a man. Tall, broad-shouldered, big-boned and long-legged, she moved straight for Doss with giraffe-like strides.

"I'm General Ritter-Starling," she said in a deep, commanding voice. "I demand you order your men to stand down. These soldiers are with me. We're here lawfully, providing security for this gathering."

"A gathering, is it?" Doss asked contemptuously. "Huh, interesting choice of words. I know who you are, General. For your own good, return to your seat."

"Alpha Leader, Charlie Leader, we are in the lobby."

"Roger, Charlie Leader. Be down in five."

The general didn't budge. "Who are you? You aren't ATF. Even if you were, you have no authority over me. Again, I order you to stand down, mister!"

Then one of Doss's men tapped him on the shoulder and pointed at the general's hand in her trousers. "She's triggered something in her pocket, sir."

Ritter-Starling voluntarily removed a remote from her pocket and smiled. "Panic button of sorts. I've brought more men than you. A Quick Reaction Force out of Nellis will be here momentarily. Poor Adelman. He thought the base commander at Nellis was his friend when, in fact, Major General Norm Thompson is my friend. Something about all this did not feel right to me. Still, Brighton had the correct authentication codes, so I wasn't sure until now. You, someone else, have flipped Brighton. So, you see, I came prepared."

Doss ignored the general. "Bravo, Charlie, Delta Leaders," he said calmly into his mic, "Bravo take face photos of the blues and zip 'em, we'll leave them behind, then we get everyone else into the vans. Delta Leader, scratch Nellis. The base is compromised. We'll rendezvous at alternate extraction Whiskey-Hotel. Acknowledge."

"Doss, Mother. You have another problem. A convoy of three Cougar MRAPs, ten cargo trucks and a dozen Humvees with Air Force markings is coming to your location. You have about five minutes."

"Charlie Leader, this is Alpha Leader, move to my position now!"

"Charlie Leader on the way!"

Doss turned to the general. "Delta Leader, hoist extraction ASAP, roof, Bellagio. Three for transport. All team leaders, scratch the vans, we'll rendezvous at the golf course for evac."

Ritter-Starling snickered. "Even in this public place, my men will cut you and your men down to free me."

"Alpha, Delta. We're airborne. Will arrive at Whiskey-Hotel in five with one Black Hawk to your position for hoist extraction."

Doss walked over to the President's Chief of Staff, grabbed him by the shoulder and yanked him roughly out of his chair. "You and the good general here are taking a little ride. Bravo Leader - take three men and get to the roof. I want the general, MacAfee and Brighton on that Black Hawk! We'll cover you from here."

"Oorah!" Bijeau exclaimed loudly, picked two men and one

woman from her team and raced out of the room with her three prisoners in tow.

Doss then turned to the rest of the attendees in the room. "We know who you are, where you live and work. We know where you keep your money. We have detailed dossiers on each of you. We'll be in touch soon. I wouldn't try to flee the country and I wouldn't free the blues either if I were you. They just might shoot you. Now scram!"

As the conference attendees hastily fled from the room in fear, Beauvilliers and her team arrived with the duffle bags and handed out automatic submachine guns, magazines, and magazine bandoliers.

"Mother, Doss, find me a way out of here."

"Freight corridor," Mother replied, "then garage. Hurry, the convoy is about to pull into the front of the main lobby."

"Delta, sit rep!" Doss commanded.

"Bellagio in view. Have visual on the packages."

Doss turned to Beauvilliers. "Maddie, we hold this level until Alejandra is clear."

Beauvilliers gave Doss a somber nod, then took her team and dispersed them down different hallways to cover the elevators and staircases leading up to the Grand Patio. Doss led the rest to secure the freight elevators and back stairwells. And then the shooting started.

"Charlie Leader, report!" Doss ordered.

"Soldiers, estimate company strength, engaging us."

Doss knew Beauvilliers and her team of ten could not hold off 100 men or more for long. But the success or failure of the mission was now in Bijeau's hands and Bijeau needed time. And then he heard Bijeau's voice in his ear.

"Alpha Leader, Bravo Leader. Delta has all three packages."

"Bravo Leader," Doss replied, "area too hot. Evac with Delta."

"Negative. Can link up with you."

Doss could hear the automatic weapons fire intensifying; then a fragmentation grenade exploded nearby. "You won't make it Alejandra. About to be overrun. Evac with Delta. Will hold our position for a mike or two until you're clear. See you back at the ranch. Charlie Leader, fall back to my position now! We'll cover you."

When Beauvilliers and her team, down to five men and one woman, made it to the freight elevators, Doss removed a compact

Android Tablet from his backpack. He showed her the escape route Mother had devised and then sent her and the rest down a back stairwell towards the garage on the ground level while he remained behind with five men as rear guard. More shots rang out as soldiers drew closer. Doss could hear panicked hotel guests and employees screaming and running. Then someone pulled a fire alarm. He and his men took cover next to the double service doors between the freight elevator corridor and the hallways linking the hotel's ballrooms on the Renaissance Level. When Doss saw a mass of soldiers advancing towards them down a narrow hallway, he and his men emptied their magazines into bodies packed too close together, into raw recruits with no combat experience and poorly led. Dozens toppled over.

Then Doss led his men down the back stairwell. He froze when he heard the metallic sound of a grenade bouncing down the concrete steps. The explosion knocked him off his feet. One of his men laid down suppressive fire at the stairwell door above them as another helped him up. He felt sharp pains in his thigh as he stood, glanced down, and saw blood oozing from multiple tears in his light sage trousers. He turned around, saw three of his men riddled with shrapnel and covered in blood, huddled together on the concrete steps as if asleep, but their lives had been ruthlessly ripped away. He was lucky, they were not. Such is war. He left the bodies behind, along with a tripwire across the stairwell connected to a grenade, and moved on.

Just as Doss and his men reached the garage, they heard a sharp BOOM in the stairwell behind them. They ditched their automatic weapons and magazine belts and walked north up Las Vegas Boulevard, overflowing with frightened people, at a brisk, but not too obvious pace, trying to avoid attention. Doss saw Beauvilliers up ahead with the rest of his team. Behind him, he saw a thick column of smoke rising above the Bellagio along with dozens of first responders and law enforcement with blue lights flashing and sirens wailing converging on the hotel. When he stumbled over a street curb at Sands Avenue, one of his men lifted him up by one arm while a second grabbed him by the other and helped him hobble over to the golf course behind the Wynn Hotel. And there they saw six Apaches circling overhead providing overwatch while the Black Hawks swooped down in pairs, landing on the fairways in turns, to evacuate his men.

Chapter Twenty-Four

Excerpts from Hermann Adelman's private journal:
The Great Turmoil

The director of M3 sat back in his chair at his office in Washington, D.C., pausing a moment to consider his old rival sitting across the desk from him. He poured freshly brewed coffee from a glass carafe into two plain mugs.

"General Barbara Ritter-Starling, welcome back to D.C.," he said and offered her coffee.

"Adelman, you old Nazi, how the hell are you?" she asked with a confident grin and declined the coffee with a flick of her hand.

"Better than you," Adelman answered evenly.

"We both know I won't be staying long enough for coffee."

"Oh?" Adelman asked, set the coffee aside and walked over to her to hand her a file. "You are still young and healthy. You have a long, long life ahead of you, I suspect. A long life to reflect and think back upon your sins. In that file is your story. Talk to me or don't. The President's Chief of Staff is down the hall with Doss, and I hear he's a chatty one."

She took the file from Adelman and defiantly tossed it across the floor. "Never understood what Calhoun saw in you, Adelman. No matter. The wind is up. You're sitting in a leaky rowboat with no oars far away from any land with a gale barreling down on you, a gale you can't survive. That dimwitted, country bumpkin is dead and soon you will be as good as dead once you are relieved from this farce you call an agency."

"President Calhoun might disagree with you there, General. You didn't get the memo? That's right - he's very much alive. I am, for now, transferring you to a place known as the Village. Your good friend, Major General Norm Thompson, is already there. I had him arrested yesterday."

"Always playing your silly games, Adelman. But you have no cards left to play. Save your idle bluster, your empty threats. Calhoun is dead, Dreyfus is President and I answer to her and her alone."

When Adelman handed her his cell phone, she, out of curiosity, placed the phone to her ear. "Hello Barbara," Calhoun said. "Yep, this dimwitted, country bumpkin is alive and kicking. I'd cooperate with Adelman if I were you, I'd try to keep my place at the Village. Prison is such a depressing alternative."

"Is this a joke?" the general scoffed in utter disbelief, certain the call was a hoax created with AI.

Adelman moved over to his desk and swung his computer monitor around to show Ritter-Starling a live video of Calhoun on the screen with his phone in hand and a TV behind him with the day's morning news.

"Certainly not Barbara. I'm in no mood for jokes. By selling yourself to the New World Order, you've committed high treason against your country, a country I dearly love. Perhaps murder too when you consider what your men did in Vegas."

"I've committed no treason and my men were engaged with armed terrorists!"

"If you say so, Barbara," Calhoun replied sharply. "I'll not waste time with someone who won't accept their new reality, goodbye," he said and then abruptly disconnected the call.

She tried to stop her hands from shaking as she mulled things over. Learning that Calhoun was alive set an explosion off in her head. She now understood that her predicament was grim. Adelman was dangerous enough, but with Calhoun back in command, well, he was a force of nature, firm in his convictions, relentless and unstoppable. Dreyfus would be no match for him. Maybe the Order would prevail and save her in the end, then again, maybe not. She needed time, time she knew that Adelman would never give her.

"What," she finally asked Adelman sheepishly after a long silence between them, "is the Village?"

The world held its breath as Temüjin the Blessed convalesced from his wounds. None of the premier intelligence agencies from any country had a clue of what he might do next. Some hoped Temüjin would end his journey of conquest after the staggering losses his armies had suffered in Turkey. Others speculated that the Khan of Khans might invade Africa next, a continent overflowing with riches but hopelessly divided and with no great armies to defend itself, a priceless jewel ripe for the plucking.

But as the peaceful calm all along the Z Line continued, a quiet war far away in the heavens raged on. The satellite-producing countries of the world had been losing satellites faster than they could replace them, slowly leaving their governments deaf, dumb and blind. No one knew who was disabling the satellites, but the one who benefited the most from this was Temüjin - or was it Stromquist?

Calhoun carefully considered everything Adelman had briefed him on. He pulled two Czech pilsners out from a small fridge next to his desk in his office at his secret shadow White House deep within Cheyenne Mountain and handed Adelman a beer.

"How confident Hermann is Duc that he will have *Blue Swan* at least partially operational within a month or two?"

"Highly confident Abe."

"When will this Project Onryō, this joint venture between the Indians and Japanese, be able to launch their hunter-killer space drones to find and obliterate whatever is decimating our satellites?"

"Weather and the absence of technical issues permitting, this Friday from the Yoshinobu Launch Complex at Tanegashima."

"Remind me, what does Onryō mean?"

"Vengeful Spirt."

"Ah, I like it. And Dreyfus adamantly refused to contribute money, expertise, or labor to the project?"

"Yes."

"Jesus. And no one knows what this Temüjin's fellow will do next? What does your gut tell you?"

"Presumably his injuries have forced him to delay his plans, then again, maybe not. I still think he is biding his time until he has alien technology at his fingertips before resuming his offensive. If he does succeed in obtaining an alien mega weapon, my guess is he'll launch an all-out frontal assault against the Zhukov Line. He strikes me as someone who prefers the blunt trauma of a sledgehammer over the finesse of a scalpel."

"And Max? He thinks he is close to being able to execute Operation Homecoming?"

"Yes. Ritter-Starling, MacAfee, Thompson, and the others we have in custody have provided a fairly comprehensive organizational structure of the Order with a few names of key decision-makers here and in Europe. As the Order has grown and become more active, its members have become more exposed and are easier to identify."

"Good, very good. We must achieve flawless execution of the plan - or close to it - if we are to survive."

"Flawless, Abe? With a plan of this complexity, there will always be hic-ups, miscues and missteps. You know this. Still, your point is not lost on me. We will have the resources we need in place and leave as little to chance as possible."

"I can ask no more than this," Calhoun said softly, then looked away, deep in thought. "Do you believe in providence, Hermann?"

"Divine Providence?"

Calhoun turned and smiled good-naturedly. "Always the scientist, always rooted in logic. Either way."

"The better question, Abe, is do you?"

"Barely surviving an assassination attempt, especially when you are the leader of the free world, certainly makes one wonder. I imagine Temüjin and I have this in common. I imagine he, too, has been doing some deep introspection."

"And this helps or hurts us?"

"Damned if I know," Calhoun replied and grabbed two more beers.

Three months pass before the Khan of Khans is seen by the West again. And when he appears in a short video posted on the internet, he speaks only about two things: he prays for the soul of Pope Joseph

I, he condemns the Pope's assassins to eternal torments and lamentations and proclaims that all true believers may take comfort knowing that all wrongs will be made right in the afterworld. And then he tells Europe it has one week, seven full days, to abandon the Z Line and surrender western Russia, Belarus, and Ukraine to him.

Dreyfus, surprisingly for once, moves quickly and decisively. She calls up all reservists, activates the draft, and orders more soldiers, fleets of warships and squadrons of fighters and bombers over to Europe, though she knows these things will take time to set into motion. She makes these decisions unilaterally, without asking Congress to declare war. The entire country, Union and League, is on edge.

When Europe refuses Temüjin's demands, Temüjin responds by launching the greatest military assault in the history of the world. The images coming out of the warzone all along the Z Line are nearly impossible to describe. A pair of enormous siege towers, each built atop two behemoth crawler transporters, grotesque beasts, and armed with a new, devastating sonic blasting device, are employed against the massive concrete, stone and steel walls outside Moscow and start chipping away. Countless heavy tanks, fighter planes and artillery, the spoils of war captured from the Russians and Chinese, unleash hell all along the Z Line from the Baltic Sea down to the Black Sea. Where Temüjin's battalions make minor breakthroughs here and there, his warriors torch everything they find, they obliterate hills and demolish whole city blocks before the Europeans can counterattack and push the invaders back. Night and day the heavens weep blood as thunderous explosions up and down a 1,000-mile front rock the Earth and it is by no means clear who is winning and who is losing the colossal tug of war between East and West.

For eleven days, Temüjin's mindboggling numbers of war machines and his millions of fanatical followers bludgeon Europe's defenses, inflicting unimaginable carnage. But when the waves of destruction crashing against the Z Line recede, when the fires and enormous plumes of smoke dissipate and the vast piles of burning dead, too many to count, are captured on camera for the first time for the whole world to see, Temüjin's forces have failed to make any decisive breakthrough anywhere along the Z Line. The massive wall outside Moscow in places is scarred, cracked and fragmented, but remains intact.

Curiously, the Khan of Khans appears unfazed. He calmly orders his armies to halt operations briefly. He orders them to replenish, rearm, and regroup. The first phase of Temüjin's battle plan has been merely to probe and soften up Europe's defenses. The lull in the barbarism does not last long.

Led by a full battalion - the first ever - of totally robotic, autonomous AI soldiers, dubbed the *Super Soldat* by their Russian inventor with the unfortunate moniker, by design or inadvertently, of the letters SS engraved in silver on their black metal skulls, followed by his ferocious, unforgiving Mongolians, Temüjin launches a single, concentrated attack along a narrow 100-mile front against Moscow. His robotic shock troops, machines with no sense of right or wrong, machines that never tire, fighting beside his frenzied Mongolian warriors, men whose religion is death and who never bring mercy to battle, do their worst. They make impressive gains at first, pouring through multiple breaches in the enormous concrete wall created by the twin siege towers. They level interior fortifications, fill in anti-tank ditches and trenches, clear minefields and negotiate their way around a variety of ingenious obstacles the Europeans have painstakingly built behind their great wall to demoralize and slow the invader down.

The Europeans fall back in good order. They bend but do not break - not even when Temüjin sends in his heavy tanks, his armored infantry vehicles and some of his finest elite tümens to add their energy and muscle to the desperate struggle. After several days of unimaginable savagery, with appalling losses on both sides, it appears the Mongolian offensive has once again stalled. It looks as if the Mongolians are about to suffer another horrific, humiliating defeat. And then, with exquisite timing - before the Europeans can catch a breath or regroup - Temüjin plays his wild card.

As menacing, dark clouds with faint streaks of lightning gather over Moscow, a single, peculiar noctilucent cloud of diffuse yellow light suddenly emerges from the stormfront - the strange cloud rolls forward ahead of the pack. Then an object, in the shape and size of a narrow blimp, emerges from the cloud and hovers over the deadliest sector of the fighting for a bit. A bright aura of light, like tongues of flame - yellows, blues and reds - seems to consume the vessel. The light intensifies until she is too bright to look at, until she is brighter than the brightest sun. This marvel is followed by a reddish-orange lightning bolt - a lightning bolt from hell - that strikes the ground well in front of Temüjin's advancing forces, leaving in its wake a charred, smoldering swath of black soil, of utter devastation, a half-mile wide and ten miles deep into the Z Line. The weapon incinerates everything in its path: metal, brick, concrete, asphalt, wood, glass, flesh, bone and stone.

When the aura of bright light dissipates and the vessel reappears, she floats effortlessly across the storm clouds, moving a few miles farther south. She hovers for a bit before a ball of blinding light again engulfs her. She shoots another lightning bolt and carves a second gaping hole a half mile wide and ten miles deep into European lines. The object moves farther south yet again and strikes a third time, inflicting the same horrific results.

Desperate, the Europeans scramble entire squadrons of their precious fighter jets. One by one, the sleek, lethal interceptors swoop down like vicious birds of prey on the unearthly object and unloose their deadly arrows - all for naught. Cameras integrated into each fighter's fire control system capture the flight trajectory of every air-to-air missile. As the first missile approaches the target, a thin shell of white light instantly envelops the blimp-like vessel. After the missile passes through the shell, it vanishes, leaving behind colorful sparkles and harmless curlicues of white vapor. Every missile following the first missile suffers the same fate. Undaunted, the fighter pilots return to their respective bases to refuel and rearm. Ground crews rush to mount a single, tactical nuclear missile with a two-kiloton yield, dubbed the Slim Jim by its U.S. manufacturer, to the belly of each aircraft. Once the job is done, Europe's valiant knights of the sky immediately take off into the darkening storm, eager to reengage and destroy the enemy. When the first wave of 12 fighters simultaneously launch their Slim Jims at the target from a dozen different directions, a thin shell of white light again envelops the blimp-like vessel and as the tactical nuclear missiles pass through the shell they too disappear, leaving behind colorful sparkles and harmless curlicues of white vapor. Stunned by this catastrophic failure, Europe's First Air Marshal calls off the airstrike to save his remaining tactical nukes for another day.

Temüjin is enough of a strategist, enough of a student of military history, to know you never squander an advantage in battle by sitting idly by like Marshal Ney did after the battle at Quatre Bras when he decided to have lunch, which cost Napoleon Waterloo, or like Meade at Gettysburg when he let General Lee limp away with the sad remnants of an army and lost a chance to end the American Civil War. Temüjin now decides to send massive numbers of men and vehicles of every sort - everything he has, including the last of his reserves - across the three land bridges of glowing embers and ash. Confused, terrified, and bloodied by Temüjin's devastating new wonder weapon, and unable to plug the triple breaches, the armies of Europe abandon the entire Z Line. They fall back in good order with hopes of regrouping and making a stand along a new defensive line stretching from Riga to Vilnius to Minsk and then to Kyiv and on down to Odessa. In all the confusion no one thinks to inform the American 1st Armored Division, sitting in reserve just outside of Moscow in Elektrostal, of the massive withdrawal.

With the armies of the West in full retreat, the Mongols and their allies resume their general attack all along the 1,000-mile front while Temüjin takes the cream of his forces in the center and divides them into three separate army groups. The Khan of Khans sends one army group south and another north to envelope the crown jewel of Moscow while he personally leads the army group in the center, spearheaded by his heavy tanks, straight at the great city. His armies in the south and north move swiftly across open ground with little opposition. But Temüjin is surprised when his army group in the center smacks into the American 1st Armored Division a few miles outside of Moscow, and he soon learns a hard lesson.

The Americans build wonderful tanks, tanks unmatched in speed, armament and survivability, crewed by men and women with an unrivaled esprit de corps, with an uncompromising dedication to duty and a selfless love of country. The Americans ravage whole battalions of Temüjin's heavy tanks and lesser armor before Temüjin learns his lesson. Temüjin is forced to pull his mauled, demoralized armor units back. But again, he is unfazed by these trivial setbacks. He summons his wonder weapon to return and obliterate the Americans.

And when the peculiar noctilucent cloud of diffuse yellow light suddenly appears over the Americans, the Americans don't know what to make of the bizarre phenomenon. They ignore the oddity and press on with their deadly, gruesome work. They continue demolishing scores of enemy armored vehicles with little damage to themselves. Then a strange object, in the shape and size of a narrow blimp, emerges from the odd cloud and hovers over the Americans. A bright aura of light, like tongues of flame - yellows, blues and reds - suddenly envelops the blimp. The light intensifies until the vessel is too bright to look at, until it is brighter than the brightest sun.

But then a second noctilucent cloud of diffuse light with a blueish hue suddenly appears in the sky and a blue object, in the shape of an angry bird, emerges from the strange cloud. With outstretched wings and a long, curved neck supporting an isosceles triangle resembling, with a little imagination, the head and beak of an eagle, the peculiar vessel shoots a beam of pulsating blue light at the blimp-like vessel. The blue beam is met by a thin shell of white light that instantly surrounds the blimp-like vessel, and nothing happens at first. But soon the blue beam begins boring through the shell. The shell reacts and expands to counter the penetration. As the blue beam penetrates deeper and deeper into the shell, the shell grows brighter and larger to preserve its continuity until suddenly the shell appears to overload. Then, in a brilliant flash of light stretching far across the horizon, the shell spectacularly collapses into itself, leaving behind no trace of Temüjin's wonder weapon.

The commanding general of the American 1st Armored Division, himself a direct descendent of one of the greatest cavalry commanders of all time, a Confederate general named Jeb Stuart, couldn't understand what he and his tankers had just witnessed. But when the blue vessel starts shooting blue beams of light at the enemy - he knows what to do. Just as the heavens open and unleash a deluge of water, and with night closing in, he orders a full attack and invites his European allies to turn around and join him.

When the blue extraterrestrial vessel obliterates the SS battalion and carves gaping holes in the Mongolian ranks and the Americans - full of fury - crash into the Mongolian formations with their monstrous tanks, panic seizes Temüjin's armies. It begins as a trickle at first. A handful of frightened soldiers turn towards the Z Line and start running in the dark, in the cold, blinding rains. Soon whole companies melt away in the chaos and follow them. Before long, the trickle turns into a raging flood of unstoppable men and machines, and Temüjin's army group center disintegrates into a terrified rabble on the run.

In all the confusion, Temüjin's personal eight-wheeled command vehicle, an enormous steel beast made of rolled homogenous armor, swerves into a deep ditch and flips over on its side. His bodyguards, standing just out of reach up on the road after rushing out of their escort vehicle, watch in horror as Temüjin, with the beast suddenly bursting into flame, desperately tries dragging himself out of the bottom of the hull through an escape hatch with his one good leg and one good arm. Without warning, the command vehicle suddenly shifts in the slime and the muck, falls on top of the Khan of Khans and crushes him.

News of Temüjin's demise is the final blow to the Armies of the Second Mongol Empire. From the Baltic Sea to the Black Sea, soldiers abandon most of their heavy equipment and flee and don't stop running until they reach the western borders of Greater Mongolia. Yes, the Khan of Khans is dead. And yet, Temüjin has departed the world stage as he had stepped onto it, suddenly, dramatically and unexpectedly, triggering in death as he had in life far-reaching, world-shaping consequences for generations to come.

Chapter Twenty-Five

Calhoun hadn't known real joy or optimism about much of anything since the day assassins tried to end him. He had lived his life incognito for well over a year in hospitals and then inside a drab, austere bunker deep beneath a mountain. He had set aside the Presidency, a job he loved passionately, along with the power and fame that went with it to give the nation a chance at survival while he played dead, while he let his body heal.

He was elated by the news of Temüjin's catastrophic defeat in Russia. He treated himself to a fine Cuban cigar and a rare Louis XIII cognac from the 1950s when he learned of Temüjin's demise. The mind-numbing volume of pictures and video of the colossal clash between the two titans at the Z Line, of the unfathomable devastation and the grotesque mounds of unburied dead, astonished and shocked him. The cost to expose the Khan of Khans as little more than a carnival con would forever remain incalculable. Even so, the end of Temüjin's reign gave Calhoun newfound optimism. He stood away from his desk to properly greet his guests after a Marine captain announced their arrival.

"Hermann, Max, I wish I could stand atop this mountain and sing your praises to the people," Calhoun declared with a huge smile as he warmly embraced both men. "God knows you've earned the gratitude of the nation. I very much wish I could meet Duc and his entire team and honor them as well. But, alas, I'm still dead. *Blue Swan* has returned unscathed?"

"She has Abe," Adelman replied, "not a scratch on her."

"Dreyfus is still under the impression *Swan* is some new, fantastical weapon built by the Germans?"

"Yes."

"Good. This alien machine has ushered in a new era. For better or worse, our lives are about to change dramatically. For the sake of all mankind, I pray we are good stewards of this newfound technology.

What of the Mongolian machine?"

"We aren't sure. The ship vanished in a brilliant ball of light. She may have been vaporized or it is also possible she transported herself to another place. The video we have of the battle between the two alien ironclads is inconclusive."

"I see. Well, I'm glad that Zubayr fellow got it all wrong with his prophecies."

"Actually, Abe, he may have gotten it right."

"Oh? How so Hermann?"

"We had a man inside the Select Few, not a mole but a cleric who distrusted Temüjin and who happens to have family in America. The man provided us with a complete copy of the book. He highlighted the famous passage about the rise of Temüjin, of course, but he also highlighted a curious passage on the very last page. Only fragments of the passage have survived the centuries, but towards the end of Zubayr's book he wrote: *all ... seen ... come ... pass ... I swear before Allah ... unless ... blue ... breathes ...*"

"And what the hell does that gibberish mean? Sounds as clear as mud to me."

"The word after *blue* was mostly illegible, but could have been the Quranic Arabic word for *flying serpent* or *dragon*. By extrapolating things a bit, the passage could have originally read: *All I have seen shall come to pass ... something, something ... I swear before Allah ... something, something ... unless the blue dragon ... something, something ... breathes ... something, something.* This would explain why Temüjin was a man in a hurry. He would have known of this passage and of its possible implications. He knew he needed to fulfill his destiny before one of the Western countries sent a blue alien vessel into the battle."

"Dear God. Doesn't this revelation send shivers down one's spine? The Mongolian ship, could she have escaped by warp drive?"

"I don't think so. We believe she was too small to house such an engine."

"And *Blue Swan* is powered by a warp drive?"

"Not exactly. Duc calls her power plant a *sling engine*, as she can sling herself from place to place around the globe almost instantly by manipulating gravity and channeling the Earth's magnetic fields."

"Does Duc have any thoughts or theories on how to build a warp drive?"

"Not yet but he and his team are confident that it is only a matter of time before we have a warp drive."

"Wonderful! So, the U.S. has the world's only operational alien spacecraft?"

"As best we know, yes, Abe. Though the Germans still have the *Cigar*."

"And that worries you?"

"Of course it does."

"I thought we gutted the damn thing?"

"I still worry. Never underestimate the brilliance of German engineering."

"Now there's good advice. You are confident we have sufficient, rigorous security protocols in place to prevent anyone from stealing or sabotaging *Swan*?"

"We've taken every precaution we can think of."

"Our pilots operated *Swan* with Duc onboard as a tech advisor?"

"I think he'd cringe at your job description for him, but yes."

"Well, spend more money, as much as you need, to double, triple security. We can't afford to let *Swan* fall into the wrong hands."

"Yes, sir. To the Veechka, that is what the aliens call themselves, humankind is known as the Tribes of Kagii and our planet is called Kagnoontootla, meaning the *beautiful place* or *beautiful jewel*."

"I'm King Kag?" Calhoun asked and burst into a hardy laugh.

Adelman smiled and bowed his head. "We are the Kagii people, your grace. Mother is busy translating everything we've recovered from the ship. We have a treasure trove of information yet to decipher. One more thing. When Duc and his team fully powered up *Swan*, one of her systems activated a beacon of sorts. We may have located the mothership."

"Where?"

"The object, we can't tell what it is yet, is sitting on the far side of Jupiter IV, one of the four Galilean moons named Callisto. This is why none of our telescopes has ever spotted the object."

"My God. Is anybody answering the transmission from *Swan*?"

"No."

"*Sitting*, you say, stationary not orbiting? Doesn't that mean the object has power?"

"Yes. The object is in what we call a geosynchronous orbit with no deterioration in altitude. She may even have warp drive power or something equivalent that we can't even imagine yet."

"Fascinating. What of the autopsies? We learn anything?"

"Nothing. The commander's last entry into the ship's log appears routine. We know these aliens didn't die from old age. One skeleton we recovered was that of a child, probably a boy. He had a metal band around his neck with an amulet or talisman of sorts attached. We have no clue what it means."

"That Papenfuss fellow took more than *Cigar* out of Ethiopia, as I recall. I wonder if the Germans are holding any of the pieces to this puzzle?"

"That possibility has not been lost on us, Mr. President."

"Well, there is nothing to be done but move forward. The genie is out of the bottle now. Max, you're awfully quiet."

"Sorry, Abe. Just listening. I had no part in the *Battle for the Zhukov Line*."

"Huh? I beg to differ. You most certainly did, my friend."

"I can take no credit."

"What rubbish. You saved us all when you went to Austria and robbed the New World Order of those alien components. It is time for you to lose this guilt you are carrying around over the Austrian casualties, Max. Evil killed those men, women, and children, not you."

"Soldiering - at my core, I am a soldier - this is who I am. That's it. How else could a dysfunctional guy like me survive in a dysfunctional world like this?"

"Ah, ha. You on painkillers, Max? Never mind. Speaking of the Order, I think the time for a reckoning is at hand. I think the time has come for us to take back our country. Everything is in place, Max?"

"Yes, Mr. President."

"Gentlemen, with great enthusiasm I hereby approve initiating Operation Homecoming. As we succeed or fail, so does the nation we cherish so dearly. The stakes couldn't be greater for the freedoms of all people. We must not, we cannot fail."

Doss had set up a large operations room, another war room, within Section M3. He had five thousand men and women under his command scattered across the country. With Mother's help, his task force had spent months gathering information and preparing. When all was ready, and with Calhoun's blessing, he sent his agents into motion, all at once, across all fifty states.

Within days, his task force took nearly two thousand key players involved in the rebellion into custody. Governors, senators, congressmen and congresswomen, state assembly folks, judges, mayors, chiefs of police, district attorneys, senior military officers and those who had financed the rebellion were apprehended. Each conspirator had been indicted by their own deeds or public statements, or by former colleagues who had agreed to cooperate with Doss. Many had secretly pledged themselves to the success of the New World Order and believed themselves loyal patriots fighting for a just and noble cause, a cause of world peace, equity and unity. Doss's task force was unable to snag everyone involved, of course. But that didn't matter. Everyone was stripped of their power and their wealth was seized.

At the same time, Calhoun sent Adelman over to the White House to personally confront Dreyfus. She had agreed to meet Adelman in private in the Oval Office after he informed her that he was coming over to tender his resignation and hand over the keys, so to speak, to Section M3.

"Good day, Elaine," Adelman said as he walked into the Oval Office and plopped down on a couch across from the President's desk without an invitation to sit.

"Elaine, is it?" she asked scornfully and raised an eyebrow, taken aback by his brazen impertinence. "We aren't that close, Hermann. Madam President will do. Though I am enjoying this moment, I have a full calendar, so let me have your resignation letter and whatever sensitive information you want to leave with me and then you can be on your way."

"I've changed my mind, Elaine."

"What?"

"I have evidence, irrefutable evidence, that your sympathies, your loyalties, lie with the NWO. President Calhoun is alive and -."

"Bullshit Adelman. You have sixty seconds to tell me what you are really doing here or I'll have my Secret Service gorillas physically toss you out of a White House window and I'll invite the press to watch. I have my finger on the panic button. Start talking."

Adelman walked over to the President's desk and handed his phone over to her with Calhoun on the other end of a Facetime call.

"Hello, Elaine."

"Abe? But, but how?"

"The short and long of it is that I survived my wounds and I'm taking back my White House and I require your resignation in writing, effectively immediately. You can tell the world you resigned for medical reasons or for personal reasons or to pursue other interests - I really don't give a damn. But you will never hold public office again. This is the only way you can save face and leave with your dignity intact. Refuse and, well, I'll have you arrested for treason before dinner. As we speak, I am retaking control of the military. I am taking the principal ringleaders of the rebellion into custody. I'm cleaning house. You have no allies."

"You're bluffing. I'm not going anywhere, Abe. I am the lawful President of the United States, have been for well over a year."

"Then this will get very messy and very ugly very fast and you will leave me with no choice but to destroy you. Hermann, show Elaine the file, then accept her written resignation on my behalf and thank her for her service."

After Calhoun abruptly disconnected the call, Adelman handed Dreyfus a thumb drive. "I can't prove you were directly involved in the conspiracy to assassinate the President, Elaine, at least not yet. But I can prove you knew about the scheme to remove Calhoun from office. I can prove that most of the actions you have taken as President were in furtherance of a plot to weaken and eventually dissolve the United States as a sovereign nation to allow the New World Order to achieve its goal of global domination. Please, take a peek at the files."

Adelman could see the life draining from Dreyfus's face as she perused the files on her laptop from the thumb drive. He knew it was juvenile to enjoy watching her squirm, but couldn't help himself. He had to bite his lip to stop himself from smiling.

After she quietly closed her laptop, she tried to hand Adleman the thumb drive. "I could fight this, you know," she said softly. "But

Abe is right, this will just get ugly, and the truth is, I doubt I would win any legal battle to keep the Presidency under these circumstances. But know this: the Order offers world peace through unification while you Nationalists cling to your antiquated notions of borders which will only perpetuate inequities, wars and suffering. The Order at its core is fundamentally altruistic and inclusive and offers hope to all mankind. Nationalism at its core is selfish and exclusive to the detriment of all mankind."

"Perhaps in a more enlightened world, you might have a point, but not in our world. Our species simply isn't ready. Too many greedy, jealous narcissists among us. You need only look at history."

"History? I've made history as the first female President. My legacy will inspire women everywhere. What legacy will you leave behind?"

"Good spies like anonymity, no legacy for me, thank you. As for you, Washington, Lincoln, both Roosevelts, Kennedy, Regan, Obama, Trump, these are examples of Presidents who, like them or dislike them, made history. You didn't make history, Elaine; you only made the news."

"Damn you. I should have destroyed you when I had the chance. You've always been a quirky, odious little fellow. You'll have my resignation in the morning. Now get out!"

"You keep the thumb drive as my parting gift," Adelman said as he removed a folded sheet of paper tucked inside his suit coat. "I've already taken the liberty," he continued and handed Dreyfus her resignation letter on White House stationery. "The President insists you sign the letter now. I will see to it that the folks listed at the bottom receive their copies this afternoon. Think very carefully what you say to anyone, including the press. You must vacate the White House within the hour. We will take care of packing and moving your personal belongings. I have six female Secret Service agents waiting outside. They will escort you upstairs. You may grab your purse, wallet, jewelry, any medications, a few clothes, cosmetics, etc. but nothing else, and then the agents will take you to your home in Kennebunkport. Your former security detail has already been relieved. I'll take your phone now."

"Good evening, my fellow Americans. Yes, the rumors you've heard are true. There has indeed been a transition of power at the White House - but not a coup as some news outlets have incorrectly, irresponsibly reported. By the grace of God, or just dumb luck if you prefer, I survived the assassination attempt on my life and today I have resumed my duties as the President of the United States of America. Earlier this morning, I accepted the resignation of the acting President, my former Vice President, Elaine Dreyfus, as she has decided to retire from public service for personal reasons. I will send Congress my choice of a new Vice President tomorrow morning.

"I realize each of you must have a thousand questions. Over the coming weeks, I hope to answer all your questions as best I can, as truthfully and as transparently as I can. I ask you to be patient.

"Nearly two hundred years ago our nation was fighting a horrific, bloody, protracted civil war. During that desperate time, when brother fought brother and father fought son, President Abraham Lincoln took a number of harsh, desperate actions, some illegal, to save the nation. He suspended, in part, certain constitutional rights such as freedom of the press and habeas corpus. He did these things not for power or political gain. He took these drastic measures because he was convinced that they were necessary to preserve the Union. Regrettably, I have found it necessary to do the same.

"Over the past few days, on my orders, roughly two thousand individuals across the country have been arrested and removed from public office or removed from duty. These actions were taken without any due process. Without any trials. I am speaking with you tonight to tell you this purge is over. Those who instigated the secession, who broke their oath of loyalty to the country and to the Constitution, will be permanently barred from ever holding public office again. That's it. That's their punishment. There will be no trials, no executions, no imprisonment, or further retributions of any kind. Today, I am granting universal pardons to all those who took part in the rebellion. As I said, this matter is behind us. We, as a nation, considering the perilous times we are living in, need this unfortunate ugliness behind us without delay.

"This universal pardon is, however, not unconditional. I have been informed that many folks at the local, state, and federal levels used the chaos caused by the rebellion to line their own pockets. Billions are missing. Local, state, and federal law enforcement are free to prosecute these individuals for taking bribes, embezzlement, or any other crimes committed outside the scope of my pardon.

"We all witnessed the rise of evil across the world when America abdicated her role as the guardian of freedom and democracy. Tyrants rose up to take her place. Now all of us must come together and heal the wounds between us. Love America or hate America, the world is a safer, better place with America.

"It matters not to me if you are black, white, or brown, or something else. It matters not to me if you are a Christian, a Muslim, or a Jew, or something else. Whether you are educated or uneducated, rich or poor, a captain of industry or a worker on the assembly line, I welcome all into my tent who have a good heart and who are red, white and blue.

"What do I mean by this? Having a good heart speaks for itself. A good person lives by the Golden Rule and strives to do right. By red, white and blue I mean you, me, all of us, must love our country and honor the Constitution. With all of our warts and faults, despite our past sins, our past transgressions, despite our imperfections - and what country is without them? - we are still the greatest and most successful nation in the history of the world. If you are red, white and blue and have a good heart, I call you my brother, I call you my sister regardless of your race, your religion, or your station in life and I will protect your freedoms under the Constitution with my life as I trust you will protect mine.

"The Constitution is a sacred contract, an unbreakable agreement between this nation and its citizens. We may be many diverse people, but we are and will always be one family. As of tonight, I am proud to report, I am profoundly honored to report, that we are again one indivisible nation.

"Well, I think I've given you enough to chew on for now. I will speak to you soon about other matters of great importance to you, your families, to me and to the nation as a whole. May God keep you and bless our country. Good night, America."

With Operation Homecoming drawing to a close, and Calhoun - to the shock of a bloodied, broken world - back in the White House, Doss left for France with Adelman's blessing where he had unfinished business. He took Bijeau, Beauvilliers and a team of 20 agents with him.

Mother found an old farmhouse for rent just west of Compiègne, an ideal place for Doss to set up shop. The farmhouse, with a nearby barn, was nestled in a quiet, remote region of northern France. It was large enough to accommodate his team and not too far from Paris.

Doss wanted to question three men: Marc Laurent, Richard Rubenfeld, and Henri Murat, the Director of DGES who promised Adelman he'd put his house in order but never did. Doss decided to start with the low-hanging fruit, Laurent. Mother found him in Marseille with a house on the Avenue de Monaco and a boat tied to a slip at the Marina Marseille. Doss left the farmhouse with five men to pick him up. Laurent had made no effort to hide or conceal himself in any way and Doss easily caught him on his boat, about to take her out fishing.

"*Putain, que es tu?*" Laurent asked indignantly when Doss pulled the black hood off his head after an all-day drive from Marseille. Laurent found himself tied to a chair in a small kitchen of what looked like a country house. He recognized the large, muscular man from Marseille staring down at him and noticed the two incredibly attractive women standing off to the side, then quickly realized one of the women was Beauvilliers.

He glanced down at the sheet of clear plastic stretched across a tiled floor, the kind used to wrap bodies in after an execution, and looked over at Doss. "*Vous, les abrutis, n'avez aucune idée aveq qui vous jouez!*"

"English please," Doss said as he took a seat across from Laurent.

"American? Who the fuck are you? You fool, you are threatening the wrong man. I am with the French government. Madeline, tell them who I am."

"You are an independent contractor for DGSE," Doss corrected him as he removed three pictures from his pocket. "You were hired to kill this man, yes? But you killed this woman, his wife, instead, and nearly killed his sixteen-year-old daughter."

Laurent said nothing and showed no emotion, not even fear, as he glanced at the pictures. Doss quickly sized him up as either a sociopath or a psychopath.

"Nothing to say?" Doss asked.

"No."

"Why did you try to kill Adelman's daughter?"

"I never tried to kill the girl."

"You ran the car she was in off the road. The car rolled down a steep embankment, killing the driver and injuring the girl."

"I only wanted to speak with Adelman. It was dark, I was delayed by an accident and meant to intercept Adleman's car before the bridge. I did not intend for the vehicle to swerve off the road and down a hill. The driver did that."

"Of course, it was the driver's fault. Why did you think Adelman was in that car that night?"

"Paris gave me the intel. I have nothing more to say to you."

"That's ok, I'm not here to talk about your crimes. I only want one more thing from you."

"What do you want?"

"I want to know where Richard Rubenfeld is."

Laurent shrugged his shoulders.

"Everyone has a breaking point, my friend. I have a list of names of people who can help me with these simple questions. You are the first. If you cannot help me, then I don't need you. Smith!"

"Sir!" one of his men answered and stepped into the kitchen.

"I cannot use this man. Bury the body deep in the cornfield. Then return to Marseille, burn his boat and his house. Bijeau!"

"Sir!"

"Laurent has two checking accounts, three savings accounts and two brokerage accounts, correct?"

"Yes, sir, one of the savings accounts is in the Caymans. It is a rather large account with his daughter Jaqueline listed as sole beneficiary."

"She's the young lawyer in Paris?"

"Affirmative."

"Take it all Bijeau and to you, Mr. Laurent, goodbye," Doss said briskly, then stood to leave the room.

The man named Smith walked over to Laurent with a plastic bag and slipped the bag over Laurent's head. Laurent stamped his feet to get Doss's attention.

Doss turned and had Smith remove the bag. "What?"

"My daughter, swear you will not harm her. Let her keep the money."

"I will not harm your daughter. The money, well, I know another young lady who could use that money more than your daughter."

"Fine, ok, ok. Rubenfeld is hiding in the French Polynesians on the island of Tahiti."

"When was the last time you spoke to him?"

"A few days ago. He wanted to hire me for a job in India."

"India, interesting. Did you take it?"

"I told him I would think about it."

Doss grabbed his phone and dialed Mother. "Mother, Tahiti, can you confirm?"

An hour later, Mother was able to confirm that Rubenfeld was in Tahiti. An hour after that, Doss and a team of three were in Paris driving towards the Charles De Gaulle Airport where Mother already had their jet fueled and ready. Doss brought Bijeau and Beauvilliers with him and took Kraft too, Bijeau's off-and-on sex toy, since Rubenfeld knew his face and Beauvilliers's face and because Bijeau was, well, not a people person. He left the rest of his team at the farmhouse with plenty to do, tracking the movements of Murat and, out of curiosity, he had them track Stromquist too. From Paris to Los Angeles, where they stopped to refuel and change crews, took eleven and a half hours, and from Los Angeles to Tahiti took another eight and a half hours. They landed at the Tahiti International Airport in the late afternoon stiff, bored and exhausted.

After picking up a rental car Mother had arranged, a Peugeot Dacia Duster, they dropped their bags off at the Hilton where Mother had booked four rooms, showered, changed into fresh clothing and regrouped back in the hotel lobby. Doss had decided to push on and drive along Tahiti's eastern coastal road straight to Taravao, a village some twenty miles away on the south side of the island where Rubenfeld kept a bungalow. When the women suddenly turned quiet in the backseat, Doss glanced up at the rearview mirror while driving and saw them both asleep with Beauvilliers's head resting against Bijeau's bare shoulder. He felt a twinge of jealousy, yawned, and reprimanded himself for letting his mind wander during a mission.

Rubenfeld was not hard to find. Before leaving the farmhouse in Compiègne, Doss had Laurent call Rubenfeld to confirm that he'd take the job in India, and Mother traced the call back to a quaint little restaurant in Taravao called *Le Manoa*. Doss figured Rubenfeld was probably a regular at the restaurant as Taravao is a tiny village, and decided to look for Rubenfeld in the restaurant before going to his bungalow.

He sent Kraft into *Le Manoa* while he and the women remained outside to keep an eye out for any muscle. Kraft spotted Rubenfeld, a bald, short, stocky fellow with disproportionately powerful, hulking arms in contrast to the rest of him, wearing cutoff shorts and a tacky Hawaiian shirt sitting at a booth at a small table eating supper by himself. Kraft plopped down in the booth across from him.

"*Excusez-moi, cette table est prise monsieur* - this table is taken."

"Don't mind me," Kraft replied, "please, finish your supper, Monsieur Rubenfeld."

Rubenfeld stiffened and glanced around the restaurant, but saw no police or other threats. "You seem to know who I am. What do you want?"

"I'll explain everything to you later at the airport. I have a private jet waiting for us."

"To go where?"

"The U.S."

"I'm not going anywhere with you."

"Then you will die here within the next twenty-four hours."

"Fuck off, American."

There had been no time for Mother to smuggle weapons into Tahiti, so Kraft had to improvise. "I'm not the only one who has found you. Paris, the DGSE specifically, has sent a kill team to Tahiti just for you. Marc Laurent betrayed you. No one can save you but me."

Mentioning both the DGSE and Laurent had the desired effect. Rubenfeld began squirming uncomfortably in his booth as his eyes darted anxiously back and forth, again looking for any trouble.

"What do you want from me?" Rubenfeld finally asked.

"I need your help," Kraft replied evasively.

"Help with what?"

"These matters are best discussed in private. I don't want to be in Tahiti when the team from Paris lands. A ride with me to the airport tonight or a bullet in the head tomorrow? Decide now."

"Very well. I agree to go as far as the airport with you. If you can convince me during the drive to board the plane, I will. If not, I will take my chances here. I need to stop at my bungalow first."

"Of course," Kraft agreed, paid the check and followed Rubenfeld out of the restaurant.

Rubenfeld was surprised and confused when he saw Doss and Beauvilliers standing outside with another woman. "*Maddie, tu es avec les Américains?*"

"*Oui*," Beauvilliers replied. "After the debacle in Nassau, Director Murat sent me to America as punishment, I suppose, for a botched mission. I did not understand why you left DGSE. I did not know how to reach you."

Rubenfeld seemed satisfied with her answer and relaxed a bit. "I am glad you are alive; I was told something different," he said and leaned over as if to kiss her on the cheek, but whispered in her ear instead. "*Ne faites confiance à personne, surtout aux Américains.*" And then he turned to Doss. "You are the man we wanted to talk to in Nassau."

"That's right. That didn't turn out too well for your men."

"No hard feelings I trust?"

"None at all. A misunderstanding. We really must go."

They all hopped into the Peugeot, with Rubenfeld squeezed between Bijeau and Beauvilliers in the backseat, and stopped at his bungalow two blocks away. Doss accompanied Rubenfeld inside, where he grabbed a leather satchel of emergency cash, his passport and a .45 caliber handgun, which Doss snatched away from him and left on a table, and then they headed for the airport. Rubenfeld grew more uneasy and restless when no one explained anything to him.

When they reached the terminal twenty minutes later, Doss parked the Peugeot and left the keys. "We have a private jet fueled and ready to go Richard."

"You people haven't told me anything. As I told this fellow in the restaurant, if you can't convince me to trust you, I'm staying in Tahiti."

"It's real simple Richard," Doss said. "We are flying to Washington, where you may be able to help us understand what the hell is going on over at DGSE."

"Who is *us*?"

"CIA."

"I'm sorry, but your cryptic explanation is not good enough for me."

"I think you know the man leading the kill team, Marc Laurent?"

Beauvilliers moved to his side and slipped her arm inside the arm of the man who, she was certain, would have had her killed in Nassau. "You will be dead Richard before sunset tomorrow if you stay. Please come with us and live. The Americans have been very good to me."

Rubenfeld hesitated until Bijeau reached over and snatched his leather satchel out of his hands. "You want this back? Get on the fucking plane. We're dead meat standing out here in the open. I've read Laurent's dossier. He's a fucking nut job who kills for pleasure."

Rubenfeld weighed his options, nodded and reluctantly boarded the plane.

Thirty minutes into the flight, Doss walked down the aisle and plopped down in a seat next to Rubenfeld. "We might as well start now."

"Start what?"

"The interrogation."

"I am happy to work with CIA and answer your questions, though I left the DGSE some time ago. Things and people have changed at DGSE. Information quickly turns stale. I may not be of much value to you."

"Drink?"

"Please, scotch whisky, no ice?"

"This is a self-service flight," Doss said and turned to look down the aisle. "Maddie, would you be so kind as to pour Richard a drink?"

"Certainly," she said pleasantly from a few seats back and returned a few minutes later with a tumbler of scotch whisky. "Cheers," she said affably and handed Rubenfeld his drink.

"So," Doss said, patting Rubenfeld on the shoulder as Rubenfeld sipped his drink. "How are you affiliated with the New World Order?"

Rubenfeld's face turned red as he choked when his whisky went down the wrong pipe. "What?" he asked after he caught his breath.

"I am not CIA. I work for another agency, a less civilized agency. If you don't start answering my questions, and answer them truthfully, I'll instruct the pilot to descend to ten thousand feet and then I'll open the cabin door and drop you into the Pacific. We already have Laurent. He helped us get to you."

Rubenfeld's face went from beet-red to ashen-gray. "Many, many people in France, indeed across all of Europe, support the goals of the New World Order. This is no crime."

"You wanted me dead in Nassau. You would have killed Maddie, too. If that is not a crime, I consider it a personal insult. Who authorized Nassau and why, you certainly didn't authorize it on your own."

"Yes, yes, well, I, um. I had nothing personal against you. I am a professional. The Council only wanted to talk. They wanted information from you. They wanted to find Billy Duc."

"Who at the Council wanted Billy Duc?"

"I, I, don't know. The higher-ups use code names, not real names."

"Why did the Council want Duc?"

"I do not know. He is a scientist, an inventor of some kind. He is important to them. This is what I know."

"How much were you paid?"

When Rubenfeld hesitated, Doss pulled a knife he had grabbed from the galley earlier and pressed the blade against the fleshy part of Rubenfeld's thigh.

"One hundred, one hundred thousand Euros."

"We can go into the details of those matters later. Tell me about Adelman."

"What about him?"

"You hired Laurent to kill him, why?"

"Laurent told you that? That's a lie. Again, we only wanted to talk."

Doss started pressing the blade into Rubenfeld's flesh. "Don't mess with me."

"Ah, well, when Adelman defected, the Germans became suspicious and, and nervous."

"Defected? How can Adelman defect when the U.S. and Germany are free democracies and allies?"

"Adelman is no ordinary citizen, as I suspect you already know. Would America have allowed Edward Teller to, with all his knowledge of thermonuclear weapons, immigrate to the Soviet Union? No. The Germans were convinced Adelman was building some extraordinary new weapon for the U.S. from plans stolen from them and behold - a strange flying vessel, far more advanced than anything the world has ever seen, singlehandedly turned the tide at the *Battle for the Zhukov Line*. For years there have been rumors about the existence of alien technology. I think that vessel must be alien and we both know it came from America. Perhaps Duc was somehow involved, too."

"Who wanted to talk with Adelman?"

"Someone in the German BND."

"You mean Stromquist and the Council wanted Adelman dead."

"The Council, German BND, there's not much difference. But I had no instructions about killing him."

"Laurent nearly killed a sixteen-year-old girl."

"A tragic mistake."

"Adelman was Laurent's assignment, not his daughter?"

"Of course, Adelman was the assignment, not the daughter. We are hardly barbarians."

"Adelman's daughter was going to her prom that night. Why did Laurent believe Adelman would be in the car with his daughter?"

"We were able to hack into his wife's phone. We read her text messages. We learned from her that Adelman would accompany their daughter to the prom as a chaperone. Laurent was supposed to force the vehicle off the road and bring Adleman in, nothing more."

"Why murder Adelman's wife?"

"A second tragic mistake. Laurent is obviously incompetent, but he is useful from time to time when DGES does not wish to soil its own hands. He exceeded his authority, at least the authority I had given him, using poison. He is not certified to administer poisons and negligently used a lethal dose. Unless - someone within the Council gave the order without my knowledge."

"These are softball questions I am asking you now. Back in the States, your interrogation team won't be as pleasant. I doubt they'll serve you whisky. How you cooperate will determine your fate and, just to be clear, I am the one who decides. Say you understand."

"I understand."

"Good. Tell me who is protecting you?"

"No one."

"Now Richard, this kind of lie is what will buy you a one-way ticket to the worst maximum-security prison in the States. American prisons are so much worse than French prisons. It was fairly easy for me to find you and if I can find you, DGSE or the Council will find you without my protection. This is your moment of truth. Your life is in your hands. I will ask you one last time, who is protecting you?"

"Murat."

"He serves the Council, the Order?"

"Yes, but as I have said, many of us serve the Order. It is the same as belonging to one political party or another and now, look, most of Europe has embraced the Order, including France."

"Maybe, but when you and Murat pledged your allegiances to the Order, for cash, you said, you both betrayed your allegiances to France."

"No, no. I did what everyone is doing."

"Beauvilliers didn't."

"We are doing what is best for the greater good. You Americans are so unsophisticated, so childlike, as was Beauvilliers when she betrayed me in Nassau."

"That's a twisted view. The thugs you hired in Nassau intended to torture and kill me. We both know they would have disposed of Maddie too as a loose end."

"Again, I gave no such order."

"I think you did, and if you didn't, Murat did. Rubenfeld is a Jewish surname, yes?"

"Yes, what of it?"

"If the Order suddenly turned on the Jews, that would be agreeable to you?"

"Of course not. You grossly misunderstand the core principles of the Order."

"We'll see. We've intercepted various chatter that some within the Order are urging Stromquist to initiate purges now that the

Mongolians are no longer a threat. Against whom I do not yet know."

Doss, who had gone without sleep for 36 hours, suddenly felt lightheaded, stood and looked down the aisle at Beauvilliers. "Maddie, would you secure our guest? Refill his glass if he wants another. I need to rest my eyes."

"With pleasure," Beauvilliers replied.

Doss wearily dragged himself back to his seat and closed his tired eyes. But when he heard a muffled scream a moment later, he jumped to his feet just as Rubenfeld was pushing a plastic shiv he had sown inside his belt deep into Beauvilliers's carotid artery. She looked at Doss wide-eyed, with her hands wrapped around Rubenfeld's wrist, frantically trying to stop him as her blood spurted across the seats. Doss mindlessly charged at Rubenfeld, smashed his fist into his face with everything he had, and then grabbed Beauvilliers around the waist before she fell. He held her in his arms, brushed her hair off her face, and tenderly kissed her forehead. Powerless to do more, he held her close and watched her eyes flutter for a bit before she faded away forever.

Dazed but still standing, Rubenfeld was smiling triumphantly down at Doss when Bijeau leapt over his seat and straddled his chest. He began foaming at the mouth after biting down on a capsule hidden inside a molar. Seized with blinding rage, possessed with an unstoppable lust to kill, Bijeau took her boot knife and sliced his throat open with one superhuman, vigorous swing, nearly decapitating him, before the poison could do its work. She held Rubenfeld up against the seatback with pure hatred in her eyes and took pleasure in watching him die.

Chapter Twenty-Six

Excerpts from Hermann Adelman's private journal:
The Great Turmoil

After Adelman finished reviewing Doss's after-action report on Laurent and Rubenfeld while his plane was cruising at thirty thousand feet above the Atlantic Ocean en route for Europe, he picked up the forensic report on Beauvilliers's company phone and laptop, standard operating procedure when any agent had been killed in the field, and began reading. He wished he hadn't. From her emails, text messages and a personal, electronic diary she had kept, it was clear Beauvilliers had been very much in love with both Doss and Bijeau and they apparently had been separately in love with her. He had an uneasy feeling in the pit of his stomach that he had somehow violated something sacred, or at least had desecrated their privacy, and ordered a beer, then changed his mind and asked for a martini. After he drained the glass, he asked for a second and then called Mother. At the Section's expense, he told her, Doss and Bijeau were to take thirty days of mandatory leave and Mother was to make certain they took it.

A black, late-model Audi limo from the U.S. Embassy picked Adelman up at Berlin's Brandenburg Airport and whisked him away to the Grand Hyatt Hotel to freshen up. Two hours later, the limo took him directly to the Federal Chancellery building a short distance from the hotel where Stromquist had agreed to meet him.

"Herr Direktor, it is a great pleasure to make your acquaintance at last," Stromquist said affably in English as he and Adelman shook hands. "You are highly respected within both Germany's scientific and intelligence communities. A rare and impressive accomplishment."

"Imperator, on behalf of the President of the United States, I am, we are, grateful for your time."

"Please help yourself to tea, coffee, juice, or a bottle of spring water from the credenza and have a seat."

Stromquist's office was surprisingly plain, even spartan Adelman noted. Except for the man's extraordinarily hypnotic eyes and a deep, commanding voice, Stromquist himself was also surprisingly plain. Of average height and a lanky build, with thinning blonde hair, pasty skin and a weak, receding chin, he appeared altogether ordinary.

Stromquist poured himself a cup of coffee after Adelman helped himself to a glass of orange juice and took a seat on a small couch directly across from Adelman.

"The White House provided me no agenda for your visit," he said matter-of-factly. "I assume this is not a social call or some diplomatic mission as your ambassador is not with you? How may I be of service?"

"My dear Imperator, I wanted to tell you in person that two days ago at precisely nineteen hundred hours Tokyo Standard Time, at GMT plus nine, the Indians and Japanese intercepted and destroyed all twenty-four of your killer satellites. This is why, in case you were wondering, your Aerospace Center in Cologne has lost contact with them."

Stromquist looked at Adelman with a mix of surprise and indignation. "What makes you think these so-called killer satellites belonged to us?"

"They are the same satellites that vaporized two of our F-51 fighters over the U.S. a while back. They are the same satellites that vaporized a number of Chinese aircraft during China's brief war with Mongolia when you believed China was a greater threat to you than Mongolia. You forced China to ground its entire fleet of fighters and bombers, severely crippling China's military capabilities. Your satellites were built with technology obtained from *Cigar*, the alien spacecraft in Germany's possession."

"Even if what you say is true, these events happened well before I came to power."

"You didn't sanction this operation in the U.S. in your attempt to capture Billy Duc when you were the supreme head of the Council?"

"Hermann, may I call you Hermann? I did not agree to this meeting so that you could interrogate me, so the United States could make outlandish accusations against me, to accuse me of being a part of some diabolical, criminal international conspiracy."

"I suppose you will deny the Council had anything to do with the assassination attempt on President Calhoun, too? I must warn you, we possess compelling evidence to the contrary."

"Warn me!" Stromquist exclaimed angrily and jumped to his feet. "How dare you come into my office to warn me of anything. Your impertinence is intolerable! I deny these absurd allegations. You have overstayed your welcome, Herr Direktor. I have more important matters to attend to. *Auf wiedersehen.*"

Adelman didn't budge from his chair. "The former Director of the DGES, Henri Murat, tells a different story regarding Billy Duc. That's right, he is now in our custody, along with most of his cronies. The Council was paying Murat, the head of France's intelligence services, to help destabilize the former French government, among other evil deeds. Scandalous. What shocking news that will make. France is already having second thoughts about her membership in the New World Order. What will you do if the French vote to opt out of the Order? Will you crush them as Temüjin would have done had he taken Europe? If yes, what is the difference between you and Temüjin?"

Stromquist's expression turned from indignation to unkind, even sinister. The sudden transformation stunned Adelman.

"Murat is an insect. No member country may opt out of the Order any more than any of your states can secede from the Union. And you have the gall to ask what the difference is, or was, between Temüjin and myself? Ha! The so-called Khan of Khans came to enslave the world. I am here to free the world. I am here to help usher in a new age of peace, prosperity, and hope for all mankind."

"How noble of you. Well, ordinarily I'd congratulate you Imperator on your historic victory over Temüjin, except that we both know it was not your victory. The United States single-handedly routed the Mongolians at the Zhukov Line, not Europe - and we both know how. Our civil war, such as it was, is over. America is whole again and on the rise. She is now poised to resume her rightful place as a great power, as the first among nations. Economically, militarily, industrially, technologically, with her political stability and vast natural resources, she excels all others."

"Ah, I see now. I underestimated your hillbilly, President Calhoun, Herr Direktor. You are here to put me on notice, to put me in my place. Do you think the United States can bully me, can arrogantly dictate terms to me? This New World Order I am building is powerful, too. True, Greater Mongolia is still a threat, but the empire will fracture into many inconsequential nations soon enough without the Khan of Khans to hold them together, just as the empire of Genghis Khan eventually broke into dozens of inferior parts. China will take years, perhaps decades, to recover. Russia as a nation-state is *kaput*, dead forever. All Russian territories west of the Urals have been incorporated into the New World Order. Soon countries in Africa, Southeast Asia and South America will join the Order. The United States and the New World Order are the only superpowers still standing."

"But Kurt, may I call you Kurt? We are hardly equals. Not even close. The United States has *Blue Swan*. What does the New World Order have? The *Cigar*? I'm the one who had her gutted. I strongly suggest you think about this new reality long and hard before you do anything rash. *Guten Tag, Herr Stromquist.*"

Chapter Twenty-Seven

The hardcore, badass Terminatrix threw her arms around Doss's neck and wept when she saw him standing alone in a hallway at Section M3 after thirty days of leave. Doss embraced her, held her tight and let her weep until she could weep no more. She excused herself, went to the restroom to wash her face, and then joined Doss in Adelman's office.

"Alejandra, Max, welcome back," Adelman said gently and motioned them to sit. "I've informed Maddie's family. I've told them of the high regard we all had for her. I told them of her exceptional heroism. She will posthumously be awarded France's highest medal for valor: the *Ordre national de la Légion d'honneur*."

"She is dead because of me," Doss offered soberly, without emotion.

"Max, what the devil are you talking about?"

"I pushed the team too hard. I pushed myself too hard. We were all exhausted when we landed in Tahiti. I got sloppy. We should've rested at the hotel before pursuing Rubenfeld. He wasn't going anywhere."

"I've lost agents too, Max. It hurts. You second-guess yourself. You tell yourself if only I had done this or that. But had you stayed at the hotel that night and rested, you don't know if Rubenfeld would have been around in the morning. Someone might have tipped him off. He could have left on his own for other reasons. You put the mission first, ahead of your team's welfare - that's your job, plain and simple. Maybe Maddie was careless. Maybe she was just damn unlucky. Either way, her death is not on you. Are we clear?"

"Ok."

"Not ok. Are we clear, yes, or no?"

"Yes."

"Good. Do you need more time? I will understand if you do."

"No."

"Very well then. Are you one hundred percent? Your head is in the game?"

"Yes."

"Alejandra?"

"One hundred percent Herr Direktor and I'm itching to fuck somebody up."

"Good," Adelman said and moved on, without revealing he understood why Doss and Bijeau were still hurting. "The President is honoring Billy Duc and the key members of his team today at a secret ceremony in the Oval Office. No doubt there will be the White House's famous white cake. You are both welcome to attend or not."

"We are ready for a new assignment," Doss said forcefully.

"Excellent. Well, here it is then. I allowed Laurent to escape from the farm in France."

Doss looked at Adelman in disbelief. "Beg pardon, sir?"

Adelman offered a hint of a smile. "I once heard someone say: if you give a rat some peanut butter and chocolate, you can usually follow it back to the nest. Sounded like good advice to me. Laurent was just a triggerman. I want the nest. If you are up for it, I want you to find him and extinguish him and all the vermin associated with him. Mother has tracked Laurent to French Guiana."

"According to Rubenfeld," Doss noted, "Murat was protecting him."

"True, but Murat denies sanctioning the hit on me. Not that I necessarily believe him, but if not Murat, who? Stromquist?"

"I don't know, but this sounds like a cream puff job anyone can handle. Alejandra and I are up for something more challenging."

"There is some chatter going around, as you know, that suggests Stromquist is planning an operation, possibly something major. Where, for what purpose, I do not know. Laurent, I suspect, will have some role to play. This is the job. Do you want it or not?"

"Very well, sir, we'll take it. What of Murat?"

"Murat? Why he's the Village's newest guest, though he won't be staying long. I have proof he was the mastermind behind Moscow."

"He planned the assignation attempt on Temüjin? He killed the Pope?"

"Yes. Murat had a Vatican security officer on the payroll. The officer fed Murat information to get to Temüjin. After the Pope was killed the officer confessed his sins in a letter and then hung himself."

"Murat did this on behalf of the Council?"

"Yes. As you've been busy, Stone put all the pieces together on this one."

"I have no words. What will you do with Murat?"

"If the Italians had a death penalty, I'd turn Murat over to them. Calhoun has agreed to let me extradite him to Mongolia. Let the Mongolians decide his punishment after we inform them of his crimes. Sometimes the old ways are best. Seems like justice to me."

Doss and Bijeau led an elite team of 20 men and women down to Cayenne on a private 737-800, customized by the CIA for special ops missions, and set up shop. They followed Laurent around for a week until he caught an Air France flight to Paris's Orly Airport under the alias Martin Lebleu. Doss and his team boarded their 737-800 and followed him to Paris though, with a smaller aircraft, they had to make a refueling stop in Casablanca and lost some time.

With Mother's help, they reacquired Laurent at an apartment within the commune of Massy, just south of Paris. Doss rented a small warehouse nearby and for nearly a week his team subtly tailed Laurent from place to place, giving him plenty of space using multiple vehicles and multiple faces. When Laurent packed a suitcase and headed for the Charles De Gaulle Airport to catch a plane for Warsaw, Doss and his team packed their things too, managed to pin a tracker on him before he boarded his flight and then boarded their 737-800 and followed him. Mother took care of getting their gear and weapons through Polish customs under U.S. Embassy diplomatic immunity credentials before they landed.

"Mother, Doss."

"Max, it appears you are following a world traveler."

"Yep. Tedious, boring job."

"I'm certain Herr Direktor has sound reasons for giving you this mission. No one could ever accuse our fearless leader of being capricious - or mismanaging his best asset."

"You still tracking Laurent?"

"No. He must have found the tracker or ditched his clothing after he landed."

"No matter. I don't think he is here on holiday. Anything going on in Warsaw that might interest Laurent?"

"Let me see. There is an international art show in Warsaw this weekend, both Saturday and Sunday, at Łazienki Park. The Mayor of Warsaw expects at least one hundred thousand people to attend. And, searching, searching, ah, the President of Poland, Piotr Nowak, is hosting an early dinner tonight for the Prime Minister of Denmark, Bjorn Kirkegaard, and his wife, together with the new President-elect of France, Alain Girard, and his wife."

"Where?"

"Belweder Palace, one of two presidential residences in Warsaw."

"I don't know anything about the palace, but the place must be a highly secure location, too secure for Laurent to cause any trouble. Are Nowak and his guests attending any public events?"

"As a matter of fact, Nowak and his fiancée are taking Kirkegaard, Girard and their wives to see the ballet *Giselle* tonight after an early dinner at Belweder Palace."

"The venue?"

"Warsaw's Grand Theatre, though the public is unaware that the President will be attending the ballet."

"Interesting. When does the ballet begin?"

"Curtains up at eight o'clock."

"Adelman and his hunches. He knew Laurent was up to something major."

"You think Laurent is in Poland to assassinate Nowak?"

"I know from Adelman that France is not a happy member of the NWO. Girard won the election on his promise to restore French independence while Poland has always staunchly maintained her own independence. Anything on where the people of Denmark stand?"

"Checking. Movements to leave the NWO, protests, strikes, walkouts, even riots are gaining traction and becoming more frequent among the Danish people. Kirkegaard's government has done nothing to curtail or stop any of it."

"Fascinating coincidence. To answer your question, I think

Laurent may be going for a trifecta. If I'm right, he'll try to hit Nowak and his party at the Grand Theatre. We have less than four hours to find Laurent and stop him. We are in our car rentals and are leaving the airport now. I'll position my team near Belweder Palace and stand by. Brief Adelman immediately. Ask him for further instructions."

As Doss waited for Adelman's call, a dizzying array of thoughts raced through his head. The Poles, the French and the Danish authorities all had to be warned, of course. If the three leaders didn't make the ballet, Laurent and his team, if he had a team, would pack up and leave and simply wait for another opportunity. He'd need to deal with them somehow before they left Warsaw. If Nowak did not take the threat seriously and decided to attend the ballet, perhaps with increased security, Doss wasn't sure what he would do.

An agonizing thirty minutes passed before Adelman called. "Max, I just learned that six days ago, thieves were able to break into a weapons bunker at a Polish military base near Powidz. They stole mostly small arms, a few assault rifles, ammunition, etc. but they also ran off with a dozen RPGs and four .50 caliber heavy machine guns. I think you are spot on. Laurent will hit the opera house tonight. He must have a team of professionals with him to pull this off."

"Cancel the ballet."

"Tried that. You don't know Nowak. Poland's President is a soldier's soldier. He secretly fought at the Z Line with the Polish Army and led a mechanized infantry battalion during a counterattack into one of the deadliest sectors of the fighting. He believes the link between the weapons theft and Laurent is weak and, as the public is unaware of his evening plans, he insists on attending the ballet. I've presented a plan to him and he has given the plan his blessing."

"Must be a helluva plan, sir."

"There's risk, high risk. He and his guests will attend the ballet as planned, but his fiancée and the others will slip out of their formal attire, change into casual clothing, and secretly leave the theatre through a back entrance. Doubles from the Polish secret service will dress in their clothes and replace them. Nowak insists on remaining behind in case Laurent has a spotter inside the theatre to confirm that he and his party are in their seats. You will deploy your team to the most likely locations Laurent and his assassins will be positioned."

"And if they have RPGs, Herr Direktor? I have nothing to stop one let alone twelve."

"Of course you don't, but I do. *Blue Swan* can intercept all twelve rockets. She is hovering over the theatre as we speak, hidden within the clouds."

"How long has *Swan* been over Polish airspace?"

"She left Kings Bay not long after you called Mother."

"So, this is what sling drive power looks like?"

"Quite so."

"It's a brave new world, sir. This new toy of yours is full of surprises."

"You don't know the half of it yet, Max. A Polish Secret Service officer named Captain Felix Bartosz will accompany your team and serve as your liaison with Polish security forces. He's solid. He's a minute or two away from your location. You have about thirty minutes to get into position, Max. I suggest you move your ass."

The sky was overcast and night came early when Bartosz arrived outside the gates of Belweder Palace. Bartosz brought ten men, twenty-two security badges, and five unmarked vans with him. Doss and his team grabbed their gear, left their rentals behind and headed towards the Grand Theatre in the vans. Doss had studied a map of the area on his tablet while waiting for Adelman's call. He already had a plan.

Doss had Bartosz drive to Ogród Saski, Saxon Gardens, a block away from the Grand Theatre and park. He had everyone grab their gear and follow him over to a large shade tree near a small building known as the Water Tower, where he laid his tablet on the ground with a map of the area on the screen just as light snow flurries began falling.

"This is Captain Bartosz and his ten men from Polish Secret Service," he said after everyone had gathered around. "Sorry Captain, I won't even try pronouncing the name of your agency in Polish. Captain Bartosz is here to support us. He has direct communications with the President's security detail. We are here. The Grand Theatre is here. Directly across from the Grand Theatre is Jabłonowskich

Palace. To the right of the palace is the Ministry of Sport and Tourism and to the left is the Church of St. Andres the Apostle and St. Brother Albert. If Laurent is in Warsaw with a team to assassinate the President of Poland and his guests, I think they'll use one or all three of these buildings to launch their assault. I could, of course, be wrong.

"The President of Poland wants Laurent to show his hand, and he is willing to be the bait. That's why we're here. I'll position myself somewhere inside the front of the theatre. Bijeau, you will set up across from the Ministry of Sport with Alpha Team and position a countersniper over here if he can reach it. Kraft, you and Bravo Team will position here and here to watch the palace. Deploy your counter-sniper however you deem best. Captain Bartosz, you and your men will position yourselves across from the church. We wait out of sight, we watch, we remain flexible. We react to the situation as it develops. We'll have some serious air support and, of course, there will be Polish security forces standing close by. Questions?"

Kraft shook his head. "No offense boss, but this plan is pretty thin, one might say fucked-up. Lots of guessing, no hard intel, RPGs, .50 cals, Jesus..."

"The leaders of Poland, France and Denmark are about thirty minutes out from the theatre," Doss replied. "If you have a better plan, other than to tell the President of Poland to get his ass back to a secure location, let's hear it."

"No sir, but we're breaking just about every goddamn cardinal rule in the book with this op."

"I suspect so. No question, we are doing this on the fly."

"*Improvise, adapt and overcome,*" Bijeau offered in a low voice.

Doss nodded. "Let's ditch the civvies for fatigues and body armor, check weapons and commo and move out. Keep to the shadows, remember your training and be prepared for anything. Remember to lower your weapons and flash your badges at Polish security if they approach. Then again, stay sharp. Some might be working for Laurent."

Doss's team moved out ten minutes later in thickening snow and positioned themselves as planned, while Doss entered the theatre from the back and made his way to the main lobby. He drew stares from various patrons with his weapons, black fatigues and a ski mask, but no one bothered him. Poles were accustomed to seeing heavily armed security personnel wandering about. He found a small, unoccupied room off to the side where he could watch the buildings across from the theatre and waited. The buildings were dark and appeared unoccupied. When the presidential motorcade pulled in front of the Grand Theatre and stopped under a large security canopy ten minutes later, Doss returned to the lobby, ditched his ski mask and took cover behind a three-legged easel supporting a large, six-foot poster of an attractive, nearly naked woman modeling women's sexy lingerie.

He watched Nowak and his guests with his security detail walk by, then noticed a big, muscular man dressed in an ill-fitting gray suit standing across the lobby watching them too. The man didn't look like secret service to Doss, even when he whispered a few words into a mic pinned to his lapel. Doss decided to follow him when he started following Nowak and his entourage. When Nowak and the others turned down a side hallway instead of heading directly into the theatre, the man in the gray suit continued following them.

Doss decided to make his move. He came up behind the man and ripped his mic off first. The man spun around and threw a punch at Doss's face, but Doss expected the move and easily blocked the blow. He threw his own punch into the man's stomach, but his fist landed against a bulletproof vest underneath the man's shirt and did no damage. When the man tried to pull his service weapon, Doss knocked the gun out of his hand. The man then backhanded Doss across the face and tried to knee him in the groin but missed. The man was heavyset and strong but Doss was taller, quicker and with a longer reach landed a single uppercut on the chin followed by two fast, powerful jabs, one to the eye and one to the nose. The man staggered backward, lost his footing, and slipped. Doss straddled his chest, pulled his 9mm and placed the muzzle against the man's temple.

"Who are you with?" Doss demanded.

"*Ich spreche kein Englisch.*"

Doss patted the man down for ID, found none and pushed his 9mm hard against the man's skin. "Bullshit. Who are you with?"

The man smiled, bit down on a tooth just as Rubenfeld had done, went into convulsions and died. Doss was confident he had at least found Laurent's spotter.

Then he heard Bartosz's voice in his ear. The French President-elect and the Danish Prime Minister had safely exited the building with their wives, he reported, and Nowak was heading into the theatre with the doubles.

A moment later, he heard from Bijeau. "Mission Leader, we have activity on the top floor of Jabłonowskich Palace."

"Can you confirm hostiles?" Doss asked and moved over to a window.

"Negative. But unless they're Polish security, something's not right."

"This is Bartosz, we have no security in the palace."

When twelve men on the palace roof stood up in unison and simultaneously launched a dozen RPGs at the theatre, a cone of soft blue light from the clouds directly over the theatre instantly surrounded the entire building. As the twelve rockets passed through the paper-thin wall of light, the rockets vanished, leaving behind colorful sparkles and harmless curlicues of white light. The blue cone then vanished.

"What the fuck!" someone yelled excitedly into their mic.

"All personnel, maintain radio discipline on this command channel!" Doss ordered gruffly. "Alpha Team, move into the palace. Bravo Team, provide suppressing fire."

Doss ran out the theatre's front doors just as Bijeau and her team began crossing Senatorska Street. The air was thick with flurries and the ground between the theatre and the palace was blanketed in snow. Bijeau and her team were taking heavy fire from a dozen or more assault weapons, firing down on them from the palace roof and from windows along the third floor. Two .50-caliber machine guns, one positioned at one corner of the roof and the other inside the palace tower, also opened fire. Doss's counter-snipers quickly silenced both machine guns first and then turned their attention to the men on the roof.

"Bravo Leader. Maintain suppressive fire until Alpha Team is inside the palace. Bartosz, time to call in your teams. Surround the entire city block as we secure the palace. Is the President safe?"

"Mission Leader, Bravo Leader, Roger that."

"Mission Leader, Bartosz, Polish Security units are on the move to secure a block perimeter. President has safely left the theatre and is en route to a secure location."

"All Team Leaders, Mission Leader, have your Polish IDs out.

"Mission Leader, Alpha Leader. We're inside the palace. First floor is clear."

"Bartosz, Mission Leader. Hold in place, cover Bravo Team. Bravo Leader advance into the palace. Alpha Leader, work your way up to the roof!"

"This is Bartosz, will do."

"Bravo Team moving forward."

"Mission Leader, Alpha Leader, securing second floor."

Doss caught up to Kraft and his team as they crossed the open ground between the theatre and the palace. The shooting had stopped and they crossed the street and entered the building without difficulty. As a young cavalry officer, Doss had trained in house-to-house fighting, a dirty, dangerous business but, unlike Kraft, had never actually used what he had learned in combat so called Kraft to his side as he removed his tablet from his backpack.

"Mother, Doss."

"Doss, Mother."

"I have the blueprints for Jabłonowskich Palace you sent earlier, Mother. Can you access any of the building's security?"

"Negative, the system has been disabled."

"Alpha Team, Mission Leader, sit rep."

"Have reached the third floor Mission Leader. Appears clear. Plenty of spent brass casings, some blood, but no sign of any hostiles. Permission to advance to the roof."

Doss looked over at Kraft and handed him his tablet. "Alpha Leader, hold. Kraft, suggestions?"

Kraft quickly scrolled through the blueprints. "Unless these guys are fanatics and came here to die, there must be some other way out," he said. "If we have the Poles cut power to the building, we could slowly, deliberately, search every room on every floor until we reached the roof, but I wouldn't. There are only twenty of us and a lot of them and it's a big building with two wings and a central courtyard. We need drones, we need more boots, sir. Huh."

"Kraft?"

"The courtyard - from the roof I'd repel down the exterior walls to the inner courtyard and go underground if I could!"

"Alpha Leader, can you get eyes on the courtyard?"

"Wait one... Mission Leader, hostiles are repelling down the walls into the courtyard!"

"All teams converge on the courtyard now!" Doss ordered. "Look for hidden doors or entrances to a tunnel. Many of these old palaces have them. Bartosz, any thoughts on where the hostiles might be headed?"

"Bartosz here, on it."

Kraft and his team, already on the ground level, reached the courtyard first. The snow was coming down fast and hard and accumulating quickly. The entire building was dark. When they caught sight of armed men running into the opposite wing of the palace, Kraft and his team raced after them. Doss followed but fell behind with his bad knee. When Doss reached the opposite wing, Kraft and his men were already inside. And then muzzle flashes lit up the widows all along the ground floor of the wing, accompanied by the crackle of automatic weapons fire. But before Doss could step inside and join the fight, out of the corner of his eye, he caught three dark silhouettes across the courtyard brushing away a layer of snow and dirt off a trapdoor.

Doss raised his H&K MP5 and fired a quick burst. One man fell. The other two disappeared underground. Doss rushed over to the trapdoor, saw the man he had shot was dead, and hurried down an ancient stone staircase and into an old, brick tunnel. He turned his flashlight on, saw a trail of blood, and followed.

"All teams, Mission Leader, chasing two hostiles inside a tunnel. You will see a trapdoor in the courtyard. Alpha, sit rep."

"Nine hostiles KIA, moving to your position now."

"Bravo, report."

"This is Johnson, Mission Leader. Bravo Leader is down, three more wounded, engaged with an unknown number of hostiles inside the east wing of the palace."

"Disengage Johnson, fall back out of the line of fire and hold your position. Hostiles aren't going anywhere. Bartosz, can your men move to Bravo Team's position and reinforce?"

"Bartosz, moving now. Just received word, no city records of any tunnel. Suspect the tunnel will bring you to either a subway rail to the north named Ratuza Arsenal or east to the Vistula River."

"Have Polish security forces converge on both locations," Doss said and hurried down the tunnel as fast as his bad knee would let him. He covered about a hundred yards before the brick tunnel ended at a freshly dug dirt tunnel supported by heavy timber beams and rafters. He saw a sliver of light up ahead and raced towards it. When he reached the light poking through a tear in a piece of heavy tarp, he pulled the tarp back and stepped through a hole in a concrete wall made by explosives, and found himself inside a utility room. He opened a metal door on the other side of the room, stepped out into a small deck overlooking a subway tunnel and spotted two men hobbling down the tracks linked arm-in-arm, heading for a passenger platform a short distance away. Doss jumped onto the tracks and chased after them.

When he reached the platform, he shouldered his carbine, drew his 9mm handgun and started climbing a set of metal loop steps slick with fresh blood. When he reached the top of the platform, he saw two men propping each other up, pushing through a crowd of commuters.

Then Doss heard a train approaching and fired several warning shots at the ceiling to clear the area. Men, women, and children panicked and scattered.

"Laurent," he cried out and pointed his 9mm at the Frenchman. "Stop. It's over."

Laurent turned to face Doss. "Over? The stupidity of you Americans is astonishing, something I'll never understand. But for that witchcraft of yours at the theatre, I would have won this night."

"If you say so, Laurent. Don't move, don't even flinch."

"Ha! This evening's games are only just beginning."

When Laurent released his grip on the other man, clearly his twin brother, Laurent's brother dropped to his knees and slumped over. Then Laurent, with a trickle of blood flowing down his right arm from a bullet wound to his shoulder, struggled to raise his carbine and managed to fire a single wild burst before Doss shot him dead.

"Alpha Leader, Bravo Leader, this is Mission Leader, Laurent is down. Report."

"Max, Alajandra, we're in the tunnel following a trail of blood.

Are you wounded?"

"No. You? Any in your team?"

"Negative, we were lucky, bossman. Guess what they say is true, only the good die young."

"Yeah."

"Mission Leader, Johnson here. Have three KIA, three wounded. Kraft didn't make it. Have thirteen dead hostiles and eleven prisoners. With Polish security forces outside, don't believe any escaped from the building."

"Bartosz, can you send medical personnel to Bravo Team ASAP?" Doss asked.

"Mission Leader, Bartosz, sorry about your losses. Difficult operation. I know President Nowak will want to thank you and your team in person. We can take it from here. Fall back and rest. We will see to your casualties and secure the prisoners."

"Thank you, Captain Bartosz; good working with you and I hope I can return your hospitality someday," Doss said and then dialed Mother. "Mother, Doss, is Adelman available?"

A moment passed before Adelman answered. "Max, my Polish counterpart in Warsaw, has just informed me that we had a successful evening. You found the rat and its nest."

"Laurent is dead, sir. Before he died, he said something odd. Laurent said the games for the evening are just beginning. Do you know what the hell he meant?"

"Unfortunately, I do, Max," Adelman replied with a heavy sigh. "How good is your knowledge of modern European history?"

"Not my strong suit."

"Have you ever heard of Operation Hummingbird, the Night of the Long Knives?"

"No sir, not that I recall," Doss replied wearily, puzzled by Adelman's odd question.

"July, 1934. Germany. Across the land, Hitler unleashed his SS squads and ruthlessly purged any political rivals who threatened him. We have, I have, grossly underestimated Stromquist's capacity for brutality. As you were busy taking down Laurent and his cell, Stromquist's assassination squads have been busy all across Europe tonight murdering high-level political rivals, key military officers, journalists, rich industrialists and financial investor types who refused to give him their unwavering loyalty. Many others have been arrested. He's cleaning house. He's tying up loose ends. You and your team saved three, along with a great number of civilians attending the ballet."

"Most unfortunate, sir. History seems to be repeating itself. Didn't something similar happen to the Knights Templar, on a Friday the 13th as I recall?"

"Indeed. Calhoun is outraged. His blood is up and he's itching for a fight. He's placed all American military installations and U.S. Embassies across Europe on high alert. Wait, Max. Please hold."

"Max?"

"Mr. President."

"Rough day at the office, I hear."

"You could say that, sir."

"Still leaving a trail of dead bodies behind wherever you go."

"I'm always trying to do better, Mr. President."

"Ha! I've heard that before. Well, you've made a new friend, Max. President Nowak called me and is singing your praises tonight."

"He's lucky to be alive."

"That he is. He wants to shake your hand. He'll probably pin a medal on you. The Poles make such ornate, pretty medals. You've been invited to the Presidential Palace for lunch tomorrow."

"Perhaps another time, Mr. President?"

"That's fine, I understand. Nowak will understand too."

"Thank you, sir. While I have your ear, I'd like to suggest Alejandra as my replacement."

"Replacement? What's this now?"

"I think it might be time for me to move on, sir."

"Move on? I owe you my life, Max. I love you like a brother. But I love our country more and your country needs you. There's more work to do. We can discuss this nonsense after you've taken some well-deserved downtime, after you've cleared your head. Understood?"

"Very well, sir. Understood."

"Max?"

"Sir?"

"Come home."

Epilogue

Excerpts from Hermann Adelman's private journal:
The Great Turmoil

2054 - Lake Vostok, Antarctica

Dr. Shi Huan was profoundly proud of his team and of himself. He and his mix of Chinese and Russian colleagues, thirteen scientists in all, had been wandering across the frozen wastelands around Lake Vostok for six grueling weeks. They had braved the Antarctica's sub-zero temperatures with little shelter, had lived on bland, meager rations with little sleep, and had suffered through a myriad of other privations and ailments together.

They longed to see their homes, their friends and their families again. Huan and his colleagues were accustomed to working in comfortable labs and offices and liked sleeping in soft, warm beds. They were scientists, not soldiers trained to survive in harsh, unforgiving conditions for weeks on end. Despite their lack of preparedness for life in Antarctica, under Huan's compassionate leadership, they had endured great hardships together without complaint and their spirits had never wavered.

Two months earlier an Australian expert in glaciology, a man named Jenkins, had publicly reported in one minor scientific journal or another of detecting an odd anomaly. He had heard faint, peculiar humming sounds, sounds not produced in nature, somewhere beneath the surface near Lake Vostok. This seemingly minor discovery had piqued the curiosity of Huan, a fifty-something-year-old professor at China's University of Science and Technology in Hefei. To his great surprise, Huan was able to persuade the University to fund an expedition to investigate the origins of the curious sounds. The General Secretary himself had approved the funds. Unfortunately for Huan, Jenkins had not provided the precise coordinates of his discovery, making Huan's task all the more difficult.

For the last few days, howling winds and heavy snows had roughly abused the expedition, making even the simplest tasks challenging. But once the winds subsided, one of the many piezoelectric sensors Huan and his team had buried in the ice and snow began detecting the very same faint sounds Jenkins had described. Huan pressed on with enthusiasm and renewed vigor - convinced his expedition was on the verge of discovering something extraordinary, perhaps even historic.

Huan and his colleagues huddled close together behind a huge Japanese Ohara SM1 00S Antarctic camper painted in tomato red parked a safe distance away as the demolition crew made the final preparations. Huan braced himself for stinging pain as he took off his heavy gloves, his protective goggles and unzipped his parka to remove a laptop strapped against his chest. The frigid cold stung his flesh like needles. He ignored the discomfort and opened his laptop to check the various acoustical and sonar monitors scattered across one square mile of territory. Within that square mile, the low, pulsating humming sounds were constant and appeared to be coming from inside a large void over a kilometer below the surface. His instruments revealed two large shafts leading down from the surface into the void, both set at forty-five-degree angles, and he was about to blow the ice and rock sealing the entrance to one of them. Satisfied with the data on the screen, he slipped his laptop back inside his parka and gave a thumbs-up to the demolition crew.

With a great *BOOOOM!* and a terrific ball of fire, the earth shuddered, flinging chunks of rock and ice far into the air. After the smoke cleared, with the help of ropes, block and tackle secured to the Ohara camper, Huan excitedly made his way down a shaft large enough to run a train through, a shaft with perfectly - impossibly - smooth rock walls and flawless square angles. When Huan and his team reached the bottom of the shaft, they found a thick wall of stone and ice blocking their way. One of the scientists drilled a small hole through the wall and tested the air on the other side of the wall for any contaminants, including radiation. After Huan's colleague declared the air was good, another scientist took core samples of the ice wall, ran a quick, crude geochemical analysis, and concluded that the ice and stone wall sealing off the shaft was at least 4,000 years old.

Six men assigned to the expedition as security, tough, brawny military types, veterans of the Mongolian wars, started chipping away at the ice and stone with pickaxes. Once they had cut a large enough hole, Huan stepped through the opening first, with his team following close behind.

Nearly a mile below the rock and ice of Antarctica, the expedition stood huddled close together inside a mammoth cavern, staring in awestruck wonder at a city like no other, gazing upon a majestic, sublime metropolis of almost indescribable beauty. The celestial buildings, towers, spheres, spires, and other stunning structures, draped in suspended ice crystals like cobwebs, appeared abandoned. But whoever had built the fantastical buildings eons ago deep within the earth had thoughtfully left the lights on. From end to end, the cavern was awash in a welcoming glow of soft blue light teeming with curious, tiny white sparkles slowly twirling and bouncing through the air like dancing snowflakes on a calm winter's night.

Made in the USA
Columbia, SC
03 April 2025